# *TEARS*
# *of*
# *AMBER*

## OTHER TITLES BY SOFÍA SEGOVIA

*The Murmur of Bees*

# TEARS of AMBER

SOFÍA SEGOVIA

TRANSLATED BY SIMON BRUNI

AMAZON CROSSING

This is a work of fiction. Some characters were inspired by living people—including Ilse Hahlbrock Schipper, whose name is used here with her permission—but the story is the product of the author's imagination.



Previously published as *Peregrinos* by Penguin Random House Grupo Editorial, SA de CV, in Mexico in 2018. Translated from Spanish by Simon Bruni. First published in English by Amazon Crossing in 2021.

Published by Amazon Crossing, Seattle

www.apub.com



ISBN-13: 9781542027915
ISBN-10: 1542027918

Cover design by Shasti O'Leary Soudant

Printed in the United States of America

*For all pilgrims*
*in search of life*
*and peace,*
*and for all lands*
*that welcome them*

*For Ilse and Arno*

*For José and our children,*
*forever*

*People need to see and hear the details of what is going on because their imagination is incapable of grasping general facts correctly. When a disaster consumes five million victims, this does not mean anything: the number is empty. However, if I show a single, individual man in his perfection, his faith, his hopes and his difficulties, if I show you how he dies, then you will remember this story forever.*

*Erich Maria Remarque*

*The most shocking fact about war is that its victims and its instruments are individual human beings, and that these individual beings are condemned by the monstrous conventions of politics to murder or be murdered in quarrels not their own.*

Aldous Huxley

# *Cast of Characters*

## *The Hahlbrock family*

Ilse: Second daughter of Hartwig and Wanda Hahlbrock

Hartwig: Father
Wanda: Mother
Irmgard: Elder sister
Freddy: Younger brother
Edeline: Younger sister
Helmut: Younger brother

Grandma Hannah: Wanda's mother

Jadwiga: Polish Zivilarbeiter
Janusz: Polish Zivilarbeiter

## *The Schipper family*

Arno: Youngest son of Karl and Ethel Schipper

Karl: Father
Ethel: Mother
Helga: Elder sister
Fritz: Elder brother
Johann: Elder brother

# 1. The girl

## Ilse

***December 12, 1935, to March 25, 1938***

At the first breath, life hurts.

How could you not cry, the first time the light hits your eyes, or the first time you feel the dry brush of the air on your skin? How could you not cry when your lungs are filled with cold, unfamiliar oxygen, or when the soft sounds that used to reach your flooded ears arrive hard, unfiltered? How could you not protest when the world turns infinite and does nothing to contain the body that, until that day, had been so tightly held, so closely hugged in the dark softness of your mother's interior?

The girl was beginning to acclimatize, even to enjoy life in her mother's arms, when they took her to the church to give her a name.

That day when everything still lay ahead, when she and her people were unaware that their days were numbered, unaware of the baptism of fire that would erase the name of their land from the earth, the holy water blessed her forehead and spilled onto East Prussian ground. Since 1918, proud Prussia had stood apart from Germany—not of its own volition, but as a punishment imposed on it by the world. And its inhabitants, including this newly baptized girl, had been ostracized, like a splinter separated from its stick: you are, but you're not; you belong, but I've almost forgotten you. They yearned for their Germanic siblings to the west—separated by sea, but more so by land. Separated by their former territories, which had once been Prussia, too, and which the world was now intent on calling the Polish Corridor.

The day of the girl's baptism of water, there was still a long way to go before the baptism of fire, but in the decades to come, the world would strive to understand the order of events, the importance of the variables; it would call upon great minds to assign blame and establish how cruel the culprits had been. Sometimes it would fall silent, hoping to make people forget how intolerable the crime had been. Other times it would promise what happened would never happen again. Rarely would it be mentioned that this promise had already been made once, then broken when the aggressor, the loser, was punished.

The girl would always like the name chosen for her, but that day, the priest let it fall unceremoniously in a sudden gush of cold. The name was hers forever thanks to that water and the thousands of blessings, but the ice-cold shock was brutal and prompted screams that didn't stop until the ceremony was over.

Her parents celebrated in a way that hadn't been possible when their eldest daughter was baptized. What a difference five years made, they thought while they set the table for six guests, the delicious smell of roast goose wafting around them. How far they'd come from the hunger of their childhood and youth. How well chosen their chancellor was: he had saved Germany.

At the same time, far away, a French journalist named Madame Titayna was conducting a rare interview with their taciturn leader, who expressed himself thus: There is not a single German who wants war. The last one cost us two million dead and seven and a half million wounded. Even if we had been victorious, no victory would have been worth that price, he declared, and she returned to her country convinced that neither the man nor his people were a threat to peace.

The chancellor wanted peace, and Ilse's parents did, too. Hartwig and Wanda Hahlbrock had survived the devastation of the war to end all wars. Now, all they wanted was to see their daughters grow up happy. And they finally believed it was possible. Three years of the Führer, three years of order, three years, at last, of a present without hunger and a future with promise. And so: a new and beloved daughter. Ilse.

Two years and three months later, though she remembered neither the pain of her birth nor the icy water of her baptism, Ilse was already a little bundle of acquired knowledge, because children never learn as much as in the first three years of life. They learn, they live, but they never remember having learned or lived.

It was in that time that Ilse discovered the people of her small and isolated world; she learned to identify hunger's twinges but also to be patient: food would come—her mother would ensure it did; there was no need to cry, because she'd learned the words *I*, *am*, and *hungry*, among many others. In those first years, she learned that the stove gave off cozy warmth at a distance, but when she got closer, it burned. She learned to stand, to walk, to climb steps and go down them. She learned to name things. To name herself: Ilse Hahlbrock, though the surname still tied her tongue in a knot.

She also learned not to cry, because tears only annoyed her mother, who always said to her, Ilse, we don't cry. She discovered what it was to desire something that wasn't hers—she thought her sister's doll more beautiful than her own—but also how to let go and to make do without complaint.

In that time, she learned to fear geese and dogs, though nobody could understand it: Kaiser doesn't bite, Ilse. He's a good boy; you can pet him.

But the girl had her reasons to be afraid, though she had no memory of them.

Because on one occasion—a rare occasion when she'd left the house without her mother noticing—Ilse approached the lake, lured by honking.

The night before, her parents had promised to take her to see the goslings soon, but Ilse didn't know how long *soon* was, and it felt as if that promise had been made an eternity ago, so she set off, with plans to play with the babies and keep them warm: the lake was always freezing, and if she hated cold water, she thought they must feel the same.

But the geese didn't give her the chance. Seeing the human fledgling approach, they came out flapping and kicking until they reached dry land. Then they ran, honking.

Ilse wasn't new to the world: she could differentiate the soft *Ilse* she heard when she managed to keep still for a while and let her mother work in peace from the *Ilse!* that reverberated through the house when she refused to get in the tub, come the moment she was called, or eat all her salami.

That's how Ilse knew with certainty that their honks were not a greeting. With a leaden weight in her stomach that came from nowhere, Ilse turned and ran as fast as her two-and-a-quarter-year-old legs would allow.

As she fled, a powerful scream rose within her. It sealed her throat and seeped into her little body, never to come out.

Ilse knew—how did she know?—that the geese were faster than she was, that they would reach her, that they would bite her, that they would tear off her skin and even her hair.

She didn't dare look back.

*Schnell laufen.* Run faster, she told herself. *Schnell, schnell laufen!*

The hot breath of the enraged birds warmed her ankles.

Then, from the corner of her eye, she saw Kaiser approach at full speed, enormous, formidable. Had she turned, she would've seen the dog throw himself between her and her winged assailants, but no: with her eyes fixed ahead, she only felt the Alsatian's tail brush against her legs, and, in her panic, thought it was his great fangs.

In her frightened mind, he joined the pack, his *woof, woof, woof* merging with the geese's *honk, honk, honk*. And Ilse ran faster.

She took refuge in the barn, surprised to have won the race, and there, in the dark, felt her heart slow. As time passed, she was overcome with a new fear: that her mother would catch her, with her harsh *Ilse*, the one her mother used when she'd been a bad girl. *Nein, Ilse. Nicht allein.* Her mother's word was law in the house: You never go out alone, Ilse.

Had it not been for her stomach, the great motivator, she would've spent the evening there, perhaps the whole night. But hunger persuaded her to return to face whatever she had to face. And because, when Ilse was hungry, she could think of nothing else, her mind forgot what her body never would: the reason for her fear of geese and dogs.

What had seemed like an eternity to the little girl had taken just half an hour. Her mother, busy embroidering her daughters' pinafores and slips, never noticed her absence, thinking both girls were taking their nap. Ilse made no complaint, just devoured her toast with the creamy butter they made on the farm. Then she played all afternoon with Irmgard, the older sister who kept her entertained (and stopped her from leaving the house alone) while their mother sewed, wove, embroidered, cleaned, and cooked.

When their father arrived, Ilse knew it was time for dinner, and good thing, because she was hungry again. Their mother served sauerkraut with beef sausage: her favorite.

But then she saw Kaiser, who came inside only at her father's invitation, staring—as if, she thought, he wanted to eat her. Ilse, whose body would forevermore hold that afternoon's scream, lost interest in food and sought refuge on her father's lap.

And it was true that Kaiser had hunger in his eyes, but not for her: he was gazing at the sausage with love. He felt he deserved a prize for heroism, for standing between the geese and the girl, for the sharp pecks those feathered demons had landed during their pitched battle.

He waited patiently, but dinner ended without anyone offering so much as a piece of stale bread. Not that Ilse would've dared to hold a hand near that enormous, quivering snout, and in any case, though still petrified, she didn't dare leave a single crumb. If her mother ordered *Alles essen*, the girl knew she'd better clean her plate.

Ilse would never know that the events of March 25, 1938, had been stored in her more as instinct than as conscious memory. Nor could she imagine how that day would be etched in the memories of her people—not because a Prussian girl had been chased by some geese, but because the master of their country's destiny was in Königsberg, making his intentions clearer to the Germans and to the world.

# 2. The boy and the flying banners

## Arno

***March 25, 1938***

It was the first time in his life he'd been to Königsberg, but on that day, his third birthday, he didn't know it. Nor would he remember the flurry of preparations his family had made to spend time away from their small farm.

That morning, nobody had to wake him; he was the youngest of four and still followed the rule all babies know as soon as they're born: the day begins when they wake.

First the baby, then the mother, then the sun. Next, the cockerel's cry and the dairy cow demanding to be milked, followed by the father, to help the mother who had to relieve the cow that, once awake, wouldn't stop mooing. And after them, the rest of the family, though they wished their heads could remain stuck to their pillows a little longer, that there could be light coming through the window before they had to open their eyes.

But that was impossible: the new day had arrived, and with it, the usual flurry of activity on the Schippers' farm.

Of course, now that he was three, Arno no longer began his day with tears. He'd left those behind when he'd found the words he needed.

*Mutter! Vater! Ich möchte mein Frühstück!*

The morning began the way mornings always did: with the youngest of the family demanding breakfast, and the rest craving more time in bed. Then came hurried farm chores, and finally, elegance: wearing their Sunday best, they would go together to the city.

"It's a historic day and it's your birthday, Arno," said Karl, his father, while they buttoned their overcoats.

It was March 25 already, but in those parts, spring took a long time to take the hint. With luck, they would have a little sun by midday. With luck, it would snow neither on the short journey to Königsberg nor on their return.

Arno picked up on the excitement of his older brothers, who understood the occasion better than he. For eight-year-old Fritz and seven-year-old Johann, who saw themselves as experienced travelers, the day promised more than anything they'd known until then, more than the things they'd enjoyed each time their father took them to the city: the luxurious houses and buildings with big windows, the bells of Frauenburg Cathedral, the cobbled streets, the seven bridges, the games in the gardens of Königsberg Castle. It all paled next to today's historic event. On this visit, they would even forget the lure of the fruit-shaped *Schwermer* marzipan they'd tried on that rare occasion when their father had had money, time, and a good mood all at once.

Though they were frequent travelers in comparison with Arno (who'd never left the vicinity of the farm) and with Helga (whom, as a girl, despite being older, their father never took to the city when he worked there as a carpenter), Fritz and Johann were very young. The journey still seemed long to them, and they were easily distracted. On the snow-spattered road, they played the good older brothers and guides, moving with Arno from one side of the cart to the other to point things out: if it wasn't the big ox on the right, it was the lambs that blocked the road ahead, or the dead dog in an advanced state of putrefaction on the left.

"Did you see his eyes, Arno?"

Arno wanted to see everything, but his mother was afraid he'd fall, and they knew not to get her worked up; she must not overexert herself.

"Come here," Helga said, sitting him on her lap. "Keep still, now."

Helga held Arno close until he calmed down: her arms were the most familiar, the most comforting. His mother sat beside him every night for a while before he slept, and she told him stories, but it was ten-year-old Helga who carried him in her arms, who soothed him when he had nightmares, who told him off when he misbehaved, and who gave him baths. There, with his sister's arms keeping the cold at bay, he fell asleep, lulled by the cart's rhythmic rocking and the eternity it seemed to be taking them to arrive at the unknown destination.

"We're here."

Arno opened his eyes, instantly on alert. They were surrounded by activity. He'd never seen so many people in one place. His mother and father were arguing.

"The cart will get stolen if we leave it here," she said.

"No, nobody would dare today. And we can't go any farther with it. Look, everyone's doing the same."

That day, Königsberg's broad streets were packed with visitors from the surrounding area. It was a historic day, and no one wanted to miss it: the excitement shone in their faces. Around the Schippers, other families were lining up their vehicles outside the city walls, as close to one another as the horses would tolerate. Then they unloaded their baskets or bags to walk the rest of the way. The Schippers copied them, with Arno on his father's shoulders, or we'll lose you forever in this crowd, *mein Sohn*.

Arno sometimes felt confused, because if he was the baby, why did adults like to say, what a tall boy! If he were tall, he'd be big; he'd be the eldest. And everyone in his house was taller than him. If he were tall, he'd be able to reach the butter that his mother kept away from him on the shelf. If he were tall, he'd be able to reach the wooden horse his father had made him when Fritz snatched it away and held it up as high as he could. If he were tall, Fritz wouldn't dare play pranks like that.

On his father's shoulders, for the first time, Arno really did feel tall. Even though his father was smaller than many in the crowd, Arno could see everything from there: the bald patches on some hatless men and the feathers in the hats of the elegant ladies; he liked seeing his siblings walking far below. Up here, he was the first to hear the music floating out from the city's streets. The wind blew through his bright blond hair. He looked all around, eager not to miss a single detail, not caring when his father told him, "Hold still, Arno."

Ahead, it was as if everything were walls: from the ones that encircled the city to the biggest buildings he'd ever seen. He'd never seen anything so high, other than the geese that flew over his house, a house that now seemed tiny.

Looking up, Arno gaped in astonishment, but his father said, "Sohn, close your mouth before you catch a fly." And he closed it, but it was stubborn, and sometimes it opened again by itself, because it wasn't just the size of the buildings and churches that surprised him: wherever he looked, flags were flying like red wings painted with black and white—big ones, small ones, gigantic ones—soaring up to the sky in the wind.

High-spirited women were selling flowers and flags just the right size for his little hands. And he wanted one.

*"Vater, ich möchte eine Flagge!"*

*"Nicht jetzt."*

Those were the most frustrating words Arno knew: Not now. Could he have a cookie? Not now. Could he play? Not now. Could he shout? Not now. Could he eat his bread? Not now. Could he have the flag that all the other children had? Not now, not now. At three years of age, Arno was already tired of those words, but he knew that, once his parents had said them, they would never go back on them. "So not now, but maybe later?"

"*Ja.* We'll see."

His father didn't want to stop, even when Arno signaled him with his legs, as if riding a horse. They seemed to be in a hurry. They walked as quickly as their mother was able.

Arno knew that not all mothers were like his. He knew that big, fat Frau Filipek, for instance, who walked to the farm once a week to exchange butter and sausage for some eggs, had more children than his mother, and sometimes she carried one of them all the way there, along with her bartering goods and her own weight.

The children took advantage of every second to play, while the mothers took more time than necessary to perform the transaction, chatting. But they were busy, practical women, and the conversation ended before long: there was a lot to do, and the Filipeks had to keep going.

Content, Frau Filipek packed her basket and walked off as energetic as she'd arrived, rosy cheeked, while his mother silently watched her stride away before returning to the kitchen to rest, breathless, without attempting to carry the boy, who, sometimes, couldn't understand why his mother never picked him up.

"Do you remember when you skinned your knee? Do you remember how much it hurt? Well, your mother's heart hurts just like that," his father explained to him more than once.

"And will she get better?"

"No."

That was why they had to take care of her. Because life is hard with a skinned heart. But Arno kept forgetting.

Every day, before leaving for work, his father said to him, look after your mother; help her; don't cause problems. Arno began the day with these intentions, but he soon forgot. He wanted to play, and he forgot about his mother's skinned heart. He wanted to run and to climb even when his siblings were at school and his father was at work, and there was no one else but his mother to look after him.

His body fled from the resolution he'd made just a few minutes before; he soon went too close to the stove, though he knew perfectly well he should not; he went to see the cow or to roll in the wheat, even though his mother had forbidden it. And he only remembered his promises when he saw his mother—pale, agitated, breathless—approach as quickly as her body would allow to dissuade, rescue, or scold him.

Tall, as he felt now on his father's shoulders, and grown-up, as tall boys that didn't forget their promises were, from time to time Arno observed his mother, a frail woman from whom he'd inherited his blond hair and blue eyes, walking slowly but steadily. He'd alert his father if he saw her become unwell, he decided. That was one thing he *could* do: spot the exact moment when her discomfort began. He was an expert at spotting that: he'd lived with it since he was born.

The Schippers soon merged with the tide of people. There were more and more flags, and the chants started off small, but grew in size.

Arno didn't know the songs. They were quite different from the ones his mother sang so sweetly when she had enough air to lend to a melody, but he liked them. He didn't know the words, so he pretended, timidly at first, until he started to feel part of the growing, evermore vociferous crowd that, gradually, became a homogenous mass.

And the steam that came from the mouth of each individual with each note mingled with the rest; it accumulated and grew large. It took on a life of its own, turning into a blast and then a swell of mist that enveloped him, that made him imagine he was floating.

And he thought his mother was walking with a little more strength in her body and more color in her face, and that his siblings had grown a little taller, through nothing more than some songs. Other children were up high like he was, sitting astride their fathers' shoulders, and they held up their arms as if commanding the seas; boys and girls he'd never seen before, but who recognized one another in their expressions, their smiles, the songs' words that almost none of them pronounced correctly, and which none understood beyond the fact that they promised bread. And they liked that.

But with all the walking, his father's shoulders seemed to have developed corners, and Arno's discomfort was now greater than his taste for the songs. He was thirsty, and his hunger was now greater than his desire for a flag.

*"Vater, ich bin hungrig!"*

"Hold on, we're nearly there. When we arrive, we'll give you something to eat."

But like everyone around them, they went no farther: some soldiers directed the crowd to the two sides of the broad avenue, lining it. The stadium was full; this was the closest they'd get.

The Schipper family was lucky: the children were able to sit at the cordon on the sidewalk, and the adults had no one in front to block their view of the parade that was about to begin. Frau Schipper gave the children bread and sausage.

"Eat slowly, Arno. Don't make yourself choke."

The children ate sitting; the adults, standing. Arno spilled tea on his long woolen socks, so while they dried, he returned to his father's arms, wrapped in his overcoat and his warmth.

The songs continued, now accompanied by bands. There were voices that stood out from the others—from those of mere mortals—on loudspeakers, commanding the crowd to repeat slogans, to respond in unison, to raise an arm, and to yell together over and over, until the words reached the boy's ears with total clarity: *Ha hidler.* Arno asked his father to put him down and, standing on the curb, he joined the chorus each time they were instructed: *"Zig ail! Zig ail!"* he shouted. And then, *"Ha hidler! Ha hidler!"*

Without wondering and without asking what it was that they were repeating with such fervor, he joined in raising his arm almost to the sky. But his throat soon dried up from all the yelling, and his arm tired from all the raising and lowering.

The game lost its charm before it really started.

He felt the heaviness that he'd recently learned to detect in time to avoid wetting himself, and insisted until his father took him behind a building to let it out in a steaming stream.

But then they returned to their place. To more of the same. Arno sat down and stood up again and again. Obliged, he remained there, but his body wanted to be somewhere else. He couldn't understand why he wasn't allowed to run into the middle of the broad, empty avenue, a space that beckoned him unrelentingly. He knew he'd be able to start a game of tag with the other children his age, who seemed equally fed up with all the walking, all the yelling, all the waiting. They could have fun together. But no: Don't move, Arno; stay on the sidewalk, don't get lost; come on, keep singing. And he must not upset his mother. It would've been easy to forget had it not been for his father's firm hand on his shoulder whenever he sensed his son about to make a break for freedom.

*"Nein, Arno."*

Arno sat down. Again. To wait. Again. But wait for what? He didn't know.

By the end of the day, the fervor, the songs, and the slogans had lost the right to linger in his mind. Tiredness even erased the excitement of being tall on his father's shoulders.

He'd always remember the red of the flags, though he'd never speak of it, not even with his wife when they lived far from there. For the rest of his life, that day remained a painful and almost forbidden subject.

In any case, what was there to say about such a dim memory? It had been etched in him more as a feeling than a recollection, consisting only of images that visited him in the depths of bad dreams on nights he let his guard down. He'd never know it was on this precise day that he'd first witnessed the red and black flying.

By now, all Arno wanted was to go back to his little world on the farm: to sit at the table for dinner and then climb into his warm bed without having to be asked twice. Down on the sidewalk, his parents' feet like a cocoon around him, protecting his small frame from being trampled, he'd even tired of looking up to ask, can we go home, *bitte*? since they would just say, a bit longer, Sohn.

So Arno had stopped asking. He'd stopped wishing he could run into the middle of the avenue. He was sitting where he'd been told to sit, no longer looking ahead, or up, and certainly not behind, because all he'd see was a dark and endless forest of legs and crotches.

Earlier, he'd tried to strike up a remote conversation, in signs, with a boy sitting like he was, in the same position and with the same tired expression, at his parents' feet, far away on the opposite sidewalk. But they hadn't been able to understand each other, and Arno had given up trying.

Protected but bored, he rested his chin on his knees and, with a flimsy stick, tried to scratch his name in the dirt. Helga taught him at home, but his letters didn't come out like his sister's. Frustrated, he was about to ask her for help when something changed: his little cocoon filled with a sudden, expectant silence. Even a three-year-old like Arno could tell: something momentous was about to happen.

*"Was ist los, Vater?"*

"Come on, Arno! Quick!"

The silence ended, and the people around him began to yell and cheer loudly again as his father lifted him up in his arms. Now Arno saw the front of the parade: riders mounted on enormous horses, then the soldiers going past. At first, their precise march impressed the boy, but there were so many of them and their step was so rhythmic that it became hypnotic. The crowd raised and lowered their right arms, and they yelled the chants they'd been practicing for hours.

His father's body shook with the effort of his own shouting, with the reverberation of the voices and the loudspeakers, and with the vibration from the military vehicles that followed. Vehicles of different sizes, so many of them, bigger than any Arno had ever seen, and they were all new and impressive, without a spot of mud: together, marching, powerful.

And that was when Arno's fatigue fell away, how he discovered a new passion that would stay with him for the rest of his life and trigger his first permanent memory, one that, years later, when his fiancée asked him, what's your first memory? he'd deny, because it would've meant accepting that his earliest recollection was of war.

In that moment, he couldn't take his eyes off the revolving tires, off the tank wheels that acted as cogs moving their chains in a never-ending ellipse. Arno tried but was unable to make out where the chain's cycle began and where it ended. Then a tank moved its turret from side to side in a greeting, and its gun up and down in a bow, and in an instant, Arno was breathless.

He didn't understand their function as weapons. He cared about them as mechanical objects.

"How do they move, Vater?"

But his father didn't answer, occupied as he was with the object of his own interest—which was at that moment passing in front of them—and because the boy's voice was drowned out by the swell of voices.

*"Heil Hitler! Heil Hitler!"* the crowds chanted.

"Arno, look," said his father, and Arno obeyed. He looked and looked. He observed. He studied. But he didn't look where his father did, because nothing would distract him from those marvelous machines and from the questions that resounded in his head as loud as the engines and cogs; from the questions that resounded louder than any mass chant: How do they work? How do they move?

And owing to the intensity with which he tried to solve the mystery, everything else went unnoticed in Arno Schipper's first memory, including the short man standing high in a convertible car, feeling even taller than the boy had on his father's shoulders. Taller than anyone.

From his perceived giant's height, the man turned from side to side to wave, like the turret on the tank that belonged to him. But unlike the vehicle's gun that had fascinated Arno so, the man kept his arm up high, because someone like him would never humble himself by bowing. Not even before the people who'd granted him power with their votes and their faith, and who sustained him at the heights he seemed to enjoy so much.

Distracted as he was observing vehicle after vehicle, Arno paid him no attention, nor did he care, an hour later, when the lethargy and the desire to be elsewhere returned, about the man's impassioned speech, which could be heard not just over the loudspeakers but all across Germany by radio transmission. That was how he achieved the Anschluss—annexing Austria for the glory of Germany and at the request of the Austrians—without firing a single shot.

During the speech there was total silence. When Arno went to ask something, his father said, "Quiet. We must pay attention to every word." Arno couldn't understand anything that the voice coming out of the loudspeaker said; each word blended into the next, and none of them seemed to take him closer to what he wanted: his home. Surprised, he saw his father crying, with a smile on his face.

"Are you sad, Vater?"

"No. My eyes are just watering from the freezing air."

After the first five minutes, he rested his head on his father's shoulder. And well before the speech was over, Arno was in a light sleep, immune to the leader's spell, deaf to the carefully controlled words that flowed from his mouth, and which, all together, promised peace and the divine support of the German god (whose existence most of those listening had been unaware of until that day), oblivious to the masterful, dramatic finish, delivered in a style so often used by the speaker, one of the greatest orators and persuaders in history.

"In the course of my political struggle, I have been given a great deal of love from my people. Yet when I recently crossed the former border of the Reich, I met with a wave of love stronger than I have ever before experienced. Not as tyrants have we come, but as liberators. An entire people cried out in joy. It was not brutal force that triumphed here, but our swastika. When these soldiers marched into Austria, I remembered a song from my youth. Back then I frequently sang it, with faith in my heart, this proud battle song: *The people are rising, the storm is breaking loose!* With faith in Germany and in this idea, millions of our fellow countrymen in the New Ostmark in the south of our Reich have held their banners high and remained loyal to the Reich and the German people. One People and one Reich: Germany!"

*Sieg Heil!* Long live Germany! *Heil Hitler! Heil Hitler!*

The crowds, and all the people of Germany wherever they were when they heard those words, resumed the chants with renewed fervor, but Arno would never remember that part of the day. In the days, months, and years that followed, his surprised parents and siblings asked, but he went right past us, just a few meters away, don't you remember? No. He didn't remember because, when the Führer passed by, Arno was busy looking at cogs, and when he spoke, Arno fell asleep in his father's arms, and Karl stroked his head and whispered in his ear, happy birthday, son.

# 3. Memories of the sun

## Ilse and the Hahlbrocks

***March 25, 1940***

The scissors called to her. She was trying to be a good girl, a big girl, a four-year-old, but the temptation was huge. So huge that she completely forgot she only needed to cut a ribbon. So huge that she almost forgot her mother's warning: Dolls' hair doesn't grow like yours does. If you cut it, you'll be left with a bald, ugly doll forever.

Her mother had gone up to listen to the radio while she finished her embroidery, with the volume low to avoid waking the new baby boy, to whom she gave so much care and love, and who made their mother so sad. Ilse only liked the radio when it played music, and not all of it. So instead of following her mother, she decided to tie up her doll's hair with her own ribbon. But the ribbon was knotted up, so Ilse had to cut it loose. It was the best thing to do, she was sure of it.

She knew where her mother hid the scissors because you'll hurt yourself, Ilse. She pulled up a chair, climbed onto it, and opened the drawer. There they were, shiny, sharp, pointy. Irresistible. Forbidden. Within her reach.

She tried to talk herself out of it, to tell herself that she was as obedient as her sister, but temptation won. I'm a good girl, she reminded herself, but the scissors now in her hand made her forget all about the ribbon. Not the doll's hair because it doesn't grow. You can't cut a doll's hair, Mama told me so. Not the doll's, not the doll's.

So she cut her own hair.

Just a little. Just the tip of one of her braids, so that no one would notice.

It wasn't easy. The scissors were sharp, but the braid was thick. She had to draw on her newly discovered patience to pull the handles open and squeeze them shut, open and shut, until at last it came away.

She studied the severed part, and only then did it occur to her that she hadn't known whether cutting it would hurt. Had it hurt, she wouldn't have been able to hide it: her mother, the farmworkers, and even the geese would've known. But no, the tuft of light-brown hair she now waved in her hand didn't hurt, nor did the hair still attached to her.

She hid the evidence under some fresh potato peelings. She darted off, afraid her mother would discover her rummaging through the waste, but dashed back when she remembered that she'd also thrown away the ribbon that had tied the braid in place. Her hair might grow back by tomorrow—after all, she wasn't a doll—but ribbons were precious, and her mother would surely notice if one was missing.

She took out the tuft, which was rather slimy and smelly from the juices of garbage both fresh and old, and pulled off the ribbon. Then she made sure the loose hairs were properly covered up again. She hesitated: she was unsure whether the pigs would like eating peelings seasoned with hair. Would it hurt them? No one had ever said anything on the subject.

She'd find out tomorrow. Or the next day.

Satisfied with her efforts to cover up what she'd done, Ilse tied the ribbon as well as she could to the mutilated end of her braid, which she tried without much success to weave together again. She was unable to redo the bow, but it didn't matter: her ribbons often ended the day as nothing more than knots, the strips hanging down. She undid her other braid's bow, certain that, this way, her mother wouldn't notice anything amiss. But she'd better make sure: she climbed onto the chair again to look at herself in the elegant oval mirror with its golden frame, which, like the scissors, her mother had positioned high above Ilse's head.

Had her face changed? No. She was the same girl she saw every day in the simple mirror in her parents' room. A chestnut-haired girl with large amber-colored eyes, a pretty face (she knew it was pretty because her father told her so every day) even if, as always, it was a little less than clean: there was a dark streak on one cheek, though she hadn't even been outside yet.

But something was different, because now Ilse was missing a sizable piece of her braid. Not even her ploy with the ribbons had worked. She lifted her shoulder in an attempt to shorten the distance between it and the braid but didn't like what she saw: she looked like the old storekeeper Lutz's son, the one with the bent back.

Then she turned to see the scissors where she'd left them: on the kitchen table. They were still as shiny, sharp, pointy, irresistible, and within her reach as before. What if she cut the other braid? Now she knew it didn't hurt at all.

But at that moment, something distracted her from the lure of the scissors and the tragedy of her misshapen braid. Something she thought she'd never seen before: a brightness that came in through the window.

She ran to look out: the world outside shone in radiant colors, and like a fan slowly opening, the grays that had defined her whole life vanished before her eyes.

It was the sun.

The elusive sun that Ilse had forgotten was real, had come to believe existed only in her imagination. It was no longer the weak, timid celestial body that had persuaded her the sun was like the mythical Erdhenne, a spirit that children talked about without ever having seen it. Her mother had told her: There are no invisible spirits inside things. They are made up. And adults had to be believed.

But this sun was just like in the stories: bright, hot, inviting. This sun was real and unobstructed by a single cloud, and the colors were finally as they were meant to be and not the sad imitations that had been offered her until that day.

It wasn't that Ilse had only lived during winter; this would be her fourth spring, her fourth summer. It was that she only remembered the last few months: an overcast life, freezing skin, the cold air that dried everything out, the snow that snuck in uninvited. And darkness. Most of all she remembered the darkness.

Six months in the life of a four-year-old child can be an eternity, and Ilse had ended up thinking the world would be the same forever; that daylight was fleeting and it was always cold, even at night, covered in a thick eiderdown.

She couldn't remember what it meant to go out in the yard without her heavy overcoat, stockings, and hat; she couldn't remember the feeling of short sleeves or of grass beneath bare feet.

Peering out through the window, Ilse forgot about braids long or short; she forgot about her doll; she forgot about the boredom. She even forgot about the seductive scissors, because now it was the sun that called to her.

Ilse dragged the chair over to the door and unlocked the bolt. Then she opened the door and stepped out into the bright light to surround herself with colors, to feel the heat on her skin. And because of the intense emotion she felt, this moment became the first permanent memory of her life.

Of course, the girl didn't think, this is my first memory. That's not how these things happen. But years later, when her only sweetheart asked, what's your first memory? she'd reply that it was the sun, the warmth of the sun on her forehead despite the day's freezing air. And with that memory came the memory of the colors. And her wild desire to run aimlessly after the clouds that were finally discrete and not one thick mass like flour-and-water paste in the sky.

By then, that day when Ilse went out to discover the sun's colors, Germany had already seized the Polish Corridor with the lightning of its *Blitzkrieg*, and future historians would take the view that, in reclaiming the territory the world had given away to Poland, Germany triggered the chain of events that would ensue.

Triggered another world war: the second one.

But perhaps they were wrong: perhaps that war was predetermined, the actors already in position. Perhaps everything clicked into place with the pact between the Germans and Italians, or when Germany split the Polish territory with the Soviets. Perhaps everything began with the German invasion of the Sudetenland, or with the Anschluss; or earlier, with the creation of the Gestapo; or earlier still, with the recognition of Hitler as Führer and with the power he invested in his Brownshirts; or even before that, when he wrote *Mein Kampf* in jail; or with the destitution of Germany's postwar period; or with the Treaty of Versailles; or with the first war, the one the world naively thought would end all wars.

Ilse herself wouldn't be exempt from wondering when the tipping point had come. But not until years later. That day of her first sunlit memory, she had no notion of how that chain of events would affect her, how it would affect humanity.

And so, as a grown woman, she'd reply honestly to her sweetheart when he asked about the first memory of a German girl, who, like him, had been caught up in the merciless whirlwind of war, and tell him that her earliest memory was the sun. Then she'd go on: And I went to find Janusz.

Like the winter gloom, Ilse believed Janusz had been there forever. Like her, like everything she knew. She didn't remember that her dear Janusz had arrived the last time the sun went away, arrived with the cold and the darkness after the Blitzkrieg, arrived as a prisoner in a military truck along with Józef, Radosz, and Tadeusz.

# 4. *Tales of gold*

*"Nein, Ilse."*

It wasn't easy to refuse the child, especially when seeing her reminded him so much of better times. But he knew they would both be in trouble if he let her roll around on the wheat in the granary.

Janusz was understanding more and more German; perhaps one day he'd work up the courage to speak it, but for the time being, he remained silent; he paid attention, though he pretended to be focused on his chores, though he appeared to be a dopey teenager with no interest beyond the drawings he made and unmade on the golden canvas of loose wheat.

Nobody complained about his work: moving the wheat, turning it over to keep it from rotting. But while the other Poles would've done it grudgingly, investing no more effort than was required, Janusz moved the wheat with love. That was how the job had become almost entirely his: under his care, every last grain was given the attention it needed before going to the mill.

And he did it with speed: nobody could accuse him of laziness.

He woke with a story in his mind, then told it in the heaps of golden wheat. He'd barely finished when it was time to start again: he'd erase his gigantic work of early-morning art and begin a new tale, another product of his imagination and the stories his mother had told him until her last day, for as long as she'd had the strength.

The work was infinite, but he didn't mind; the task that seemed so boring to others connected him with his far-off home.

And the girl wanted to be with him while he worked.

Without uttering a single word, he told her stories born from a cabin in the depths of a Polish forest—*his* forest—where all there would've been, were it not for these tales, was silence, hunger, cold, and tears.

It was on stories and on little else that a mother, a son, and a sickly little sister had lived in that solitary cabin. But the stories came to an end on the day when that sister died and that mother went out for a walk from which she never returned. The son, twelve, waited and waited. But, in time, silence elbowed its way in, bringing hunger, cold, and, finally, tears.

Loneliness drove the boy to the villages, but the company he found there didn't know the power of stories; the people didn't know that their scarce food could also feed him, stretched by stories that help the spirit leave the body and forget its needs; could help him become the raven prince saved from enchantment by a kind princess; could help him hear, in the breeze from the far-off sea, the sad song of Jurata, queen of the Baltic, buried forever under an amber castle as punishment for a forbidden love.

The boy tried to explain it to them. But he didn't have the words.

And then, after his four years of hunger and loneliness, of wandering, the Russians arrived. So the boy fled along unknown roads, running until he could no longer hear those harsh, terrifying voices.

The fear faded, but the hunger and loneliness did not. They only grew. Wherever he went, he found plundered houses. Sometimes, he saw fearful faces peer through windows. No one would open a door to him, not even to say good morning, let alone offer him work in exchange for some bread.

The soldiers took him by surprise. But they weren't Russian, and that comforted him.

They, too, were surprised at the lack of resistance from the tall lad, whom, from a distance, they'd taken for a man, and they put him in the truck full of other passengers, all men, all Polish.

Inside, nobody spoke, so Janusz kept quiet, too: he asked no questions. Whether they were taking him north or south, east or west, he no longer cared. What destination could there be with no one waiting for him? If nobody had ever showed him the way?

In the truck, he felt as if somebody had set his course.

Janusz sat in the small, dark space afforded to him by the warm, earth-smelling bodies, and he accepted it. He closed his eyes and took a rest—from running, from solitude, from cold.

They were left by the side of the road. Again and again, the truck stopped. Sometimes it was day and sometimes it was night, but all Janusz could make out when the soldiers lifted the heavy canvas was a group of four men being dropped off at each point.

Only then did some break the silence. They couldn't stop themselves. Their uncertainty and fear were too great. Or perhaps the uncertainty increased their fear.

*"Gdzie jesteśmy?"*

But the German soldiers did not answer. Perhaps even they didn't know where they were.

Janusz had no idea whether it was a good thing to be chosen: no one seemed happy about it, but they obeyed all the same. He, too, would be left at the side of the road, but he wouldn't ask where he was. He already knew where he wasn't. He wasn't in the land he'd wandered like a vagrant since his mother's death. He wasn't in the land the Soviets had invaded, and anything was better than that. Almost since he'd learned to walk the paths of the Białowieża Forest, his mother had warned him: If you see a Russian wolf, son, run.

And that is what he'd done. Until he'd been captured by the voices with German bodies. His mother had never warned him about German cruelty, so he supposed he was better off with them than with the wolves, who almost always featured in the strange horror stories his mother whispered in his ear, in secret, so as not to frighten his sister.

After two full days traveling, the journey to nowhere ended. Only four captives remained: Janusz, Tadeusz, Józef, and Radosz. Of course, Janusz didn't know their names yet; he hadn't even heard their voices.

Janusz concentrated on imitating his companions' silence, their sidelong looks, their stoicism. He hadn't complained even when the hard wood bench began to feel as if it had sprouted thorns, or when his legs, burning, fell asleep. He never asked for food or drink, accustomed as he was to hunger and thirst eating him away from inside.

Like the others, he fell in and out of sleep, drank rainwater that tasted of canvas and soil, and emptied his bladder when he feared it might explode. He was careful, directing his stream toward the gap between the wooden boards on the floor. He didn't always succeed, especially when the vehicle jolted, but no one complained. Just as the others were sprinkled with his liquid, he also had theirs on him.

And that was what Janusz and his companions smelled of on the night when they climbed down to be received by a reluctant Herr Hahlbrock. Beside him was a soldier who spoke in harsh, clipped Polish: They were in Germany now; Poland no longer existed. They were prisoners of war, but they were lucky: they would work the land.

The alternative was death.

They were shown to their hut. It was small but heated by a stove for which they would be given enough firewood to keep them warm at night. Each prisoner had a cot with sheets and blankets. On each, they found work uniforms and an overcoat, as well as gloves and a woolen hat.

On the round table with four chairs there was bread.

Bread.

For their labor, they would be paid a few coins each month, with which they could buy cheese or sausages in town, but bread would be given to them daily.

The soldier continued to explain rules of conduct, of discipline, but Janusz could no longer concentrate: he only had eyes for the loaf. The smell of the cold bread rose above the other smells, even the urine, almost making him groan; but the groan would've broken into a sob, so he held it in.

And perhaps it was on that night, when he stood there in a daze with his eyes fixed on a single point, appearing to lack the intellect to understand the instructions given in bad Polish, that everyone concluded Janusz was an idiot. Or could it have been the next day, when, after sleeping for a few hours (the warmest and softest hours he'd slept in years), with his stomach full with his ration of bread, dressed in clothes that were too small but the best he'd worn since leaving home, he'd gone out into the freezing air to work, as a prisoner in a foreign land, smiling from ear to ear.

Yes, perhaps it was this that led his Polish companions to conclude that the young giant with a child's face was crazy, and to fear that they would have to divide the work of four men between three, because they couldn't imagine how someone could smile under their circumstances: their country destroyed, families scattered, friends dead, themselves enslaved.

You would have to be crazy. Or an idiot.

Janusz walked out on that first day of freezing German captivity with a smile. That day, he smiled despite his stomachache, a pain caused by the unusual sensation of fullness that was far better than the bottomless suffering of hunger. And if this land belonged to Poland by ancestral right—as his countrymen tried to explain in their attempt to indoctrinate him into hating their captors—Janusz didn't care: he felt safe from the Soviets, and, what was more, nobody, since his mother's death, had given him so much or protected him from the cold.

He understood the others: they'd left people behind; they'd tried to prevent the Germans from invading their villages; they'd been subdued by force. Janusz, on the other hand, had left behind everything that mattered a long time ago: the old cabin deep in the forest, his sister's grave, and his mother's ghost, which he'd never had the fortune—or misfortune—to see.

He was bound to nothing other than himself and what he carried inside: his mother's stories. Stories that he now told in his drawings of wheat.

He'd started telling them for himself, but he'd continued, with more detail, with greater care, for her, the girl who was so much like his dead sister. Not in her coloring: all the Hahlbrocks had brown hair and eyes, while his sister, like him, had inherited their mother's black hair and blue eyes; nor in her stature: his mother said her children had inherited their height from a giant. But in the sparkle of her eyes.

She came back every day for the stories in the wheat, and that was why he felt he loved her, despite knowing it was inappropriate, despite the disapproving looks from the other prisoners; despite the fact that, every afternoon, a frightened Frau Wanda Hahlbrock came in search of the little girl with big, kind eyes.

# 5. The Wanda of legend

Ilse was downstairs, playing with her doll. Wanda had suggested it needed a new hairstyle. The complexity of weaving a braid should keep Ilse busy for a while. Her daughter was safe inside the house.

Wanda liked the radio when it wasn't news. Whenever they played music, she put it on low to lend rhythm to her sewing and to prolong her little Freddy's sleep, since he struggled so to rest away from his mother's arms. Wanda listened to forget what she needed to forget. To keep herself from thinking about the people prowling around outside her house.

They were lucky: Hartwig was the farm's administrator, a role for which he received a salary plus use of the house they'd built after she refused to live in the estate's castle.

It's been in my family for seven hundred years, Von Witzleben, the landowner, had told her in the hope that his administrator's young wife would feel flattered and be persuaded to take up residence.

But Wanda, a practical woman, made a quick calculation of how long it would take her to do the daily cleaning in that place, and decided that all that history wasn't for her. She didn't want to live with the constant worry that the girls—Ilse—would break an antique, or disappear into the dungeon.

The little castle had been left uninhabited, and the Hahlbrocks were very happy in their small but practical home.

Wanda had been born in West Prussia, and her parents taught her to feel proud of her ancestral roots. You're German, they'd said since she was a child, but first and foremost, Prussian. And that was why they'd named her Wanda, after the legendary queen who'd defended their lands to the death in the eighth century.

You have a warrior's name, her father would say. Take pride; you have the heart of a warrior who defends her land.

She'd believed it when she was young. I'm a warrior, like Queen Wanda, she'd told herself. Then someone had told her the real story of the legendary queen, or one of many in which the only recurring theme was that Wanda, a Pole, had chosen to die rather than surrender herself and her land to the invading Alemanni tribes. Whereas she was just a modern-day Alemanni Wanda.

The Germans and Poles had been disputing this same land for at least twelve centuries, with Germans controlling it for the last two. But after losing the Great War in 1918, Germany had been forced to cede land to the Poles, such that West Prussia no longer existed and East Prussia was an enclave surrounded by enemies. Like an island encircled by stormy waters.

Her father, who'd survived the horrors of the trenches, had not wanted the family to live under the humiliation of Polish rule even a day longer than necessary, and so they headed for German soil. Her father gave up his land, his roots. He walked away but looked back constantly, promising himself that he'd return, as the ancient Alemanni had done after being defeated by Queen Wanda.

What followed were years of exile and hunger for the family, but the first love letters from the man who was now Wanda's husband had vanquished that bitter time. It wasn't that hardship had ceased; it was just that, with Hartwig by her side, it all didn't seem as hard.

Newlywed Wanda had been pleased when her husband was offered work in a remote corner of East Prussia as the administrator of a large estate not too far from Königsberg. It was a chance to return home, to tell the children that she'd bear: You were born in Prussia, like me. Moreover, the job meant financial stability at a time when few had work and even fewer had enough to eat.

Wanda couldn't forget the time of need after the Great War, but now it seemed that the situation had changed; the modern Alemanni had returned with a vengeance, annexing and unifying all of Prussia.

Her father's beloved East Prussia existed once more, and he'd lived to see it. He found the strength to reclaim their small farm from the same Polish invader who had occupied it when he and his family had left years before.

Then, with the satisfaction of having reconquered what was his, her father had died in the bed where he'd conceived almost all his children—and where the Pole had probably conceived his—two months after settling in. Now it was Wanda's mother who bred rabbits and grew maize for livestock, to be sold exclusively to the government. Thanks to the system Chancellor Hitler had introduced, both large farms like Wanda's and small ones like her mother's enjoyed a surplus. German stomachs, especially those of self-sufficient farmers, had never been so full.

Wanda, a cautious woman, kept the jingle of her coins and the silence of her bills in a tin box that she hid in the bottom of a chest. She was determined to make things with her own hands, from materials on the farm. The future looked bright, but she never forgot the hardship of her youth. Her children, she vowed, would never know hunger.

Not that it was all virgin snow: Freddy had been born with a cleft palate and took up much of her attention, and Ilse wasn't like Irmgard, who was a chatterbox but calm and obedient. While she looked like her elder sister—both of them brown eyed with their father's fine features—Ilse was silent, never cried, never complained, but she moved as if by magic. Her mother would leave her playing for a moment, and in a blink, the girl was gone.

Wanda didn't know where such speed came from. Or such silence.

But the force of that silence sparkled in her eyes and manifested in the mischief she caused without warning and without giving herself away. When she was younger, there wasn't much to worry about: a few outings to the castle, which she couldn't enter because it was locked; more often, she made a mess drawing in the mud. Wanda would search for Ilse with the certainty that she'd find her up to no good, but she would find her. Did the girl think her clothes washed themselves? And your shoes, Ilse. How many times have I told you to look after them? Shoes don't grow on trees, you know. Then Hartwig would say, don't worry, leave it, stop nagging her. He found everything Ilse did amusing or touching.

But these days, it was no longer so safe for a girl to go out in her own yard. Hartwig, you can't tell me not to worry anymore.

Germany, victorious, had invaded Poland and reestablished Prussia. That was what the Führer, the news, and her husband said; it was what everyone was saying. If that was the case, then why was Wanda the one who felt invaded?

It was impossible to go out now without seeing them, without remembering that they were there against their will. That they were prisoners. The Poles. Her prisoners, the Poles. My prisoners, my prisoners, my slaves. But as much as she tried to make it stick in her mind, to understand it, to accept it, she could not.

"I'm a farmer's wife. That's what I know. Are we jailers now, Hartwig?"

"I don't like it any more than you do, Wanda, but we have no choice."

And they didn't. The Führer had ordered it.

Still, she didn't understand it. However much Hartwig tried to explain the situation, she didn't understand why their Polish prisoners slept in warmth, with bread in their stomachs, while German men were dying in the war.

"We couldn't run the farm without them."

Farmland was a priority for the Reich because, if there was one lesson they'd learned from the previous conflict, it was that no one can endure a war without food. The German farmhands were sent off to war, but if manpower were needed to work the land, the Führer would provide it, no matter where it came from. Hence their Polish prisoners.

And they were also lucky on two counts: not only did they have their salary, but the government needed Hartwig, as manager of such a large farm, home, safe, and producing food. Nobody would summon him to take up arms for the *Vaterland*.

"Someone has to stay and feed our soldiers, don't they?"

Hartwig tried to persuade himself, though Wanda knew it weighed on him, that his friends—his brother Josef—would face danger far from their families while he enjoyed his daughters' antics. But it was a time when one did what one was ordered to do, and he was no exception.

You're a patriot, Wanda would tell him. You're working for the glory of Germany, too, if not on the battlefields, then in the wheat fields.

She was grateful. Every day, she felt relieved to wake up in the warmth from her husband's body. How many German women no longer had that comfort? How many more would lose it before the war ended?

Yes, Wanda was grateful, but the matter of the four Polish *Zivilarbeiter* and the soldiers who guarded them made her sleepless at night and breathless all day. When they were close by, when Hartwig sent them to her with firewood, the day's milk, or the week's meat, she couldn't look them in the face. Leave it here or leave it there, and careful, don't get my floor dirty! With gestures and simple words, because she'd forgotten almost all the Polish she'd known as a child, Wanda gave orders (she had no choice, if she wanted things to be done properly), but the months passed and she couldn't have said what shade their eyes were, what color their skin, what shape their noses. She couldn't distinguish one from another, because she never looked directly at them. Why? She didn't know. Was she afraid of what she'd see? The hatred? The resentment? Calling them Zivilarbeiter—civilian workers—was a much kinder designation than what these Poles really were: slaves.

And each night, before bed, she said the same thing.

"They have to go, Hartwig."

"I've told you, that's not possible. They were brought here, and here they stay. There's nothing we can do about it."

Wanda understood there was nothing they could do and reproached herself for upsetting her husband with her insistence. She wasn't stupid. But she was stubborn: Did she not have as much right to defend her home as Adolf Hitler said he had to defend the country?

Don't let anyone hear you say that, Wanda, Hartwig told her the first and only time she voiced her resentment.

She was also afraid for Ilse. Once her sister had left for school, the child had for some reason attached herself to the foreigners, especially the young one. Perhaps it was boredom. And however much her mother told her, you're forbidden from going out, they don't want you there, Ilse, the little girl didn't understand. How could she? If at the age of four Ilse was only beginning to understand a family's love, how could Wanda explain the hatred between enemies to her daughter's young soul?

"If it worries you so much, find a woman to help mind her. A Polish woman."

But no. Wanda would have no help in the house. She wouldn't spend her hidden coins and bills on that. She hadn't wanted it before the war and she didn't want it now. Her grandmother hadn't had help; her mother hadn't needed anyone. Nor did she. She liked keeping house for her family; she liked to have everything in its place and to know that clean really meant clean.

She tried to keep a close eye on the girl, but housework and the problems with Freddy distracted her from her vigilance.

Wanda's needle stopped. She turned off the radio to listen.

As always, it wasn't a sound that alerted her, it was the emptiness. Ilse could be silent, but her mere presence made the atmosphere vibrate. And in the house now, even the air was still. Wanda left the needle hanging from the curtain hem, glanced at the sleeping baby, and ran with a clear destination in mind: the same as yesterday and the day before. Now, just as then, she feared she'd find Ilse dead. From a knife, from a stick, from an axe, from a fall—from whatever it had been. Dead. Dead at the hands of Poles forced to work land that wasn't theirs, at the hands of Poles dragged into a war they hadn't anticipated and had lost in a blink, and who now lived at the mercy of a reluctant German family.

When she arrived, she saw her daughter watching the precise movements the Polish boy was making as he turned the wheat.

When she saw her, air came rushing back into her lungs. Ilse wasn't dead. Wanda had known it deep inside, of course; and of course, she'd overreacted, Hartwig would tell her later: Their daughter was fine. She seemed happy. She seemed . . .

"Ilse! What did you do to your hair?"

# *6. Not all slavery is the same*

Janusz watched them walk off, the mother pulling the girl by the arm.

"How many times have I told you, child? Don't come here. It's dangerous."

"Why?"

"Don't answer back."

He felt sad about Frau Hahlbrock's unfounded fear. He couldn't understand it: How could she think he'd harm Ilse? Nothing would happen to the girl while he was near. He wanted to put the woman's mind at rest, but his tongue didn't have the words in German yet, or at least, not with the clarity to inspire confidence.

"Be careful."

Janusz turned around, alarmed. He hadn't noticed Tadeusz, Józef, and Radosz returning. If they were there, it meant the day had ended, that it was time to rest and, best of all, eat dinner.

He was hungry; he was always hungry. That hadn't changed during his time on the Hahlbrocks' farm. Just when he thought that hunger had gone, never to return, after he'd eaten bread with creamy butter or a stew of potato and onion, it came back to remind him that, while for the first time in his life it rested and allowed him to rest, there was no way to tame that monster completely.

Still, the reprieves made Janusz feel liberated; he now had the time and energy to think about other things. About the old stories he could still, with total clarity, hear in his mother's voice, but also new ones now, stories whose origin he didn't know. Did they come from nowhere? From him?

"Are you deaf or something?"

"Hmm?"

"How many times have we told you to send that girl home? Can't you see they don't want you?"

"Who?"

"Who do you think, *głupi*? No one here wants you. You're a Zivilarbeiter."

Of the four prisoners, Radosz complained the most, because while missing their homes and families left the others paralyzed, his soul was inflamed. Radosz had given everything up for lost.

"I don't know why you all still cry. Do you think I can't hear you? I hear you when we put out the light every night, and I see you when you eat bread your wives didn't bake at lunchtime. You cry. And if you don't cry, you want to. But what for? What for, if your wife's as dead as mine? If your bread will never taste of Poland again? If Poland doesn't exist anymore, because it's as dead as we are, even if you don't want to believe it, even if you can't accept that every day we walk on its corpse?"

Józef and Tadeusz knew Radosz from before. They'd played together as boys and taken their first drinks together as young men. But they'd been neither able nor willing to keep up with him.

"You should know, Janusz," said Józef. "Radosz is used to keeping his spirits up with *krupnik*. And now there isn't any . . ."

Nor were there any good spirits.

Janusz had never tried the vodka sweetened with honey and herbs, but he remembered his mother saying that his father had abandoned them rather than give up the drink. Poison, his mother called it, pure poison for a man. And now Radosz had been cut off not only from his family but also from the drink. And he missed his family, but he missed the krupnik more.

In his terror, Radosz had endured the journey and hidden his withdrawal, but as soon as the soldiers had driven away in the empty truck, he collapsed, seized by a cold fever that made him tremble, mumble nonsense, even cry.

For the first few days, he went out to work in this state, weak and shivery; he couldn't tell his captors that he needed more than bread, that his body was vigorously protesting the thirst. The others helped him pretend he was working, but when they were unsupervised, Radosz would drop to the ground, breathless.

In time, the trembling had stopped, as had the desperation, but not the longing or resentment, and so nights in the Polish farmers' hut always ended the same way; they'd put out the oil lamp and close their eyes, lulled restlessly to sleep by variations of the same complaint.

"All I have is myself, or at least, what these damned Germans have left of me: a shell, a slave. Get up, Radosz; move; do this, do that; not later, not tomorrow: right now, today. Even on Sunday, even on your saint's day. Not one day off, not even one. In the rain, in the cold, in the mud, with sores and blood on your hands. And not even one drink to see out the day, not even one to warm the soul. This war will never end, and they'll never release me. And if they do, what will it be for?"

And in the day, he worked with a bitterness that also sought to infect his fellow exiles, especially Janusz, who tried as hard as he could to turn a deaf ear. The more the man spoke to him, the more Janusz immersed himself in his stories—the old ones, the new ones—and in this way, he brightened the days and nights, banishing Radosz and his gloom from his mind.

He understood what yearning was, what it meant to miss one's mother, to fear for one's sister. He understood the pain of losing everything and not being able to forget. He'd lost everything a long time ago, and he never forgot. But he'd learned to be glad for life for its own sake;

glad to live another day, and another, and another. Hungry, but alive to enjoy food another day. Cold, but alive to enjoy warmth when it came. Alone, but alive to enjoy company when it found him.

For his companions in this imposed exile, the loss was more recent, but time passed, and Janusz didn't understand why they couldn't find even a single reason to be happy: they could have been in Russian hands or as dead as Radosz said the rest of Poland was.

Dead enough that they would never enjoy anything ever again.

He couldn't understand why it upset them to see someone find peace in the midst of war; he couldn't understand why they wanted to persuade him to give it up, to join them in their bitterness.

The last four Poles in the land, united by bitterness.

"No one wants you here, głupi," Radosz repeated as if he were incapable of understanding.

They could call him głupi all they wanted. Janusz knew he wasn't stupid. He heard because he had no choice. He didn't listen, because he didn't want to.

Because he didn't want those words to unlock the drawer where bitterness was kept, afraid that, if they did, he'd end up believing that if no one wanted him here, no one wanted him anywhere. In Poland, there was no Ilse, and if she was in Germany, that was where he wanted to be, because on that farm, he'd found the closest feeling to the one he'd known in the bosom of his family. He'd found someone to tell his stories to, a girl with the eyes of the sister he no longer had, a girl who now wanted him there, even if Radosz was intent on convincing him otherwise.

"Is it dinnertime already?" he asked.

# 7. *The children's anthem*

***March 25, 1941***

The war continued, as war does every day, and no one could ignore it, no matter how hard they tried; no matter how they pretended in front of the children; even in the most remote part of the country; even without turning on the radio; even when dinner conversation avoided the subject; even when the parents pretended not to notice that their eldest, their Irmgard, now arrived home from boarding school for weekend visits dressed in the military uniform of the Jungmädel, and refused to sing anything that hadn't been taught in her National Socialist girls' group.

Die Strasse frei den braunen Bataillonen.
Die Strasse frei dem Sturmabteilungsmann!
Es schau'n aufs Hakenkreuz voll Hoffnung schon Millionen.
Der Tag für Freiheit und für Brot bricht an!

The war continued, the Reich made its demands, and they did their part: Produce more, they were told, and they worked harder. Have more children for the glory of the Vaterland, and they complied: they were trying for their fourth. But they couldn't understand why Germany needed children to forget how to be children; to forget play and subject themselves to military discipline; to replace lullabies with "Horst Wessel Lied" and its call to arms.

> Clear the streets for the brown battalions,
> Clear the streets for the storm division!
> Millions are looking upon the swastika full of hope,
> The day of freedom and bread dawns!

Why did a ten-year-old girl have to sing these lines? What possible benefit did it bring for the country? Why did she also have to teach them to her siblings, who, like her and thanks to her, no longer sang anything else?

The war continued, and the Hahlbrocks did everything that was demanded of them; they gave everything, but they didn't understand why they also had to hand over their daughters' and son's childhoods. But they remained silent, because they had no choice.

The Hahlbrock family lived in a remote corner of the country, essential due to its fertile soil but far from the Prussian capital and its new social and political tenets: Jews were the scourge of the earth; Germany would see to it they were defeated; the Reich was gaining more and more territory; they'd invaded Greece; the battle for France had been a stroll in the park; it wouldn't be long before they overcame the stupid British via aerial bombardment and total control of the seas; the Vaterland would build a greater empire than the Romans.

None of this changed the fact that the cows had to be milked when they had to be milked, that the planting and harvesting had to be done at precise times, that the lambs needed shearing every summer. Everything had to be maintained: the house, the fields, the barn, the stables, the castle. But the countryside had no time for national greatness. Crop infestations didn't care that the government demanded a bigger and bigger cut. *Sieg Heil!* Wanda and Hartwig yelled at the obligatory meetings and rallies. *Sieg Heil! Sieg Heil!* Victory was guaranteed; Germany's greatness, assured. Glorious Germany.

They hated the Party meetings. They both thought their time was better spent on the farm, leaving politics in the hands of whoever was interested. But missing meetings was considered worse than missing church. Absence was interpreted as a show of dissent, because politics was the new religion; Adolf Hitler, the new messiah. Friendly neighbors, fellow churchgoers, now wouldn't hesitate to report as traitors anyone who failed to show sufficient fervor in their Nazi salute.

The Hahlbrocks didn't understand the paranoia, but they understood they had to live with it. So they went to the meetings; they sent their daughter to the youth group—and they did it without complaint. By now, they'd almost stopped complaining even in the privacy of their bedroom for fear that Irmgard would hear them.

And they dreamed of the day when the war would end, when everything could go back to normal; when, as the anthem they were so sick of hearing said, there would be bread but also peace. Peace among Germans, between neighbors.

The Hahlbrocks worked to this end; they contributed in order to reach a better time, a better Germany. So they put up with the chants that Ilse now repeated at her sister's instruction.

"Learn it properly, then when you're ten and you can go, you'll be the best."

She taught her to march just as she'd been taught. She taught her the exercises. She told her terrifying modern fables, hectoring Ilse until she listened to every word.

"Ilse, you must pay attention and learn what to do if you come up against one of those yellow-starred snakes. Come on. Sing the anthem again. And don't mess it up this time."

"Later. It's time for dinner, and we don't sing at the table," said Wanda.

She was grateful for any excuse to avoid listening to the song they were using to turn her daughters into fanatics.

"But, Mama—"

"We don't even sing church songs at the table; you know that, Irmgard."

# 8. Like a leaf on a river

## The Schippers

***June 22, 1941***

Karl Schipper would remember Arno's third birthday for the rest of his life. It's a historic day, he'd told his children. And how right he'd been, but even if he'd been wrong—after all, what does a simple carpenter know about history?—that day would've been engraved in his mind like the cuts in the fine furniture he made to order.

Clear the streets for the brown battalions,
Clear the streets for the storm division!

The communion of everyone and everything, the anthem echoing off Königsberg's walls and even the icy wind that blew that spring, had moved him.

Millions are looking upon the swastika full of hope,
The day of freedom and bread dawns!

With each step, despite the weight of Arno on his shoulders, Karl gradually forgot the twenty years of humiliation that Germany had suffered.

Already Hitler's banners fly over all streets.
The time of bondage will soon be past.

He forgot East Prussia's isolation; he forgot the harassment from Poles reluctant to allow a German to cross their new borders.

"Vater," Fritz complained that day, "Arno's messing up the song."

"It doesn't matter, Fritz: let him sing," he replied with a smile, not taking his eyes from the red-and-black banners that filled the present and promised a glorious future.

*Already Hitler's banners fly over all streets: the time of bondage will soon be past.* With that promise, the hardship he'd suffered—first as his family's eldest son in a devastated Germany and then under the Great Depression—seemed to vanish. His mind was freed from the torture he'd endured as a new husband and father, when being a carpenter was useless because no one had money for repairs, let alone to commission something new, and when the only thing that saved them from starvation was the tiny farm his wife had inherited.

Things were changing. So much so that he could barely resist the urge to rush to his father's grave and say I told you so.

The topic of Adolf Hitler had always been a sore point between them.

"Son, you can't just believe any old boor that makes promises."

"Then who should I believe? Old people like you who keep us plunged in misery? The ones who gave away the country? Men who, in losing the war, also lost their dignity?"

On more than one occasion, young Karl had declared to his father and anyone who'd listen that he'd sooner have died than laid down his weapon or signed that shameful unconditional surrender, as the old guard had done before settling for the useless Weimar Republic, which had achieved nothing but to keep Germany on its knees.

And Karl spoke not only for himself; this was the voice of his generation. Hitler's promises resonated in those young hearts eager for revenge, eager to see Germany unified again, to regain the honor of a people scattered beyond the borders of the old empire, in the Sudetenland, in the Rhineland, in Memel, in the lands of West Prussia that the world was intent on calling Poland.

Hitler's road to power had been long, and Herr Schipper had died before his son was proved right. But reason had prevailed, young Karl thought, when he and almost all of Prussia had flocked to the polling stations to vote for their leader, because in him the voice of the German people would resound with new strength in every corner of the world.

And so, that March day in 1938, Karl Schipper walked side by side with his wife, his children, and his countrymen as they celebrated the beginning of Germany's restoration. He carried his youngest son high on his shoulders, looking down from the sky as a proud German. Karl wanted to arrive early at the stadium, so he walked with a firm step that day; there was no way to stop: they were being carried off on a human river, like a leaf fallen from a tree, pulled by its unstoppable current. It didn't bother Karl. To hear the words of their Führer in person, to be a part of this story and this brotherhood, he'd allow himself to be carried wherever the river flowed.

And the message that Karl heard that day was one of peace, of love of country, and it was as if it came from the German god that the Führer himself invoked, almost as if God were whispering in Hitler's ear.

And Karl believed it, because how could he not when each word throbbed with the conviction of truth?

Again he wished his father were alive so he could tell him, see how wrong you were? Because not only had Herr Schipper opposed the leader of the Nazi Party, accusing him of false prophecy, but he'd also made gloomy predictions: this man will take us into another war, just watch.

Yet now, just over three years later, still at the mercy of that powerful river, Karl remembered that day full of banners and full of hope, and decided that, if life gave him the opportunity to speak to his father just one more time, he would ask him for forgiveness.

The last remnants of his idealism and youthful credulity had long since been washed away by disappointment and anxiety; now it seemed he'd inherited his father's gift for premonition.

And yes, now he would ask for forgiveness and gladly admit that he'd believed what he'd wanted to believe; that he'd heard that marvelous speech but understood what he'd wanted to understand, ignoring inconvenient truths, seduced by the promise of a full larder and full pockets. And he'd hoped—how he had hoped!—that the next region to be restored would be West Prussia.

He had imagined it would be like the Austrian Anschluss: the Army would march in with strides of glory and peace, and everyone—the Germans and Poles who'd always inhabited these lands—would welcome them with open arms.

There would be peace and progress. Once-scattered Germans would rediscover their lost pride. Their children would live without fear, without hunger. With the freedom to determine their future.

But the German god hadn't granted Karl's wish: not long after Hitler's great speech, in Germany and even in Prussia, mobs had attacked Jewish shops, schools, homes. The Kristallnacht, they called that night of broken glass and murder.

The next day, Herr Stern, who often hired Karl for small jobs, had summoned him to repair some shelves. Stern's store, the city's most elegant, was in ruins, its wares looted. But on his way in, Karl had been intercepted by some unfamiliar men: If you work for Jews, they said, you're an enemy of the Party.

As word got around, Karl lost at least half the clientele that he had built up in the recent years of prosperity. He was mystified: The Jewish community had always been an integral part of Königsberg. Were they enemies now, too?

Not long after, they began to disappear. One day when he'd finished work and was passing the synagogue, Karl realized that, on each trip to the city, he saw fewer and fewer yellow stars. Perhaps they'd taken refuge elsewhere, he thought, since minds were becoming ever more inflamed against them on the streets of Königsberg.

And it all came from the Führer's speech.

He'd forever regret the naivety that had led him to hear only a message of peace and love that March 25. He'd understood its true meaning one evening in Königsberg when he witnessed a violent raid in which soldiers threw entire families into canvas-covered trucks.

This was how Jews were disappearing: against their will.

He looked around to see if anyone would defend the few rights that their neighbors still had, but there was nobody; on that usually busy street: nobody.

He, too, turned his horse around to hurry away from there, saddened and disappointed—with himself for being so afraid, and with Germany for filling him with such fear.

Months later, part of his wish for a unified nation had been granted. But neither had the German Army arrived with the slightest intention of peace, nor did the Poles welcome them. Quite the opposite: by surprise, in alliance with the Soviets, and with violence, Germany had launched its lightning war against Poland on September 1, 1939.

The days of the Blitzkrieg were, for the Schippers, days of hiding from the sound of artillery; of inventing chores and games to keep the children inside and help them forget their fear of the explosions. The bombs weren't aimed at their farm, they knew: they were landing on the other side of the border, in the part of West Prussia the world now called Poland. But the attacks grew more intense, and as much as they tried to persuade themselves they were safe, they couldn't quite manage.

Then there was that sleepless night listening to engines rumbling nearer and nearer until they stopped at their farm; until military footsteps approached the house; until they banged fiercely on the door.

*"Sie sind Pole?"*

"No. I'm German."

*"Papiere."*

While the soldier inspected the papers that proved that both he and his wife, Ethel, were pure Germans—not Poles—Karl had time to see three trucks with their engines running. He was reminded of the trucks into which they'd thrown the Jews, the canvas that had hidden the human cargo. And Karl's heart contracted with fear: Were they here for him? Had they identified him as a witness to those abductions?

*"Danke schön. Heil Hitler!"*

The soldier returned his papers, turned on his heel, and marched off upright and proud, as if Germany's future depended on him, as if the Führer himself and not a frightened husband and father, a simple farm-dwelling carpenter, were witnessing each step. When the convoy of trucks had gone, Karl Schipper's head spun with relief. He didn't know who they had behind the canvas, but that day, they'd left *him* in peace.

Days later, his wife was anxious: Frau Filipek hadn't visited them on Tuesday, as she usually did.

"Go check on her, Karl, take her the eggs."

And he went without saying anything to his wife, not wanting to alarm her, but he suspected he'd find the farm empty. He was wrong: a German family from Eisenhüttenstadt, a town near Berlin, had already settled on the Filipeks' family farm. He decided not to ask after their former neighbors. What for? Karl wasn't so naive anymore: he had gathered that the trucks that stopped at his house that night had been full of Poles.

What was more, asking questions was dangerous.

He had no choice but to hand over the basket of eggs as a welcome gift and leave open the possibility of future trades between his wife and Frau Färber.

"All right," she said, "but not this week: I'll be very busy cleaning up the garbage those Polish pigs who lived here left."

What could he do? Declare that his family had been friends with those Poles she now called pigs? That his wife would miss the plump woman who'd won her heart first with her creamy butter and then with her conversation? That their children—especially Arno—would miss playing with the Filipek kids?

Even if Karl wanted to do something, it was too late. Germany had swallowed them up. And he himself had helped pave the way, because he had believed; he'd raised his voice and his arm, intoxicated by the Führer's vision. He'd handed over everything, even his free will, even his peace of mind.

It was too late.

Now, to speak in support of any persona non grata was to declare oneself an enemy of the Reich. It was dangerous not to raise one's arm in salute whenever the occasion demanded; it was dangerous to utter words or sing songs other than those decreed. If Karl wanted to work, he had to be a member of the Nazi Party, to fly its flag. They also had to buy the Führer's portrait and hang it in a place of honor in the house. And none of this was cheap: they had to postpone buying new shoes because of their patriotic duty to show what good Germans they were.

The Führer had taken them where Karl's father had feared he would. He'd unleashed the storm he'd promised in that messianic speech Karl had failed to understand. Germany—joyful, credulous, reckless—was following its leader in search of promised glory. And this time, with the audacious invasion of Poland, the world hadn't turned a blind eye, as it had done with the annexation of Austria, or the Sudetenland, or Czechoslovakia.

The invasion of Poland brought war.

And Karl feared for the future. But it was dangerous to express any doubts, so he exorcised his thoughts as much as he could—not even in the privacy of his inner being did he feel safe—and allowed himself to be carried off again like a leaf in the current, but afraid, now, of the destination.

At first, they hadn't felt it. Not as war, not in Königsberg or Prussia. Despite all the preparations families had made in the early days, the war was happening elsewhere, and while many fervent young men had enlisted as soldiers to fight in France or Africa, military service wasn't obligatory for men Karl's age.

Karl and many heads of households like him could stay at home to take care of their families and be grateful that they lived so far from the bombs.

At first, it had seemed as if there were only gains: not just because of the triumphant announcements on the radio but also because they'd freed themselves of the impenetrable Polish borders that had kept Prussian agriculture contained and depressed. They had recovered the port of Danzig and could finally come and go freely, lowering the cost of transporting goods. Now they all remembered that Prussia was part of the Vaterland, and with delegates from the government and visits from the Führer, support and subsidies that they'd lacked for years began to arrive.

Germany conquered everything that lay to the northeast and west. The Soviet Union protected them in the east, in the part of Poland it had claimed.

And with so much abundance, Karl was busy once more. Sometimes he made objects as simple as frames for the Führer's portrait. Sometimes he built or repaired practical items like doors, tables, windows, roofs, cart wheels in the summer, and sled runners in the winter. This work supported the family, so he did it with pleasure and care.

But what Karl liked most was being commissioned to make furniture. He threw all his talent into these projects, sparing no cost, with no concern for profit. The profit he wanted was of another kind: the satisfaction of knowing he'd made something with his hands that would last; something that would transcend time, like the marvelous furniture of Fräulein Stieglitz, one of his oldest customers. He wanted to leave a legacy for his sons: they would follow in his footsteps, he hoped, and become the finest carpenters and cabinetmakers in the country; the best families would seek them out to furnish their castles with their carving and marquetry.

But.

But the war continued. They'd all believed it would be no time before every country bowed to Germany's undeniable power. But no: the years passed, and the war continued. And it devoured men.

As it would now devour him. The papers had reached Karl at the farm one Sunday: *Conscript.*

The soldiers had knocked on his door more gently than on that night when he'd had to prove his German blood. This time, they didn't arrive in the trucks covered with canvas behind which so many disappeared, but for him, the notification meant the same thing: they would tear him from his home, from everything he knew.

Where was this war heading, the war that now took men who weren't so young, heads of families with no military skill whatsoever?

He went to the Wehrmacht offices to explain: He was a simple carpenter who'd never held a weapon, a worker on a family farm, father of four children and husband to a seriously ill wife. His family needed him.

"Are you primarily responsible for the farm?" the man from High Command asked.

"No. My wife is."

His request for exemption was refused. "But I help her," he told them. "She can't do it alone." They paid no attention. He was to report immediately for basic training: they would teach him to hold and fire a weapon. His carpentry skills would be very useful on the front. *Heil Hitler!*

On which front? Where were they sending him? He received no answer.

As ordered, Karl turned up on May 1 at the barracks on the outskirts of Königsberg. They would allow him to visit his family on Sunday afternoons. He tried to make the most of those afternoons, surrounded by his family while he put the finishing touches on a chest of drawers that, for once, was within budget. He'd leave his family with a little money, at least, but first he'd have a photograph taken of himself, not as large as the Führer's portrait, but certainly more loved.

He wanted them to remember him.

What they spoke of least on his visits were soldiers and war. As new members of the Deutsches Jungvolk, Fritz and Johann wanted to know everything, happy that their father was proving himself, but Karl was grateful that their mother stopped them from asking questions. In that house, without needing to scream or threaten like the Führer, it was Ethel who was in charge. She might have had a sick heart, but no one could call her weakhearted. One look was enough.

Thirteen-year-old Helga was forever knitting in silence. She was also now a member of the Jungmädel, but only because she had no choice. Helga thought it a waste of time when there was so much work to do on the farm, with a sick mother and a little brother to care for.

Six-year-old Arno watched every movement his father made as he worked. He knew the name of every tool and was starting to see the difference between elm and cedar. He was the only one of his sons, Karl thought, who showed signs of having inherited his calling. *Mein kleiner Helfer*—my little helper—he called him, touched when he arrived for his weekly visit to find Arno waiting with his toolbox ready.

But time always flew when he was home, and, inevitably, the moment came when he had to leave.

Picking up Arno to hold him a little longer, he told eleven-year-old Fritz and ten-year-old Johann: Always check the cart's wheels, keep them well oiled. You know where I keep the tools. Don't forget to make sure there's enough firewood chopped before winter comes. And he never left without also saying: Help your mother with the animals and look after your brother. To Helga, he always said: Help your mother with the sewing, with the preserves, with Arno. And she handed him the wool socks she'd knitted. Two or three pairs per visit.

His wife, he just hugged, and she hugged him. Ethel asked nothing of him; there was no need. What was more, they both knew nothing was certain: by the next Sunday, he might be at war, her heart might have failed.

Karl drew out the goodbyes as long as possible, but then it was time; he put Arno down and walked away without looking back, because it hurt to leave them, and even more so when, after just a few steps, he felt Arno's body thump into his, clamping itself to his legs from behind.

*"Nicht verlassen, Vater!"*

And Karl didn't want to go. He wanted to hold his youngest just as tight. The son they'd been so afraid for, ever since he was in the belly of his mother whose heart barely kept her alive, let alone him.

If you reach full term, the baby will be born weak, tiny, sick, the doctor had predicted. But Arno was born big and strong, full of energy. The boy's a bull, the doctor declared in surprise. And his father's heart had filled with pride: against all the odds, his son was a survivor.

And he'd filled the house with joy.

Would he remember the father whom war had dragged away? Would Arno remember his face, his voice, his words? Maybe. He'd have that photograph taken this week, leave something to remember him by. He freed himself from the boy's arms. The Reich demanded it.

"I'll be back next Sunday, Arno. I'll bring you a surprise. Take care of your mother."

That was all he could say to his youngest, though he wanted to say much more.

Away from his family for the first time, every night, Karl prayed, but not to the Führer's German god: he prayed to the god of his ancestors, of his church, to the only one, to God.

"Let this war end before I have to go," he repeated until he slept.

He didn't ask to win the war: he asked for it to end, without conditions. But he supposed there were many more Germans praying for victory each night, because his prayers were ignored: to win, they had to stay in the fight.

Karl couldn't sleep the next Saturday night. He had the photograph ready. He knew his wife would smile and that his children would be thrilled to see the family's first portrait. They would have one taken all together when he returned from the war. He'd suggest it to them tomorrow. Then, Fritz and Johann would go with him to deliver the chest of drawers; Helga would bake bread for him to share at the barracks, and give him another pair of socks; Arno would make him laugh with the funny things he said; and he'd hold Ethel once more.

He'd find the strength to turn his back and leave. Then he'd spend another week doing the drills that, they assured him, would make him a model soldier of the Reich. He did everything they asked of him like an automaton; he never ventured an opinion, never said much. All he lived for was to complete the endless tasks his sergeant assigned. Time passed in this way, without thought and so without worry, while Karl waited for the next Sunday, the next visit home.

But at four o'clock on the morning of Sunday, June 22, 1941, the alarm sounded: everyone dressed, everyone armed, everyone outside, everyone ready for deployment.

To where?

No one answered. His fellow soldiers because they knew no more than he. And his superiors, to keep the big secret: Why did they need so many soldiers in a war they were winning? All Karl knew for certain was that he wouldn't see his family again, that he'd drown in the violent current of the river that he'd initially thought so beautiful.

The boys wouldn't help him deliver the chest of drawers. He wouldn't leave them his portrait.

The photograph would go to war with its subject. He'd try to send it by military post if he could. And he'd write, try to explain that they hadn't given him the chance to say a final goodbye. What would his children think that Sunday when he never arrived?

The truck that was to transport his battalion took two hours to arrive. Two hours standing there with his military equipment and some extra socks on his back, not for a moment allowing his expression to slip, the one he'd seen so often on the faces of soldiers in the news bulletins and on posters: pride, courage, love and sacrifice for the country, his eyes fixed on the horizon where certain victory awaited, so that no one would realize that all he really wanted was to run home and be held by his wife, and to wake up to the smell of freshly baked bread, ready to work with some fine wood.

Karl wanted this even more when, about to climb into yet another canvas-covered truck, he heard the sergeant proudly informing the driver of their destination.

Unlike the Jews and Poles, who surely hadn't been told where their trucks were headed, Karl knew: they were sending him to the east. And his children, he feared, would live afraid, hungry. Fatherless. Without the freedom to chart their own course.

This war wasn't nearly won; quite the opposite: it had grown into a monster, a hydra, and no sooner was one of its heads cut off than a new one would grow.

And the newest head was Russia.

How right his father had been.

From that day on, Karl prayed that the war would end before his sons were of fighting age.

# 9. The day will come when everything is understood

Normally, going to church was not on Arno's list of favorite activities; he never understood anything the priest said, and he always preferred the kind of music on the radio.

"You're only six. By the time you have your first communion, you'll understand everything," Helga would tell him.

"Everything?"

"Yes. Everything."

Arno was looking forward to the day when he'd finally understand it all: the priest's words; his mother's illness; her amicable hostility toward Frau Färber. What a stuck-up woman, she often said, and her butter isn't even that good. Or, she thinks she can give me less butter for my eggs! He wanted to receive communion so he'd understand why the Army wanted to take away his carpenter father but not the farmer Herr Färber; he wanted to comprehend his brothers' passion for war games and why he always had to be the prisoner and they the winners. That's war, they told him. The Germans always win. To which he replied, I'm German, too; I want to win, too! But what he most wanted to make sense of was his father's painful absence every day that wasn't Sunday.

He often went to bed at night missing him, upset by his mother's irritable state, sore from the ropes he'd been tied up with in the day's games. He fell asleep abandoned by Helga, who now spent all her free time knitting socks for their father. The only thing that consoled him a little was remembering her promise: By your first communion, you'll understand.

What's more, Sunday morning church had become a signal: Vater will be here soon. So now he liked it a little more.

That Sunday, he dressed quickly, and was already on the cart when his mother called for him. He made out a slight smile on her face, a rarity in this lonely time.

Arno didn't care about the service, which was just a lot of words that he sat through waiting for the *amen*; nor the time after, when the adults would chat, time he passed playing with Werner Färber, though it felt as if he were betraying his mother a little by having fun with their crazy neighbor's son. Arno was just waiting for the moment when they got back home, when he could fetch the tools.

There hadn't been so many Sundays like this, but Arno felt as if it had been this way his whole life. It seemed that one step perhaps led to the next: the service to the chatting, the chatting to the games, the noisy games prompting the adults to head home, the cart to the road, the road to their home, their home to their chores—some of them cooking; others cleaning; him, fetching the tools.

When all the steps were completed, his father would appear. That's how it worked. So that day, Arno went out onto the road carrying the heavy, noisy tools, thrilled once again to be the first to see him arrive.

At any moment.

And then his mother would serve them lunch and his father would say, mmm, this is the best I've ever tasted, though it was the same stew his mother made every Sunday. Thinking about the stew made Arno's mouth water and his stomach tighten.

At any moment his father would appear with the smile that was never missing from his face.

And from standing there so long, Arno's legs began to grow tired, but he was in his Sunday best, and he didn't want to upset his mother, just as he didn't want to disappoint his father, who always said to him, look after your mother, and one way to look after her was to avoid making her cross or giving her more work by muddying his clothes. He also wanted his father to see him dressed up nice, to tell him that he'd done it all by himself, and for Vater to say to him—because he definitely would—and look how handsome you are.

He was about to come around the bend, Arno was sure, and he didn't want to take his eyes off the road; he didn't want to miss the moment.

But it was Herr Färber who appeared on his cart.

"Young man, fetch your mother."

Arno didn't want to fetch his mother; he had a mission to carry out. But he heard his parents' voices: Respect your elders. He tore his eyes from the road to go in search of his mother, and then returned as quickly as he could to his post.

His mother arrived, surprised that it was Herr Färber looking for her.

"Frau Schipper, I just heard the news: all the troops stationed in Königsberg have been mobilized."

The conversation continued, and Arno could hear the distress in his mother's voice, and would have liked to have told the man to stop talking, to stop upsetting her, but adults had to be respected and he had to keep his eyes on the road. His father would appear at any moment, and he would take charge of driving the neighbor away.

Then Herr Färber left without needing to be told.

"Arno."

His mother was speaking, but he couldn't look at her.

"Arno. Let's go in."

"Vater hasn't arrived."

"No. He hasn't arrived. But let's go in. You must be hungry. You don't want Vater to find you all skinny, do you?"

No, he didn't want that. And yes, he was hungry. Very. He would eat quickly. He'd be back soon.

But Arno never returned to the road to wait for his father, not that Sunday or any other. His father was now a real soldier, his mother explained. Would he come next Sunday? No. When? I don't know. But be proud: he's gone to defend the fatherland so you can grow up and we can be happy.

What? Hadn't they been happy with their father at home?

Arno tried to be proud. He tried to be glad. But he couldn't, and he didn't think his mother could, either. She tried to hide it, but Arno could tell she was sad, and it seemed to Arno that her telling him again and again to be proud was mostly to convince herself.

Why did his father have to leave for him to be happy? Would he understand that, too, by the day of his first communion?

His father had left without saying goodbye. Without revealing the surprise that he'd promised; without accepting Helga's last socks, her best ones; without Arno giving him one last hug. His best.

# 10. A flock of ill omen

## The Hahlbrocks

***June 23 to August 1941***

Ilse's short but definitive list of things to fear didn't include the motorcycle. She liked observing her father's hands as they rode. They were strong, firm hands, and with them in control, Ilse was never afraid. She enjoyed traveling in the sidecar, like a bold adventurer, but what she liked most was being with her father.

Her father had bought the bike as a newlywed, before moving to Prussia. Before all the children and all the expense, her mother said. It was the only one in the region, and on warm days, they all managed to climb on to go to church or visit another farm. Her mother sat in the sidecar with Freddy, and Irmgard and Ilse rode one in front of their father and one behind. In this jumble of bodies, he always said perhaps it wasn't the most practical vehicle now that they were a family of five with one on the way.

"Maybe I should sell it."

"No, Papa, no!"

Ilse knew that her father said it half in jest, but she protested strenuously, because when things are said half in jest, they're also said half in seriousness.

What would they do when the new baby arrived? They'd travel by cart, like everyone else, like they also did in the winter. But the motorcycle should still be there. So that Ilse could make out the sound of its engine in the distance, announcing her father's arrival; so that he could take her for rides; so that he could take her to school, precious time with just the two of them, even more precious now that her father had more work, more meetings, more Party obligations. Less time.

The motorcycle was her father's, but it was hers, too, because with Irmgard at boarding school all week and Freddy so little and delicate, she was the only one who went out for special rides with him. And she delighted in those shared journeys, even if it was almost impossible to have a conversation over the roar of the engine and the wind in their ears. But it was closeness that they sought, and looks were enough to tell each other: Look at that cow with bulging eyes, or look what's on that roof, or what about that gigantic fallen tree, or that woman chasing a petticoat snatched by the wind, or that cloud shaped like a running rabbit?

Whatever they had to say with words could wait until they reached their destination.

But on their journey that perfect morning, almost at the end of the school year, when the first light of the day filtered through the trees, her father gave her no looks. He was focused beyond the road, on the world that sometimes absorbed him so much that, if Ilse assailed him with her insistence to look, Papa, look-look-look-look-look, he would, with great difficulty, turn to her with confusion in his eyes. Who are you and what're you doing here, those eyes seemed to ask for an instant. And that instant cut straight through her. So that day, Ilse let him sink into his musings and, in solidarity, she sank into her own.

When they reached the Witzleben estate, her father left her in the kitchen in the care of Frau Wollatz.

*"Guten Morgen,"* he said to the woman, then turned to Ilse. "Wait for me here. I won't be long. Then I'll get you to school."

"On time?"

"Of course."

Ilse didn't mind waiting for him there. She knew the estate well, because her parents often left her with Frau Wollatz, the housekeeper, when they had to take Freddy to the doctor.

"Do you want some breakfast, Ilse?" the woman asked her.

"Yes. Bitte."

Though there were no children to play with, Ilse was never bored at the Witzlebens'. Frau Wollatz, who'd grown up there in the shadow of her mother, from whom she'd inherited her position, knew the story of every wall that had for generations formed the home of the Witzleben family. When the two of them walked into a room, she'd say to Ilse, look, the countess brought that vase home from a trip to China in 1909. Or, that portrait of the current heir's great-uncle, he was hunchbacked, but they made him look straighter in the painting, see?

While Frau Wollatz oversaw the cleaning of the parquet floor in the ballroom, Ilse could almost hear music playing—a waltz by Johann Strauss they often played on the radio—and she spun and spun, stopping only to drop from dizziness or when Frau Wollatz instructed her to go to the kitchen. Then she raced off, her dizziness forgotten, because the cookies she knew were waiting enticed her more than any fantasy.

But what she liked most about the castle was the rose garden. Frau Wollatz always let her cut one for her mother, and her father said that a single rose was enough to make her incredibly happy.

"Why can't we have roses like this on our farm, Papa?" she asked on one occasion.

"Because the geese would eat them. And then it'd give them the runs, and they'd dye the lake water pink. And water should never be pink, should it? Or would you like to be the only girl in the world with a pink lake?"

"No." Ilse didn't like the color pink. "But the goose poop would smell of roses."

They both laughed.

Ilse finished her snack, but Papa still hadn't come back. She'd be late for school, and the teacher would punish her, because the thing that displeased her most, aside from children with dark hair, was tardiness. Tardiness is for savages, she'd say. And then she'd send the unfortunate pupil to sit with the little ones if they were the oldest, or with the oldest ones if they were the youngest, or to spend the day facing the wall. The punishment depended on what she thought would hurt most.

The sun was shining bright outside and even without asking the time, Ilse knew it was getting late. She was about to go in search of her father when he came in.

"Let's go, Ilse. Say thank you."

*"Danke schön, Frau Wollatz!"*

Ilse had to hurry to keep up with her father, who didn't adjust his long strides in consideration of her short ones.

He lifted her into the sidecar without ceremony, then climbed onto the motorcycle and started it up. It wasn't the soft, gradual start that Ilse was used to. It was sudden, violent. As if the vehicle had forgotten who the owner was or the owner had forgotten himself.

They were going too fast for Ilse. And her father didn't turn to her once: he was in his private world again, where there was no space for her, where every connection was severed. Ilse wanted to shout, Papa, slow down, even if I'm late. But he drove like an automaton. Ilse would've liked to take his arm, but she was afraid, because her father had told her that, once they were riding, Ilse, you mustn't move from your seat or you'll fly out, crack your head open, and die.

Ilse didn't want to fly out, crack her head open, and die, so she held on tight and maintained the distance that the tension on her father's face demanded.

The trees streaked by like a green stain, as if fleeing in the opposite direction. And then they passed the lake still full of wild geese, lethargic perhaps from the previous day's migration. Ilse was pleased, without knowing why, to see that they, too, were scared of the metallic beast that almost drowned out their alarmed *wah-wah-wah*. She followed the mass takeoff with her eyes and watched their coordinated flight until they'd almost disappeared over the horizon. But suddenly it looked like the flock was returning, as if it had found the courage to confront the invading monster. Little by little, Ilse could make out the individual bodies, and then she saw that, though they had wings, they weren't geese. They were aircraft. Dozens of them in a flock, headed for the same destination.

Like giant geese.

And just as she was about to raise her arm to point out the spectacle to her father, he braked so hard that Ilse had to grab on to prevent herself from being thrown. The motorcycle stalled out, but now the sound of other engines filled their ears. Her father was looking up at the sky, and Ilse expected him to turn with a smile on his face, to say something, something like, imagine the color the pond would turn if the rose-eating geese were that big!

But no.

"Luftwaffe" was all he said before restarting the engine and setting off at full throttle.

That day, Ilse didn't have to worry about tardiness. Her father took her straight home. The grown-ups seemed to forget that it was a school day; they even forgot to say, don't go there, don't do that, and don't say such things, and Ilse, infected by their gravity, didn't go there, or do that, or say such things. That day, she kept silent, not bothering anyone, so that they wouldn't notice her presence. She listened; she tried to understand, but she couldn't.

Because that day, the adults spoke only of how life would change now that the war had flown over their remote corner of Germany on the way to Russia. That day, there was no freshly baked bread for dinner.

The next day, Ilse got up and dressed for school, but when she went down, her father was already gone.

"There's no school today," her mother told her. "Summer vacation's started."

Ilse knew vacation wasn't for another week, but didn't question her mother. Later that day, Irmgard returned from boarding school.

"You're on vacation, too?"

"Yep," said Irmgard.

She didn't seem very happy about it.

By nightfall, they both had a bag of clothes on their bed: an everyday dress, a Sunday one, underwear, and Sunday shoes. There were also toothbrushes, hairbrushes, and ribbons.

"Frau Wanda told me to pack them for you," said Jadwiga, their mother's new helper.

"But why?"

The girls were going on vacation, their mother explained when she came up. To their aunt Ida's house. She was the wife of Uncle Josef (their father's brother), who lived in Schneidemühl.

"You'll have a wonderful time, Ilse. You'll meet your cousins."

"But who's going to help Janusz with the wheat? Who's going to play with Freddy? Can I take some stories?"

Irmgard, who took the train to and from school each week, had told Ilse that they could read on the journey, and since there was no way to dissuade her mother from sending her away, Ilse wanted to experience this for herself.

Early the next day, they were taken to the station. While their father bought the tickets, their mother enveloped both of them at the same time in a long hug. The two girls fitted perfectly into her cocoon of silence, heartbeats, clothes, and summer skin. Ilse felt her mother's arms press against hers, skin against skin, as if wanting to ward off an imaginary chill, and the feeling was very novel: an undistracted mother, completely focused on their shared embrace, those arms all for her, for once not busy chopping fruit, slicing potatoes, churning butter, sewing, cleaning.

Ilse wished that hug would never end, but the train's whistle forced them apart. Quick now. Their parents helped them board the train and lifted their luggage onto the rack. At their feet, they left the basket containing an envelope with their identity papers, food for the journey, and ham, salamis, potatoes, and preserves as a gift for Aunt Ida, who would be waiting for them at the station.

"I don't know her."

"As soon as she sees you, she'll know who you are: you look like me. So does Irmgard," her father told her.

She always liked it when he told her: You have my face, my eyes. Only, when Ilse looked in the mirror, she couldn't see the resemblance: she saw big brown eyes, similar to her father's, but not his, just hers. Her little nose and smooth skin were nothing like her father's rough cheeks that scratched her when he gave her a goodnight kiss. And he had short hair, while she had braids. She doubted that Aunt Ida would recognize her, though he assured her she would. The fear persisted.

"What if she doesn't come?"

"She'll be there," her mother promised. "Just remember: you have to get off at Schneidemühl."

"How will we know when we're there?"

"Railway stations have a sign at the entrance with the town's name. You have to look for it at each station. But it'll be hours before you arrive."

"What if we miss it?"

"You won't. Irmgard will look for it."

"What if she falls asleep?"

In the end, they decided to leave the girls in the care of a couple who were traveling beyond Schneidemühl.

"They'll tell you when to get off. Irmgard will take care of you. Do as she says."

The train's whistle announcing their departure made Ilse forget her nerves and concentrate on the wonder of the journey ahead. There was time for another brief hug.

"God bless you, Ilse," she heard her father murmur softly against her head.

When they reached Schneidemühl, both girls were awake and alert, and the couple taking care of them, asleep. They saw the sign, gathered their belongings, and got off. Ida spotted her nieces easily: they were the only unaccompanied girls. Ilse thought she had a kind face, but she looked tired: her mouth smiled, but her eyes didn't.

"My mama sends you this, Tante Ida," Irmgard said, handing her the basket.

Their aunt peered into the basket, and then the smile reached her eyes. Just. A flicker.

At the brisk pace set by their aunt, they walked all the way to the house where they'd spend their vacation. On the way, Ilse observed everything. She'd never seen so many cars and houses all together. Nor had she seen so many people in one place. Women of all ages and some elderly men, all coming and going in a hurry; they crossed the street with long strides, they walked alone or in groups, but all of them seemed to have one thing in common with their aunt Ida: a tiredness that stole the color from their cheeks, and an opaqueness in their gaze that made Ilse want to look away, at anything that wasn't their eyes.

When they reached the home of the other Hahlbrocks and their three cousins came out to greet them, Ilse noticed that they had the same sullen look. She wondered if the problem might be that these people lived too far from the countryside. Or too far from Janusz's stories. Later, when she tried to share the story of the Wawel Dragon, hoping to cheer them up, her aunt stopped her.

"What're you telling them, Ilse? We don't have time for stories here."

In the evening, they ate ham and potatoes in portions measured precisely according to their ages, and smaller than the ones Irmgard and Ilse were accustomed to. The ham had to last at least five days, Aunt Ida explained.

Martha, her ten-year-old cousin, would give them her bed for the length of their stay. She would sleep with her mother.

"Where's your papa?"

"He went to war," said Martha.

"Why?"

"Ilse, stop asking questions," Irmgard told her.

Ilse did as she was told, but she couldn't understand why a papa would choose to go far away and, worse, to war. Many of her schoolmates' papas had gone, too, but she hadn't said anything to them; she didn't want to hurt their feelings by saying, your papa's an idiot, especially when they seemed so proud. War is for idiots: that was what her mama said when she thought no one was listening, when she was so worried she talked to herself.

How sad that Onkel Josef was an idiot, too. Ilse resolved not to ask about him again.

Despite her exhaustion, Ilse struggled to sleep that first night. She missed home: the smells and the sounds, yes, but it hurt to imagine her mother without anything to do because she wasn't there—nothing to knit, nothing to embroider. How would she fill her time while Ilse was away? She missed being held by her father, who would no doubt be disappointed each evening when Ilse wasn't there to greet him. It upset her to think of Jadwiga being lonely when she slept by herself at night, and Freddy having no one to play with all day.

"I miss Mama," she said, but her words were lost in the darkness. Irmgard, more accustomed to being away from home, was already fast asleep.

Ilse missed everything. She even missed the dog she feared without knowing why, the dog that always looked at her with his enormous brown eyes as if puzzled, as if wondering why he had to share the father's attention with a creature like her.

And she missed going to bed without worry. At home, they told her: Go to bed, say your prayers, goodnight. And there was always time for a story. In the house of these other Hahlbrocks, they told her: Go to bed, lay out your clothes exactly right so you can put them on in the event of an emergency; that's not the right order, this is the right order; go to sleep now and wake up if you hear the siren.

What was a siren? What did it mean? What if she was asleep and missed it?

Maybe that was why everyone in this place looked tired: If they had to listen for a siren every night, how did they rest?

Ilse fell asleep. The next morning, she woke up in a panic.

"Irmgard! We didn't hear the siren!"

"That's because there wasn't one."

For Ilse, that was the worst thing: Some nights there was a siren and some there wasn't? So was it always a surprise?

"What does the siren mean, Tante Ida?"

"Run."

# *11. Sometimes it's good not to find what you're looking for*

Ilse had learned the routine of this town so far from home. In Schneidemühl, almost the entire day was spent gathering necessities, from food to information.

The day started early with a visit from a neighbor who knew where there was bread that was fairly fresh—and made with flour that was almost clean—or which butcher some fresh meat might reach. It made little difference: finding protein to fill their stomachs was always a matter of luck. While Ilse's aunt went out with ration coupons in hand, Martha was left with the task of watching the street from the window, looking out for a neighbor passing with full bags. Then she had to rush out and ask, what've you got there and where did you find it?

Ilse thought that Tante Ida must scour the entire town, which to the young girl seemed enormous, before returning, sometimes, with empty hands.

By the time I arrived, it was all gone, she'd say in a hollow voice.

Soap, flour, coffee, tea, potatoes, spinach, cabbage, pork shanks, chicken livers, and bones for stock were on the most-desired list. If she heard there was coffee somewhere, Tante Ida dropped everything to go out in search of it.

On nights when she'd had no luck—when, exhausted, she made do with preparing a thin vegetable broth accompanied by yesterday's bread—after giving thanks for their food, she'd say: If there's nothing here, it means there's something wherever Papa is. Can you picture him? I bet he's having pork shank for dinner.

"I have an idea, Tante: if you like, I'll go look for potatoes in the yard. My papa says I'm very good at it."

"Nothing edible grows here, Ilse."

Now Ilse understood the fleeting joy she'd seen in Tante Ida when she received the basket her mother had sent, and the other time when, two weeks later, Wanda had sent another package containing flour, onions, more potatoes, and a dozen bratwurst, and in a big tin, several dozen ginger cookies.

Ilse could've eaten until she exploded owing to the simple fact that her mother's hands had touched them, but Aunt Ida only gave them one each.

"We must save them. You can have another tomorrow."

In the afternoons, the children could go to the park.

"Stay there for a while. I'm going to the Wehrmacht office."

Because another thing that kept Tante Ida occupied was her daily search through a list of names—a new list each day, if they were lucky—at the High Command. Ilse had concluded, after several days observing, that finding the list was a good thing, but that finding the name was not.

"What is it that all those crying women find on there, Tante Ida?" she asked one day.

All the color drained from her aunt's face.

"Their dead."

This response set off a whirl of questions in Ilse's head, but with the help of a pinch from Irmgard, she contained it and put them all away.

The park was what Ilse liked most about her vacation in Schneidemühl. In part, it was because the green of the grass and trees reminded her of home, but it was also where time passed most quickly and where the heaviness lifted from her cousins' faces, if only for a while. Playing games in the open air, they stopped worrying about what they'd eat that day or what their mother would find on the list. There, the fear vanished; there, they didn't have to talk about bombs, the destructive marvel of the *Panzerkampfwagen*, or the threat of the *Untermensch*, who, according to her cousins and the posters, abounded in this region. For an hour, Martha taught them to play the circle games that she and Irmgard didn't know, though sometimes Ilse left them to go play marbles with her younger cousins. For a little while, their only concern was who jumped the highest or ran the fastest, who won the most marbles.

But then Aunt Ida returned, relieved that she hadn't found what she'd searched for so anxiously on the Wehrmacht list. It was time to go back for dinner, wash, and go to bed. They went to sleep with the sun still on the horizon, taking advantage of the last light of the long summer's day: lately, they had been forbidden from turning on the lights after dark.

And so they all had early nights, even Tante Ida. They all arranged their clothes just so in preparation for the emergency that had not yet come.

"It's a needless alarm. There's nothing of interest to them here," Ilse heard their neighbor Frau Klara tell Aunt Ida.

"There's a prisoner-of-war camp on the outskirts of town."

"Then all the less reason: Why would they want to attack their own people?"

But Tante Ida didn't seem convinced: she prepared each night as if, that night, the siren would definitely sound.

Several weeks after their arrival—now that Ilse was accustomed to her aunt's nocturnal rituals, now that she mechanically arranged her clothes just right, now that she slept the moment her head hit the pillow—the siren went off.

# 12. The Volksempfänger never lies

How empty the house felt without the girls, and how empty life was.

Jadwiga's presence helped, but it wasn't enough. The chores on the farm and Freddy's problems eating and breathing had persuaded Wanda that she needed help; that sometimes one woman can't do it all; and that it was better to accept it than collapse, not least when another baby was on the way.

She'd found the girl in the nearest Polish village.

I don't want an exile living in our house, she had told her husband. I want a woman who has family close by, who can go visit them on Sundays.

Jadwiga and her sister lived with their mother and grandmother. Their father and brother had been taken to work in a factory near Berlin. What kind of factory? No one knew. The women received letters written in the father's hand, but they were so censored that sometimes they couldn't understand a single sentence. It didn't matter. The letters served their purpose: their men were still together; they were still alive.

The mother and elder sister had only been saved from being taken away with them because, on the Sunday of the raid, the grandmother had fallen ill, and they had stayed home to take care of her.

Don't you miss church as well, Jadwiga, her mother had said. We don't need three to look after one.

And that was how Jadwiga, as she came out of the service, found herself surrounded by soldiers. There was no persuading them that the father and the brother were already Zivilarbeiter, already employed on a nearby German farm. She was the only one left behind when they found that she was not yet fourteen and therefore not legally obliged to do forced labor.

She'd returned home alone, sobbing.

But before long, she turned fourteen and had to register, and when her mother had heard the Hahlbrocks were looking for help, she'd gone herself to offer her daughter's services.

"She'll be a good worker, Frau Hahlbrock. You need someone and we need the money."

"I'm not allowed to pay more than the law sets for Polish workers."

"Frau Hahlbrock: anything will help, but more than that, I'm asking you to hire Jadwiga so they don't take her away. She's a good girl; she's young, but very hardworking. She'll be a great help to you."

Wanda had accepted, and now she couldn't fathom how she'd managed for so long without help. Jadwiga was a very good girl and the children loved her; even Irmgard, though she only saw her on weekends, and despite the supremacist ideas they filled her head with in the Jungmädel and at school.

But Irmgard was a kind girl, and, in any case, neither rudeness nor mistreatment were permitted in the Hahlbrock household. Not toward anyone. And Wanda liked to think that their compassion wasn't just down to her fear of what Freddy would endure when he was older because of his facial defect, but because nothing, not even the Führer, could make them forget the golden rule: to treat others as you'd like others to treat you.

Since she arrived, Jadwiga had shared Ilse's bedroom, and she woke her up on school days, but was forbidden from helping her dress or brush her hair. If Ilse's shoes were muddy, she had to wait until the younger girl had cleaned them herself; if her sweater was covered with twigs or dirt, it was Ilse who had to remove them before she was allowed to go out to play. But she read stories to the child, they sang songs, and laughter sometimes came from the bedroom when they were supposed to be asleep.

Girls! Go to sleep now! Wanda would shout, as if they were both her daughters.

It was easy to forget the reality of Jadwiga's status, and, knowing her well, loving her, it was difficult to understand the scientific reasoning that, according to the Party, proved Slavs were inferior.

For Wanda, it was hard to see inferiority in someone with a heart as good as this Polish girl's, and her intelligence was undeniable; she'd made Ilse's mathematics homework an adventure for the young girl; she devoted so much time and patience to teaching Freddy words he could barely pronounce, but which she understood perfectly when he repeated.

At the same time, wherever one looked, there were posters depicting the vileness of the Jews, and the newspapers and movies portrayed the Poles as an ignorant and inept people, dirty and backward. All one had to do was turn on the *Volksempfänger* radio receiver to hear an announcer or scientist proclaiming the greatness of the German bloodline and the savagery of undesirable bloods.

Wanda didn't know any Jews, but she'd lived among Poles as a child and now again as a married woman. It was clear to her that there were dirty and ignorant Poles, of course, but there were also Germans like that; and just as there were industrious and intelligent Germans, there were also such Poles.

Wanda thought it best to turn off the Volksempfänger and throw the leaflets she was given straight in the trash unread. Nobody was going to force her to hate.

But Ilse's school made it difficult to banish these ideas from the house completely.

There were lessons in which Ilse had to write, a hundred times: *Judas the Jew betrayed Jesus the German.* Since when was Jesus German? Wanda wondered. Since the Nazi Party had seized control of everything, she supposed, from the alphabet to history. It was impossible to contradict them. Impossible to close the book and ignore the homework that had to be handed in the next day, with good handwriting and spelling. It was impossible to go to the teacher and demand: Fräulein, stop teaching my daughter this garbage.

On one occasion, she'd found Ilse practicing, with the help of Jadwiga and Janusz, the lesson she had to memorize and present to the class on the characteristics of the Untermensch. "The greatest enemy of the dominant species on earth, mankind: The subhuman is a biological creature, crafted by nature, which has hands, legs, eyes, and mouth, even the semblance of a brain. Nevertheless, this terrible creature is only a partial human being. Although it has features similar to a human, the subhuman is lower on the spiritual and psychological scale than any animal. Not all of those who appear human are in fact so."

Wanda had interrupted her before she reached the explanation of who these Untermensch were: gypsies, Jews, and Poles, among others.

"Not here, Ilse."

"Why, Mama?"

"Because I'm going to help you inside. Jadwiga: look after Freddy for a while, yes?"

It was also impossible to tell Ilse that everything they were teaching her was pure nonsense. Knowing her, the next day, she would march into school and announce, my mama says everything you teach is nonsense, Fräulein. The danger wasn't that she might offend the teacher; the true danger was in offending the Party, which didn't tolerate any slight, let alone insubordination. And the teacher would rush to inform on them. Wanda no longer had any doubt about that.

On that day, she decided that Jadwiga would thereafter only help the girl with mathematics, because it didn't involve opinions or discrimination, at least at the elementary level. Wanda knew that for Irmgard at boarding school, not even mathematics was exempt: The Jews are aliens in Germany. In 1933, there were 66 million inhabitants of the German Reich, of whom 499,682 were Jews. What was the percentage of aliens in Germany in 1933? What had happened to the arithmetic that used apples and peaches for its calculations?

"And you, Ilse, don't talk about the Untermensch at home. Leave that for school."

"Do we know any?"

"Of course not."

At home, with the Volksempfänger switched off, the Party leaflets in the trash, Ilse's homework censored as much as possible, and their hands and their time occupied with the farm and with Freddy—Wanda tried to pretend that there was no war.

But all she had to do was go outside and bump into the Polish workers for it to hit her—like a bucket of freezing water—that not even Jadwiga would be with them if she had the choice. All Wanda had to do was go to the village with Freddy to be faced with staring eyes, prying questions—is he talking yet?—to feel cornered by the Vaterland's uncompromising attitude toward imperfection.

And since the day when Hartwig and Ilse saw the warplanes heading toward the new eastern front, all Wanda had had to do was go out and look up at the sky.

Many had thought the conflict was as good as won from the very day when war was declared on the Soviet Union, but Hartwig didn't understand why: the Russians must have had their reputation for a reason. And in the years of armed struggle, he'd always been grateful that the battles were taking place in every direction except against Russia, but he'd kept it to himself because doubting German power was akin to treason.

Hartwig would later admit to Wanda that he'd gone to see Von Witzleben, the owner of the estate he managed, on the morning after war was declared, worried he'd be dismissed and sent to the front.

"Certainly not," he told Hartwig. "We're going away for a while. And I'm entrusting you with everything."

In addition to running his own farm, Hartwig would now be responsible for supervising several others.

"As long as they're doing their job," Witzleben assured him, "the Reich needs farmers to stay put. It's to be expected that demand will increase. You must deliver. *Viel Glück.*" Good luck.

Hartwig understood: the Witzlebens were fleeing. Some in the region still remembered the Russian invasion during the Great War, and feared it would be repeated.

He left there with the weight of the world on his shoulders: it seemed as if there was no longer anywhere on Earth where it was not raining fire. Then he saw the air force fly overhead.

"For an instant, Wanda, I swear I thought it was the Russians coming to drop their bombs on us."

And then he told her how he rode off determined to do something; determined to save some of his family, even if it wasn't possible to save them all.

Hartwig didn't know where Von Witzleben thought he'd be safe, given the constant bombing of German cities, but guessed that his boss clearly preferred the prospect of British bombs to Russian hordes.

"Wanda, Von Witzleben's leaving East Prussia, and he's no idiot."

Wanda hated discussing the war, but with the attack on Russia, there was no avoiding it. The Hahlbrocks decided: they couldn't abandon their obligations, but they could send the girls somewhere safer, just for a while. Little Freddy would stay; he needed his mother.

Wanda's heart shrank when they went to the train station. A vacation in West Prussia, they said. They'd meet their cousins. It would be fun. What they didn't tell them, what their daughters didn't ask, was when they'd return.

They knew the British were bombing Germany's towns and cities, but there was nothing of military interest in Schneidemühl. Surely the British wouldn't waste their explosives. And right then, it seemed riskier at home, so close to Russia. Ida would be happy to have the girls, she assured Hartwig and Wanda, especially if they arrived with provisions.

So they said goodbye without knowing when they'd see their daughters again. Or whether they'd see them again, though neither Wanda nor Hartwig voiced that fear, even to the other.

Since then, the Messerschmitts had flown overhead, and convoys of trucks and even tanks had passed near the farm, but they always kept on going. The war still existed somewhere else: in the distant west, and east, in Soviet territory, which the Germans were seizing at devastating speed: the eastern front was moving farther east with each day.

The Soviets seemed to have folded like paper.

Edeline was born just a month after the first attack on the Soviets. This baby had been born under a lucky star, they thought, because while the Russians hadn't yet surrendered, they continued to retreat. Their initial certainty that their lives would change forever—that fire would rain down on them, that battles would flatten their wheat fields—now seemed unfounded.

The bullets and bombs were raining on Soviet heads.

The Russians won't last more than a few weeks, Party officials declared with disdain.

They're a backward people, said others.

Wanda and Hartwig wanted the optimists to be right, so they bit back their doubts. Still, the war's new front meant more soldiers and, thus, more work for Von Witzleben's farms. There were more troops stationed there and constant visits from officials, who scrutinized the accounts and required an ever-larger percentage of production.

Hartwig was more and more occupied outside the home, and Wanda felt more and more alone without her Irmgard and her Ilse. But she tried to be positive. She had Freddy, and now Edeline. Germany was laying siege to Leningrad, and the Soviet Army was in full retreat. The new school year would begin soon. It was time for their daughters to come home. That night, she asked Hartwig to send them a telegram.

But the next morning, as she fed Edeline, Hartwig returned pale faced.

"Back so soon from the telegram office?"

"I didn't make it. Wanda, the British bombed Schneidemühl."

# 13. Freddy cries amid thundering wheat

Ilse was running barefoot on soft summer grass. She ran with ease even though she'd been going for hours, without aim or purpose. As she ran, she wasn't short of breath, and there were no stones or nettles to hurt her. The sun's rays filtering through white morning clouds warmed her way. Her mother, she knew, was in the house cooking sauerkraut. Ilse would go back when her mama's voice called. Or when the smell of the food, accompanied by the scents of the flowers, grass, and pines, reached her here at the top of the hill.

She would sit and wait. In the distance, she could see everything: the house, the barn, the stables, the pink goose lake; her father in his motorcycle helmet and goggles, astride his horse, waving to her with his riding crop.

"Let's go for a ride, Ilse," he said quietly, knowing the wind would carry his invitation intact.

She didn't like to say no to her father, but when it came to horses, she made an exception.

"Not on the horse; you know that, Papa," she whispered back across the distance.

Her father turned and led his horse away over the onion field. He mustn't do that, Ilse said to herself.

"You mustn't do that!" she told him.

But the horse had disappeared, and now her father was making intersecting furrows with his motorcycle. The sidecar was empty. He was going without her.

"Wait! I *do* want to come!" said Ilse.

But it was too late; her father couldn't hear over the sound of the engine.

"Don't cry," Janusz said to her from the field of living wheat in which, with his scythe, he drew a golden, whinnying horse. "Here's your horse."

But that made her sob even more. Janusz knew she didn't like horses.

"Draw me a story, instead, Janusz."

*"Nie chcę. Nie dzisiaj,"* Janusz said in words he used with the other workers.

"What?" said Ilse. "I don't understand Polish!"

But Janusz just smiled, and, singing, he stayed in his wheat field drawing the horse, then adding a fox at its feet and clouds above its head.

*Chodzi lisek koło drogi,*
*Cichuteńko stawia nogi,*
*Cichuteńko się zakrada,*
*Nic nikomu nie powiada.*

Ilse wished Janusz would keep quiet. When they worked in silence on the stories in the harvested wheat, she understood him. But that day, his strange words stole the meaning from her. Or from him; she didn't know which.

And the clouds over the horse's head moved in the wind, which now also took away the smell of her mother's sauerkraut, and far-off peals of thunder reached her. Ilse had never heard thundering wheat before. It was almost like a purr. But like every storm, this one migrated, coming closer and closer.

And then, louder, the wails of a frightened, hungry child reached her ears. Freddy. Who else? Freddy, woken by thunder, crying alone without answer, because his mother was no longer there. Without her comforting hand, because she'd left on the bike with his father; without soothing songs, because they'd been extinguished by the approaching storm.

Ilse wanted to tell him: Freddy, don't cry. It's just wheat rain. Janusz will get his horse to take it away. Right, Janusz?

But the young man was gone and so was his golden steed. Ilse frowned; Janusz would never leave her like this, alone, so far from the house.

What was she doing so far away when Freddy was crying?

"Don't cry, Freddy. Don't cry now. Freddy! Don't cry!"

But Freddy couldn't hear her, and Ilse didn't know whether it was because of the thunder or because, with her father gone, with Janusz gone, the magic spell had broken.

"I'm coming!"

She tried to run as lightly as before to get back to the house, to get into the crib with him, as she sometimes did even though her mother forbade it.

Ilse ran, but she didn't get anywhere. She grew tired, the soft grass disappeared, replaced by sharp thistles and stones. And Freddy cried and cried and cried.

And she was shaking. She was being shaken. Was it Frau Wollatz's horse, the one that always looked at her, was the horse shaking her?

"Ilse!"

"Let me go!"

"Ilse! Wake up!"

Ilse made out Irmgard's voice. She opened her eyes, but the darkness was so thick she could almost grab hold of it. The green field had faded; the golden field of wheat had disappeared, but the crying in her dream had followed her.

"Freddy's crying."

"No, Ilse. Freddy's with Mama."

"What is that, then?"

"It's the siren!"

"The siren? What do we do?"

"Get dressed. *Schnell!*"

Yes, the nightly instructions: If the siren goes off, get dressed fast. Atop the precise piles, first underpants, then camisoles, petticoats, stockings, and pinafores. On the floor, their shoes.

But nobody had told her that she'd have to get dressed in the dark, disoriented and half-asleep. And the siren, the siren made her arms tremble, it made her hands clumsy. Dropping clothes on the floor, struggling to find them.

"Faster, Ilse!"

She put each layer on as well as she could, not knowing whether the buttons were in the right holes.

*"Schnell!"*

Or whether she'd put her underpants on backward.

"Hurry, Tante Ida's going!"

Scrabbling at her shoes as the sirens shrieked and the thunder rumbled closer.

Ilse was breathless by the time they went out. The dark street was full of people who seemed as confused as she was. There were children crying, women yelling the same orders as her aunt: Stay together, hold hands, stop crying, run.

Tante Ida's nieces and children followed her down streets and alleyways in the midst of a storm unlike any that Ilse had known before. The sky vibrated not with thunder but engines.

"Is it the Luftwaffe?"

No, it couldn't be; it didn't sound like the German flock Ilse had seen flying that morning with her father. These were monsters, dragons. How many? It was impossible to know, impossible to stop to look up, but whatever it was they were dropping fell with a strange whistle. It was when these things hit the ground, a building, or a bell tower that the sound roared, blowing out bricks and glass. The thunder wasn't coming from the sky: it was coming from the earth; it made the solid world around them crumble, and Ilse, panting from fear and the thickness of the air, ran holding Irmgard's hand. Wherever Irmgard went, she'd go, trusting her sister wouldn't lose sight of their aunt, because Ilse could no longer distinguish between one figure and another, between Tante Ida and a lady who at that instant was buried under a collapsing wall. Who one moment was there, and the next, gone.

Ilse froze as her heart skipped a beat, and the little air she'd managed to take in escaped. Maybe it'd been Tante Ida. Maybe not. Should they stop to help her? And their cousins? Were they lost?

"Irmgard!"

"Run, Ilse!"

Her parents had told her: Irmgard will take care of you. Do as she says. So she did as she said. She'd follow her sister blindly, blinded—by the night, the dazzling explosions, the dust. All she could see, all she wanted to see now, after seeing too much, was Irmgard's firm hand in her own and the ground she trod.

Some roads were now blocked with rubble. Irmgard jerked Ilse's hand back and forth with her own, signaling some sudden change in their path. Ilse obeyed but felt the scraping on her shoes, which weren't her Sunday ones, but even so, take care of all your shoes, Ilse; you know why, Ilse: take care of them so someone else can wear them when they don't fit you anymore, child; watch where you walk!

That voice, louder than all the chaos, distracted her from her distress.

Ilse! Take care of your shoes!

It was her mother's voice calling to her from the safety of the past, from Ilse's first forays up the stairs: Be careful, don't scrape them; on her visits to the pig pen: Don't get them muddy; when she ran through the fields, or on the gravel path, or dipped her feet into the goose lake, or when she went to see Janusz: Don't scrape them, don't get them dirty, don't get them wet; you must keep them clean, child!

Ilse heard her mother's voice, and she imagined that Mama was there, and it gave her the strength to take one careful step at a time over the pieces of what had been someone's home; to block out the roar of the monsters overhead; to not ask why Schneidemühl was crumbling around her; to erase from her mind, at least until she reached her unknown destination, that she'd witnessed death. Perhaps her own aunt's.

She had to run. Irmgard said so. Without scraping her shoes, as Mama ordered.

That night, Ilse didn't run easily like she had in her dream: The journey took her breath away, pricking her bare legs with gravel and flying glass. The dust filled her throat, her lungs. There were no green fields to admire, no smell of her mother's sauerkraut promising a feast. On the contrary, an acrid smell had taken her senses by storm, and it didn't leave her in peace even after the last bomb, or after that night, or after they'd left Schneidemühl. Her nose would recover, but her memory wouldn't: the smell would stay with her for years.

But that night, during those minutes when the sky seemed to fall on top of her, all Ilse wanted—all she could do—was to look after her shoes so that someone else could use them in the future; so her mother wouldn't scold her.

That was her shield and her fire.

How long did it take them to reach the shelter? Just long enough for the foundations of a little girl's sense of safety to crumble. How far did they travel? It could have been a few blocks or three entire towns. It was all the same. By the time they arrived, Ilse had no idea that they had taken the same route they did every day to go to the park.

As they climbed down into the shelter, she saw with relief that her aunt and cousins were with them. Her aunt wasn't buried and her cousins weren't lost; they'd only been transformed: now, they were gray.

All the color, from their hair to their clothes, had disappeared under layers of dust.

"We'll be safe here," Aunt Ida said as she brushed herself down.

Ilse turned and saw that her sister was the same; she looked like a living statue, struggling to breathe. Each wrenching breath was accompanied by a dry groan, a tearless sob. Irmgard was clearly trying not to cry, and the effort was making her squeeze her sister's hand—which she hadn't let go of since leaving the house—more and more tightly.

"Ouch! Let go!"

They all walked together to the far end of the damp, dimly lit basement. On a normal day, it would never have occurred to Ilse to go down into this underground room even to explore, let alone sleep.

The place filled with people trying to be calm, even as the explosions outside shook the cramped space. Here, a woman was crying inconsolably, because on the way she'd lost hold of her son's hand; there, an elderly man collapsed; somewhere else, a girl began to recite a prayer.

*"Vater unser—"* Our Father . . .

The anticipation of the familiar words soothed Ilse. Everything would be fine, because the words were for God and they'd please Him, but also because they'd transport her mother there, to the dark corner that the Hahlbrocks were settling into.

*"Im Himmel—"* In heaven.

Her mother told her to pray each night before bed. It was easy to do it together. Then, Ilse knew every word and never got the cadence wrong. Her mother's voice and her own merged into one, and Ilse thought it must be true: prayers reach God and He listens.

But when her mother wasn't there, the words wouldn't take shape in her mouth. She searched her mind and found them scattered, vague, and unpronounceable. Without the magic of the mother-daughter duet, they didn't make sense.

"Help me, Jadwiga," she'd sometimes ask the older girl.

"I can't, pretty one. I only know it in Polish. And anyway, I'm Catholic and you're Lutheran. Our Lord's Prayers must be different . . ."

So on that dark night, Ilse was grateful to be led by someone who could guide her safely through. She was about to join in when, a little out of time, in a bold voice eager to prove its patriotism, a second girl countered with the version Ilse had learned at school. Although the prayers were directed at two different figures, the words and the cadence were the same. Ilse's head swam.

Our Father,

Adolf Hitler,

which art in heaven,

thou art our great Führer,

hallowed be thy name,

thy name makes the enemy tremble,

thy kingdom come,

thy Third Reich comes,

thy will be done,

thy will alone

in Earth as it is in heaven.

is the law on Earth.

The war of prayers ended before Ilse could join either side; with the onslaught on two fronts, she lost the words. Perhaps she'd dropped them on the way, forgotten them in that warm place of green fields that now seemed as distant as a dream.

The girls and their cousins sat in silence, waiting for the bombardment of Schneidemühl to end. Tante Ida, who'd planned ahead, passed a bottle of water for them to share. A swig of cool water had never tasted so delicious to Ilse. When her breathing had slowed, when her cousins had stopped crying, Ilse huddled against Irmgard and fell asleep.

The attack had been over for hours when Ida woke them, anxious to return home, if indeed there was anything left of it. She'd waited until morning so they wouldn't get in the way of the first aid volunteers. They climbed out of the shelter, squinting in the bright daylight, and picked their way back through the rubble.

When they reached the house, Tante Ida faltered, looking ready to burst into tears.

*"Was ist los, Mama?"*

"It's fine, Martha. I'm just happy to be home, that's all," she said, inspecting the intact windows. "We were lucky."

"When will we have breakfast, Tante?"

"Into the bathtub first, Ilse."

"I don't want a bath. I'm too hungry and tired."

"Look in the mirror, Ilse. Go on."

Standing before the mirror in her aunt's room, Ilse took stock: She was as gray as the others, and the tiny cuts on her legs were beginning to burn. Her eyes looked strange, red and glassy, full of dust despite the tears welling up. Had she been there, her mother would've told her there was no reason to cry. Deep breaths, Ilse, she'd say as she applied some kind of ointment—but not before sending her to the bath.

Ilse went to the room she shared with Irmgard and took off her shoes. Could they be saved? She hoped so. She didn't want to see her mother's face when she found out that her daughter was wandering around Schneidemühl in her socks because she'd mistreated her shoes.

The next layer was her petticoat. Wait, that couldn't be right. She looked around and saw her pinafore under the chair, where it had fallen last night. Had she worn the petticoat as a pinafore?

Ilse forgot her anxiety about the shoes. Her mother had always told her: Ilse, never let your petticoat show. Irmgard would warn her in urgent whispers: Ilse! It's showing! Why hadn't she said anything last night? Now Ilse hadn't just let her petticoat peek out, which might happen when she jumped or climbed a tree, but she'd shown the whole thing all over town, from the red flowers her mother had embroidered on the chest to the lace hem. Everything.

Ilse took off the petticoat of shame, threw on her nightclothes, and went in search of her sister.

"Irmgard! I want to go home!"

"Be patient, Ilse. It won't be much longer."

"No. I want to go now!"

After Ilse's first experience with the siren, she didn't want to stay in Schneidemühl to repeat it. What was more, everyone there had seen her in her petticoat.

In Schneidemühl, her eyes were in danger of becoming like her cousins': forever sullen.

Would her father still recognize them when she returned home?

# 14. The past is best left there

The boss left very early that morning. He didn't give them any explanations; he just said: "Do the plowing for the potatoes. You know how. Janusz: take me to the train station."

Herr Hahlbrock didn't say a word on the way, either, but Janusz could see the anguish in his face.

When he returned, Janusz went to the house to return a jacket the boss had left on the seat. Jadwiga opened the door with Edeline in her arms. The little girl was crying inconsolably. He could see that Jadwiga had been, too.

*"Wszystko w porządku?"* Are you all right? he asked her in the language they shared.

*"Nie."*

The night before, Schneidemühl had been bombed.

"And the girls? Ilse?" said Janusz, his voice rising.

"We don't know anything. That's why Herr Hahlbrock went there."

A clatter came from somewhere inside, and the girl grimaced. Contrary to what might be expected, Frau Wanda wasn't crying. She wasn't speaking. She'd handed over Edeline and set about scrubbing every nook and cranny of the already-clean house.

"I offered her something to eat, some tea, but she doesn't even respond. Do you think the girls are all right?"

Janusz didn't know. How could he know? But he wanted to follow Wanda Hahlbrock's example and immerse himself in work to stop from thinking. He supposed he should join the other men preparing the potato field. But he didn't want to see them. He didn't want to work shoulder to shoulder with people who'd guess at his state of mind, and who'd take pleasure in their boss's misfortune.

Nor did he want to be alone.

"Shall I help you take care of Freddy?"

The relief on Jadwiga's face was instant. The baby wouldn't stop crying, and she wasn't going to stop, Jadwiga thought, until her mother stopped her cleaning frenzy; until the girls returned and tranquility was restored.

"She was feeding her when she received the news, you see."

Jadwiga was certain that Wanda had passed that fear to the baby in her milk, and that was why the child was now crying almost in rhythm to the brush on the floor. Little Freddy was still asleep. But when he woke, Jadwiga knew, a toddler whirlwind would be unleashed.

"I'm not going to be able to manage both of them by myself."

As if he'd overheard, Freddy chose that moment to wake up and start shouting.

"Take Edeline," Jadwiga said, and rushed off.

Janusz was left in the doorway with the screaming bundle in his arms, unsure what to do. He'd never been invited into the house; nor had they ever taken the baby out in the cool morning air. He walked in and closed the door behind him.

He couldn't remember ever having held such a small person, and felt like a giant with more goodwill than dexterity. Afraid of dropping her, he sat on the rocking chair by the hearth.

The fire wasn't lit now, but for Janusz, hearths meant home, family.

His little family of three had often sat around a fire, contemplating the swaying flames that consumed the wood he had collected in the forest. In minutes the fire ate up what had taken him hours to gather, but he didn't mind: it was a luxury that made those idle moments—those moments of togetherness and storytelling—glow. It was the only luxury they'd had in that poor corner of Poland that was now disputed territory once more.

What was there that interested both Russians and Germans so much?

It had been in front of that fire, the flames low, the stories about to end, that his mother, her little daughter asleep in her arms, had warned him to run when the Russians came. *Dlaczego, matka?* She shook her head with annoyance, her eyes staring into the past. Don't ask why, just do it.

In the horror stories she sometimes told, the monster always emerged from Russia's frozen forests. But she offered no personal details. The past was best left there, wherever it was.

And Janusz had honored his mother by escaping in time, by keeping away from the Russians. Now he had to concentrate on this little girl who wouldn't stop crying, who understood neither German nor Polish, who was unlikely to be soothed by a story in any language.

To rock her, he rocked himself; to calm her down, he calmed himself; to console her, he hummed the only tune he could remember of his mother's.

"What're you doing?"

Wanda's question surprised him and silenced his song. Still gripping a scrub brush, she repeated the panicked question with her eyes. Janusz got up carefully from the rocking chair to respond.

"I'm sorry, Frau Hahlbrock," he said. "I brought back a jacket that your husband forgot to take, and Jadwiga asked me to help her with Freddy, but she left me with the baby. She wouldn't stop crying, you see."

But now Edeline was quiet and the panic had gone out of Wanda's eyes.

"I know. Poor thing. Her mother can't think about her today."

"The girls will be fine, Frau Hahlbrock."

"Yes. They'll be home today."

And with the harmony that shared hope brings, Frau Hahlbrock set about cleaning the room, and Janusz sat back down in the rocking chair. He could hear Jadwiga playing with Freddy upstairs. Would they come down soon? He tried to remain serene for Edeline's benefit, but he wasn't used to being so still. He had implicit permission to stay where he was, with no task other than to hold the baby, but his idleness in front of his boss's wife perturbed him.

Concentrating on the movement of her arm as she brushed the floor, Frau Hahlbrock seemed not to mind that it was she who was punishing her body with work, instead of her Polish servant.

Should he say something? Try to help her, to lighten the load of her anxiety? But what could he say? Assuring her that the girls had been unscathed by a shower of bombs had already been quite forward.

And what did he know? What guarantees could he offer? Nothing. None.

Janusz tried to transport himself to Schneidemühl, to search for Ilse, to travel to her like the fairy-tale voice of Queen Jurata of the Baltic Sea traveled to him. He wanted to hear her voice, to find her mischievous eyes and keen ears. He'd tell her a story; he'd draw it for her in wheat. And if there wasn't any there, he'd draw it in whatever there was, even ash.

He'd make her smile. Another story, Janusz, she'd plead. Another and another and another. And he'd tell them. He'd tell her the old ones and also the new ones that had besieged his mind in recent weeks, unsatisfied because, absent their usual audience of one, they could only churn around and around in his head.

If someone had given him a pencil and paper at that moment, he would've written a story about a boy named Janusz who flew and in an instant arrived to rescue his little friend. Ilse would've been proud, he knew, because she'd been the one who'd taught him his letters in the wheat and on her little blackboard as she learned them herself. And maybe, just for a moment, she would believe the story as she read, expecting him to appear out of thin air.

But he was just an orphan who, though he believed in all the stories' wonders, knew that they must remain there: in the world of stories. Long ago he'd learned that great deeds and magical acts were not for him; the only power he possessed was his remarkable ability to retell them. He loved stories—they made life bearable—but Janusz had no illusions: he didn't live in a story where anything was possible.

He was sitting there, his arms filled with a new life to whom he had nothing to say, while Ilse was far away, perhaps lost forever. That was reality.

He'd missed her from the moment she was gone. He hadn't even had the chance to say goodbye. And at first, he hadn't understood why she had left.

The Poles were forbidden from having radios, but they risked their lives for information. In the village, searches were carried out from time to time. When a device was found, it was confiscated and the owner taken away.

But even in complete radio silence, the Polish townspeople learned everything, albeit through slower methods than the Volksempfänger: through word of mouth.

Many had been delighted to hear the announcement of war with Russia, celebrating what they saw as the beginning of the end for Germany. Józef, Radosz, and Tadeusz were among these. They were certain: soon the Soviets would win and the Poles could return to their homes!

When? asked Janusz. When would the Russians arrive? He needed to know so he'd have time to run.

Once he'd understood the imminent danger, he'd been relieved that Ilse and Irmgard, at least, were safe from the Russians, that they'd gone to their aunt's.

But there in Schneidemühl, instead of furious Russians, British bombs had fallen on them.

And waiting for news was killing him. Or rather, inaction while he waited was killing him. He wished he could put Edeline in her crib and snatch the brush from Frau Hahlbrock so he could scrub the floor himself to let out his pent-up energy. But he didn't dare do the former, because it would mean going upstairs—where he'd never be invited—let alone the latter.

Poor Frau Hahlbrock: to stop herself dying of anguish, she was showing the floor no mercy.

# 15. The summer war

## The Schippers

***Summer 1941***

"Why'd you bring so many socks when it's summer?" his fellow soldiers asked.

They assumed the war would end before fall; it was what they'd been promised, so why carry so many thick woolen socks?

"My daughter made them."

Karl Schipper didn't need to give any other answer. His daughter had knitted them as best she could: crooked, uneven, made from coarse wool that irritated the skin. And they were heavy. After Karl marched for hundreds of kilometers, his backpack weighed more than seemed possible, and wool was heavy as lead. But his daughter had knitted them for him, and, in each tight, loose, or missing stitch, she had woven the warmth of home, her desire for her father to come back. He felt that love in each sock, and he treasured it.

At first, it had been summer, and no: he hadn't been assailed by such a yearning for home that he'd worn them on his feet. He wore the regulation socks, which fit better inside his boots, and which kept his feet cool on those long summer treks, sometimes walking through mud, sometimes climbing, sometimes crossing sandy terrain.

So he hadn't worn them at first. But he smelled them; he stroked them; he squeezed the woolen balls in his hands and pressed them against his mouth when the echoes of the bombs that had deafened him all day didn't let him sleep; the nights when the endless cries of pain (from Germans and Soviets) tormented him; the nights—all of them—when he could not suppress the fear that was his constant companion. Sometimes, they became the bank in which Karl Schipper deposited his screams.

They were his anchor and his compass. With them in his hands, he slept and he awoke. He squeezed them and they comforted him; they gave him the strength to get up the next day, and the next, and the next.

Today—today, at least—you're alive, he told himself with his nose buried in the woolen folds. Then he stuffed the socks deep in his backpack, inside a tin box that he'd found lying on the road. Yes, it made his pack heavier, but it protected his socks from the water and the dust, and, as far as possible, from the war.

His daughter had knitted them, and they lightened life in the war that weighed on him far more than the burden on his back.

Karl spent all summer carrying around winter socks. Why do you have them, when we're going home soon? A foolish question with an unvarying answer.

He carried them because he knew, from the moment he reported for duty in Königsberg, that even a few days would be too long for someone who'd never slept apart from his wife since the priest had blessed their union. Who'd never gone to bed without giving his children his own blessing followed by a kiss.

The heaviest thing in his backpack was the portrait he'd had taken for them, which he also kept in the tin box between two pieces of cardboard. He never took that out. What for? To see and not be able to recognize himself? To long for better times?

Without looking, he knew that not even his own mother would recognize him if he caught up with her in heaven. Just by touch he could feel the new angles of his face, the unwanted angles sculpted with the sharp chisels of hardship and anguish. With the keen knowledge that, a few paces away, just out of sight, there was always someone who wanted to kill him despite not knowing his name.

At first, a few months ago, but an eternity to Karl, the journey had been relatively easy despite the pain—of longing, of leaving behind his family, and of Königsberg. They'd said to him: You're with the 18th. In his division, everyone had been assigned a task. The Army was, he thought, like a well-oiled machine in which each cog moved of its own accord, without failure and without doubting that the others were also playing their part. Because failing in their duty would never occur to them. It would be like failing the Führer himself.

With such machinery, how could they not win the war in what remained of summer?

Karl was new to the art of war, but when he saw how smoothly things were run, he felt confident, reminded of his carpentry. Cupboard doors that close without a sound, a drawer that slides without getting jammed, two pieces of wood that join together perfectly, complex marquetry fitted seamlessly into fine wood . . . That was what the German Army was like. And he felt hopeful. They would win.

Soon, he hoped. Very soon, he prayed. And in the early days of the conflict, everything suggested they had God's blessing, even the blessing of the Soviets, who did little to resist them.

He would walk, they told him. Eastward. And he walked. They'd all advance to victory. And he walked. He learned to sleep outdoors without letting his guard down. He learned to keep watch despite having marched all day. He learned to fall asleep the moment he laid his head on the hard pillow of the ground, despite the snoring and the sobs of a fellow soldier who, even in his dreams, was gripped by the horror of battle. And after each night's sleep, he learned to face the next morning, the new orders, the new directions in which they had to walk and shoot.

He marched across land that his feet had never trod and imagined how, in better times, he would've stopped to admire the scenery, to talk to the locals. But it was impossible to stop and admire anything, even the rhythm of their march: the war scorched the earth as they passed.

With each step and each battle, his shoulders gradually familiarized themselves with the weight of his backpack, his hands with the feel of his *Karabiner*, and his entire body with the weapon's kickback. He aimed and fired as he'd been trained but never—not even once—paused to notice the destruction, or how his bullet hit its target. He did his part for Germany, but he didn't have to enjoy the death he caused. No number of accumulated footsteps, no number of bullets, had made Karl Schipper forget himself.

The German Army cut through Lithuania like a bolt of lightning, and then Latvia, because Soviet forces had neither their armaments nor their organization. Nor their fervor, it seemed. They ceded their most recently acquired part of Poland to the German advance guard. And as Karl marched to the northeast with the 18th, some walking like him, some in trucks, others in panzers, they scattered.

But even with all this success, Karl never forgot that, one day, he might well stop a bullet with his body. It could happen to anyone, from the least experienced private to a lieutenant colonel; no medal, rank, wish, or prayer served as armor against bullets and bombs.

When they reached Riga, Karl was certain that on that very day they would announce a total victory. The entire city turned out to welcome them. Parading with his division through the crowded streets, where the Latvians' cheers rose up into the sky, gave him the strength to walk a little more upright than he'd managed in recent days: after so much time on the road, his regulation socks had worn thin, and his feet were covered in bleeding sores.

The Latvians welcomed them as liberators, and he—a carpenter from a humble village—had contributed to that liberation. Perhaps this was the secret of those who loved war, he thought: all that fighting and loss in exchange for the satisfaction of changing the world. That day, it seemed worthwhile. That day, he almost understood the Führer's motives for taking on the whole world; he almost believed that Germany had regained its former glory.

And that day, he couldn't help but forget his contrition for defying his father a little, shrug off his fear for his children, to relive the youthful pride that had persuaded him to believe in Adolf Hitler.

Marching in the celebratory parade, Karl briefly believed these would be the last steps on the road of war. All along the route, beautiful women approached to give him bunches of flowers, which he accepted, and kisses, which he rejected. He was a married man; that, he didn't forget for a moment.

His division stopped for a few days in Riga. They followed their orders by day, and at night they drank beer or sought out female companionship.

But not Karl. Once the euphoria of their triumphant entry into Riga had passed, Karl realized that nothing had changed, that this was just one more point on a map. Those who knew about war attached little importance to the gains they'd made so far. The earth they'd scorched was small potatoes. They wanted more.

Karl didn't know when they'd be ordered to set off again. In the meantime, he carried out his duties without coveting anything more than the moments of rest, the rare privacy and reprieve he found in a half-ruined stable. He didn't even mind sharing it with its owner, a good-natured old horse.

"Listen, horse: if you don't step on me, I won't saddle you up or take you to war. Don't kick me, and I'll leave you here to die happily of old age. *Jawohl?*"

Even in that modern war, motorized vehicles couldn't do everything: to transport all the armaments and provisions for such a large army, another army of horses was needed to pull carts. Two hundred thousand, at least, a groom had told him, depressed from seeing so many die so horribly.

Because if a man's life was worth little in war, a horse's was worth less. They were left to die from bullet wounds, exhaustion, and colic. They were pushed off the road, left behind without anyone bothering to clean up the entrails or brains, and that was what the unfortunate horses that still lived trod on as they headed into another battle.

The dead were replaced with new ones seized in captured towns and villages.

Karl didn't expect, in what remained of his life, to get over the shock of seeing a man die. It could happen in a blink. And what a waste of possibility, the possibility of a new world with each man gunned down. But it was men who waged wars, and while many wouldn't have chosen to fight, at least they had some understanding of the purpose and risk. At least they had the option of pressing their chest to the ground to try to stay alive a little longer, with a bit of luck or the enemy's poor aim.

But a horse did not. These farm horses had been snatched from their fields without explanation, without training to help them endure the sound of the bullets that flew around them, bullets that found their neighbor's flesh or their own.

"Don't step on me, horse. Stay here in your home."

There, by the light of an oil lamp, Karl wrote his first letter to his family.

> *Dear family,*

He stopped. What should he tell them?

> *I'm well. We've marched a lot. Now we've stopped to rest in Riga, where we were welcomed as heroes.*

The fleeting excitement that seduced him during the parade had faded as soon as the clamor was over; when the pain in his feet and the echo of bullets had returned, all the bullets that had hit a countryman or the enemy. Enemies. Karl Schipper had never dreamed that one day he'd have enemies.

He couldn't write about that to his family. He glanced up at the horse.

> *I'm here with a new Latvian friend, who, very kindly, is sharing his quarters with me. I talk to him in German about how beautiful my wife is, and how clever all my children are, how devoted to their mother. I tell him how proud I am of all of you and how sad I am to be away for so many weeks. I imagine that, by now, you've all grown like the summer grass I've seen from the road. And I laugh when I tell him that I imagine Arno as tall as the oak tree that gives us shade.*
>
> *Because of the language barrier, my friend doesn't understand me, but he listens attentively. In return, he tells me about the beautiful fields of his country, the whole of which he seems to have traveled, if the damage to his feet and the arthritis in his knees are anything to go by. He tells me about family dinners after giving thanks to God for the food. He tells me that what they want here is freedom; for the wars to end forever. He's glad that he's old so he doesn't have to fight, because all he wants is to stay in the home he's always known.*
>
> *I don't understand his words, either, but I sense their meaning.*
>
> *On this journey that's taken me so far away from you, in the company of this friend, who now snores and snorts beside me, I've come to the conclusion that, whatever our*

> *language, we have more things in common with each other than things that divide us. And all I want is for those who are promising that this war will end soon to speak the truth, because my only wish is to return to you, to our family dinners, and to tread only on my land, German land.*

He didn't want to write any more. He had no more words of hope.

"And you, horse. Any suggestions?"

The horse snorted.

"Ah, yes. You're right."

The horse was asking him to stop his complaining, put out the oil lamp, and let him sleep so that he could snore and snort as Karl had alleged. But a letter to the family couldn't end without a goodbye and some advice.

> *The days here begin even earlier than at home. I'm a carpenter even in the war, would you believe? There's always something to build or repair. Now I have to go mail this letter so that it's sent to you tomorrow, and then rest. There are many cart wheels waiting for me that need reinforcing.*
>
> *Make sure you do your jobs on the farm, at school, and for your mother. Help her and don't give her any trouble. Don't forget to check our cart's wheels and take good care of our horse.*
>
> *Your loving father and husband,*
>
> *Karl Schipper*

He was about to seal the envelope when something occurred to him. Something very important. He only hoped that, if anyone else read the note, they wouldn't be offended that he had left it until the end.

*PS: Heil Hitler!*

He'd wait for another opportunity to send his photograph. It didn't fit in the envelope he'd been given, and he didn't want to fold it.

Karl's bleeding feet healed a bit during the respite in Riga. Before entering Russia proper, there was much to repair: engines, axles, damaged hammers. Fortunately, there were engineers and mechanics. And Karl's carpentry skills had been in demand from the moment the first cart had been damaged, and later, when the need arose, he'd improvised a temporary officers' quarters with wooden boards. *These quarters are bombproof, Schipper*, the division commander had marveled.

And so it turned out that Karl Schipper, reluctant soldier, had his own expertise to contribute to the war.

He'd missed his carpenter's calluses, seen his hands grow soft with nothing more taxing than aiming and shooting. So in Riga, as ordered, he devoted himself from dawn to dusk to enthusiastically repairing damaged carts and wheels. It comforted him to put aside his Karabiner and replace it with a saw or mallet, though they weren't the ones he knew so intimately and didn't have the familiar weight and scratches that were like known, loved, necessary scars. In time, thanks to them, his calluses regained their hard-won size and hardness.

At night, with no energy left for any beer-warmed talk of war or conquest, he returned to his stable in spite of the friendly voices saying to him, *are you leaving, Schipper? Why so early? Have a drink with us!* He rested at the feet of the horse who offered him not just respite each night but also a friendly ear.

In this war where each cog performed its duty, the long-missed duties of carpentry gave Karl the excuse not to look up from the sawdust to observe the rows of Latvian civilians that his division escorted to the outskirts of town. He used his mallet and handsaw to silence the wails and the ominous tramp of footsteps. Later, at the end of the day, his exhaustion gave him an excuse not to ask—even to ask himself—what had happened to those people, his fellow soldiers having returned alone to lose themselves in the warmth of the beer and of other Latvian bodies.

He didn't want to know. He didn't even want to suspect. Better to just take refuge in his stable and cling to his socks.

Having repaired what needed repairing, the 18th Army resumed its advance to the northeast. Karl walked again, as he was ordered, behind the column of vehicles, motorized and horse-drawn.

On the outskirts of Riga, no engine, no whinnying horse, no amount of denial could distract him from the hundreds of carrion birds hovering happily over a feast some distance from the road. And nothing, not the horses' excrement nor the engines' fumes, could mask the stench of death. The wind moaned through the pine forest in the voices of all those souls marched to their demise by German weapons.

Karl vomited, and he wasn't the only one. No one said anything.

In Riga, they'd been welcomed as liberators.

# 16. Ice kills patience

***January 1942***

Arno was the only Schipper who could contend with the ram. At that age? his sweetheart would one day marvel. The youngest, and you were the one who had to fetch the ram? It wasn't that he had a special power over animals in general or over troublesome rams in particular; it was that Arno could be more obstinate than the ram himself.

It wasn't easy: first they had to catch him with his nose busy in search of sweet grass to eat; otherwise, they'd spend the whole day playing catch-me-if-you-can. The ram knew the smell of humans—the Schippers in particular—and fled when he smelled them near. But he wanted his grass and didn't want to leave until he was sated.

Arno soon learned to approach from an angle opposite the direction of the wind, so it would steal his smell and carry it away. But having taken the animal by surprise, he had to be decisive and seize the ram by the horns. He would not be persuaded by gentle urging, nor even by a lead around his neck. It seemed that the ram would sooner choke to death than move an inch from his favorite spot on the Bäckers' farm or the flowerbeds Frau Hitzig used to tend so lovingly. Before she lost her husband and three sons in the war.

Is my papa lost in the war, too, Arno asked his mother sometimes when he went to bed, and sometimes when he woke up. He always expected to receive the same answer: No! Your papa isn't lost. We just haven't received a letter for a while.

Not receiving a letter was a bad sign, Arno deduced, but his father's name had not appeared on the list at the Wehrmacht office. And until his name appeared in black on white, Arno's papa wasn't lost; he was just away from the family, absent and silent.

This confused Arno because if that didn't signal that he was lost, if his absence and his silence didn't declare him lost, then what right did paper marked with ink have to make such a declaration?

As he'd done all his life, Arno observed his mother. Now it wasn't just to see when her heart stuttered, but to track any change in her look. Dora Hitzig hadn't just lost her sons and husband to the war: she'd also lost the gaze that had once been kind, that had once signaled cookies to share even before she spoke, that had once stroked the face of a little visitor when her hands were too busy making *Apfelstrudel.*

Arno loved her apple cake, which tasted of laughter. Now there was no smell of baking in Frau Hitzig's home. Now, in those eyes, there was only a void that reflected the emptiness of her house.

Frau Hitzig's sad, Arno.

That was why she no longer made strudels or cookies. What for? It was why she'd stopped cleaning her house or gathering her hair in the coiled buns that hid her ears. Who for? The light in all the eyes she cared about had been lost in the Russian ice, taking her own light with it.

Arno didn't want that to happen to his mother. Or to him or Helga, or his brothers, who were already talking about the day when they'd go to war. When they said this, his mother's look did change, but not because it was lost; quite the opposite: she searched in some secret trunk in her body and found a look full of fury. And she forgot not to get herself worked up. She picked up whatever was at hand—a frying pan, a chopping board—to smack her elder sons on the buttocks. Let's see if this stops you wanting to go to war, she told them.

But not even the smacking put them off. Every day, they went to the Nazi Boys' Group, who, according to their mother, did nothing but fill children's heads with war rubbish, teach them to worship a man they'd never meet, and forget their duty to their church, their mother, and their farm.

Helga also had to attend the League of German Girls, though she did so unhappily. Her mother never had to give her smacks on the backside to remind her that God and the family came first. The only day she came home content afterward was Saturday, when after their gymnastics exercises, her group was taken to Königsberg to visit recovering soldiers at the military hospital. She liked to think, she said, that if her father was wounded far from home, some kind girl there would visit him.

But she hated everything else. She resented being trained to be a housewife when she'd only recently given up playing with dolls and, worse still, being forced every fifteen days to burst into people's homes and demand donations of money or goods. Don't take no for an answer, her superiors told her; reward them with badges on their doors if they donate, but punish them by adding them to the offenders list if they don't.

They don't care if the family's poor; if they've just lost their father; if they barely have enough to eat, Helga told her mother, furious that she'd had to add so many names to the list that day and left so many doors bare to shame the miserly families in the eyes of the community.

Though few in number, there were those who, like Frau Hitzig, didn't care if they were disgraced; they didn't care if they had to live another month without their donor's badge. I've already given them a husband and three sons, what else can they ask of me, she told Helga before firmly closing the door on her.

Helga arrived home after her collection rounds crestfallen and depressed to knit the woolen socks she handed over for donation so that their door wouldn't lack the latest badge, badges that she repositioned tidily in consideration of her father, who would hate to see the beautiful oak covered in tacky stickers.

They had no money, but they had the wool their sheep donated and Helga's now-skilled needles. And Arno kept her company when she knitted, because he knew that was when she thought about the socks that, with a novice's clumsiness, she'd made for their father. He knew that she missed him terribly, and it was something they shared, because not a single day went by in which Arno didn't long for his father.

But while Helga was forced to recite or sing or proclaim or yell at full volume her love for the fatherland and for the Führer above all else, at home she said nothing. Fritz and Johann, on the other hand, returned with a frenzied crackle in their eyes. It mattered little if their mother asked them to lower their voices, to weigh their words. They came home full of songs and slogans. They adopted the grand ideas as their own. The time they had to wait to graduate to the Hitlerjugend at the age of fourteen and then to be old enough to go to war seemed eternal to them. The training games at their Jungvolk meetings seemed like child's play to them now. Even you could do them, Arno, his brothers said. At the Jungvolk, they'd found more friends than the simple life of the farm and school had afforded. They'd found the fervor in their eyes, the rebelliousness that their mother had to fight with thrashings, the worst of which came after Frau Hitzig knocked on the door to accuse Fritz and Johann of vandalizing her home.

"Everyone does it, Mutter. It's her punishment for not contributing anything to the Vaterland."

"Some fatherland! Family comes first, and I've taught you to behave like good Christians, not animals."

"Careful what you say, Mutter, or you'll be investigated for treason."

"Let them take me away, then we'll see who takes care of you."

In the end, Arno's brothers apologized to their mother and left to clean up the damage to Frau Hitzig's house. Ethel sank into a chair, hand pressed to her chest.

"Arno, my only consolation is that the war will end before you have to go to the Jungvolk. At least one of my children will escape this madness."

Because his mother—who never lied—said it, because he wanted his father home, and because he had no interest in war, Arno believed it. He didn't want to go to the Jungvolk. Sometimes, he didn't even want to go to school, where he never found answers to his questions. He'd learned to read easily, and he enjoyed numbers. But what he wanted to know was how pulleys and cogs worked, how objects moved and how they stopped. He wanted to know why engines needed gasoline to run. He wanted to learn how voices came out of the Volksempfänger with such clarity.

But the only answer he received was stop asking so many questions, child, and finish copying the words, prayers, oaths, even the biography of the Führer. The good teachers had gone to war, his mother told him. It was true. Only ill-prepared young women or elderly men and women—brought back from retirement—remained, teachers with little patience for true curiosity.

"Don't pester them with questions, Arno. Ask your father when he comes home instead, all right?"

"Does he know the answers?"

"*Ja.* He knows everything. And if not, he'll take you to Königsberg Library and you can find out there. They have books on every subject. Until he's back, you just have to go to school and learn what they teach you."

Arno tried to be patient. He practiced. He tried to allow days to pass before asking when his father would be home, which wasn't the same as asking if he was lost. He worked on his patience and, though it didn't help him bear his father's absence any better, it did help him catch the wandering ram.

Practicing patience, he'd had the time to observe the animal and learn his ways. It was why catching him was now his task. His brothers, busy as they were with school, their usual jobs on the farm, and Jungvolk activities, had washed their hands of the animal's fate.

That day, the wind kept changing direction, and Arno had already spent more time on the task than usual. His patience wore thinner with every freezing gust. His hands were stiff even with gloves on, and his feet disappeared in the snow. He stuck his hands under his armpits, but there was nothing he could do about his feet.

Why had the ram decided to wander off on that icy day when the greens were still hidden under whites and grays? What was he searching for, seeing as he must have sensed that his favorite pasture wouldn't appear for many weeks yet? Arno didn't know. Maybe he'd grown tired of waiting. Maybe he'd grown bored of his stable's walls and the monotonous company of his little herd.

Whatever the ram's motivation, Arno didn't find it funny. He didn't have the protection of a natural overcoat of wool like the ram, wandering around out there, insensible to the cold. Nor did he have hooves to lift him above the snow. Arno's coat was thirdhand, its insulation thin; he was the fourth Schipper to wear these boots. All those children's footsteps had left them with a hole and a loose sole. Only his father knew how to mend them, and anyway it was hard to find leather or tire rubber these days.

Arno knew he couldn't waste any more time or his feet would freeze.

"The cold kills them," his brothers had warned. "One moment you can feel them, the next you can't: they've gone black. And when they've gone black, the butcher has to chop them off with his axe."

"And then?"

"Then nothing, because not even blood comes out. Have you seen how Herr Ganske limps? It's because the butcher chopped off all the toes on his right foot."

Arno shivered. Were his feet already turning black? He didn't want to limp for the rest of his life. If he didn't catch the ram soon, he'd have to go home empty-handed for the first time. And then his mother would have to go out herself to try to fetch the beast.

Arno hugged his body; he forced himself to stop shivering and forget about his feet. He concentrated on the direction of the wind, approached stealthily, and grabbed him by the horns. The ram looked up in surprise, as if asking, how did you do that?

*"Gehen wir nach Hause."*

The ram seemed to understand if not the words then the firm intention of the most stubborn of the Schippers. He knew that his day's wandering was over, that Arno wouldn't let him go even if he jerked his head violently, nor would he allow him to continue sniffing the frozen ground. So in an almost docile state—almost, because surrendering completely went against his nature, against his status as the king of the herd—he followed his owner back to the stable where his sheep anxiously waited.

And Arno talked to him on the way, as he always did: calmly.

"*Schnell.* Come on. Let's go. We'll be home soon. You can warm your hooves in the stable. Come on. It's not far now."

He wasn't upset with the animal. Why would he be when he understood him perfectly? The ram was waiting for something that, in the depths of winter, seemed like it would never come. And he was out of patience.

Like Arno.

# 17. *Nothing stops time*

***January 1942***

The 18th Army reached the outskirts of Leningrad in September. They bombarded from afar and fired from the periphery, but although the Russian bombardment was largely ineffective, they didn't go in, didn't capture the city. The Soviets were putting up more resistance than expected.

Karl Schipper spent the first few days of the siege building quarters for the officers.

Don't go to too much trouble, Schipper, we won't be here for long, his commander told him.

But months passed. It was winter now and a new year, and the war that was only supposed to last the summer wasn't ending. And Karl, camouflaged among boards and sawdust as he worked to strengthen a structure or seal a crack through which the Soviet winter's unfriendly air seeped, caught the frustration on his superiors' faces and the worry in their voices, though they took care to hide these from the troops.

At first, they'd believed they were only holding the position until reinforcements arrived. Not that they were informed of anything: the official information didn't trickle down to the lower ranks, so they could only speculate. It'll be tomorrow or the next day, some suggested, imagining the victory parade; they'd enter like a bolt of lightning, and, faced with their strength—with their undeniable superiority—the inhabitants would meekly hand over the keys to the city. It would be like Riga. No, others speculated: the German Army was preparing for the city's total annihilation, but from a distance—why risk German lives?

But days and weeks passed, and the city defended itself; months passed, and it didn't fall like an autumn leaf, as Adolf Hitler had predicted. What everyone had believed would be quick turned into a siege without end. Cut off the city, starve it into surrender—that's what the Führer had planned, ordered, desired. It infuriated him to discover that, no matter how thin they made the German line around the enormous city with access by land, sea, and lake, it was impossible to surround Leningrad entirely.

The city was hungry and cold; its inhabitants were dying by the thousands, the officers said as words of encouragement to the rank and file. Very soon, we shall see them on their knees! But the German Army was also feeling the cold, because weather is never interested in war and never takes sides. And time doesn't stop even when ordered or threatened: one season ends and another begins; time neither listens to reason, nor obeys orders, nor forgives carelessness.

Now fall had passed, one day at a time, as it had since the dawn of history, and the Russian winter had arrived. And the 18th, the 16th, Finland's volunteer armies, and the Spanish Blue Division went nowhere, unable to enter the city, unable to take shelter under roofs or between solid walls that could protect them from the cold better than any tent.

They were attackers, but they were also under attack, because with their front facing the city, the Soviet Army, now organized, now well led and very determined indeed, attacked relentlessly, and they were better equipped than the German rear guard. Well equipped with weapons and well equipped with warm clothes. Well envied by their German enemies, because if Leningrad was freezing to death, so were its invaders, unaccustomed to temperatures of forty below and ill prepared, because they'd left expecting to fight in summer. Not in fall, let alone winter.

The message that the Führer sent to the Soviet front early in the siege and that they listened to on the radio began simply: Soldiers!

How important all of them felt as the object of the leader's interest; that great, resounding voice addressing them that day; not all the soldiers—not those in France or Africa—but them, the ones fighting on the eastern front. Hearing it, many felt as if, when he said *Soldiers*, he'd addressed each of them by name, as if he knew them, like a father.

He continued: When I called on you on June 22 to ward off the terrible danger menacing our homeland, you faced the biggest military power of all time. But within a few weeks, its three most important industrial regions will be completely in our hands . . . Your names, soldiers of the German armed forces, and the names of our brave allies, the names of your divisions and regiments and your tank forces and air squadrons, will be associated forever with the most tremendous victories in history.

And they'd believed it, because the Führer had said it almost into each of their ears. But after endless nights stranded on cold Russian soil, their belief had turned to ice.

With all the bullets of cold and lead that had assailed them since that transmission at the beginning of October, Hitler's words of encouragement now rang hollow in their memories. Sometimes—when they had no choice but to huddle against the ailing body of a fellow soldier as they slept, praying they wouldn't sleep so deeply that the soul left its vessel of flesh, bone, and yearning—those words even sounded fraudulent.

And although the commanders kept up the pretense that Leningrad would soon fall, not even the most naive of their soldiers were under that delusion anymore. Something had gone wrong; someone had miscalculated. The commanders' voices were often heard coming out of their improvised quarters, which, though Karl had gone to great pains to seal them as well as possible, failed to contain the shouting between them or over the field radio, when they suggested, then requested, and finally demanded more reinforcements, more equipment, more food, sufficient and appropriate winter clothing.

To every request they made to Berlin, the answer was yes, but what arrived was never enough. Some overcoats, most of them dark, which made them an easy target for the enemy camouflaged in white against the frozen landscape. Some food, but rotten and paltry. The supplies reached them by ship or overland, and the men who received them always hoped to hear the fresh and arrogant footsteps of new divisions, but no, no troops arrived.

The besieged city was slowly starving and freezing to death, but its assailants, abandoned by their Führer, were, too. They were dying of cold, of weariness, of hunger, of loneliness, of illness, of continuous darkness, from bullets, from grenades, from mortars. They were dying from broken promises.

It was impossible to send a letter home when one's hand trembled so much it couldn't hold a pen. Impossible to write when the spirit was no longer able—no longer wished—to maintain a delusion. To participate in the delusion.

Karl did as he was ordered. Every day, he hammered and he machine-gunned; he machine-gunned and he hammered. He wanted to hit his target just to take someone's hunger away, to save a body from the pain of hunger and cold.

And he felt unending desire, now that the socks that had given him so much emotional comfort had a practical use warming hands and feet, now that other soldiers tried to give him a portion of their week's bread in exchange for a pair of the socks that had seemed so useless to them just weeks before. Like everything else, the socks were filthy, but it didn't matter: they wanted them. They wanted them to save parts of their bodies from frostbite. And their offers tempted Karl, since the wool no longer preserved the smell of his daughter's hands. Now that they smelled of gunpowder, of mud, of the moisture from his feet,

Karl sometimes wondered what he desired most: the relief of a satisfied stomach or the scratch of itchy but beloved wool on his skin. He had more socks than it was possible to wear, whether on his feet in their hard boots, on his hands under the thin gloves that recently arrived, or as a mask to protect his nose and eyes. The cramps from hunger almost made him give in. But Karl resisted the temptation: he was hungry for bread, but hungrier for home.

And if he had to die of hunger, of cold, and of neglect, he wanted to take his home to the grave with him.

# 18. A mother cries in silence

***January 1942***

Arno left the ram in the protection of the barn and went into the warmth of his house. His mother was sitting with her elbows on the kitchen table and her face in her hands. She was crying in silence. In his life, Arno had seen his mother weak or pale, he'd seen her furious, but he'd never once seen her cry, not even when his father left without warning or when they received the first or the last letter; not even when she read the letters over and over after dinner.

Did mothers only cry when their children couldn't see them?

"Mutter, the ram's in his shed."

He didn't know why she was crying, but he was sure that it wasn't over the ram.

"*Was ist los?* Are you ill?"

*"Nein, Arno."*

He forgot his freezing feet. He tried to be patient, to stay strong for his mother, but he felt the words rising in his throat.

"Did we lose Vater in the war?"

# 19. Lost

***January 1942***

Karl was lost in white silence. As he walked, he thought how silence never managed to be so absolute in the familiar German winter. He took another difficult step forward, and it occurred to him that perhaps even sound freezes just a short distance from its source, because all he could hear were his own footsteps on the snow, which he could also barely see.

Karl was lost, and it gave him no comfort that his division accompanied him in this soundless, colorless, formless world. In this world of viscous white, everyone was deaf; everyone was blind.

On the commander's orders, he'd set off with a small group before dawn. In the night, a squad had recovered an important position it had lost ten days before.

The war was like that: one step forward one day, another step back the next.

"The 28th Division suffered many casualties. They need reinforcements and ammunition."

Before retreating, the Soviets had burned down their barracks.

"We'll have to build new ones. Schipper, bring wood."

*"Jawohl."*

Karl tied on his mask made from dark socks before climbing onto the sled with the wood. He'd made the mask for himself one freezing night to protect his eyelids and nose, and the next morning, he'd decided to make slits and wear it during the day. He could see just enough through the slits while protecting his eyes from being blinded by the light reflecting off the small but infinite crystals that covered everything.

They were nearly at the Nevsky Pyatachok bridgehead, where the 28th awaited them, but the progress was slow. During the muddy fall, various vehicles had left deep ruts that later froze and made the road almost impassable, even for sleds. Beneath the deceptive white cloak of snow lurked deep, icy furrows, any of which could become a trap, a barricade, or a grave. Even knowing this, the men driving Karl's sled were unable to avoid falling into one that seemed as deep as a trench.

They put down the horse, its front legs broken by the hole it hadn't seen. Another sacrifice for the glory of Germany. Karl no longer cared about a horse's life. After months of violence, hunger, and cold, all he could feel was disappointment that they were leaving behind—and leaving for the Soviets, no less—a massive quantity of meat. But there was no other way. The enemy was stalking them. There wasn't even time to rescue the sled and timber. Against his comrades' advice, Karl picked up his toolbox. That, he could not leave.

"Leave it, Schipper. Or bury it under the snow by the road. You won't get anywhere with that on your back."

It was true. The priority was ammunition, and every soldier had already strapped boxes to his back. Karl was up to his waist in snow, and the extra weight would sink him further, but he couldn't leave his beloved tools at the mercy of God—and much less at the mercy of the Russians and their infernal winter. After the past few months of being a little more carpenter than soldier once again, he'd grown fond of each tool. His hands didn't care anymore that they weren't the tools waiting for him at home. These were the saws and hammers that had brought back his calluses, and he couldn't throw away their intimacy just like that.

"I can't take the wood, so I'll have to cut new pieces when we arrive. I need the tools."

His superiors reluctantly accepted this justification. So they walked. Deaf. And blind.

Karl wanted to take off his mask. Perhaps he'd see better without it. Perhaps the light wouldn't harm his eyes if it was only for a short while. But Karl's hands were full, and he couldn't stop. And he knew it wouldn't help: it wasn't his sight that was failing. The white light reflecting off the snow and fog blinded all of them. It was like a veil they had to pass through. Each step plunged them deeper into the sea of whiteness that had no beginning or end. It occurred to him to take out his small saw to cut through the air.

When they reached the woods, they were ambushed.

The bullets, which came from all directions, shattered the icy silence.

"Shoot!"

Given the order, Karl, like everyone else, fired. And fired. But it was madness. Don't waste munitions, they'd been warned from their first lesson; if you can't see the enemy, don't shoot. Now, all of them—experts and novices alike—fired into the void because the void was firing at them. Forgetting everything beyond instinct, they fired with little success; if, through the noise, they could hear German bullets happen to hit something, it was only the trees of the Russian forest, which withstood the battering without begging for mercy and without offering any.

And in the middle of that white chaos, Karl's fear intensified, because it was as if the Russian trees were conspiring with their countrymen. For the first time, Karl felt—more than saw, because in the confusion, his mask of socks and the slits he saw through shifted—that the perfect order of the German Army, the one he'd so admired, was falling to pieces. Blind, Karl heard yelling and conflicting orders—hold your position, retreat, fire, save your ammunition. He heard bodies fall, groans of pain. He smelled blood and death but remained blind. Fire, came the order. Fire! And Karl fired until he ran out of bullets.

The madness ended, the silence was restored, and the white blindness turned dark when Karl heard the last bullet; the bullet that, after hitting and rebounding off the metal of his toolbox, found its final destination in his carpenter's body.

The last German body to fall in the forest that day.

# 20. Work hard, Ilse

## The Hahlbrocks

***January 1942***

Ilse didn't think about the Schneidemühl bombs anymore. Her mother had told her not to talk about them because it would frighten Freddy, so she'd kept quiet and pushed the corrosive memory into her mind's deepest recesses. The events in Schneidemühl—so distant now that she was back in the tranquil Prussian countryside—seemed part of a bad dream. A dream of which the things one remembers best are the things that mattered least: a ruined pair of shoes and the shame of an exposed petticoat. A dream faltering, doubted: Did I see a woman buried by rubble? No. Impossible.

Not talking about it was better, as far as Ilse was concerned. In the day, her memories were locked away in a cell full of buffeting cotton, no cutting edge exposed.

But the night can't be so easily fooled. Fast asleep, Ilse didn't know that night unlocked the door to let the images, sounds, and fear roam unhindered through her mind and body. She didn't know why she sometimes woke up sweating, agitated, and with an acrid smell in her nose: the only evidence the memories left of their time wandering free to torment their jailer.

When she was older, her beloved would feel her tense in her sleep, clutch the sheets, and mutter faintly about fire. He would stroke her head to soothe the nightmare away. But though she was still a child, no one realized: neither Jadwiga, who slept beside her, nor her mother, who would've heard if she'd woken in the night with a scream.

But Ilse didn't scream. Not even that night when she'd raced behind Irmgard in her effort to stay alive. She'd learned as a little girl to keep her screams inside, and nothing could make her unlearn that lesson. After the torture of a nightmare, she woke in silence with her hands clenched, with her fingernails marked in the skin of her palms like a line of painful crescent moons, and with her jaw knotted, but she didn't know why. She didn't know that, in her dreams, the night had been cruel and creative, showing her not just violent memories, but also new and inventive images in which, over and over, she saw an entire building fall on her sister.

Suddenly opening her eyes had the effect of an eraser on a blackboard. Ilse would then lie on her side, catch her breath, and instantly fall back asleep. When she woke up the next day, without even remembering that she'd sat up in agitation, she didn't understand why her arms and legs hurt so much. It was as if her muscles had plowed and harvested an entire field while she slept. Had she been cold? She got out of bed feeling a little numb, but by the time she had gone down to breakfast, even the discomfort in her body had disappeared.

She stiffened again as she left the house, but it was for a very different reason: she had to go to school, which wasn't easy even on the best days of the winter, even with the best coat or the thickest sheepskin sack. On those freezing January days, her father put her on the cart and told her to get in the woolen sack—tailor-made by her mother—after also putting a hot brick in there.

"*Auf Wiedersehen!* Work hard at school, my girl."

"Yes, Papa. *Auf Wiedersehen!*"

Ilse liked warm days, when her father sped her to school on the motorcycle; when she could sleep a little longer, not needing to set off so early. But now it was winter and so hard to leave the goose-feather cocoon of her bed. Now Janusz took her to school early, moving slowly in the cart, since it was impossible to go on the motorcycle, because as her father said, we'd be blue by the time we got there and we'd be stuck to the seat, like ice. Ilse hated the cold, but she missed the morning adventure with her father.

"Mama would come out with hot water to unstick us."

"But then we'd melt and end up in the lake."

"And the geese would drink us."

"And they'd dump us like hot rain when they flew . . ."

"Oh, Papa!"

Ilse wished it was spring again so she could ride with him, but if she had to go to school and her father couldn't take her, she couldn't have chosen a better escort than Janusz. He didn't laugh or joke like her father, but he talked incessantly. With her, that is. With others, he was sparing and succinct.

He drove the cart slowly, very carefully. He was following her father's instructions: Take care of the horses and my little girl, Janusz. Better to arrive late than not at all. And what could the teacher say? Nothing. There was less obligation to arrive before the bell when the snow was falling so thick they couldn't see beyond their noses, when they were often the first on the road after a blizzard, pushing their way through the dense powder with hooves and sled runners.

Sometimes, Ilse thought they were like explorers of unknown lands who found a new path each morning, a new landscape, forever changing between the greenish blacks of the trees and the gray-blue whites of the snow. And they moved slowly in that silence unbroken even by bird-song, never knowing if the road ahead would be blocked by a branch collapsed under the weight of snow.

Because the journey was long in winter, they left so early that their eyes hurt, first from tiredness and then from the dry, freezing air. Ilse made the most of Janusz's company; when they talked, she almost forgot the cold. Recently, he'd had less and less time for her, having to work harder than ever because of the war, but as long as this journey lasted, no other tasks could force him to leave her side. On the way to and from school, his time was all hers; his stories and the figures he pointed out to her in the clouds warmed them more than the bricks inside their sacks.

"Tell me the story of Queen Jurata and her tears of amber," she asked him most mornings.

Janusz knew that it was her favorite because he'd told her once that her eyes reminded him of Jurata's amber.

"The Baltic Sea is freezing now, as her tears must be. Don't you think that's a story best left for a warmer day? How about if I tell you the story of the silver fox that wouldn't let the big brown bear hibernate? It's a new one."

But no matter the stories, the snowfall, or the obstacles in their way, they always reached the school. Ilse liked going into the simple but warm building and taking off her coat and all the layers of wool that made her feel like a rag doll, saying hello with a quick *Heil Hitler*, to which the teacher, exasperated at having to repeat the same ritual every day, replied: Nein, Ilse, the Führer must always be greeted with the respect that is due to him, before making her repeat the salute with correct posture, in the proper manner, like a good German girl, Ilse.

But she was always more eager to greet her classmates—the older ones, who were numerous, and the ones younger than her, of whom there were only a few—than to greet a sullen man she only ever saw in photos. At school, they had his portrait hanging on the wall, just like her father did in his office. The difference was that her father would never reprimand her for playing or laughing or taking off her coat in front of it. But at school, you must do what you're told and not answer back, he told her when Ilse complained. So that was what she did.

"Good morning, Fräulein. *Heil Hitler!*"

After her apology, the salute, and cheerful hellos to her classmates, Ilse liked to take out her notebook, excited to show off the homework she'd done the evening before.

When they'd said goodbye that morning, her father had told her what he always did: Work hard at school. And so she would. Papa knew about these things, Ilse presumed. That was why he was still at home: because he worked so hard. Soldiers came to see him, but they didn't take him away to fight like the fathers of the other boys and girls. He worked hard, and now, day and night, there were soldiers watching over the whole farm, from their most prized bull to the smallest piece of straw. The Vaterland needs people like us in the fields, Ilse, her father would say. Because they worked hard, she concluded. Unlike the fathers of her classmates, it seemed. Many of them would never return, Ilse's mother had explained one day when her friend Anna hadn't come to school. The same thing happened to the Aldinger brothers, the Achens, and Maria and Klaus Biermann. They all lost a part of themselves on the day when news came that their fathers had died.

Ilse felt sorry for them, but she was proud that her father was so well respected for his work. Work hard, he advised her, and Ilse thought he must know how diligently she worked, so she worked without complaint and with pleasure. She learned everything, wrote fast, calculated numbers, memorized oaths, read stories. She liked going to school even in the middle of winter, because good workers live, and if they stop working so hard, the war takes them away to die.

Ilse wanted to live. Ilse didn't want the war to come for her. Ilse worked, read, learned, wrote, and enjoyed doing addition, though not so much subtraction. With subtraction, she thought, the lost numbers disappeared into the infinity between the earth and sky.

"*Guten Morgen, Kinder.* Today our thoughts will be with Gertie's father, who died for the fatherland and for the Führer."

Ilse bowed her head, joined her hands in prayer, and sighed: another day of subtraction.

"Let's begin. And I want to hear you loud and clear," said the teacher. "Adolf Hitler, thou art our great Führer. Thy name makes the enemy tremble . . ."

# 21. Winter wolves

The body became accustomed to the cold. Or at least to tolerating it for a while, if promised that it'd soon be given warmth. The cold no longer frightened him, or not as much as it had when he was a boy, because it was an enemy whose tricks he now knew, but it was an enemy he'd learned never to underestimate. The years had passed, but Janusz didn't forget his earliest lessons, his mother's lessons: In winter, son, sometimes you have to half die so you can live.

From birth, Janusz had known those winters, had known having few opportunities to warm up. Only when he was lucky, when the depths of the forest deigned to give him some dry branches; only with the fire he could build himself after penetrating the freezing outdoors in search of wood.

Don't stop, don't rest; you don't want to freeze to death, he learned to tell himself with each difficult footstep after his mother had said to him: Janusz, fetch firewood. In the few hours of winter light, fetch firewood. Put your feet in a pair of boots that don't fit you, that don't protect you, that allow the snow to find the warmth inside. Walk, even if the snow threatens to swallow you whole. Walk, climb out of the snow you're trapped in, or you'll be left planted like a tree of crystallized flesh and bone until the next thaw.

Sometimes, he had to walk for hours to scrounge just enough wood for them to make it through the night and be able to open their eyes the next day, because as his mother told him, the cold is a venomous monster that injects itself silently into your skin, that makes you forget to fear it. It'll seduce you to close your eyes, Janusz, and take you to a dream from which you'll never wake. Don't listen to it, Janusz. Don't listen to its sweet lullaby. Do that and you'll die.

Janusz learned that the cold attacked while he was collecting firewood and came back when the fire went out. He had to suffer the cold, risk his life, to later enjoy the heat and survive. The daily risk was worth it, because if he managed to return with wood and with his life, the promised moments of warmth borrowed—or was it stolen?—from the forest would become reality. He and his loved ones would live thanks to the wood that his eyes had detected, that his arms had chopped with the little axe that was a weapon only against slender trunks and branches, and that his torso and his legs had carried.

But the eyes didn't distinguish a temporary reprieve from a permanent one. The eyes, exhausted, closed at night in the belief that warmth would last forever; in the belief that he'd wake the next day in the same heat that had wished him a good night, only to find that he hadn't. When they'd shut, the fire had gone out, and now the cold, its power restored, wanted to persuade them to stay shut, to never again shed tears, whether from hunger, or fear, or cold. No more cold. Sleep. Close your eyes. Rest. No more cold.

But Janusz learned to fight against the enemy's seductions. He forced himself to think of his mother and his sister, huddled together in the other bed. He opened his eyes. He shook himself awake. He threw off his heavy blankets and skins. He confronted the cold with pain in his ears, chest, hands, legs, feet, and nose, and he fed the last sticks—if any remained—into the frozen fireplace. He lit them, and then he knew that they would live another day. Son, sometimes you have to half die so you can live, his mother told him one day as she cut two dead toes from his right foot. Then she'd gathered them from the ground where they'd dropped like dry leaves and she'd thrown them into the fire, where Janusz had watched them burn away, quickly at first and then slowly, until they turned to ash, until they were dust. That day, part of his body had helped to heat his family's little home. Like the forest's trees that donated their branches, Janusz had donated his toes. The difference was that, unlike the trees, there would be no regrowth.

Janusz would never forget that lesson.

And while his skin may have grown thicker from age, loneliness, and years of exposure, he was never fooled now: no skin, no matter how thick, could keep out the cold, and there was nothing better than a good overcoat, a good hat, some good gloves, and heavy boots. Like the ones he wore now. Nothing better than going out in winter to work knowing that, at night, there would be warmth, the responsibility for it shared with other men. Nothing better than knowing that the logs sent from some sawmill could easily be chopped into firewood, and that in the absence of wood, there'd be coal. Or better than the sweet certainty he'd open his eyes to see the next day, even if Józef, Radosz, and Tadeusz insisted they always feared for their lives.

Janusz believed them. They were afraid. Time passed, and the fear held firm, despite the daily evidence that, while the Hahlbrocks were German, they were first and foremost decent people; that while they asked them to work—and to do it well—they kept at bay the soldiers who were more and more numerous and who supervised them more and more closely.

"I can't breathe when they look at me," said Radosz.

But Janusz had learned that, if he didn't look at them, he could pretend they didn't exist. He closed his ears when they tried to provoke him. I can't see, I can't hear, I don't understand, he told himself, repeating it in time with the saw or the brush or the wheelbarrow tires. Without hearing, without seeing, pretending that he didn't understand, it was easy to make the soldiers vanish.

He did his work on the German farm and he felt safe.

Janusz knew he had to work to survive, but in all the time he'd been working for Hartwig Hahlbrock, his boss had never seemed as dangerous as the cold. Or as dangerous as loneliness. So Janusz did what he was told to do. Time passed. The clothes he'd been given on arrival were tighter, but they continued to protect him. At night his eyes closed, and, in the morning, they opened without surprise, without effort, without being lured toward ruin: in the efficient stove burned the embers of the fire they'd made before sleep, and to one side, there was always more fuel to revive them. Time passed and he woke up every day.

On the Hahlbrocks' farm, one didn't have to half die in order to live.

Now, he was asked to take Ilse to school every day, but it was easy in spite of the weather. Her ever-cheerful company warmed even the coldest journey, and he knew that he didn't have to sink into the snow to walk, because the horses would do the walking for him. Janusz came out of his quarters each morning into the frigid air, but he knew Frau Hahlbrock would have a soft woolen sack ready for him, and inside it, a hot brick that he and Ilse liked to joke kept the interior as warm as a summer's morning.

And they set off like that: happily, with Ilse sheathed head to toe in a sack that had been Irmgard's, and Janusz to his waist in one that was clearly sized for Herr Hahlbrock, happy to have earned the family's trust.

Janusz made the same trip four times a day, but he only enjoyed two of them: when Ilse was beside him on the way there and on the way back. As well equipped as he was, it wasn't the cold that bothered him; it was that, without her, his mind went on its dark journeys; his ears heard footsteps following him among the trees that lined the road; his eyes sometimes saw silhouettes of wolves or even men in the shadows. It was that his neck broke out in goose bumps when he felt the—real or imagined?—gaze of predators just waiting to catch him off guard. Wolves or men? Men or wolves?

Russians. He couldn't just wish them away.

With Ilse, he filled the journeys with words, stringing them into the stories she liked so much, but when he was alone, the words escaped. He tried tossing tales into the air, but without her by his side to receive them, the words became wild, deranged, and the wind carried them deep into the forest. Once there, Janusz imagined, they perished of loneliness and cold, because he'd never seen a word that could survive alone, without anyone welcoming it into the warmth of an ear; without being threaded into a chain of sisters preceding and following it, giving it meaning, and with meaning, life. These, cast into the wind, were wasted words, sent to die like a common soldier.

When Janusz was alone, he was afraid again of the seductive monster with jaws of ice; he felt his mother's knife on his dead and unfeeling toes, felt that constant childhood fear of failing to gather enough wood to save himself and his family. Alone, he could never rid himself of the certainty that someone or something was about to come around the bend or out from behind a tree.

Soviet wolves, thirsty for blood; Polish men, thirsty for revenge.

Janusz listened closely to the Poles in the village, who never spoke directly to him. His silence made them eye him with a suspicion that his readiness to work and attachment to the German girl confirmed: That kid's not natural; he's not normal; he's not a patriot; he's a Germanophile, a spy.

At night, taking off his boots after a day's work, Radosz often muttered that if he wasn't so old, so tired, so dejected, so defeated, he'd go with all the young Poles who, like drops of water, escaped through the Germans' hands to make a dash for the surrounding forests, where their new friends and liberators, the Soviets, awaited them in silence.

"What I'd give to be free like them!"

"No one is free in winter," Janusz told Radosz one night, daring to interrupt the monologue.

"What're you talking about, you idiot?"

"And the Russians are worse."

From Radosz's scowl, seconded by the other two men's, Janusz knew that his comments hadn't been well received. Better to be quiet and pretend to be asleep.

The Russians were prowling around, they were close, and Janusz saw shadows in the shadows. He was afraid: of enemies even more deceitful than the winter cold.

# 22. Poor Freddy

Every day when Ilse went to school, Wanda was left with a tightness in her chest that only eased when she saw Janusz return in one piece. That told her that, for a few hours, at least, Ilse was where she should be and safe. Only then could she concentrate on the house, on Edeline, and on Freddy, her poor boy.

That day, Freddy was sick: a common flu that would not badly trouble another child suffocated him, preventing him from eating or lying down. Wanda had spent the whole night in a rocking chair with the small boy in her arms, heating and reheating water so that the steam would clear his airways, as the elderly Dr. Veldmann had advised her before dying.

Wanda was sorry he was gone. Doctors were scarce now, but compassionate doctors were extinct. After Veldmann's death, she vowed never to take Freddy to another doctor, because she knew that, convinced by the modern "science" that now prevailed, they wouldn't show so much as a pinch of the compassion old Dr. Veldmann had for Freddy and his cleft palate.

*Friedrich is lucky to live on a farm, Frau Hahlbrock, far from the cities beset with Nazi fervor. We all love the Führer—don't get me wrong and don't repeat what I say—but in this new Germany, there's no place for someone like your son. Keep him out of sight. Don't take him* to hospitals or believe anyone who tells you there's a cure: you'll never see him again; it's what happened to Herr Lutz with his son.

It was true: Herr Lutz's son had been taken away for a highly innovative operation to straighten his back, at no cost.

We will notify you of the scheduled date soon. *Heil Hitler!* officials from the medical corps told the grateful father as he stood at the entrance to his store, imagining that, the next time he saw the boy, he'd be as tall and straight as the ideal German man.

A few weeks later, the poor shopkeeper had received a message of condolence: *Your son Eric Lutz died from measles.*

Wanda would take care of Freddy herself, and even if the simple flu turned into pneumonia and threatened his life, she would never take him to another doctor. She'd prefer for him to die in the arms of the mother who loved him than hand him over to a medical system that sought to eradicate imperfection.

Eric Lutz had been badly hunchbacked, but anyone who'd had dealings with him, anyone who looked past his difficulties walking and even breathing, quickly understood that the boy possessed an agile mind and a kind and cheerful nature. He didn't have the body of a Teutonic knight, but Germany could surely have benefited from citizens like Eric, now that generosity was in increasingly short supply, and young, brilliant minds were being exterminated in the war.

The same could be said of Freddy, though he was two years old. He was brilliant—mothers know these things—and had the most cheerful nature Wanda had ever seen. He'd be a great German citizen, if only Germany would allow it; if only the Führer gave him the opportunity to grow, to develop, to live.

She would give him the opportunity, if the Vaterland would not. Wanda did as the doctor advised and took Freddy out as little as possible. Last summer, they had taken him to church, but after what happened to the Lutz family, she wouldn't take him again; the looks they received were increasingly cold, and few smiled back at a boy who did little but smile—even at strangers.

Now, more soldiers had arrived on the farm, patrolling ever closer to the house.

"Anyone would think they're guarding the empress's jewels, not some wheat and cows."

It was late in the evening, there was no danger their sleeping children would overhear their mother question the Third Reich, but still she lowered her voice. Hartwig did, too. "They have to protect the crops, Wanda."

"Yes, but why send more men now? Who's going to attack us if the war's nearly won?"

Hartwig said nothing, perhaps because he didn't know the answer, either.

Hence poor Freddy was now confined to the house, so nobody would see him. It was a harsh winter, so he didn't resent it much, but soon, spring would arrive, and Wanda was afraid that her active little son would insist on following Ilse out on her adventures. And the girl wouldn't understand why he couldn't. How could Wanda explain that her dear brother, whom she took such good care of, was in danger? That in this country that the school taught her so insistently to love, someone like Freddy had no more value than an Untermensch?

For the time being, at least, Ilse was a great help distracting the toddler.

She had him painting: No, Freddy, the flags must be red; red with a black cross in the middle, like mine; see? And they have to be square!

She invited him to hop up and down the stairs again and again: We're rabbits, Freddy! Bet you can't beat me! Jump!

And now she'd taken over the task of making him practice words, imitating the tone her teacher used: Repeat after me: *Ich möchte eine Wurst.* Ich. Möchte. Eine. Wurst. Hmm, maybe something easier: *Mein Name ist Freddy.* Almost! Try again: Mein. Name. Ist. Freddy!

They were both tireless and Wanda admired them for it, because she was tired. She was tired of wanting the madness to end; tired of life in a country that could feel so much repulsion for a human being, for a child, for *her* child. She was exhausted from so much fear of the war—fear of losing it, fear of winning it. She knew that her little family wouldn't win under any circumstances.

She decided that, when spring arrived, she would ask Janusz to help her make sure Freddy didn't escape the confines of the house as his sister used to do at his age, that he'd never play outside in full view of anyone.

She'd guard her son inside. Janusz would watch out in case he wandered outside and promptly return him to the house.

Poor Freddy.

# 23. The end of the war

## The Schippers

***January 1942***

"Did we lose Vater in the war?"

The tremor in the question stopped her crying. It made her lift her flushed face; it forced her to look Arno in the eye. What a brave son she had. How tough these recent months had been for him without his father and how little he'd complained. Even now, under the circumstances he most feared, he asked his question softly, trying to hide the expectant pain, taking care not to hurt the delicate mother that life had given him.

So she untangled the knot in her throat and quickly told him that she was crying with relief.

Arno believed her. His mother's blue eyes were moist, but there was a rare happiness in them.

"He's back, Arno."

"Where is he?"

Arno wanted to run to him. In his bedroom or his workshop? Where is a father just returned from such long absence to be found?

"Not home. He's in Königsberg. Back, but in the hospital. Wounded."

That day, she hadn't had to search for his name on a list. A message had come directly to the house.

"Is he hurting a lot?"

"I don't know. I don't know how serious it is, but he's back. We'll take care of him. The war's over for him. Whatever happens, the war's over for us. And that's good."

But they couldn't go right away. They had to wait for Helga, Johann, and Fritz to return from their meetings. It was a long wait. To Arno, it seemed longer than all the time his father had been gone.

When his siblings finally arrived, the waiting continued, because, Arno, it's too late for you to go out; it'll be dark before we get there; the hospital won't let you in to see him. So he stayed home with Helga as his babysitter; she, frantically knitting socks, and he, staring at his toes. How do you knit socks for toeless feet, wondered Arno with a knot in his throat. He'd taken off his boots when it was announced that he wouldn't be going to see his father, when the disappointment of having to stay behind forced him to return to his freezing body.

When, bravely, he took off his moist socks, he saw that his toes were red, not black; they hurt, but they were still alive. He put on clean, dry socks, and rubbed them. And there, beside his sister and the constant, gentle collision—*click, click, click*—of her knitting needles, Arno fell asleep.

# 24. Lost

***January 1942***

Karl Schipper was lost in pain.

He wouldn't remember it later, but in the haze of his confused mind, in that silence that smelled of gunpowder, at first, he believed he was lost in death. He felt a moment of sorrow for his wife and his children. So many fatherless children. His would just be a few more in this new world of orphans. Then, he remembered the promise that his fatherland had made: in the new Germany, no family would be abandoned, no child left without food or education.

He could go reassured, then, he thought. If he could open his eyes. If he could rise, leave his body's weight behind, he'd go. He hadn't yet reached the level of consciousness necessary to ask himself, why do I need strength to go to the eternal life? Why do I need sight? Isn't it supposed to be easy?

He'd barely had time to think, thank God it's over, that the bullets have stopped flying, that life no longer reeks of dead flesh, that my hands will never again hold a rifle, that my body will never again know cold, when he became suddenly aware of his body—frozen eyelashes under a makeshift mask, breathless, motionless, lying faceup in the middle of the forest.

There were voices around him, and, more than anything else, it was they that anchored him to life. German voices.

"This one's breathing!" said a voice above him.

Karl was happy for the man who'd be going home, who'd see his children again. What he'd give to be able to see his own! But when he felt hands lifting his body, covering it with a blanket, he understood that the voice was referring to him, the only survivor of that massacre in the forest.

As the anesthetic of ice wore off beneath the blanket, Karl's body began to convulse with shivers. As he was transported first on a stretcher and then in a truck, the living monster named pain arrived, a monster that burned, bludgeoned, tore, bit—and with it the desire to die so that he no longer had to suffer.

But desire alone was not enough.

And, as bad as the pain was, worse still was feeling none in his legs.

"You were lucky. The bullet didn't hit a single organ," a doctor would tell him later. "As for your legs, you fell backward onto another soldier. You pressed a nerve against his rifle or his binoculars. Who knows? You were there for hours. And the cold did its bit, too. There's damage to the nervous system, severe inflammation, and your toes froze. There's no way of knowing whether you'll recover the feeling in your legs, but we think we can save your feet. Good thing you were wearing thick socks. Time will tell. For now, rest. Don't move, Schipper!"

As if he could. Karl couldn't even speak, his jawbone was so tightly clenched, as if trying to kill the pain, and more than that, kill the terror of the contrast between pain and its absence. Uncontrollable pain, unbearable nothingness.

Karl Schipper had emerged from the Russian forest with raw, perforated flesh above lifeless legs. Ragged branches above a dead trunk. All he could do now was scream and groan, but inside, where nobody else could hear.

A bullet had taken him out of one war and plunged him into another: the one between his torso and his legs, between two monsters, one of excess and the other of nothingness. His only relief was the Demerol.

"Look at it this way, Schipper: you're lucky. Your legs could be hurting, too."

Lucky. He was lucky.

Between episodes of Demerol delirium, he could see very clearly that, in his body, life was fighting against death, good against evil, everything against nothing. He was the only witness to these battles and the only victim. He tried to explain it to his doctors, to his nurses, but no one seemed to understand.

"Listen to me!"

But no matter how he begged, nobody helped him.

"It's all right, Schipper, don't worry. You'll be home soon, and we saved your feet."

There were days—many, most of them—when he would have preferred the numbness in his legs to conquer the territory held by pain. To kill it all and give him rest. But the wounded branches of the tree that was Karl Schipper were intent on living. Little by little, electric current by electric current, they made strategic advances and, in doing so, enlisted more pain.

It made little difference that they transported him by ship and not by road. The steadiness of his journey made little difference if the pain emanated from inside, and if between the pain and the Demerol, Karl lost his head and even his memories. It made little difference when they told him: Cheer up, Schipper, you're going home, to the first-class hospital in Königsberg. It made little difference that he'd see his wife and his children. Little or none, because Karl Schipper was in the clutches of a monster that writhed and made him writhe, that with its infinite tentacles had now reached his toes, showing no mercy and offering no respite.

Hence, when his wife and older children arrived to visit him at Königsberg Hospital, they found him unable to believe they were there, and were not just a new form of torture that his private monster had conceived.

Hence, they returned to the farm in silence, and hence why it took Arno so long to persuade his mother to take him to visit.

"They won't let you go in, but send him a letter."

Arno did something he thought was better: he sent his collection of tank drawings in the hope that his father would pin them on the wall, admire them, and then explain to his artist son how they worked.

His father looked at the drawings without looking, for an instant and without admiration, because the war, the pain, and the craving for Demerol had robbed him of the ability. He had no wall to pin them on, separated only by curtains that allowed a concert of moans to pass through unmuffled, his own voice joining in when he let his guard down.

Days ago—terrible, endless days—they'd withdrawn the drug. Apparently, he was showing signs of improvement, and it would be good for him to bear the pain without pharmaceutical assistance. Demerol was in short supply and others needed it more, they said when he begged. The man that still lived deep inside him understood and felt pity for those other soldiers, but the man beset with pain yearned for that fog. He wanted to feel nothing, remember nothing: not heroes' welcomes, nor timber left to rot in the snow; not steaming horse entrails, nor grenades; not faceless bodies, nor bullet wounds; not hunger in the belly, nor wool socks; not even that useless photograph of a smiling man with meat under his skin. He didn't want to imagine his lost tools, rusting first from blood and then from melted snow. He didn't want to remember everything he'd lost, but time passed as Karl stared at the blue hospital curtain and took stock. He understood that he was bankrupt. He had nothing other than pain. That, and a single desire: relief.

He measured time by the stabs of pain that prevented him from breathing, sleeping, eating, or looking up. He thought he remembered that, the previous day, there had been one thousand three hundred and forty-one pulses of pain, but he knew his count was off, because he'd lost track when sleep took him by surprise.

He'd forbidden his wife from bringing the children on her visits: he didn't want to see the innocence ebb from their faces; he didn't want requests for stories of wartime adventures; he didn't want to hear Helga's soft voice, or receive scarves she'd knitted, because, Vater, yesterday you were shivering. How could he return to a life in which he was responsible for the well-being of four children? How, if he couldn't even watch over his own? He should never have survived the ambush that took his whole division.

The shivers came. He couldn't think about that day without them returning, without his vision clouding over, without getting lost in the blinding whiteness.

Fräulein! I'm cold! Nurse, bitte! *Mehr Decken, bitte!*

Why did he bother to ask for blankets if the nurse never brought them? We don't have any more, Herr Schipper. She said the same thing, but with more severity, when he changed the word *blanket* for the word *Demerol. Mehr Demerol! Bitte, bitte, bitte! Bitte* was the most frequent word to come out through Karl Schipper's dry lips. Bitte: less cold, less pain. *Bitte!* Please!

All he could make out within himself was a constant desire to weep, which didn't diminish when the doctor tried to give him hope.

Easy, now, Schipper: the war's over for you.

What did this city doctor know about war? Perhaps a little more than a city carpenter, that gullible innocent. But what did the doctor know about never-ending treks, about unrelenting cold, about memories of dead friends' living voices? The doctor knew about blood and flesh, but what did he know about his own body being perforated? His. Own. Body.

The war was over for him? Karl didn't believe it and didn't want any words of comfort from the person who'd taken away his anesthetic. Take me back to the stable with the Latvian horse, he thought. Take me back to the blisters from endless walking; bring back the comfort of coarse wool that smelled of home. The war was not over for him. The war now possessed his body and his mind.

*"Mehr Decken, bitte!"*

"If you want more blankets, you'll have to ask your wife for them. You're not the only wounded man in Germany, you know."

He didn't want to see his wife, but not even the coward he'd become could deny her, because he knew she was also suffering, so he raised his head a little, and sometimes opened his mouth, just a little, to try the tasteless spoonfuls of food she fed him.

"They say it's not allowed, but I don't care, Karl. I'll bring more tomorrow. You need to put some flesh back on your bones before you come home."

He didn't want to think about that: going home.

# 25. Somewhere else

***August 1942***

Arno didn't understand his father's distance. He'd missed him when he was at war, but he missed him more now that he was close, back home three weeks already. It was as if he had left as one man and returned as another. Arno missed the father of his memories, the one always ready to smile and hug, the one who'd carried him proudly on his shoulders that day he'd never forget.

Now, he was a stooped, emaciated shell that only pretended to smile, that didn't have the strength or will to lift a hammer, let alone the son who'd grown in his absence and continued to grow before his absent gaze. The only moments when Arno recognized his father were when he helped his mother with the milking and carried the full pails from the shed to the kitchen. Arno knew it took all his strength and he would've liked to help, to say: Sit down, Vater; I know you're hurting; I'll help Mutter; look at me; I'm a big boy, now; I can do it. But on his mother's orders, he stopped himself.

"We have to help him come back, Arno."

"But he's back."

"No. That man you see isn't your father. Do you remember the one from before? Well, that's the one we're waiting for."

So Ethel, with a look or a groan, urged her husband to help her a little. It was the first time that Arno had seen his mother use her infirmity as a ploy, but it worked: he shook himself from his lethargy. He did what he could to lighten her load, then slumped back into his chair positioned in the sun, where Arno took him food his mother had prepared.

"Did he eat?" she asked afterward.

"Everything, Mutter."

"See? There is *one* thing he's interested in. He'll eat his way back to health, Arno, just watch."

At first, Arno had believed his mother. He sat with his father in the evenings, after school and his chores. He told him about his day and asked him questions about machines and pulleys. He was always there to take him his food and stay with him until he'd finished. After three weeks clearing empty plates and finding nothing but emptiness in his father's gaze, he wasn't so sure anymore. He stopped sitting with the stranger.

"Vater's lost."

# 26. The pain

***August 1942***

Karl ate, not because he was hungry, but because he remembered hunger and because his own mother had taught him: Eat everything on your plate today because you don't know whether you'll have anything tomorrow. Lessons learned in the cradle could never be forgotten, so he swallowed the last sip of soup as he fought back tears with the sunlight as his company and witness.

"Karl, if you keep sitting in the sun like that, people will mistake you for a gypsy. A skinny, haggard one, at that. Come in."

Not even his wife's teasing got through. Karl didn't budge, willing the warm summer light to chase away the winter inside him. Only when night fell did he go into the house to occupy the rocking chair beside the fireplace. He sensed the familiar rhythms of home around him, but he remained distant, out of time. He couldn't even muster the energy to yell at them all to be quiet, as he would have liked to do. With the cacophonous gunfire in his head, he already had enough to contend with. He ate his dinner and left nothing on the plate. But he didn't distinguish one food from another. Sometimes, he forgot to chew and relied on his wife to remind him: Chew, Karl, then swallow. He obeyed.

Often, he couldn't manage to keep what he'd ingested down. With the nausea, Karl's trembling and his tears returned. The weakness. The war.

But time passes even when it seems still. From day to day, and from mouthful to mouthful, the pain from the bullet wound and from the legs still coming back to life eased. Gradually, the nausea abated. He realized it one morning between blinks. Where was the pain that made him picture the furrow the bullet had made in his flesh? It was still there, but no longer at the center of his mind. His muscles were finding it less and less difficult to get him up, get him dressed, to help a little on the farm, and to keep him still, without screaming. Karl knew he should now be able to think of something that wasn't him, him, him. But he was still in pain and still trembling. Poor me, wailed every cell in his body.

If someone had asked him, where does it hurt, Schipper, why don't you move, why don't you respond to anything? what would his answer have been? His legs remained weak from disuse, from having to remind themselves with each movement that they could indeed obey the commands sent to them by the brain. His chest felt the bullet that the doctors hadn't been able to remove, but the hole left by Demerol was much greater, the bottomless hole that still screamed: Fill me or you'll die. He wanted to answer the call. Given the choice, he would never have stopped trying to fill the hole, to satisfy the need that he'd come to love more than his wife and children put together. But even after the hospital, he could barely move. How could he obtain a dose, or a thousand, without help? How, if the drug was for the exclusive use of soldiers? What am I, then? Don't I count for anything? Hadn't they promised the Vaterland would never abandon him? Karl felt abandoned, adrift.

He spent that time in the sun devising schemes to ease his suffering, and as a result didn't notice as the aftereffects of war became tolerable without chemical help. One day, he suddenly realized it was only the drug's warmth that he now longed for, that addiction and not pain was the only thing that kept him trembling and enslaved. Fill me or you'll die, the absence of Demerol told him with every beat of his heart.

The doctors had inserted one nail into him to remove another. The liquid nail had left him with a hole inside, and there was no way to get rid of it other than through willpower. Understanding this, he resolved to overcome the yearning for Demerol, and the decision made him feel proud, strong, like Karl Schipper again. The war would be over for him, as the doctor had said: The bullet you have inside is your ticket to staying home, soldier.

What he didn't know was that, by the time he'd made this decision, the drug's siren song had already softened thanks to six months of forced and arduous abstinence. That the Demerol escaped from his body in each tear, in each shiver, in each shuffling step he took to help his wife. Each day was a battle he'd won without knowing it.

They'd inserted one nail into him to remove another. Karl knew about nails. He had nails. Yes: he remembered exactly where. He knew precisely where he'd bought his last batch and how much it had cost him. He remembered the sadness he'd felt on the day when he'd been conscripted, realizing what a useless expense that had been. He wondered whether they were still where he'd left them. He'd be happy if they were, and happy if they weren't: it would mean one of his sons had heeded the call of iron and wood.

One nail to remove another. It wasn't easy, but Karl got up, he walked, he unbolted his old workshop. He opened the dusty toolbox he'd been sorry to leave when the war tore him from his family. There they were. Holding the nails, he was flooded with memories of good times. He heard sweet echoes of hammer hitting nail on the head. He recognized these nails. They were his, and they were him. He would remove the poison from the liquid nail with an iron one, or with a hundred iron ones, with however many were needed.

The smell of damp wood filled his senses and the hammer in his fist anchored him to life.

# 27. Grandma

## The Hahlbrocks

***January 1944***

Ilse was bored. Her grandmother bored her. She had to love her, her mother said so, but Grandma didn't allow herself to be loved. There was no way even to ask her, Grandma, what games did you play when you were a girl, because the only response would be, impertinent child. Embroider that handkerchief, do your chores, knit more socks. Think about the soldiers, Ilse, those poor soldiers who had to leave their families; all those poor men freezing to death, losing legs. Not like your father; look at him: so happy, so healthy, so well fed.

It was impossible to reply, but, Grandma, my father's doing his part, too, because that would only inspire another *impertinent child*. Instead, Ilse said, you, too, Grandma; you've put on weight, too, since you arrived. Her mother had scolded her for being rude, but Ilse had simply told the truth: her mother's mother had arrived emaciated and now she filled all the spare room in her clothes. Before long, Ilse thought, she'd need her daughter to let out her dresses.

Fall and the darkness had arrived with Grandma Hannah. Or at least, that was how it seemed to Ilse, despite Jadwiga insisting things didn't work that way. Ilse had been almost eight, and, though she hadn't been to school for years, there was nothing better than a farm to show a person the passage of time. In any case, it seemed like her grandmother had been there forever.

Her cousin Crystl had been born in late September, on the day when they'd had to wear thick socks for the first time. Grandma had arrived before that. In October, she stayed to keep helping Uncle Franz and his new wife, Aunt Erna, with the baby's colic. No one would answer Ilse's question: If she came to see them, why doesn't she stay on their farm? She didn't leave in November, because the first snowfall came. December left them, but Grandma did not, because it was Christmas. Nor would she go in January because Ilse's new little sibling would arrive.

Ilse wanted to meet her little brother. Or little sister.

"It's a mystery that won't be solved until it's born," her father told her. "Like with the cows."

Since she'd left school, Ilse had devoted herself to helping on the farm, something that hadn't been easy for her mother to accept.

"Let her be, Wanda. Ilse's not one to do nothing."

"She could learn to embroider or bake the almond cookies she loves so much."

"You really think so?"

They looked at each other. They laughed.

"No. All right, fine. But promise you won't let her get dirty."

After Hartwig had made a promise he couldn't keep, Ilse joined his workforce for a few hours a day. She spent another hour cleaning her shoes or plunging in the tub after getting potato-field mud in her hair, stable earth under her arms, wheat in her braids, or ink on her fingers from learning to do the accounts with her father in the office.

In this new school, there were no kids her age, but Ilse enjoyed herself and learned a lot. She even thought that she now knew the secrets of life, because she knew—in detail—how calves were born. She even knew how they got in their mothers' bellies. And now her mother had a calf in her belly; they could no longer fool her with look what the stork brought us. Which prompted her to imagine how it got there. Because a farmer knows everything there is to know and never feels shocked or disgusted. Or keeps it to herself.

Then her grandmother had caught her telling Freddy about Papa being the bull and Mama the cow . . . and Ilse's freedom to discover nature abruptly ended.

Thereafter they kept her between the walls of the house, taking care of Freddy, embroidering, chopping potatoes. She did the schoolwork her mother gave her, because not going to school didn't mean she shouldn't continue, albeit at home, with Irmgard's old books. She practiced her arithmetic, but they no longer allowed her to help her father with the accounting. Let alone go out in search of Janusz. Grandma never took her eyes off her.

"Ilse, farms are for men, as are financial matters. Perhaps Friedrich can't go out to help your father, as is his proper role, but nor can you."

Now, thanks to her grandmother, Ilse spent her days frustrated and bored.

And to make matters worse, Jadwiga had been sent to sleep on a cot in the kitchen, because her bed in Ilse's room was now occupied by the eternal visitor. Ilse missed Jadwiga. Her grandmother didn't wait for Ilse to bring her words in time with her own when they prayed, as Jadwiga had done since they discovered that the Lord's Prayer was the same in Catholic as it was in Lutheran. Her grandmother didn't tolerate questions, or sing little songs to help her sleep. She didn't even want to listen to Ilse's stories.

"Janusz told it to me."

"I don't want to hear anything that came from that—"

The word caught in her grandmother's throat, as if it hurt just to speak it.

"That what, *Oma*?"

"That Pole."

That Pole. Ilse understood what she wanted to say: Untermensch. She missed that Pole. She missed her father; she needed the open air, even if it was winter. She'd had enough of embroidery and the endless lessons on manners, and she had no interest in learning how to make butter with just the right consistency. She'd had enough of the criticisms, and not just the ones directed at her, but also the ones aimed at everything her mother did or didn't do. She'd had enough of the stern looks directed at Freddy and especially the lack of patience for his peculiar way of speaking. She'd had enough of the blows to the head she received, like the time she'd said to Grandma: Freddy's smarter than you.

No. It was impossible to love Grandma.

# 28. The numbers don't add up

Poor Mother, thought Wanda as she changed thread, careful not to break the welcome silence they'd found while they embroidered.

Family is family. You don't choose it. That was what she'd always said. Wanda supposed it was an idea she'd inherited from her parents: family is predestined. So predestined that her mother hadn't argued when her parents found her a husband thirty years her elder when she was still nearly a child. Poor Mother: she'd left home for the home of a man who, though he was her father's age, was in spirit more like a stern grandfather.

Wanda had loved her father despite his severity and the hours she'd spent kneeling on coarse salt crystals with her brothers and sisters, punishment for some shared transgression. Her father's antiquated sensibilities could be wounded by anything. From a young age, Wanda knew she'd never allow such a man to choose a partner for her.

No, Wanda had decided that nobody would mark out her path but her.

You were always rebellious, Wanda, her mother had said last year when Wanda asked her to let her brother Franz choose his own wife.

I might be rebellious, Wanda would've liked to reply, but you're not, and look what they did to you.

She glanced over for a moment. Just long enough to see that her mother was embroidering the same flowers she'd done all her life, in the same pattern, with the same old colors: the red one beside the blue one.

Wanda returned to her own work. She'd better concentrate, or the baby would be wearing a jungle on its clothes instead of a field of flowers—and this in front of a grandmother scandalized by red next to orange. She liked creating new patterns, but that day, her needle moved without rhyme or reason.

I might be rebellious, Wanda thought, but I'm never rude.

They'd driven that out of her by dint of grains of salt digging into her knees while she repeated the Fifth Commandment until she cried. Honor thy father and thy mother. Now she had that lesson seared into every cell. Better to keep quiet. She kept quiet the frustration of seeing a mother aged beyond her years by a hard life. A woman convinced that defying your parents meant defying God's will. And Wanda's biggest offense was choosing Hartwig: That corrupting liberal you married.

Her mother had never accepted Hartwig, not even now when her daughter was about to have his fifth child. That, for her mother, was not reason enough. Nor was the fact that, thanks to Hartwig, their family had never known hunger, even in times of war. For her, he was still a nobody, and her daughter was a rebel.

Wanda sighed.

In contrast, the Party called them patriots for giving the Vaterland so many Aryan children—rewarded them, even, with extra rationing coupons. Wanda wouldn't turn them down, but, though she never told anyone for fear of offending the Führer's delicate sensibilities, none of her children had been conceived for the glory of that man and his interminable yelling. Her marriage was between two—and Adolf Hitler had no place in it.

She felt movement and looked down. The baby had pressed its head against the living wall, deforming it. I'm ready for you to come out, too, *Liebling*, but that's not the right way.

She didn't even let out a groan, still reluctant to break the silence.

Wanda knew she was no longer young. She was fed up with pregnancy: the heaviness and pains in her body, the strange ideas and cobwebs in her head. She felt the baby's weight on her years, on her body shaped by so many births. It wasn't just her belly that bothered her: her swollen feet and hands did, too; her breasts, the nipples; her navel seemed to want to free itself and fly off. And the children bothered her: the ones that were there, because they were there, and the one that was absent, because she was absent. When Irmgard visited, she wanted to send her straight back to school for being a know-it-all and a woman of Nazi severity, yet she wanted to keep her home to erase the severity, and so that she could help with Ilse and Freddy and Edeline, who, if they continued not going to school . . .

She'd feel better when the baby was born. Her shoes would fit again, and she'd be able to climb the stairs without her knees and pelvis hurting. She'd be able to walk without waddling like the geese from the lake. She'd be herself again: controlled, even-tempered.

It would also help if her mother ran out of excuses and went home. She had come for Crystl's birth but said she was still there to help after Wanda's baby was born. Lies. She'd never offered to help before.

Hannah's life had become one of scarcity that Wanda and Franz did all they could to ease, sending provisions whenever they had the chance. But it was never enough. And the opportunities to send provisions became ever scarcer, with fewer guarantees: sometimes because the Polish Resistance managed to destroy the railroads, and sometimes because the stout courier swore he'd been robbed by hungry Poles.

Grandma Hannah had had to make do with the little she managed to grow, the little that wasn't stolen at night from a widowed farmer's wife, as afraid of Polish workers as she was of enemy warplanes. Recently, there had been an attack on a nearby town. What prevented them from deciding to bomb her little farm one day? They're not going to waste bombs on you, her children promised her, but it was impossible to make her believe that.

Winter was worse: the little family farm—whether from theft or from the inefficiency of its old and solitary owner—didn't yield enough in spring or summer to stockpile for the winter. And the Reich came for its cut, which it took without consideration for an old woman's needs. If you can't manage the farm, hand it over to someone who can, the collectors told her when she informed them of her situation. That was the last time she said anything. She would have to get by with the rationing coupons, but what use were coupons for coffee when there was no coffee? What use were the meat ones, if meat always ran out? Sometimes, even salt and sugar couldn't be found.

Now she was here, warm, well fed, free of fear, and with the intention of making herself indispensable—by acting as if she were doing something. By tidying, but making a mess. By giving orders that created disorder. On several occasions, she'd made Jadwiga cry, but most of the time, she preferred to ignore the girl. (Wanda reached the conclusion that Hannah, in her loneliness, had allowed herself to be taken in by everything she heard on the Volksempfänger.) Every day, she undid Ilse's braids, the girl complaining that, with all her tugging, her grandmother wanted to pull her eyelids onto the top of her head.

Every day, Hartwig sent Janusz to fetch his food so he could eat in peace in the office, because neither conversation nor laughter was allowed at Wanda's parents' table, a rule that Hannah imposed wherever she went. Hartwig was tired of his mother-in-law's stern looks, but he was also polite and respectful, so he tried to stay out of the way as much as possible. He even accepted the decree that Ilse no longer help him on the farm.

Wanda sighed. It would be easier to persuade the baby to come out than its grandmother to leave. How she wished both ordeals could reach their end!

She felt guilt gnaw at her core. The woman was her mother, a widow: she would never want her to be hungry or afraid. She would welcome Hannah's stay if only she appreciated the roof that gave her shelter, the peaceful surroundings, the absence of aerial attacks, the nourishing food her daughter prepared, the son-in-law chosen by her daughter. Why couldn't she enjoy her grandchildren, perfect or imperfect? No: the children didn't speak properly; Edeline was a baby, Freddy was clumsy and deformed, and Ilse, she said, was rude.

Her mother broke their shared silence with a complaint that didn't surprise Wanda: Irmgard didn't visit enough and spent her time home moping.

"She's also an insufferable know-it-all."

She was right about that, Wanda conceded. The teenage years were difficult, but even more so when your school made you believe you were the brilliant future of the nation.

"What is it with sending children away to study? We never sent you . . ."

No. They never sent her anywhere. It would've done her a world of good if they had.

"There aren't any schools for girls her age around here. You know that, Mama."

"Well, then you should bring her back home, where a young lady should be."

That, Wanda didn't agree with. She thought with sadness of Ilse, who'd lost her school, and of Freddy, who'd never been. Irmgard would study for as long as it was possible, she promised herself, but she knew better than to throw wood on the fire of her mother's lectures.

How she wished her mother could appreciate the daughter who'd built her own home with her own rules—tough or lax—a mother who accepted that this gave her the right to be a little rebellious. She would invite her to stay, if only she didn't believe that it was impossible for her mother to change.

Wanda sighed. The baby relaxed, and her belly's roundness was restored.

She had to be fair. She couldn't blame her mother for all her uneasiness. The region's run of good luck always felt like it was about to end.

Don't worry. The Russians will never get through.

That was what Von Witzleben, who'd returned when the war seemed far enough away, always said to Hartwig. More frequently since the disaster in Stalingrad: by February 1943, all the German Army's divisions had been decimated or had surrendered.

Hartwig had come home grief stricken that day. From then on, Wanda joined him at night to listen to the radio in the deserted office—not to the Volksempfänger, which continued to proclaim Germany's imminent victory; they listened to the forbidden British broadcasts, the ones that, though perhaps intended to demoralize them, rang true: *Tick-tock, tick-tock, tick-tock, tick*—every seven seconds, a German dies in Russia. Is it your husband? Is it your son? Is it your brother?

Yes. It had been Josef, Hartwig's brother, Ida's husband. He'd disappeared with the rest of the 6th Army in icy Russia. Officially missing, Josef wasn't even counted on the list of the Wehrmacht's dead. Only his brother, only his wife in Schneidemühl counted him. Only his orphans. Seven seconds. It had been a husband, son, or brother of almost everyone they knew. Everybody was in mourning, but even if they listened to the BBC, too, no one said anything other than the Russians won't get through, we're the fatherland's granary, they won't let them get through.

Even Wanda repeated it, wanting to be complicit in the mass delusion. It was, she suspected, a collective wish; one that, repeated with enough fervor, enough times, would be granted. Not even under the influence of pregnancy did she dare contradict anyone, afraid of reprisals, of being branded a heretic or a traitor.

Even to Hartwig, she said nothing, though she often had to bite her tongue to stop herself from screaming, you always say the same thing!

Do you think I can't see the worry on your face? Do you think I haven't counted the trucks full of wounded men?

Though the war of bullets hadn't touched their corner of East Prussia, the war of hunger roared in, raising dust behind it. The first time Janusz informed them that a convoy of starving soldiers was asking for help, Wanda stopped what she was doing. Running up to a second-floor window, she saw hunger personified for the first time since her childhood.

"Herr Hahlbrock says to send what you have today—"

"Janusz, go down to the basement and bring up a sack of potatoes. And jars of fruit preserves."

She placed the freshly baked bread in a basket. Finally, she added a leg of smoked pork.

That night, the Hahlbrock family ate dinner without bread but with the satisfaction that they'd done something—directly—for the soldiers. Happy to have witnessed a moment's relief on the young faces, to see them walking straighter back to their truck. A few days later, another convoy stopped, and then another, and another. Wanda soon lost count and her enthusiasm. Her little farm had worked overtime for the war effort, producing more and more. They'd assumed that, with all the farms coordinated to this end, Germany would always have food. But it wasn't enough: her mother went hungry, the cities went hungry, the soldiers went hungry. Was there anyone, other than farmers, who wasn't hungry?

They couldn't continue to make such generous unofficial contributions, because ironically, they meant that the accounts submitted to the Army didn't add up. The farm worked for the Wehrmacht, not for the soldiers.

For Wanda, the hunger was the clearest sign that the war was going badly, whatever the Volksempfänger said. But recently, something else had alarmed her: the trucks that stopped weren't just looking for food; now they were also searching for gasoline.

Gasoline, Hartwig and the rest of the region's farmers had been informed, must be prioritized for the Army. Hartwig had stored the tractor and his motorcycle before winter arrived. Now everything at the farm was done with horsepower and human sweat. We'll just go back to the old way of doing things, Hartwig had told her. A farm could go back to the old way of doing things. With horses or oxen, a farm could function. Could a modern army do the same? More and more military vehicles were left abandoned by the roadside. Could a war be won without gasoline?

The Volksempfänger always reported victories, never defeats. Wanda was baffled by this magical mathematics that the radio voices were intent on conveying, and that every listener was intent on pretending to believe. But she understood that war, like the farm, depended on conventional arithmetic. And the arithmetic was clear: an increasing number of trucks returned from the front, like birds of ill omen. Demand was growing: more work, more crops, more soldiers, more devotion, more cold, more hunger, more orphans, more widows, more death, more silence. Then came the subtractions: For each wounded, how many were dead? For each death accounted for, how many men were missing?

There were fewer and fewer truths, thought Wanda. Even so, she bit her tongue to stop herself saying: Hartwig, wars aren't won by starving boys in stranded vehicles. Why speak the words? She knew his calculations were likewise sound—and that he said nothing.

Wanda felt the baby that clung to her belly's darkness kicking.

"Shh, Liebling. Maybe you're better off staying in there."

# 29. The howl

"Don't even think about escaping."

Herr Hahlbrock's warning was stern, but Janusz understood. He could hear the concern in his boss's voice. The sadness.

Janusz knew that not all Poles were so lucky. For years, Hartwig Hahlbrock had done everything possible to pretend that their relationship was the traditional one in which a boss employs workers, treats them well, and pays them a salary. He always offered friendly conversation, shade and water when the sun was hot, and warmth and tea when icicles formed on their noses. Janusz appreciated even more the fact that they were provided with warm or cool clothes as needed. And they certainly had been needed often in his case, because he continued to grow; you could practically watch his pants shrinking.

"Here, Janusz: a new shirt and pants. Boots, too. They belonged to the Didschus widow's husband. I traded some wool for them. I think they'll fit you, but let's see. You must be the son of giants."

Sometimes, Janusz wondered about that. His mother had disappeared into the trees years ago. What he remembered of her had nothing to do with size. He had no memory of his father, and his mother had never spoken about him except to suggest that he'd been a forest giant. One that drank. Was such a thing possible?

Janusz was grateful. It was hard to work well in clothes that were too small, especially in winter, when a strip of exposed skin was dangerous.

He'd spent weeks debating whether to ask for bigger gloves, ones more appropriate for a young giant's hands. He'd never dared ask before. He knew that he had to wait for the situation to return to normal, for there to be less suspicion.

Tadeusz, Józef, and Radosz had escaped.

One evening, they'd gone out for firewood and hadn't come back. Janusz imagined that they'd entered the woods, found themselves unsupervised, and kept going.

The next morning, nobody emerged from the workers' hut. When Hartwig went in to find out why, he had found only Janusz, dressed but motionless, sitting on his bed.

"Where are they?"

"I don't know."

"Why didn't you come to find me?"

"I fell asleep last night. When I woke up, I realized they'd gone. And I was afraid," he said honestly.

"Did they say anything to you?"

"They didn't say anything to me."

Not even goodbye. Almost five years living together, and not even one parting word?

"Listen, Janusz, the soldiers will come to interrogate you. Don't worry; I'll be with you."

Indeed, the soldiers had tried to take their anger out on the one remaining prisoner. Herr Hahlbrock hadn't allowed it.

"Leave him in peace. It's obvious the boy doesn't know anything. It's not his job to patrol; it's yours. You soldiers let them escape. And I'm going to report it to your superiors."

He did. The soldiers who'd watched over the farm, who'd established a kind of peaceful, if distant, relationship with their prisoners and who respected Herr Hahlbrock as an efficient and fair man, were sent to the eastern front. It was a hard lesson for having allowed themselves to grow complacent and lax.

But they hadn't been executed: Herr Hahlbrock had persuaded the commander that the war needed them.

"I didn't want to see those men die, Janusz. But now I don't know whether I did them a favor or made it worse."

For the eastern front was execution in a slow, roundabout way, the victim waiting to stop a projectile with his body. And while he waited, there would only be cold and mud.

The three Poles hadn't managed to erase all their footprints as they fled; they were caught shortly after joining a Polish Resistance group. Nazi bullets brought down ten men, including Józef. Tadeusz was left wounded but alive. Hartwig had been summoned to identify him and witness his punishment: he was hanged on the spot.

It was the worst thing that Hartwig had experienced. Seeing an acquaintance, if not a friend, sent deliberately to his death robbed him of any ability to put on a friendly face.

"Janusz, things are going to change."

The young man didn't know what that would mean. He imagined what was going through Herr Hahlbrock's mind: the workers were prisoners. The boss, their jailor. Janusz saw a flash of this forgotten understanding in his eyes. That the war beyond the farm's boundaries also existed within them. The almost five years of relative peace had persuaded him that his fiction was true: the Poles were employees and he their benevolent employer. And, more seriously: the Russians would never invade these peaceful lands.

Janusz was glad that the Poles' escape had made Herr Hahlbrock see how dangerous it was to live a lie. Though he feared the coming changes, this one pleased Janusz: the Russians would come one day, but now they wouldn't find it so easy to take the Hahlbrock family by surprise.

The replacement guards were neither new nor friendly. Not even with Hartwig. They'd survived several winters on the eastern front. This assignment was a reward for heroic service. They wouldn't squander it with carelessness.

The only concession they'd granted Herr Hahlbrock was not to bring more prisoners to live on the farm. Workers were needed, so they would transfer some from elsewhere—no one asked where—but have them lodge in the village. They would report for duty each morning; each night, they would leave. Hahlbrock didn't want any more familiarity with those who didn't want it with him. He'd take care of his farm and his people, and that was it. And Janusz was among those people. That day, Janusz had had to promise that he'd say nothing to Ilse or Wanda about the violence that had taken place.

"I don't want them to know what happened, you hear?"

Janusz had understood. While he missed Ilse, he was glad they'd decided to keep her in the house: she wouldn't understand the changes, the coldness of the new soldiers. Nor would she understand the grotesque convoys that stopped to beg for food and gasoline. Soldiers climbed out with bullet wounds, hobbling, moaning; others had been mutilated by the cold. It was shocking to see the missing fingers, eyelids, noses. Sometimes, these images woke Janusz in the middle of the night. He didn't want Ilse to suffer that way. She and the family had to be protected above all else.

"You can go to the village, if you want."

Janusz's heart had stopped for an instant when Herr Hahlbrock made the offer. Was he throwing him out?

"You can live there and come every day with the other workers."

Janusz's relief had been immediate.

"No. I'll stay here."

Herr Hahlbrock's relief hadn't come so easily.

"Don't even think about escaping, Janusz."

There was no menace, just concern: Don't even think about escaping, Janusz; they'll kill you.

"I'm not going anywhere."

There was no fear in Janusz's reply. It was a promise and a declaration: I don't want to be anywhere else.

"You don't mind living alone in the hut?"

It had been a long time since Janusz had been alone. But in the day, he wouldn't be: with the Hahlbrocks, he'd acquired a family. It wasn't his own, he knew. The circumstances weren't ideal. But Ilse loved him. He loved her. Herr Hahlbrock . . . perhaps he loved Herr Hahlbrock, too. He was the closest thing he'd ever had to a father, though he wasn't a giant. He'd protected him from the soldiers' vengeful rage. Janusz wouldn't feel safe anywhere else.

"I don't mind."

With the decision made, Janusz felt a moment's apprehension: it was the memory of the child that he'd been, so lonely that he preferred the company of strangers to one more day of silence, one more day of cold, of hunger, of neglect. He'd become accustomed to the taciturn company of Tadeusz and Józef, to Radosz's complaints. He'd become accustomed to their snoring, the smell they filled the entire hut with. What would the hut smell of now? What would it sound like now with only his voice, with only his sighs? What would the temperature be? Janusz had become accustomed to a warmth that had more to do with seeing living bodies than with the firewood that all of them took turns keeping alight. But then the others had left. And left Janusz, just like that.

In all likelihood, they knew he wouldn't have accepted an invitation to join them, but not being asked hurt. Perhaps they suspected he would give them away. It wasn't true: he would never, Janusz swore to himself, though he knew his oath was worthless now. It *was* true that he felt an attachment to the boss and the dear girl. It was true that Janusz, trusting the effectiveness of their prison and content with the comfort of their mere company, had pretended not to notice the ill will the three men felt toward the Hahlbrocks. While Janusz would've wished them luck in their escape, now that he knew two of the three were dead, he felt two parts relief and one part dread: Radosz remained at large. Janusz didn't know how to convey to Herr Hahlbrock his worst fear: the man had gone to the forest to howl with the wolves and he wouldn't hesitate to seek revenge on the familiar face of their oppressor.

# 30. The bonfires of the vanities
## The Schippers

***January 1944***

His boy had so many questions, and Karl had so few answers. A carpenter doesn't know about such things. A carpenter knows about woods; he knows them all by touch and smell. He knows sandpaper, nails, plugs. He knows about timing: I can deliver a unit like the one you want, *gnädige Frau*, in seventy-five days. He knows about geography and history: That ebony comes from Gabon, Fräulein Stieglitz. The table was made during the reign of Friedrich Wilhelm II. He becomes a forecaster of the weather: Enamel mustn't be applied on a rainy day, and it's going to storm tomorrow. A carpenter knows about creation, about construction, but pulleys? A little, perhaps, but what does he know about engines and cogwheels? About mass production? Nothing.

"Take me with you to Königsberg, Vater. Take me to the library," the child insisted for the third, the fifth . . . the tenth time?

"No, Arno. I'm going to work."

And he'd left him at home, with a sad face, not understanding.

But why should he take him? So that the boy could see the destruction the bombings had caused? So that he'd know fear, know war? No. Arno was the only one in the family still unscathed. The only one who still had the light of curiosity in his eyes, who still looked at his father with admiration. How precious he was! Fritz, Johann, and even Helga had seen him ruined, not by a bullet but by his need for the drug and then by the memories he couldn't escape. Karl could see the disdain on their faces. Especially when he admitted how happy he was to have returned home, especially when they had to explain why their father was the youngest and healthiest man in the area. It was difficult to remind everyone that he was only able to move by some miracle and that he'd always carry inside the bullet that almost killed him. It was difficult to explain that he'd used up all his youth while he was away.

Arno. His little farm boy. Karl refused to see the city's destruction reflected in those eyes that were bluer than the sky, and he feared seeing his disappointment at how few books remained in Königsberg—if the library was even standing.

Karl Schipper went to the city because he had no choice. He had to work. He had to risk his life to do so. There had only been a few Russian bombings of Königsberg, but if he'd learned anything about war, it was that you never knew when it would kill you. Small or large caliber bullet, grenade or mortar or aerial missile, Russian or British: every German had their name written on one. Better, then, to hide away and not be found.

That day, he decided to go on horseback to speed up the journey. If he wasn't carrying any materials, what did he need the cart for? If bombs dropped from the air, fleeing would be easier this way. He hoped, if that happened, that his mount would respond calmly to its rider's commands. Or react with its heart and four hooves to save its own skin, seeing as its rider had left his composure at the foot of a tree in a blood-soaked Russian forest. His rescuers had forgotten to lift it onto the stretcher with its broken shell, and now Karl imagined it buried alongside all the other soldiers who fell that day.

He would prefer to never leave the farm again, but he had an appointment he could not miss.

For many years, Karl had done annual maintenance at the grand Stieglitz house. The job never paid a lot, but he enjoyed the privilege of being able to caress the antique furniture and the knots in the beautiful wood, to admire the carving that the cabinetmakers of the past had achieved.

The previous year, he'd turned up at the agreed time as if he'd never left, as if the war hadn't happened. And Fräulein Stieglitz had welcomed him as if he'd never been absent. Come in, Herr Schipper. There's a lot to do. Reconnecting with his tools, his trade, had helped Karl escape the clutches of Demerol: the trembling hadn't returned, though cravings snuck in at night. Every day he was surprised to find that his body obeyed his commands and that it was only on the iciest days that he felt the old pain return. He'd hoped that, throwing off the chains of the war and the drug, he'd find salvation in the work he loved, but demand for skilled carpentry work was gone, and Karl struggled to find anything that gave him satisfaction. He helped on the farm, he eased his wife's burden, he served as the family's full-time cook.

But the carpenter inside him was fading away with each day. It came out occasionally to repair doors or sled runners, and with immense sadness it carved miniature horses to pay tribute to all those he saw die. These little sculptures were his only creative output, but he was unable to reproduce even the old Latvian horse faithfully. With each rigid horse that he created, his desire to attempt the next one diminished.

Arno was obsessed with engines and mechanics, but his father had always done everything with his own hands. Now those hands seemed to have lost the steam from their own internal engine, perhaps because recovering from the war was impossible when the war wasn't over, or perhaps because, thanks to the war, no one came to commission a new cabinet or rocking chair.

Who needed to be surrounded by beauty if they were going to die of cold or hunger? If they might die in the next bombing? It was more important to have something to eat than a table on which to eat.

Because surviving the night was more important than history or ancestors, sometimes even an heirloom table could be sent to die slowly in ephemeral flames with no consideration for the carpenter who, since he saw it for the first time years ago, had considered it an inspiration, had caressed it like a lover. Without giving him a chance to say goodbye.

The previous year, when Karl visited Fräulein Stieglitz after a winter's absence, his heart had broken.

"What do you mean, you burned the table, Fräulein? It was Gabonese ebony!"

"And it belonged to my great-grandparents. But what was I supposed to do? Dusty heirlooms, Schipper, don't fill the stomach or warm the skin," old Fräulein Stieglitz told him. "It was a museum piece, wasn't it? I would've sold it, but who would've bought it? And for what? A few coins? Enough for a bundle of cheap firewood—if I could even find one—that wouldn't last me half a night?"

Her great-grandmother's table, she went on, had burned slow, long, and hot.

"When the first leg caught fire, I could hear my ancestors' wails, and I cried. The second night, I didn't cry anymore. Who cares about the freezing tears of a lonely old woman?"

"And the ivory inlay?"

"I shouldn't have thrown that in the fire, but it was stuck fast, and I was stiff with cold. The smell wasn't very nice, I must say."

In the end, all that had remained was the gap a table had once filled—in space, in history, and in a carpenter's heart.

When the devastation after the Great War had depleted what remained of the family fortune, the Stieglitzes had resolved to keep the mansion—can you imagine, Herr Schipper, what the neighbors would say if I sold the house in which I was born?—and some jewels, but little else. With prudence and thrift, she and her siblings had lived in a noble poverty, spending money only on food and the annual repairs to the house, an investment required in order to prevent it from collapsing on top of them. Karl Schipper knew that the furniture had always been a source of pride for its owners, and rightly so.

That day a year before, Fräulein Stieglitz had told him she needed help.

"With the roof? The stairs?"

"Who cares about a few leaks when a bomb could drop on me any day? No. The table lasted, but it's gone. Winter, on the other hand, shows no signs of ending, and I have a lot I can burn."

"Not the sideboard in the entrance hall!"

That one was French, from before the Revolution, and Karl had always admired the hunting story told in its carved foxes, partridges, and wild geese. He couldn't stand more heartache.

"No! What do you take me for! That will be the last thing to burn. No one'll miss the table, but we must keep up appearances if someone comes to the door. No, Herr Schipper, I won't burn any more furniture if I can avoid it."

Karl was relieved. The woman had come to her senses.

"I'll burn books. I have lots. But I need help. Follow me."

That previous winter, in 1943, instead of the usual annual repairs, Karl had helped his only remaining customer in the city take the vast library down from the bookcases, making mountains of paper, leather, and golden letters. The vast library would help her survive the first winter of real scarcity, she'd calculated. He hoped it would last her several years. As long as the war lasted. Better books than antiques, he told himself.

"There used to be more," his employer said. "These are just the ones that were left after the bonfires of 1933. Did your family burn many books?"

His family had only ever had a copy of the Bible, and they would never burn that even to escape the cold, so Karl shook his head.

"Like some kind of Torquemada, my brother, Hugo, may he rest in peace, got carried away with that modern bonfire of the vanities and made several trips to the garden with wheelbarrows full. He could've just taken a few insignificant editions to the university bonfire to placate the authoritarians, but no: we were never given to mixing with the rabble. So he made his own private pyre as tall as himself and lit it with gasoline. Oh, Herr Schipper, how I'd like to have some gasoline now! It would make lighting the stove much easier."

Hugo Stieglitz had read the list of banned books from the Deutsche Studentenschaft and purged all the named titles from the library their grandparents and parents had left them. His sister couldn't understand where her brother's pyromania had come from. Nor his fervor for National Socialism.

"Was it fear? I don't know anymore: hate and fear are very alike and they're great motivators, don't you think? They should both be included among the great muses of destruction. I don't want to speak badly of my brother, Herr Schipper, but that day, there was no dissuading him. It was as if he'd been convinced in an instant that the old authors our grandparents and parents read were to blame for Germany's misfortune. He said: We have one of the biggest private libraries in the city; they'll come for us and our books; you'll see, Maria."

She'd managed to snatch two treasures from the fire: the last volume of the first edition of Victor Hugo's *Les Misérables*, in its original French, and Heinrich Heine's *Almansor*.

"You won't tell anyone, will you, Herr Schipper, that I saved a Frenchman and a Jew from the fire? Imagine the uproar."

Karl would never mention it, nor should she have told him: it was dangerous information for them both.

"I ran to the garden when Hugo was in the library and grabbed two at random, one in each hand. I wasn't going to allow him to turn our grandmother's books to ash at the whim of some student organization. I only found out which books I'd saved later, in the privacy of my room. I believe it was providential: for one Hugo to burn another would've brought bad luck, as would burning the work of a Jew lamenting the burning of books. Did you know that Heine wrote that where books are burned, it always ends in people being burned?"

"When did he write that?" asked Karl, a little breathless.

"More than a hundred and twenty years ago. Do you think the Jew was right? That it will come to that?"

"Just old customs, I'm sure," he said as if he knew what he was talking about, as if a seed of fear had never invaded him. "Nobody burns people anymore."

Maria Stieglitz fell silent for a moment, pensive. Uncertain? Then she told him how, the day after the fire, she'd made an inventory: she hadn't been able to save Bertolt Brecht or Stefan Zweig. Erich Maria Remarque was burned alongside Dostoyevsky. Also lost in the flames was Hemingway's *In einem andern Land*, which she'd bought herself, though she admitted that she'd never liked it much.

"Almost as dry as Marx. Almost as communist, they say."

Maria had promised herself that, when the madness subsided, she'd replace every one of the lost editions.

"The only new books I have are the ten copies of *Mein Kampf*. They're utter garbage, but don't tell anyone I said that. My brother thought it'd be a good idea to scatter them strategically just in case they came to inspect our library. But they never did.

"I didn't do anything to hide the gaps: they served as protest for the words that my brother had silenced with fire. I thought they could also serve as a reminder for me: Mann's *Der Untertan* will be here again, and there, Kafka's *Die Verwandlung*, I told myself."

But then war came, and the paper and ink of old dissent no longer mattered to her. Fräulein Stieglitz didn't even go in the library anymore.

"Who can read when you're obliged to go from store to store searching desperately for an old scrap of cheese or a coarse bar of soap? Who wants to fill their head with ideas when their belly's rumbling? I'd prefer a Wiener schnitzel to any Egon Kisch, if I'm honest."

Now, a year after that heartbreaking visit, Karl Schipper, mounted on his horse, was certain that he hadn't been summoned to repair anything this time, either. He'd left his toolbox behind, obeying the request sent by messenger: Come tomorrow. Bring your axe.

Work is work, and it's food on the table, he said as he urged on the horse. Work is work and it's flour for our bread. He hesitated before ringing the doorbell. Work is work and it's sugar in our tea. Work is work, even if it means destroying instead of creating.

When he heard the woman's heels tapping toward the door, he would've liked to turn and disappear into the icy day. Work is work and it's being able to look your family in the eyes.

Fräulein Stieglitz looked surprised.

"Aren't you at war, Schipper?"

Now he was the surprised one.

"No. I've been back a while." Did the old woman not remember his visit last year or the message she'd sent him?

"I'm glad you returned from your adventures."

"You asked me here, Fräulein. I received your message."

"Ah, yes. I have some work for you. Come in."

Work is work and it's . . . it's . . . , he repeated to himself, trying to find the courage to cross the threshold.

"Look, last year I burned all the books in the house, and I still had enough to make a good start this winter. I learned a lot, watching them burn one by one. In particular, that they're a luxury not everyone has. I managed them well, and, inspired by their warmth, I also had the idea to use old jewelry. I ate it, little by little."

She must have read the shock in Karl's eyes.

"Don't be alarmed! I mean that I traded them for potatoes and cheese on the black market. There's a good market for the brooches and earrings that I used to consider tasteless knickknacks. And I have a lot of them. Thanks to the war, Herr Schipper, I've realized that I'm very rich again. How about that?"

"You shouldn't tell me these things, Fräulein. You shouldn't tell anybody," he said to her, unhappy to be the owner of more dangerous information.

Hunger and cold had driven Fräulein Stieglitz to lose her love for her books and her things—and to lose her good sense, it appeared—but those things would drive others to lose all decency, to steal, to kill. Even Karl felt tiny tendrils of envy and temptation: what he could do with a few of those *tasteless knickknacks* . . . His breath caught in his throat. He didn't recognize himself: How had such thoughts invaded him? He'd always lived by the Commandments, but it was easy to do when his character wasn't put to the test. He realized that he didn't know how many of those divine rules he'd be capable of breaking to protect his family from hunger or cold. So that his wife would look at him like she used to.

Every man had his breaking point. Karl had witnessed it on the front: one soldier killing another in his own unit to double the thickness of his clothing. Soldiers killing a healthy horse with their mouths watering in anticipation. Not without first weaving a story about a Russian bastard, because there, everything was some Russian bastard's fault.

There were more stories like those: some soldiers became scavengers, stripping Russian and German dead bodies, while another murdered a helpless elderly civilian for his fur coat.

Then there was his own story.

Karl knew that he'd almost broken. He knew it when he felt grateful to be chosen by his commander as the recipient of a dead soldier's not-too-bloodstained overcoat. He didn't take it, he was given it, but the idea passed through his mind: yes, the coat was perforated, but it was good that the man had bled so little. He no longer felt any pity when he ate the horseflesh offered to him; now his mouth watered and his hunger screamed whenever he saw one die. Eating meat gave him at least another day of life, he told himself, excused himself. Eating meat gave him the chance of seeing his children again.

By the end of his war, he was no longer able to banish envy and desire from his thoughts: Look at that piece of bread that's bigger than mine, smell that horsemeat stew they won't share, look at that Russian coat that's better than mine.

A bullet had taken him out of the game before the predatory thoughts had won. But now he was on the home front, on the front of difficulty and shortage. He hoped he would never reach his breaking point. He ordered himself to never fall into temptation. He vowed never to tell anyone about the treasure chest that was the Stieglitzes' old mansion. He wouldn't do it, he promised himself as he looked the old woman in the eye.

Unaware of the feelings she'd stirred in her trusted carpenter, she continued to list her vast inventory of heirlooms as if she hadn't heard him tell her not to: fine rugs, silverware, Egyptian artifacts.

"I gave the Persian rug in the library, the one my great-grandfather was so proud of, to the butcher, for a month's worth of prime meat. I didn't even have to wait in line. That centuries-old treasure of silk thread, I ate after roasting it on a fire made from other treasures. It's ironic, don't you think," she said, laughing, "how I protested so much to Hugo about his pyre of books, and how I enjoyed my own! Did you know that where they burn books, they always end up burning people? I don't know where I read such a thing, but it's true, you'll see: with all these bombs raining down, the war will end up burning us all."

Put like that, Karl thought the premise that had seemed so shocking last year now seemed plausible, inevitable. We'll all burn in this war. Will it be in fleeting fires or one enormous conflagration? Which would be better? Which would mean less suffering? He shivered. He hoped, if it was going to happen, that the fire would come before he had to return to this house to work.

"Let's go to the library. Do you remember the books from the bookcases? I burned them to keep the cold at bay, did you know?"

He'd helped her make the stacks of books. And she'd just talked about it. How could she not remember?

"They even lasted until the beginning of this winter. I think the last one I burned was by a Johann? Stefan? It doesn't matter. A German author with the surname Fallada. That one was my brother's."

"And what about the two books you saved? The ones by the Frenchman and the Jew?"

"Which ones?"

Karl was silent a moment. "Never mind."

"Now I have empty bookcases. A lot of them."

Karl felt a knot in his stomach.

"Did you bring what I asked, Herr Schipper?"

A reluctant Karl showed her his axe.

"If I manage it well, that wood will last me the rest of the winter and part of the next, if a bomb doesn't drop on me first."

"But they're made of Gabonese ebony!"

On the trip he'd made the previous year to evict their paper tenants, he'd stroked the boards and carvings that covered three walls of the large room from floor to ceiling.

"I know. You should see how long it burns . . ."

# 31. Hidden truths

Arno didn't know if he was breathing on purpose, or if the freezing wind was flooding into his lungs of its own accord as he launched himself into it. He felt it go under his earflaps, but he didn't care. Nor did he care that his gloves—and boots, too—were bursting with snow. His desire to forget and have fun kept him impermeable, or at least, impervious. Perhaps it was because he was already frozen through. It was the tenth time he'd slid on a board down the steepest hill on his friend Adolf's farm.

Arno knew he'd hit flat ground soon, that his fast ride would be over, that he'd have to carry his board back uphill again. That then he *would* struggle to fill his lungs with the freezing air. He'd do it once more. Just once, he told himself, and then I'll go.

Adolf had shared some of the bread and cheese that his mother, Frau Müller, had given him when they'd arrived after school. It wasn't enough, but Arno had thanked him without daring to ask for more. Now he was hungry, but it was better than going home. It was also better than doing his afternoon chores. He guessed that, by now, his father would've returned from Königsberg: it wouldn't harm the horse to wait a little while longer in its dirty stall, and he'd be home in time to feed it, Arno told himself. To feed all the animals, even the sheep. He could put up with his own hunger, but he couldn't forgive letting his animals go hungry; they were blameless.

Nor would his mother forgive it, he knew. It would be hard enough for her to forgive his intentional absence, his thoughtless diversion of a few hours. Come home after school, mein *Kind*, was her precise instruction every day, and his mother was precise in all things. He knew that, by now, she'd be plotting all kinds of punishments and praying to a thousand gods so that avenging fire and sulfur would fall onto her wayward son. He knew because he'd witnessed the phenomenon each time Fritz and Johann disappeared on one of their adventures, which happened more and more often.

The war's going to kill them before they're even conscripted, and if it doesn't, I'll spank them to death myself the next time they're late.

She always knew where they'd gone: far from the tedium of the farm, drawn to the Jungvolk's increasingly unfettered action. One day, someone's going to find you in a ditch, you'll see. And what will I do? I'll come throw earth on top of you—what else, she'd say, but after hearing it so many times, they never took her seriously.

Arno's descent ended in a small mound of snow: more icy powder inside his gloves, boots, and jacket. Adolf was already waiting for him: his board was better and had more wax on it, so he went down as if floating. Arno brushed himself off as well as he could and picked up his board again.

"Last one to the top gets a smack in the head!"

The two boys set off at the same time. So far, Arno had won some of the races and Adolf had won others. The loser was never rewarded with the promised beating. The smacks were more likely to come from his mother, Arno thought, summiting a few steps ahead of his friend. And it must be time to sate the animals' hunger.

"I'm off, Adolf."

"One more!"

But Arno handed over the board.

"Thanks."

He left the Müllers' little farm, quickening his pace. He took the long way, not wanting to pass by the Färber family's land. Since Frau Färber had accused her of sending over fewer eggs than they'd agreed in exchange for butter, Arno's mother had broken off all contact, and their proximity had become uncomfortable. At school, Ludwig and Werner Färber, once friendly, now contrived to spill ink on Arno's work or steal the piece of bread his mother packed for lunch. Small things: not worth ratting on them to Herr Baumgartner. But after school, the Färbers were always lying in wait in front of their farm and they chased him with stones, clods of mud, or sticks. If they weren't there, they left their big dog on guard for the enemy. So Arno preferred to cross Frau Hitzig's farm whenever possible. It was better to be saddened by the loneliness of the widow who'd given everything to the Vaterland, it was better to offer her help—which he always tried to do—than arrive home with a lump on his head or with pants torn by a dog's bite.

That day, Arno saw Frau Hitzig peering through her window. Could she be looking at him? The woman closed her curtains. Arno took it she was having one of her dark days.

Arno looked around for something helpful to do, even if there was no request and would be no thank-you. He understood her sadness. Frau Hitzig needed help, she needed all her sons not to have died, she needed her neighbors to stop throwing mud at her door because of the absence of donation badges. She needed . . . she needed Arno to clean the door again.

He couldn't help with her sadness, but he could do that for her. He went to the well for some water. He knew where she kept some old rags. Without knocking, he got to work. But then, too soon, the door was clean. He had no more excuses: he had to go home to face his mother's anger, and his own anger at his father.

Arno didn't understand why he refused to take him to Königsberg. He started by telling him, Arno, there aren't any candy stores anymore.

Today he'd told him: There's just work. But Arno didn't care about the candy. With the rampant shortage, the first establishments to die off had been Königsberg's famous confectioners. There was no sugar for tea now, or for the expensive ersatz coffee made from Italian chicory that his mother kept in a tin box for when she couldn't bear it any longer. And it wasn't because of the work: he'd proved to his father many times that he was a good helper, that he was no burden, that he could be quiet, that he could wait.

He wanted to go to the library; that was all. Before or after the job. So he was angry with his father. That day, instead of going to Königsberg, he'd listened to the elderly Herr Baumgartner talk endlessly about his dead sons' heroism during the Great War, about the Führer and his heroism during the Great War, about the missed opportunities after the Great War. The teacher might begin with arithmetic as he was supposed to, but he always ended in the Great War.

Arno was tired of war—of that old one, of this new one. They said Germany would be victorious this time, but he'd already lost: his father had returned, and how lucky that he was in one piece, everyone said. But Arno knew it was a lie: he'd returned, true, but not in one piece. Maybe the bullet had hit him right where he kept his joy and had smashed it to bits.

His father's joy had died in the war. And his voice, too. He'd gotten better, though sometimes he still limped a little; he ate and drank like everyone else, but though his voice sounded like the one Arno remembered, he scarcely used it. He never used it to command Johann and Fritz to show him the respect they had before. Never to ask Helga to stop staring as if she didn't recognize him. Never to respond to his wife's nagging; never to ask her to stop. Never to answer Arno's questions. Never to tell him: Arno, I can't take you to Königsberg because . . . and never to complete that sentence with words that sounded true and convincing. And that infuriated him.

But now, almost home, Arno realized that the bitterness had died away on the snowy climbs on Adolf's farm. Or maybe on one of the descents. It didn't matter: he'd expended his resentment. But even so, he didn't want to get home. Would his mother scold him badly? If so, he'd face up to it and apologize. She was obliged to forgive, as God commands all Christians. She said so herself. Arno had always thought the tactic would work for his elder brothers. Say sorry, he'd suggested, but they never listened. He would try it.

So, no: it wasn't his mother's likely fury or his faded anger with his father that was making him want to stay away. It was the dense air inside the house, the sidelong looks, the truths hidden among the words as simple and as everyday as *pass me the salt, sure, thanks*. It was the long silences and the complaints left hanging for days like walls. How much could be said without a sound? How much of this treatment could his father bear without wanting to find his own way to escape? Arno didn't even want to imagine it.

They were all angry with his father: Helga because he wouldn't let her go out with Adelbert Weber, his brothers because he didn't let them talk about the war at home, and even more so because, at home, he refused to talk about *his* war. He never told them about the medals awarded to other soldiers, about the bullet inside him, about the vibrations of a tank. In response to a question such as, Vater, how many Russians did you kill? or, what did it feel like when the bullet hit you? he pretended not to hear. He walked out and left his sons expectant, frustrated, skeptical.

But his mother was the worst.

Before going in, Arno headed to the stable. Now it was his father's horse who looked at him with resentment.

"Yeah, yeah. I'm here."

The horse was still warm. His father had arrived just ahead of him, he realized. Arno performed the usual routine, leaving the animals happy and their space clean. How easy it was to make peace with them. If only everyone could be that good at erasing bitterness from their memory. His mother forgave because Christ demanded it of her, but she never forgot.

From outside, Arno could hear her firm voice addressing his father's dense silence. What had happened now? He slipped into the house. He didn't want to witness his mother telling his father again how useless he was, so he snuck up to the second floor without them noticing. It was impossible to close his ears: some words found their way in. They made his ears hurt, but not as much as his father's silence did.

He decided that he preferred the truths hidden among words as simple and as everyday as *pass me the salt*, *sure*, *thanks*.

# 32. War never leaves the soldier

On the way home, he had given the horse free rein. They'd arrive whenever they arrived. He knew what was waiting for him there, but his work in the city was done, and all he could do now was go back along the road. The heavy sacks that hung from the horse's sides swayed with each slow step. They would hurt the animal if he rushed it.

Karl took off a glove to dip his hand in one of the sacks. He caressed the contents.

How easy destruction was. It could break a man's heart, but it got easier after the first hack. By the second or third swing of the axe, he'd stopped apologizing to the hands from another age that had taken months or years to build what he was now desecrating so that he wouldn't go home empty-handed. By the time he had no feeling left in his arms from the countless blows of iron against wood, by the time he came out of the deep trance in which he'd taken refuge, by the time every last ebony board had surrendered, nothing mattered.

All that mattered, as he reluctantly held out his blistered hand, was receiving payment for the service provided. In coins, perhaps. If so, he'd deserve thirty. Silver ones. Like Judas.

"Herr Schipper, I don't know how to repay you."

"You have nothing to thank me for, Fräulein Stieglitz."

"No, I mean, I don't have any money to pay you with. But I have a pretty Limoges porcelain pitcher and cup set, which, according to my grandfather's grandfather, belonged to Robespierre. Though they say that he didn't enjoy it for long."

Maria Stieglitz ran her forefinger across her throat. Dread filled Karl's stomach. Perhaps this Robespierre had arrived home with porcelain instead of coins to give his wife, he thought.

"They'd break on the way; I can't accept that."

The negotiation had gone in Karl's favor, and he'd left happy. After becoming a destroyer, he'd ended the day a savior.

When he arrived, he took the horse to the stable. He was surprised to find it was dirty. What could've happened for Arno not to clean it as he should have? Then he took the heavy sacks to his workshop but didn't stop to admire their contents. He would have a whole lifetime to do that; now, he only had a few minutes to face his wife before his children arrived. He mustered all the courage he had and headed to the house.

"I'm home," he announced, though he took it as a given that she already knew, that she'd observed him from her place at the kitchen window.

"Did you see Arno on the way?"

"No."

"He didn't come home after school."

Surprised, Karl looked at the cuckoo clock. It was late, but no need to worry yet, he decided. Poor Arno: it wasn't a good day to start seeking his independence.

"I'm sure he won't be long. He'll do his chores, you'll see."

"You bet he will. Did the woman pay you?"

There was the expected—dreaded—question, asked in the bitter tone he'd discovered after returning from the war, a tone she reserved only for him. Did the woman pay you? was just another version of when are you going to contribute something? or, why don't you get to work? But it was worse, he suddenly understood. It was worse because it was asked with the last remnants of faith that she had in her husband, with hope that he'd surprise her, at last: Yes, she paid me, and here's the money.

"Yes."

Karl noticed Ethel almost smile. Almost. He was glad she didn't.

"Well! Give me the money."

"She didn't have any money."

He saw the near smile turn to a grimace.

"She owes you? How did you let that happen, Karl? No one pays their debts anymore, you know that. No one works for nothing. Only you. Only my husband."

"She paid me, but not with money."

Karl rushed to interrupt her in the hope they wouldn't end up where they always did: You're useless, Karl, or, find some work, Karl, or, I don't know what they did to you in the war to ruin you like this, Karl.

Through no choice of his own, he'd left one home and, transformed, returned to another, which he didn't recognize, one which, likewise, refused to recognize him. To accept him. While he was gone, life at home had taken on an unfamiliar rhythm. Now he was out of tune and out of sync.

His absence and then his torturous recovery had cost him dearly, leaving a hole that had quickly been filled. Now it seemed there was no space left for him. Because the loss continued. Sometimes, when he suddenly opened his eyes to come out of a nightmare, it was the fire's heat, the pillow's softness, his sleeping wife, the weight of the quilt that, in the total darkness, seemed like the illusion: he must be freezing to death, hallucinating all this.

His tears brought him back. When Karl felt their warmth, when they ran down his temples to his ears, he returned to reality. But still, he kept silent as he had in the war, first when he'd learned to stifle his screams with the beloved socks, and then when he'd allowed the lesson to become permanent, instinctual, as much a part of him as the bullet he'd take to the grave.

In the middle of the night, a soldier doesn't scream if he wants to live. In total darkness, a soldier doesn't scream if he wants to return home. A soldier cries oceans, but he learns to do it in silence if he wants to survive the war. Karl had managed it: he'd left the war, but the war refused to leave him. It had followed him to his farm; it had invaded his mind. It had turned his dreams into nightmares, his bed into ice, his hands into lifeless instruments, his heart into a rhythmless, tuneless musician. His love of wood had become impossible, and the looks from his children and the words from his wife had turned cruel and unfamiliar.

". . . but from you, nothing. Are you listening to me, Karl? The farm puts food on the table, but it's not enough. Fritz needs shoes, Arno needs soles on his, and you spend your time in that workshop with your little horses of rotten wood. And the one day you have work, what do you do? You come home without any money!"

"I help you on the farm . . ."

"You help. And what use is it? It's not because I have help that I manage to grow more potatoes or get my hens to lay more eggs. We need you to do your part."

"The Army pays—"

"What the Army pays you isn't enough, and it never arrives in time. They take a lot, too. In any case, what kind of example are you setting? My children need to know that their father works. They don't need to see you stuck to my apron."

Everything was hers: his war veteran's compensation, the farm, the field, the potatoes, the chickens and their eggs, every mouthful that the family enjoyed. The apron that Karl put on to cook three times a day. And the children: they were completely hers now. All he had was a forgotten trade, a lost energy, and a shortage of work. All he had was shame. But on that day of destruction, and despite his wife's usual words, he still had the feeling that he'd saved something, that he'd invested in the future by rescuing a little piece of the past.

"I took wood as payment," he said to interrupt the lecture.

Ethel broke off, surprised.

"Yes," Karl continued, spurred on by his wife's silence. "From the furniture that Fräulein Stieglitz asked me to make firewood from."

"What for? There's plenty of firewood on the farm," said Ethel, still not fully understanding, but certain that she wouldn't like the answer.

"This isn't firewood. I only took the decorative pieces. They're made of Gabonese ebony, carved by masters. When the war's over, I'll use them to teach the boys to become great cabinetmakers. Who knows, perhaps one day Schipper and Sons will design a great piece of furniture, like the one I destroyed today."

Mockery and something else appeared on Ethel's face.

"Bah. Schipper and Sons . . . If you can't even get paid for working as a woodcutter, why're you thinking about Schipper and Sons? And who says this war will end? Do you believe those people on the Volksempfänger? Are you gullible as well as useless? This war, Karl, is never going to end. It'll take our three sons, and you and I will watch Helga starve to death as she knits socks."

In Ethel's smile there was mockery, yes, but also pain. At that moment, Karl understood that, much like him, his wife was possessed by a demon, her own demon, her own war nightmare. The demon that made him silent drove her to bitterness. He would have liked to ask: Do you cry in silence when no one's looking? Where do you keep your screams? Then he would have held her. He would have confessed his nightmares to her. But he didn't ask. Nor did he hold her or confess. He didn't have time to consider taking such a bold step. There was a knock at the door. Three firm blows. Only three, but they were authoritative, ominous. The last three that would reach Karl's ears in that house, the last three he would hear emanating from that solid oak door with simple carvings made by some ancestor of Ethel's, the door that, in the fleeting peace between wars, he and his wife had opened after saying I do to each other before God.

Three firm blows that announced that the war had come back for Karl Schipper.

# 33. The war enters through the front door

Someone had knocked on the door, and someone had opened it. The air in the house changed. It reached Arno in his bedroom in a gale that brought a strange man's voice to his ears through the closed door, but not his words. The fervent *Heil Hitler*—that did reach him loud and clear. Then the door's soft creak as it closed. And then absolute silence, one that didn't even leave room for things that are said without saying them. A stunned silence.

Arno opened the door. He went down the stairs. He saw his parents standing there, motionless, in that shared silence at the closed front door. His mother was facing him, his father had his back to him. When his mother saw him, she didn't protest his unusual lateness. She ignored his presence, in fact.

"No, Karl. You're not going. You'll go see the doctor tomorrow to get a letter, and that's that. He can tell them that you already have a bullet in you. How could they even think of taking a useless soldier?" Her words quivered with anxiety.

"Do you think they care? There are gaps letting the bullets through, and they need to fill them. I'm upright; I have eyes, legs, and arms, and that's enough for them. See? You don't need to be more useful than that to be a soldier." His words quivered, too—with sarcasm.

Arno had never heard him speak like that to his mother or to anyone. His father gave his mother time to respond, but seeing her struck dumb, he went on.

"You're right, Ethel: the war won't be satisfied until it burns us all." Those words didn't even quiver with fear. "I'm going to fetch some oil. The hinges on the door creak."

Arno's father turned around, opened the front door, and went out in the direction of his workshop. His mother, always practical, always a diligent protector of the warmth achieved with meticulous care inside the house, closed it. Then she turned around and went to the kitchen to wash something. Arno—dumbstruck, too, and sickened, his father's words reverberating inside him—sat on the step.

# 34. One, one, one

## The Hahlbrocks

***January 10 to January 20, 1945***

Ilse woke with a start. No light was coming in through the window, but it was January, the depths of winter. Something had woken her abruptly, her jaw and muscles still knotted. For a moment she believed she was back in Schneidemühl and it had been the siren. No. There was no alarm, just voices downstairs and firm footsteps on familiar flooring. She was home; she was safe.

She fought to relax her body enough to turn over. Jadwiga wasn't in her bed. Nor was Irmgard. Where were they? Her internal clock told her there was still some time before morning.

Ilse quickly got up. At once she started trembling from the cold. Her father said it was the harshest winter he could remember.

Had Freddy had one of his fits? They were less and less frequent. Rare, even. Perhaps it wasn't Freddy who was sick. Could it be one of her younger siblings? Edeline was three and a half now, and not prone to illness. Ilse remembered that today was Helmut's first birthday. He *was* given to choking from his coughing fits. In winter, his mother kept a pot of water with special herbs in it in front of the fire, so that the steam would help Helmut breathe. Even in the house, she kept his woolen sweater and leggings on. Ilse hoped he hadn't fallen ill: it would ruin the celebration she'd insisted on organizing.

We're going to wait for the weather to improve, Ilse, her mother had said. In spring we might find sugar and the other ingredients we need to make cookies for him.

She said that babies don't remember anything, don't care whether their birthday is celebrated on the correct day. But Ilse didn't believe that Helmut wouldn't remember. He remembered her every day, wanted her and no one else to swing him between her legs, held up by the armpits. He always greeted her with a smile, raised his index finger, and said, with his baby speech that made everyone, even the grown-ups, laugh: *Eins, eins, eins* just like she'd taught him. She'd ask, how old are you going to be, Helmut? He'd learned to say it very well and quite quickly. Their mother said Helmut was very advanced for his age. How could she be so sure, then, that such a smart boy wouldn't remember? It was also obvious that he remembered Kaiser, because he threw himself at the animal every time he saw him, which Ilse couldn't understand. Kaiser's going to eat him like a sausage, she worried each time, but the dog never did.

Helmut remembered flavors: he recognized the Brussels sprout purée that he hated, pressing his lips together each time his mother held the spoon near. He'd be pleased with his party even if there were no cookies, not to mention no cake. There would only be bread, butter, and peach jam. But Helmut loved peaches.

Come on, Mama: let's celebrate. I've already made his birthday boy's crown.

Ilse admired her work while she took off her pajamas: it might've been made with simple butcher paper, brown and crumpled, but she'd saved the part that hadn't been stained with blood from the leg of lamb her mother had gotten hold of for New Year's. Ilse had put it on top of the wardrobe where little hands couldn't mistreat it until the right day, which had now arrived. There'd be a party and Helmut would remember it.

Birthdays—and other big celebrations—should never go unobserved, and each one should be memorable, Ilse would maintain from that day and forevermore. One day, her beloved would tease her about this fierce insistence on proper birthdays, but she would explain, and he would understand. He would agree.

In December, she'd had her birthday without anyone remembering to make a crown. Everyone had hugged her, because not even the war could take that from them. Then, on Christmas Day, they had invited the Bendziuses to dinner after church. Her mother had made the goose and potatoes, her aunt Erna the bread, but neither of them had managed to find ginger or almonds for cookies.

Aunt Erna's bread had proved to be only a little softer than the grown-ups' faces. To lighten the mood and keep up traditions, they'd sung "O Tannenbaum" in front of the fir tree Janusz had cut down, but it was only Irmgard, Freddy, and her. The performance hadn't been very good, and nothing had cheered up the adults.

Ilse tried to dress quickly, but it was very cold. This cold that made the skin break out in goose bumps and turned muscles to stone wasn't the kind of cold that belonged inside a house. Shivering, she chose her best dress, her Sunday one. When Helmut woke, she'd be ready for the birthday celebration that would last the whole day. She had come up with a list of competitions. They would all take part. Everyone would have fun, she decided. Where there was no longer joy, it had to be created again.

Ilse couldn't get used to her parents' low spirits: for a long time, they'd smiled without smiling, they'd said affectionate words out of obligation or habit, they'd communicated without saying anything, they'd looked without seeing. Now they allowed long and uncomfortable silences to set in at the table, in the kitchen, and around Ilse and her siblings' games. They sent them to play, pray, and sleep, but they didn't go with them: it was Irmgard and Ilse who led the younger ones, and Jadwiga who gave them baths. Even Kaiser sensed it: he followed their father around with his head bowed, without wagging his tail.

Her parents had lost the light in their eyes. They lived surrounded by children whom they loved and who loved them. They lived without sirens like the one in Schneidemühl waking them in the night, or bombs falling on them from the sky, but nonetheless, for a long time now, the war had demanded all their attention and energy.

Since when? Ilse couldn't say exactly, but she was sure it had been longer than a year. At least since they'd insisted on her staying in the house, because with Grandma's departure, this restriction hadn't loosened. Certainly since before they made Irmgard come home for good.

The war had wormed its way in and turned their parents into a pair of accomplices who whispered, they thought, out of earshot of their children. But Ilse was a sharp just-turned-nine-year-old with well-tuned ears. She knew how to be as quiet as a mouse, and which step to avoid so that she wouldn't betray her attentive espionage. Besides, she had an elder sister who was also frustrated at being left out of the parental conspiracy. Whatever one of them found out, she told the other. But only the other.

In this way, they learned that the Americans had arrived in Africa. That Italy—those traitors—had switched sides, that the war was going badly in Russia, that the enemy had managed to invade France via Normandy. That, in October, the Russians had managed to reach Nemmersdorf, but had been pushed back by German forces.

"Why don't Mama and Papa tell us anything?"

"They do say some things to me. I'm older. When they wouldn't let me go back to boarding school, they had to explain. They think you're too young."

"But I'm not."

"No. But, Ilse," Irmgard said every time, "don't tell Freddy any of this. He *is* too young. And don't worry, we have the Führer; he knows what to do. At the Jungmädel they say that for every defeat there are ten victories. Look what happened in Nemmersdorf: the Russians got in, but we ran them off. They won't come into Prussia again. We won't let them, and they won't dare: they're done for."

Ilse didn't want to think about the horrors of Nemmersdorf and said nothing to Freddy or anyone else. She felt conflicted. If the Führer and his Army were going to be victorious, they needed her and her increasingly skilled needles, so she knitted woolen socks and scarves to contribute to the winter campaign. But she didn't want to think about the conflict all the time. She knew she was a lucky girl: the war hadn't taken away her world, it hadn't wiped it out. Her father was the manager of an important farm; so was her uncle Franz. Janusz was considered a vital worker. The war left them in peace.

With trembling hands, she quickly braided her hair. War or peace, her mother didn't allow scruffy daughters to roam the house.

She felt sorry for other families. Every Sunday at church, there was at least one family saying goodbye to a dead soldier, without a body present. The priest gave the name and surname and then the place where he'd fallen. From service to service, Ilse had acquired a geography of exotic names: Tobruk, Bir Hakeim, Leningrad, Monte Cassino, Stalingrad, Normandy, Ardennes.

On one occasion, she'd heard her mother tell her father: Can you imagine what it must be like? Not saying goodbye? Never knowing how it happened . . . what happened? And on another: This village is full of dead people, but the cemetery's empty. Like her parents, Ilse mourned her uncle Josef's death in Stalingrad and imagined Aunt Ida and her cousins' sadness when, finally, they found his name on the casualty list. Had they had a funeral without a body, too? Did they know how he'd died? Ilse had never dared ask her parents.

She barely spoke about the war, not wanting to add to her parents' worries. And, if they were going to get the light back in their eyes, Ilse would have to do what she could to help in the house, especially with

Edeline and Helmut. That was why if one of them was sick she should know, she should help. Why hadn't Irmgard and Jadwiga woken her up?

She left her room and ran into her father, who was dressed but disheveled.

*"Guten Morg—"*

The look in his eyes stopped her.

"Papa?"

But he didn't reply. He went down the stairs two at a time. Ilse followed, but couldn't catch up with him: he grabbed his overcoat from the rack and left without saying a word to the three women in their nightclothes who watched in bewilderment from where they stood near the fire.

Where was he going in such a hurry? To fetch the doctor?

Neither Jadwiga nor Irmgard had dressed. Nor had her mother. Why? All three of them had a strange light in their eyes, one Ilse had never seen.

"Is it Freddy? Helmut? What is it?"

Her father's loud voice reached them from outside, urging the horse on; the well-trained animal set off at a gallop.

"The Russians are coming," her mother said in a choked voice.

# 35. Tick-tock, Wanda

"But the Führer won't let them," Ilse said.

"What?"

"The Russians are coming, but they won't get through. The Führer won't let them. That's what Irmgard says . . ."

"Yes. It's what everyone says," Wanda murmured.

Wanda had run out of time for sensitivity and pretense. Years had gone by that way—protecting her children's innocence, keeping the war outside the family home. Irmgard knew more about the war, but only the glorious lies her school and the Jungmädel had told her. And Wanda's dear little Ilse still hugged her doll, still did bunny hops with her siblings, still lost herself in Janusz's stories. Stories that she then retold for the enjoyment of her siblings, though Irmgard pretended not to listen.

However, that day, there was a lot to do if parents and children were going to live to see the next. *Tick-tock.* To survive today, they had to make use of every able body, including Ilse's.

Ilse said, "But—"

"Everyone get dressed," Wanda cut in. "*Schnell.* Without a sound. We'll let the little ones sleep as long as possible. Ilse: cut yesterday's bread and make toast for breakfast."

With great difficulty, Wanda climbed the stairs to her room. She closed the door behind her. She looked at the bed, feeling an urge to throw herself onto it and pull the quilt over her head. It wasn't the intense cold that tempted her: it was fear. It was a desire to make herself small, to curl up into a ball, to block out the light and air. The temptation was fleeting but shameful. Her bonds to the world were many and they were firm. She couldn't betray them with cowardice.

She thought of Hartwig, freezing, galloping through the still-black new day to reach the Von Witzleben estate, where they must surely have special instructions for their administrator. Perhaps, out of an instinct for survival or compassion, the government would finally give the order to leave, to evacuate.

There had been other occasions when they'd believed it would happen. The first came when, the previous summer, Erwin von Witzleben, a field marshal general and relative of their landowner, had been hanged as a conspirator in the plot to assassinate the Führer in his East Prussian bunker. For a terrible couple of days, the government's inquisitional force had fallen hard on the estate. Unlike his executed relative, Von Witzleben had persuaded everybody of his innocence, so they had neither imprisoned him nor stripped him of his land, and the Hahlbrocks hadn't been forced to flee from their own government.

After the German catastrophe at Stalingrad, the Russians recovered all their lost territory; a year ago, they'd freed Leningrad and then went after the Polish land they'd deserted in 1941. The German Army was in retreat. Moving ever closer to the farm. To Wanda's family. For the first time, the danger had become real, almost immediate.

Fleeing had seemed the most sensible thing to do, especially when the area filled with refugees flocking west. But then the Russians would stop their advance, or the Germans would regain territory, and many refugees returned to their countries. And many, like the Hahlbrocks, were left adrift, not knowing what to do.

They'd lived with this uncertainty for a year. A year in which she and Hartwig had begun to stockpile the provisions they'd need if fleeing became unavoidable; they'd started an austerity and rationing plan their children didn't understand. But then came the Russian invasion of Nemmersdorf.

All the local farmers were at the harvest festival when the news arrived. They'd run home, ready to implement their escape plans. But no: Erich Koch, the Gauleiter, had forbidden anyone from leaving.

East Prussia will always be German, Gauleiter Koch insisted from the safety of some remote bunker. Yet the towns and villages had been plastered with fresh propaganda: *Our Walls May Break, but Our Hearts Never Will.*

So there it was in writing: the walls had broken. Finally, they were admitting it. But our hearts never will? What did that mean? What was being demanded of them now? That Prussians should form a human shield against the Soviet steamroller? That was what the Third Reich seemed to want: the evacuation order hadn't arrived. Not when there was still time.

Difficult weeks had ensued in which explosions could be heard in the distance, and however much Hartwig said the bombs must be located outside their beloved Prussia, as far as Wanda was concerned, they were unacceptably close.

And then came the documentary. Soldiers and citizens alike were expected to see it: Come see the massacre committed by the Soviets in Nemmersdorf! Wanda didn't go, but Hartwig had no choice. He left before the screening had finished.

"Why do they want us to see women crucified, mutilated, raped? What good does it do for me to see murdered children? They want us to know what awaits us. They want us to join the Volkssturm."

"Is there no Army now? Do they need the civilian population to defend itself? Women, the elderly, children?"

"I'm not elderly," said Hartwig, a little indignant.

"You know what I mean. Do they think a few farmers will win the war? With spades and pickaxes? Oh, and mattocks: let's not forget those."

"Wanda. Don't worry. It won't come to that."

"Enough, Hartwig. Nobody's listening. Let's say it straight: this is unsustainable. We have to get out of here."

"We can't."

He didn't say, the situation will improve, or, let's give them time. He said, we can't. Hartwig was right: the soldiers guarding the farm had become their jailors. They had orders not to allow anyone to leave; they were suspicious even of a Sunday visit to church. They were more effective at controlling German civilians than Polish workers, who vanished in large numbers every day. Where did they go? To the forest to join the partisans, said Janusz. Meanwhile, the Army now demanded an even higher percentage of their agricultural output, which was ever more meager. Raised voices came from Hartwig's office when the collector came.

Each time, they take more. I tell them, Wanda, but they don't understand: How can the farm produce more this year than last year, if they've asked me to slaughter more and more animals? Every year, there are fewer young. The Wehrmacht is like a virus that ends up killing the thing that keeps it alive. They're like a plague of locusts. Next year, they'll polish off everything. They'll take the last goose and the last seed.

They didn't get the chance to see this prediction come true. In the early hours, Jadwiga had woken them.

"Janusz is outside, Herr Hahlbrock. He says it's urgent."

Hartwig didn't even take the time to throw on a robe. Wanda had gone down after him.

"Come in, Janusz."

"They're gone, Herr Hahlbrock," he said in a voice that trembled from the cold.

"Who?"

"The guards. I heard them say they weren't going to wait around for the Russians to come. They took the cart and four horses."

Janusz broke off when he saw that a sleepy Irmgard had joined the group.

"What does that mean, Papa?"

Nobody answered. Faced with his boss's and the women's stunned silence, Janusz continued.

"They took the eggs that were left, all the half-cured pork legs . . . some sacks of flour, and potatoes." He paused his inventory. "I didn't stop them, Herr Hahlbrock. I didn't dare."

"You couldn't. Forget it. I have to find out what happened." He looked at the clock. "There won't be anyone in Von Witzleben's office at this hour," he said to himself. "No point in calling. Saddle my horse, Janusz."

The young man lowered his head and his voice.

"They took it."

Wanda knew what that horse meant to Hartwig, and she saw the sorrow wash over his face.

"There's no time to waste," he said to Janusz. "Saddle the fastest one we have left."

Janusz ran out.

"Where're you going, Hartwig?"

"To see if Von Witzleben knows anything. I'll be back as soon as possible. Get the children ready, Wanda."

She understood what he meant. They'd discussed it those nights when the *tick-tock* on the British radio had frightened them. They'd made a plan, hoping they'd never have to implement it. *Tick-tock.* Now it seemed to have arrived. *Tick-tock.* And she felt gripped by a paralysis that began at her tongue, entered her lungs, and spread to her arms and legs.

Hartwig went upstairs to dress, and then he left.

*Tick-tock.*

In all that time, Wanda didn't move an inch, or speak, or think. She stood clutching the corners of her wrap as if it were a lifejacket, as if it held her up. Telling Ilse the truth had brought her out of her stupor. She'd told the truth, but sprinkled it with untruth: in giving her orders, she'd made her daughters believe that their mother, as always, knew what she was doing. That there was danger, yes, but that they could rely on her. What a beautiful age, when one still believes that Mama and Papa know everything, that they'll fix everything. But she couldn't fool herself.

Like the doll she'd seen in a store that moved when a cord was pulled, she forced her body into action. *Tick-tock.* But her feigned calm crumbled away when she closed the door behind her.

Wanda stood petrified. She didn't crawl into the false hiding place that was the bed, but neither did she dress. She had to get ready. She, with her warrior's name. Could she rise to the challenge and defeat an enemy horde as her legendary namesake had done? No. But she was even less capable of seeing her children die. So she moved one foot and then the other. *Tick-tock.*

She dressed.

*Tick.*

*Tock.*

# 36. Each universe to its own

He was waiting for instructions from his boss, but the man didn't even look at him. Only the horse received orders to set off at full speed. Janusz released the reins he'd been holding. Kaiser took off after his owner.

"Kaiser! *Komm!*" Janusz called, but the animal ignored him. When the other Poles left, Janusz had invited Kaiser to sleep in his hut, but for the dog, Hartwig came first.

In all his years on the farm, Janusz had never known Herr Hahlbrock to do anything impulsive, imprudent. He guessed that, if there was ever a day when his boss could justify risking not only his own neck but also a horse's, that day was today.

In the early hours, Kaiser's whimpering had alerted Janusz to the almost imperceptible sound of careful footsteps on new-fallen snow. Russians, he thought in alarm. He hushed the dog. Then he heard German and recognized a voice: it was the guards. Without turning on the light, Janusz got dressed. They had no business being inside the confines of the farm, let alone this close to the house. He waited until they were some distance away and then went out to follow cautiously. He left Kaiser inside, ordering him to be quiet.

What were the soldiers searching for? He watched as they took out the summer cart, the one they used for transporting straw, the one sled runners couldn't be fitted to. Did they want to go somewhere? They wouldn't get very far with those wheels on the snow-covered road. They might be battle-hardened veterans of the eastern front, but they knew nothing about the things that mattered, Janusz thought with scorn. He was glad that the other cart was kept in the garage nearer to the house. They wouldn't get that close, he promised himself. He'd give away their presence before they could, risk being shot to alert the family.

He was about to come out from his hiding place to shout when he saw that they were leading three horses out from the stable, and he stopped just in time. No horse was worth his life, he understood, even the first one they'd chosen.

"That's Hahlbrock's," said one soldier, the youngest.

"And a fine horse it is, too. Hahlbrock just donated it to the Vaterland," said another, fastening it to the cart.

"To the nation, or to you?" asked another.

"You know what I mean. To us. The Vaterland can go to hell."

*"Das Vaterland ist kaputt."*

Then there was total silence. Did they fear that a thunderbolt would fall from the sky to punish their heresy? That the Reich's omnipresent ears had heard them? But what was said, was said. It was a declaration. What they were doing under cover of darkness was not a military operation: it was a robbery. They were deserting, Janusz realized. They would've died for glory, but for misfortune, for ashes, they would not.

As new wolves, they'd try to disappear into the forest and wait there for the dust to settle. That was, if the older wolves didn't hunt them down. The forest would be full of deserters already were it not for the vengeful Poles and the Russians who'd been supporting them. In the village, Janusz knew, the Poles kept count of how many of these Germans had met a violent end at the hands of their partisans. And they recounted, in detail, the bloody stories of how they met it.

These men who'd survived the Russian Army and the Russian winter wouldn't last long in the Polish forests. Almost everything his six former guards were stealing would end up feeding Janusz's compatriots, he thought with irony.

"Will it be enough?" the youngest asked, trying to gauge the provisions.

"Do you know how long the war will last?" a higher-ranking one replied.

"No," said the first.

"Then we don't know whether it will be enough. But don't worry: horsemeat is very good."

And with that, they decided to fetch an extra horse to tie to the back of the cart.

When they left, Janusz let out Kaiser, then ran to alert the family. He knew that Herr Hahlbrock had been anticipating this, and that he'd surely taken precautions. Those that could be taken, at least.

Now the boss had ridden off. Janusz would have liked him just to bring out the winter cart, pack provisions, and prepare the family to leave. But no: he'd left in the direction of the Von Witzlebens'. Herr Hahlbrock still hadn't fully accepted, as the soldiers had, that his country was kaputt.

Janusz was worried. For himself, for the family, but more immediately, for Herr Hahlbrock. The trip, at full speed on an unfamiliar horse, in the dark, with snow underfoot and more coming down, was folly.

And yet, Janusz wanted to be committing the same folly. He wished Herr Hahlbrock had said, come with me. Had he done so, Janusz's mind would be occupied by the urgent task of surviving the ride, instead of throbbing with anxiety about what lay ahead.

Life is a mystery: that was the conclusion he'd reached during his long hours of plowing stories into the wheat. It lets you know where you are in the present, but never where you'll end up. A single step is enough to change everything, he thought. Look at him, born in a forest almost without human contact other than his mother and sister. Then he'd walked alone for years, and that path had led him to this war and this farm.

Where would he be if he'd never left his mother's home? Where would he be if he hadn't taken a single step? Dead at the hands of the first Russian invaders, perhaps. Sometimes, not taking a step could also change a person's destiny. Or end it. Which was what could happen today.

In spite of what his fellow prisoners had thought, he understood very well that his status on this farm was little better than slavery. But for Janusz, the slavery of hunger and, even more, the slavery of loneliness were far worse than his years here, with these people.

He'd spent the years of toil solving life's mysteries: In the trance of chopping firewood, it had become clear to him that love could overcome all obstacles, even war. During the hours spent leading oxen with the plow, he found the best stories: the most vivid, the most real. When he was working hardest, time flew; at night, alone, time was as dense as the wet sand of the Baltic. When he was working, he understood that he had a young body, but the mind of something else. An old man? No. What? It was something he couldn't figure out.

But that day, the mystery that occupied his mind was how everything could hinge on a single day: life and death in each minute, in each decision, a single horseback ride on a snowy road. A day like this made him doubt his certainty that love transcends everything, a young man's certainty that he'll live until old age, that he'll never feel alone again.

On a day like this, individuals become their own universe. On a day like this, people could turn their backs on everything in order to save their own skin. Like the soldiers, that day, Janusz was his own universe inside his own skin. It was his own survival instinct that called to him, demanded he persevere.

Before the family left—because they must surely leave soon—he could mount one of the remaining horses and speed away, without looking back. Who would stop him? Nobody, now. For a moment,

Janusz decided he would go first, abandon them, before watching them leave, before being abandoned. Again.

He imagined it: he could go deep into the forest, evade everyone, return to the solitary cabin of his childhood, disappear forever. He'd never have to utter or obey a single word in German. He'd never have to hear a single word of Russian. He wouldn't even have to speak his native tongue. He wouldn't have to speak to anyone, or look anyone in the eyes, ever again. Nor would he have to worry about anyone.

Impossible. His universe was bound to other universes. He couldn't steal their horse and reduce their chances of survival. He wouldn't desert them.

He'd wait. Herr Hahlbrock had left him standing there in the freezing darkness without doubting that he'd be there when he returned. Without doubting that he would keep watch in his absence, as sole protector of the family. There hadn't been any orders for Janusz that day, but he understood: it was implicit in the look that Herr Hahlbrock didn't have to give him.

Janusz wouldn't betray his trust. Later, he'd see. Later, when the family made its decisions. While the family was alone inside the house, he wouldn't go anywhere.

Kaiser approached. He'd abandoned his pursuit of his owner. Janusz looked out toward the farm's boundary, where the darkness was thicker. He imagined all kinds of eyes alight in the darkness, looking at him, looking at the most prosperous farm in the region. Thirsty. Hungry for revenge.

Radosz? Was he there, beyond the meager light of the new day? Or on his way? Janusz was sure he'd prowled around at times, that he wanted revenge, but the soldiers—Janusz's jailors—had provided protection. Not anymore. Janusz felt a knot in his stomach.

Up until now he'd been too preoccupied to feel the cold. Now, he was still shivering and he couldn't feel his fingers. He had to move, organize himself, if he was going to be a good lookout.

He went to fetch his overcoat, hat, and gloves from his hut. He also took his quilt: it would be a tough wait, but it didn't have to be deadly. On the way to the house he collected the axe, poor protection against any bullet fired from a distance, but it would deter any intruder who had the nerve to come close. A giant with an axe could be very intimidating, Janusz imagined, if the intruder didn't know that the giant was a gentle one.

Radosz knew him well. He'd look beyond the giant he'd become and understand that he was a youngster; enormous, perhaps, but with the mind of . . . of a child, still. A child still bound to the world of his stories, fantasies in which wondrous beings proved themselves heroes and saviors. Radosz would take one look at the axe and laugh.

When Janusz reached the house, before sitting on the wooden bench to keep watch, he peered through the kitchen window: Ilse was there, alone, dressed in her Sunday clothes. She was wearing her golden-brown braids coiled over her ears. It was the style that she wore on Sundays, the one she considered elegant and distinguished. She was making breakfast. She was singing cheerfully, despite the dark circles under her eyes. Janusz moved closer to listen: the birthday song. It was Helmut's birthday, he remembered. Little Ilse had been planning for some time: there'd be bread and jam, and she'd invited Janusz to the party. Will you tell a story? she'd asked. Two or three, he'd promised.

How lucky Helmut was to have a sister like her, Janusz thought sadly.

For Ilse, to ensure she had a future full of parties, this giant would use his axe against anyone. Without hesitating for an instant.

# 37. The list

When Wanda made it back downstairs, all the girls were there. Even Edeline was dozing in her chair, wrapped in a little pink blanket.

Ilse had done her task and more: the thick slices of black bread were already in the basket beside the butter and peach jam. On the stove, two pots of water were boiling: one for tea, Wanda supposed, and the other with eggs bobbing among the bubbles. The table was set with the elegant tableware and linen. It was their Christmas table, but without candles.

Wanda felt herself boil like the eggs fidgeting in the pot. What was Ilse thinking? Wanda had given her a very simple order: Make toast. Ilse understood that there were things in the house that were special, that weren't to be touched. It had taken Wanda three years to embroider the tablecloth and the napkins. The dishes had been a wedding gift from the Von Witzleben family, and Wanda planned to pass them on to her children. Ilse knew that the only person who touched that porcelain, the only one who washed it, was her mother. That was why not a single dish in the set was chipped.

That day, Wanda was in no mood for games or mischief. She wouldn't say anything. She wouldn't argue. She would just clear the plates before they got dirty and replace them with the everyday ones. Then she'd wrap each in its cloth, put them away, and lock the cupboard.

This time, she'd hide the key where none of her children would ever find it. Tonight, Ilse would go to bed without any dinner, she decided.

She was about to make this announcement when Jadwiga approached, speaking in a low voice so that Ilse, who was staring at the eggs, wouldn't hear.

"I'm sorry, Frau Hahlbrock. Ilse insisted on setting the elegant table and—"

Wanda was about to say, why did you let her do it today of all days? but the sound of hooves reached them from outside. They looked at each other, falling silent. Then they were alarmed to hear Hartwig yelling. All the activity in the kitchen stopped.

"Stay here, girls," said Wanda.

She ran to the door and, without considering that there could be danger, opened it. Hartwig was trying to rouse Janusz by shouting and shaking him.

"What's the matter with him?"

"He fell asleep."

"I'm sorry," said Janusz drowsily.

"Have you no sense? Don't you know the cold puts you to sleep?" said Hartwig as he lifted the younger but much larger man from the bench. "Wanda, make Janusz some tea. Jadwiga, fetch another quilt."

As Wanda turned to do as her husband asked, Ilse said, "I'll make it for him." Freddy was coming down the stairs, and Helmut started crying to be liberated from his crib.

"No, Ilse, I'll make the tea. You go get Helmut. Now," said Wanda. "Irmgard, take those eggs out of the water."

She wanted to know what news Hartwig had, but first they had to help Janusz get warm. And Hartwig. He might not have fallen asleep in the cold, but his face looked raw.

Hartwig helped Janusz to a seat near the stove. Wanda poured the water that the eggs had been boiling in into an earthenware flask, which she wrapped in cloth. She gave it to Janusz to hug to his chest under the quilts. Then, she made two cups of tea with a generous amount of camomile and honey. By the time she went to place one in the hands of the young man, he was shivering so much he couldn't hold it.

"Keep your hands inside. I'll feed it to you," she said. "And you drink up, too, Hartwig."

When Ilse came down with Helmut, he was already dressed in warm clothes, and wearing a paper crown on his head. Like a king. No: like a birthday boy! With the events of the early morning, Wanda had forgotten. It was her baby's first birthday.

"How old are you, Helmut?" said Ilse in a singsong voice.

*"Eins, eins, eins!"* replied Helmut, excited, smiling.

"Who's having a party today?"

That question was new.

*"Eins, eins, eins!"*

Ilse laughed. "No, Helmut, *ich, ich, ich*!" Me, me, me!

Even Janusz laughed at that. He was already getting some color back.

"Look, Helmut: your birthday breakfast's ready," Ilse said to him.

Wanda remembered the table and was about to say what an absurd idea it was to use the finery, that there was no time for it, that there was too much to do, but Hartwig surprised her.

"The table looks beautiful. What a wonderful way to celebrate the birthday boy."

"But, Hartwig—"

"Let's sit, Wanda. We have time for that, at least."

"But—"

"Sit down, Wanda. Enjoy it. Some celebrations can't be missed."

She obeyed without another word. There was something in Hartwig's face: a desperation. His smile wasn't false, but it was exaggerated.

"Janusz, if you're feeling better, come celebrate with us. There's space," Hartwig said.

"And there's an egg," said Ilse.

They ate and sang to celebrate the boy's birthday. They all laughed when Helmut covered his face in jam. Extra quilts and overcoats were no longer needed. Between them, they warmed the kitchen with love, but it only lasted thirty minutes.

"Tell us a story, Janusz," said Ilse.

"No," Hartwig pronounced, breaking the spell. "We have a lot of work to do. Janusz, see to the animals. I'll join you soon. Irmgard and Ilse, thank you for breakfast. Wash everything and put it away. Carefully. Jadwiga, get the children dressed."

Wanda wanted to object, but Hartwig said, "Come with me, we need to talk," and she followed like an automaton.

He quietly told his wife how, on reaching Von Witzleben's house, he'd found their soldiers gone, too, and Frau Wollatz crying: when she woke, she'd thought they'd been robbed. Von Witzleben's office was open, his desk a mess. Many pieces of silverware were missing, especially the small, portable ones. Alarmed, she went up to warn the family, but her employers had gone. Did they take anything from the larder? Hartwig asked. No. If they'd gone down to the kitchen, she'd have heard them. The Von Witzlebens had packed in the night without a word, without asking for help. Without offering it.

Frau Wollatz was sobbing, unable to understand why she'd been abandoned. "They only took the driver, who's also German, Herr Hahlbrock. I'm German, too, but they left me."

"Apparently they'd hidden gasoline for their car, Wanda. Someone clearly warned him about what's about to happen, but he didn't bother to warn us. Von Witzleben abandoned us all."

Wanda could hear the disappointment and anger in her husband's voice.

"I told Frau Wollatz to load the cart with what she needs and head west with any German staff that wants to go. Then I sent word to your brother Franz that our families will leave together at two o'clock."

"Not until two?" Wanda's voice came out in a fragile thread.

Was it enough time? Was it too long? She was almost choking on the uncertainty.

"The Russians are coming; it's the only thing that would've made Von Witzleben run like that. They're close, but as far as I know, they haven't mobilized. We have time, Wanda. We have the cart and three horses. We'll be ready. We leave at two o'clock."

"There's a lot to do . . ."

"Yes, but the important things are already done, remember. Don't worry. You take care of the children, their clothes, quilts, provisions. The pit's ready. Pack the things we decided to keep from the castle. Jadwiga can help you."

Hartwig went to implement his part of the evacuation plan. Some time ago, they'd bought expensive cigarettes on the black market, then soon found a soldier happy to trade them for an accurate map. They'd made and remade lists until they were left with the most absolute essentials. But their plan always assumed an orderly, government-coordinated evacuation. Would it work in outright flight? When soldiers and bosses had abandoned the people under their protection to save their own skin? During the worst winter in years? It had better.

Wanda shook off the paralysis that had enveloped her body again. She heard horrible clattering and almost ran to check on her daughters handling her beloved porcelain, her most precious treasure. No. Best just take a deep breath. She decided not to look, to walk on past, down to the basement. Was she starting to let go?

She thought with irony that, on the list of priorities, no tableware was included: neither the elegant set, nor the everyday. The list included neither tablecloths nor curtains, though Wanda had spent more hours embroidering them than she had telling stories to her children. Nor did it include a single ornament, even if she had saved and pondered for months before daring to spend the money on them. So much care, so much effort invested in things of no importance. Yes. She was starting to let go.

Since they'd made plans and written the list, Wanda had concentrated on doing her part. What belonged to the Wehrmacht belonged to the Wehrmacht—and now to the thieving soldiers. What belonged to the family, she stored in the basement under their house. In the last year, she'd cured more hams than usual, prepared more pâtés, more sausages. She'd put away entire Tilsit cheeses. She'd traded some of the milk the family's two cows produced for soldiers' cans of evaporated milk: Helmut wouldn't go without. She produced double the amount of butter and preserves. She did the same with the bread: baked double and put away half, wrapped in cloth. Near-frozen bread wasn't to her taste, but it would fill the belly.

She picked up the key and put on her overcoat: in summer, the basement remained cool, but in winter, and especially this winter, it was barely above freezing. Everything was ready. It didn't take long to load everything in trunks. In another, she packed bars of soap and toothpaste. She didn't know where they'd go or when they'd arrive, but they'd arrive clean. She also packed the tin box containing ginger and herbs for teas and simple remedies. It had been hard to resist using the ginger at Christmas. Their first Christmas without cookies.

"We've finished the dishes," a serious Irmgard said when she saw Wanda come up from the basement.

"We didn't break anything, and we locked it away," said Ilse.

"Did you put a cloth between each plate?"

"Yes."

"Leave the dishes there, but take the cloths. We're going to need them on the journey. And don't lock the cupboard this time."

She didn't lock the cellar, either. Let them take whatever they want, she decided.

Wanda surprised herself. She would never have believed that, in the space of a morning, she could go from treasuring something to feeling nothing more than a distant nostalgia, thankful for the last impromptu opportunity to use it thanks to a mischievous daughter's crazy idea.

Hartwig was right: some celebrations can't be missed. That day, they'd celebrated a birthday and a goodbye.

Wanda looked at herself in her grandmother's mirror. Another goodbye. A painful one. For now. It wasn't the finest mirror she'd seen. At the castle, there were many of better quality. But this one was hers, an heirloom. She'd transported it there as a newlywed, imagining that she'd pass it on to the next generation. She had never let the girls touch this, either. Why had she been so attached to fragile things? She closed her eyes to stop seeing herself in the imperfect glass. Who would the next face reflected there belong to?

"Ilse, it was a lovely breakfast. Thank you." Wanda felt her voice falter, but she cleared her throat and strengthened it. She opened her eyes, looking at her daughters. "Now go up and put on your warmest clothes, two pairs of tights. *Schnell!* We're going away. Wear your boots. Pack your Sunday shoes, underwear, tights, coats, gloves, and sweaters. Just two dresses. Tell Jadwiga to pack the same for the boys. Bring some books and your blackboards: don't think you'll stop studying just because we're going away."

*"Jawohl, Mama,"* they said in unison.

"And don't forget your toothbrushes and hair ribbons!"

She took off her coat and went upstairs. Jadwiga was in the three youngest children's bedroom, packing as she'd been instructed.

"Pack Edeline and Helmut's diapers, and the cod liver oil with zinc. Add a toy for each of them, please. Freddy, you, too: just one."

Freddy made a series of sounds in the back of his mouth, but his mother understood his anxious question.

How does one answer a beloved child without lying?

"We're going on an adventure, Freddy. All of us together. Jadwiga, when you've finished, leave the boys with Irmgard and Ilse. I need you to help me with something."

Instead of making the beds, Wanda unmade them: she stuffed feather quilts and pillows into neat sacks. She folded all the sheets.

They weren't on the list, but they'd need them. Someday, they'd sleep in a bed again, she presumed—hoped.

"Mama, may I take my doll?" Ilse called from her bedroom.

She was still so young . . . Wanda felt deep sadness. If they'd been lucky, if it had been up to her, her daughter's childhood would have lasted many more years. But it hadn't been, and it wasn't: Ilse's childhood was about to come to an abrupt end.

"Of course you can," she called back. "Hold it tight, *Kind*," she murmured to herself.

She rolled up two woolen rugs, placed them at the top of the stairs, gave them a push, and watched them slide down. The sacks followed. A day of madness: until now, she would never have allowed such carelessness, but on that day of goodbyes and last times, who cared about some rugs and feather-filled sacks rolling down the stairs? Why carry them? Who was going to tell her she was a bad housewife?

Then it occurred to her that she should have let Freddy sit on one of the sacks and slide down. It might be her boy's last memory in that house. When he was all grown up, perhaps he'd say: When I was a boy, my mother always let me slide down the stairs on pillows. It was worth it for that memory. Perhaps all the times his mother had said no would be erased from his mind. She wished it could also erase everything that was to come. She went down to fetch a sack and climbed back up again.

"Freddy, come here! Can you help me get this sack down the stairs? It's heavy. Can you think of a way?"

Freddy ran to her. Of course he could think of a way. He wasn't very talkative, her boy, but he knew how to get into mischief. Now, he was surprised to find permission in the eyes of his mother, who for the first time in his life didn't say, be careful, don't do that, don't fall, don't hurt yourself. Just with her eyes, she said, dive! What're you waiting for?

That's when Wanda realized that today was also a day of first times.

Freddy's delight consoled her for the rest of the morning as she continued with the tasks on her list. She packed for herself and for

Hartwig. She took the first aid kit from its hiding place under the floorboards. She didn't regret not handing over her bottles of sulfa to the Wehrmacht: it wasn't her fault it was scarce, like everything else. A cautious woman, she'd gotten hold of several bottles of the expensive medicine—in liquid and powder form—with which old Dr. Veldmann had saved Freddy from an infection.

From the bottom of her own trunk, she took out her saved money and rationing coupons and put them in a little canvas bag. In another, she put the family members' identity papers, along with her bankbook. She took off her dress and, over her slip, hung the money bag around her neck and the one containing the papers around her waist, so that it hung down along her leg on one side, and got dressed again. She looked at herself in the mirror and noted two things: that the bags, hidden under her dress, couldn't be seen, and that, this morning, she hadn't done her hair. Something else that seemed to have lost importance on that strange morning. But she quickly tidied it.

Downstairs, Jadwiga was already waiting for her.

"Fetch a wheelbarrow and take these sacks and rugs to Herr Hahlbrock. Tell Janusz to come fetch the trunks from the basement and the bedrooms. I'll see you later at the castle. Bring the wheelbarrow."

Then each woman went her own way. Wanda could hear Hartwig and Janusz both toiling away. She had just a few more tasks on her section of the list.

At the castle, there was already a bag waiting for her full of silver trays, serving dishes, and cutlery: the estate's treasure. It was impossible to save everything from the plundering that was to come. These pieces—valuable not just because of their age, but because of their weight in silver—would go in the pit that Janusz had dug in the garden last autumn before the ground froze.

Wanda thought she'd chosen pieces well, but she walked through the castle once more just in case. It wasn't as elegant as the Von Witzlebens', but it had been built by an ancestor who'd filled it with treasures from all over the world. She'd never forgive the Von Witzlebens for abandoning them, but if she'd struggled with giving up a simple dinner service and an old mirror, what would it have been like for them to abandon so much? Or perhaps they didn't even remember what they had in this house, one of many they owned.

According to Frau Wollatz, they'd taken a lot from their main house, but not everything. And they had favored loading their car with belongings over people. Would their overloaded car be capable of transporting them to their destination in this weather? Did the Von Witzlebens know that silver spoons wouldn't keep them alive?

Wanda thought of more things she and Hartwig hadn't written down: cups, spoons, a pot, a pan, and two knives. How could we not have included them in the list of essentials? What else have we forgotten? And napkins: she'd take the Christmas ones, why not? Things were to be used, not hoarded. What was more, she hadn't spent all that time embroidering the tablecloth just to leave it for Russian soldiers. Yes. She'd take that, too. It wouldn't take up much space. And Hartwig wouldn't know until next Christmas, when she'd surprise everyone by setting their new table with a beloved cloth embroidered with familiar flowers.

Jadwiga was coming: Wanda could hear the wheelbarrow. She'd agreed with Hartwig to let the girl know where the most valuable pieces from the castle were to be hidden. The two of them would take the sack to the pit, throw it in, and then cover it with earth.

"The Russians will plunder whatever they can see, but this here is our secret, Jadwiga. Don't tell anyone, not even your family: it's not safe. If we haven't returned in three months, come for what we buried. It's yours. Use it wisely and remember us." Wanda had planned this speech for months. Now, at the last minute, hearing Jadwiga approach, she decided to add something else. "For today, take my porcelain tableware home in that wheelbarrow; take good care of it and pass it on to a daughter of yours. You can have Grandma's mirror, too. And don't let the Russians find you here. Hurry home."

If Wanda couldn't pass these things to her own children, she was glad to be able to give them to someone who had been a good friend and almost a sister to her sons and daughters. In a few months, if the Russians didn't discover the buried treasure, the young woman would be rich. Her stomach knotted when she thought about her children realizing that they'd left Jadwiga behind forever, about how much they'd miss her. She hoped that Jadwiga would miss them, too. She hoped that she'd remember the time she spent with her family with fondness, and that, in the future, she would have kind words to say about the Hahlbrocks, despite the circumstances that had brought them together. That would be another painful goodbye, but not the last.

Wanda had a feeling that neither they nor any other German would settle in these lands that the Prussian and German kingdoms had called their own for centuries, these lands that had changed hands so many times and for which so much blood had been spilled. They'd leave that day and it would be painful, but they wouldn't spill their own blood here. Wanda was leaving in the hope that the territory would never be fought over again. If it was up to me . . . Why do I insist on imagining things are up to me? Nothing is. Nothing. Not even the fate of my children, it seems. Not even where we'll sleep tonight.

Jadwiga would sleep at home with her family that night and thereafter. But Wanda's family?

She remembered her anger that morning when she saw the table set with her precious things. She regretted planning to punish Ilse: You'll go to bed without any dinner tonight, she would have decreed. What bed? What dinner? What plate? What table? Where would her family be tonight? She didn't know, but she understood that it was not important. The important thing was not where they were but that they were alive, and together. After years of relative peace in the war, in the blink of an eye, her life had been reduced to that: to understanding that the only treasure worth anything is life.

# 38. Softly, playfully, and with simple words

Ilse stopped packing for a moment to let Edeline try on the birthday boy's crown and look at herself in the mirror.

"But be gentle with it. It's Helmut's."

"I want it!"

"No, Edeline. I'll make you one another day. This one's Helmut's."

"Oh, hush, Ilse! Who cares about your stupid crown?"

Irmgard had done everything she'd been told to do: wash the dishes, take care of her siblings. But not happily.

"*I* care. And Helmut and Edeline care; look at her."

It being brown, the same color as her hair, the crown didn't look as nice on her youngest sister, but Ilse had learned from Jadwiga that you didn't always tell small children the truth, that you always had to speak to them softly, playfully, and with simple words. As if they're stupid? Ilse had asked. A bit, she'd answered, but just until they're a little older.

"You look *very* pretty, Edeline. When it's your birthday, we'll make you a purple one, if you want."

"Pink," said Edeline.

"Of course!"

Irmgard rolled her eyes. "We're losing the war and you're promising them birthday crowns? Do you not understand what's happening?"

"I understand perfectly."

But there was nothing Ilse could do about it. All she could do was take care of her siblings as her mother had asked. All she could do was pretend she was excited to be going on a trip so that the little ones wouldn't be distressed. Why couldn't Irmgard do the same? Why had she suddenly realized that the Führer was fallible? All those Führers—Führer, my Führer, given to me by God, protect and preserve our lives . . .—that Irmgard had insisted on making her pray to, where had they gone? Why did she insist on infecting everyone with her anguish?

Ilse understood what was happening, but she didn't want to. That day, she wished she were Edeline or Helmut so that the world would still speak to her in half-truths, softly, playfully, and with simple words. She wanted to believe and to be excited, as Freddy was, that they were embarking on an adventure. She wanted to believe, as Irmgard had always assured her, that the Führer would never allow Germany to lose the war. She wanted to believe that it was just a bad day. That they would soon return, laughing, feeling stupid about having left for no good reason.

If only. Now she recognized that, in the past months, her parents had spoken to her as if she were stupid but no longer quite so stupid: not like they spoke to her younger siblings, but enough to keep her anchored to the world of children. But today, her mother had spoken to her with her anguish intact, without measuring her words. As an equal. Ilse was no longer a child; her mother had declared it with each word: The. Russians. Are. Coming.

Did that mean she had to give up playing forever? She was overcome by an intense sadness: she didn't want to give it up. Not quite yet. And that was why she'd persisted with Helmut's early-morning celebration despite the anguish on her mother's face: not even the Russians would ruin this, she told herself. Everything had turned out so well; they had all enjoyed themselves.

She'd been forced to grow up a few hours ago, but Ilse saw her childhood so vividly that it was like something she could pick up or put down as needed. That's why she needed her doll on the journey, as a tool and a shield.

"Edeline, Helmut, what noise do kittens make?"

# 39. The hours

Saying goodbye wasn't easy, even though they'd been preparing for it for over a year. The surprise that day hadn't helped, and neither had the surprise within the surprise.

They'd always expected that there would be a few days' notice for the evacuation, but no: everything had to be ready by two o'clock. It was just enough time, if not to say goodbye to every inch of their home, then at least to pack and leave the house clean, Wanda calculated. That would be her goodbye: she'd stroke the floors and bricks that had shaped her life.

When she was about to start, Janusz arrived, breathless.

"Herr Hahlbrock says the leaving time has been moved up to twelve o'clock."

Fifteen minutes from then. She ran with Janusz to meet Hartwig. Franz was there, with Erna and Crystl set up in the cart, just as planned. A neighbor had told Franz that there were rumors the Russians were close. Time to leave.

The children were excited to see their cart: "It looks like a gypsy caravan," yelled Ilse, but Freddy preferred their father's version: "We're settlers of the Old West fleeing the Apaches."

Hartwig had designed their own cart with the novels of Karl May in mind, tales of the Old West he'd told to Freddy so often. The cart had never had a covering before, but if it worked for the pioneers, it'll work for us, under sun, rain, or snow, he'd told Wanda. So he'd added three iron arches and inserted them into the fixtures installed on the cart for the purpose. Then he cut a thick canvas to throw over the top. Wanda had sewn the fittings. And just this morning, Hartwig had thrown their colorful woolen rug over the white canvas.

The rug was well fastened, with newly cut holes at the four corners and two more in the middle on each side to tie it down with thick cord. Hartwig caught Wanda's frown.

"It's below zero out here. This'll give them more protection in the back," said Hartwig by way of an excuse and apology.

"Don't you think it'll attract too much attention?" she said, nodding at the sky.

No aircraft were overhead today, but Hartwig understood.

"When we stop this evening, I'll swap the layers so the canvas is on the outside. I laid the other rug on the floor of the cart . . . it'll keep some of the cold out. In any case, with all this snow, the colors won't be visible for long."

Wanda poked her head into the cart. In one corner were sheepskin sacks and hot bricks, quilts, and pillows for each traveler. In another corner, in another sack, were the horses' blankets. The food trunks were lined up on one side and would double as seats. Outside, fastened to the sides, they had several sacks of horse feed, sheets of canvas, wheels for when the snow thawed, and various tools. In the front, under the driver's seat, there was an old shotgun and an axe.

There was nothing left to do except worry. Nothing else. Nothing important. And yet Wanda felt as if she was forgetting something. She counted her children: five. Her husband was there. They were all there. If anything was missing, it couldn't be vital. So there was nothing left to do except worry . . . and say goodbye.

They said goodbye to Jadwiga while the little ones were distracted in the cart, excited at the novelty of it and unaware of the irreversibility of what was to come. Hartwig was formal: Thank you for all these years of help and company. The older girls cried and hugged her: Ilse promised she would write. Jadwiga cried with them and told them that she'd be waiting for their letters. When it was Wanda's turn to say goodbye, she gave her planned speech, her voice choked with emotion. She didn't cry when Jadwiga did. She didn't let her thank them for the gift they were leaving. It wasn't a gift, she explained: it was compensation. She hugged her, turned around, and climbed onto the cart after her daughters. She lowered the rear curtain and fastened it to seal the interior from the cold and the memories. They would travel in semidarkness, but it didn't matter. Perhaps blocking out the view would help them leave behind what they'd believed to be their secure life.

And so, they set off for West Prussia, like explorers of the Old West. They set off on the journey without knowing what awaited them in a future that promised nothing.

In the distance, they could just make out Jadwiga yelling, but they stopped when Ilse, who'd opened a gap in the rear curtain to look out, let out a shriek.

"Kaiser!"

The dog was racing after them, leaping like a hare in the deep snow. The rope that Hartwig had tied him with in the barn had been torn to shreds and was trailing behind.

Hartwig looked at his wife. "I tried, Wanda."

"We don't have food for him," she replied.

"He's a good hunter," said Janusz. "And I can help him."

Wanda had been surprised when the young man agreed to go with them. We'll need Janusz, Hartwig had told her when they were making their plans, but I won't try to insist if he doesn't want to come.

She didn't know when the conversation between the two men had taken place. When they were fastening the rug? As they opened the sties so that the pigs could find their freedom? When they turned their backs on the fields they'd worked together? While they tied Kaiser up in the shed?

"He'll be a good guard," said Hartwig to persuade her.

"He's not riding back here," said Wanda, giving in.

The joy on Hartwig's face washed away years of anxiety. It reminded her of the man he'd been before the war. For that alone, the dog was worth taking.

"We'll keep him in the front. He'll help keep us warm."

Janusz climbed down to lift up the satisfied dog, who seemed to feel no resentment at having been left behind.

"Then let's go. And no stopping for anything else," she said.

They all pulled on their sacks, each with a brick inside that would remain hot for hours. Two hours later, Irmgard was asleep. An icy wind blew outside, but the cover held fast and protected them from the worst of it. Ilse, Freddy, and Edeline remained in good spirits: they played with their own breath, blowing it at one another, poking it with a gloved finger. They'd constructed a nest of quilts that they all shared. They laughed.

Little Helmut was asleep against Wanda's chest, inside his little sack under two quilts that covered them both. Did his mother's heartbeat comfort him? Was it still beating? That didn't seem possible. Wanda felt a weight on her chest that had nothing to do with her baby. Perhaps this was how a broken heart felt: like a stone.

She couldn't sleep. She was confident that they were well prepared but terrified to be traveling without the government's guidance or protection. In the rush, she'd climbed onto the cart without even asking what their destination was that day.

She tried to synchronize her breathing with her baby's. How peaceful it would be, breathing and sleeping like him, unsuspecting, lulled by the cart's movement and by what remained of his mother's fearful heart.

When he woke, she'd have to change his diaper. Poor thing: it would be very cold. She'd console him with his bot—

"No!" she said out loud. She knew she'd forgotten something. "Hartwig!"

"What?" Her husband's barely audible voice penetrated the shelter.

"I forgot Helmut's bottle!"

"Use a cup. We're not going back."

Wanda scowled. She wasn't asking him to go back, but couldn't he be a little more sympathetic? She lay Helmut beside her on a pillow and covered him in quilts, then climbed out of her sheepskin sack. The wave of cold took her by surprise. She couldn't stand up straight inside the cart but, bent over, she poked her head through the opening at the front.

The only uncovered part of Hartwig and Janusz was their eyes. In addition to the cover for the wagon, they'd built a small protective roof for the drivers, but the snow was blowing in sideways, so thick that it blinded them. They'd given up and were allowing the horses to dictate their own pace and footing. In front of them was only a freezing curtain, and to the sides, barely visible, the forest, its blackness standing out against the white pouring down. Everything was muted, even the colors. Everything except the howl of the gale that blew through the pines.

Wanda didn't recognize the road. There was nothing to indicate where they were heading. The new snow made her feel as if nobody had ever been there before, as if they were the only living things in the world. She knew that Franz and his family were following, and that comforted her, but looking ahead, looking without seeing, made her grasp the solidness of Hartwig's shoulder. What was beyond the ground on which the horses trod? Would they fall off the end of the world, into the great abyss?

"Where're we going, Hartwig?"

"We're moving too slowly to reach the Römers' before nightfall, as I'd intended. We'll have to go to Jürgen Klaffke's farm. It's a little way off the road, but we'll arrive by four o'clock. I think. I hope."

They arrived in the dark, at five o'clock. Klaffke, surprised but friendly, received the two families.

"There's nothing on the radio about an invasion," he told them when they explained.

"It's coming."

Klaffke didn't invite them to sleep in the house. They were already hosting his wife's family, who'd settled on a farm in Białystok when Germany declared war on the Soviet Union with the intention of seizing all the eastern territory. Months ago, they'd taken refuge in East Prussia with their relatives, because the Russians wouldn't reach here, they said. The house was small: there was no room for anyone else.

"But you can use the barn. There's a good woodstove. And an old pit latrine outside."

In the barn, there was just a horse and a cow. While Janusz settled their horses in and tended to them, Hartwig lit a fire in the little stove. The children hadn't arrived happy. Helmut and Edeline were crying with hunger.

On the way, Wanda had tried to give Helmut some milk, but when she touched the can, she realized it was frozen. He'd been impossible to soothe. Then Edeline had started crying, wanting bread. Wanda cut some with difficulty; that had frozen, too. The jam had frozen; the butter, the water, the cheese, the ham: all turned to ice. She used two warm bricks to heat the bread a little. The older children understood they had to make do, but the little ones did not: Helmut wanted his bottle and Edeline her bread and jam, and to warm up her nose: *Meine Nase ist kalt, Mama!*

Irmgard, Ilse, and Freddy, irritated by their siblings' crying, fought over nothing and everything: Don't touch me! Mama, she's touching me. Don't touch her. Freddy's mouth stinks: tell him to stop talking to me. Cut it out, Irmgard. Ilse, stop squashing me, move over. There's no room, you move that way, Irmgard. Mama, Irmgard's trying to push me out of the cart. Look, Mama, she's staring at me. All of you, stop staring. Stop touching me! All of you, stop touching. She pinched me! Mama, Mama, Mama, Mama . . .

By the end of that day's journey, the walls of the cart, which had seemed spacious at first, had closed in on them. Even Wanda wanted to tell the others to stop touching her, stop talking to her. But she was the mother and, so, feigned patience. But she didn't stop reproaching herself: I should've organized the food better. If they weren't hungry, we'd all be having a better time, she thought. When she got down from the cart and saw Erna's fed-up face and heard baby Crystl crying, she felt bad that it made her feel better. They were tired, too.

There wasn't any use in asking her sister-in-law if she had an extra bottle, because she was still breastfeeding her little girl. How Wanda wished she still had milk in her own breasts, but the tension of recent months had dried them. Helmut would have no choice but to grow up, she supposed, purely because his mother had forgotten his bottle.

Hunger forced Helmut to drink his milk despite it being offered in a cup. That night, exhausted, the children slept on the cart, their bellies full, the crying and irritation soothed, and their bodies as warm as it was possible to make them with bricks radiating heat inside their sheepskin bags. Janusz didn't need to go out to help Kaiser hunt for his food: in the nooks and crannies of the barn, there were fat rats unused to being pursued, easy prey for a hungry dog. The adults sat down around Hartwig's map.

They'd leave at six in the morning, when it was still dark. No, they wouldn't head north toward Königsberg. The city would be the Soviets' first target. In a few days, weather permitting, they'd cross the Vistula. Once in West Prussia, they'd travel to Wanda's mother's farm to rest and to persuade her to escape with them. Then they'd head to Schneidemühl for Ida and her children. They'd spend the nights on farms they'd find on the way. They'd sleep in barns if necessary, but always traveling west until they crossed the River Oder. Then they'd be safe: the Russians would never cross the Oder, Hartwig and Franz thought.

Wanda and Erna also made plans: each night, they'd take out the food they'd need for the next day. They'd defrost it in the heat of the fire and divide it into individual portions. In the mornings, they'd heat some extra bricks: there were lots in one corner of the barn. They would ask, of course, but they didn't think Herr Klaffke would mind. They would put the bundle of food and milk on the Bendziuses' cart in a warm space between the bricks, placing the horse blankets on top. That should also help heat the interior of the wagon: it hadn't occurred to Erna to bring rugs.

Close to dawn, when they were ready to leave, they heard engines in the distance. Lavochkins, said Hartwig when the aircraft broke through the clouds. The Russian warplanes were flying low. Hunting without fear of being detected, arrogant, confident that the air was free of enemies, it seemed. They were heading north, toward Königsberg, perhaps. Had the invasion already begun?

"We can't leave now," said Franz.

"No. We'll wait till nightfall."

"Do you think they'd fire at a couple of carts full of women and children?" asked Erna.

"And how would they know that, Erna?" said Franz.

"I don't think we should risk finding out," said Hartwig.

"Children, get down," said Wanda.

The Klaffkes, still skeptical, didn't want to go with them when they set off that afternoon as it grew dark. The only light they had to guide them came from the two Pertrix flashlights Hartwig and Janusz fixed to the middle horse's harness, the beams pointing ahead on the road. Franz did the same. It didn't make much difference; with the blizzard, visibility was almost nil.

The children slept. Wanda did, too, but only intermittently, because she had to make sure, above all, that the little ones didn't come uncovered, or the opposite: suffocate beneath the weight of the quilts. At midnight, under a blanket, she changed Helmut's diaper.

It was shortly before dawn when they reached another farm. They didn't know the owners, but they begged for space in their barn. There was still no news of a Russian invasion, they were told, and refugees had not stopped flowing into Königsberg, though the bombings were becoming more frequent.

"They must be evacuating people by sea, Wanda, but it's too far. I still think our best option is overland on the quietest roads."

That afternoon, as darkness fell, they continued their journey west. The next morning, they stopped again to ask for a roof at the first farm they found. The whole family was outside loading their little cart.

"The Soviet invasion's started," the farmer reported. "They said so on the Volksempfänger. We're going. You can stay in the barn, but if I was you, I'd keep moving. A neighbor told me the first thing they'll do is close the bridges over the Vistula."

But they couldn't carry on right then. Janusz and Hartwig were tired, of course, but more than that, they had to consider the already-overtaxed and bewildered horses.

"We have a three-day head start and the roads are difficult for everyone, even them. We'll rest a few hours, Janusz. We'll leave at two o'clock."

Kaiser settled down with them to sleep near the campfire.

Another barn, another rest. Five hours that Wanda and Erna took advantage of to organize things. Five hours in which they could hear the far-off explosions. Did they mean that the Vaterland was still being defended? That it would recover its territory? Five hours watching over the deep sleep of three men and a dog.

"Children, go play in that corner. And keep the noise down."

Two more hours to eat, heat bricks, and load everything into the carts. It would have to be enough for the horses and everyone else. At two o'clock on the dot, they headed west again, fearful of being spotted by Soviet aircraft.

# 40. Something worse than loneliness

They had to win the race against the Soviet advance.

"If we don't manage to arrive before them, we'll have to head for Marienburg," Hartwig said to Janusz, breaking the silence.

It was so cold that they only spoke when absolutely necessary, because doing so meant uncovering their mouths. The cod liver oil with zinc that Wanda had smeared on them helped, but still, after ten days with their skin exposed, their faces and lips were raw, even though they'd tried to cover themselves like Berbers, who lived in the desert and who had to cover themselves not against the cold, but against the sun, Hahlbrock told him. Janusz had never heard about these people, and he would've liked to ask Herr Hahlbrock more about them, to learn about the desert, to imagine himself there, in a place where the cold didn't exist, but he knew that he must save his strength and use it only for their objective: to reach somewhere that would offer them shelter during the daylight hours.

Like the horses, the men were alert during the many hours of the night and slept during the few hours of daylight. At first, it had been easy to rest: exhaustion played its part, and so did the fact that the only sound came from the two families' children. But after the invasion began in earnest, it seemed as if all of Prussia had come out to make the same pilgrimage for life.

Their progress had grown slower—more frustrating—because the roads were increasingly packed with walkers and vehicles of all kinds pulled by animals or humans.

One afternoon and for part of the night, the German Army had forced everyone off the road while they passed. None of the soldiers made eye contact; none responded to Hartwig's questions.

"Did you see, Janusz? Some of those boys were Irmgard's age."

No, Janusz hadn't seen anything, because he tried never to look at German soldiers. Five years of learning to look only at their boots couldn't be erased in an instant.

On some nights, they found the road blocked by abandoned carts and bodies.

The first time they encountered such a scene, heralded initially by Kaiser's growling, they'd stopped to help. They ran as fast as the snow allowed them. Hartwig, Franz, and Janusz were left dumbstruck by what they saw. The passengers in the cart, two children Freddy's and Edeline's ages, were dead. Frozen. There was nothing they could do for them. Shocked, saddened, they went around the wheelbarrow that someone had packed with the intention of saving their children's lives, not knowing it would become their hearse.

They continued their journey. Five hundred paces farther on, they found what they assumed was the mother.

"They say it's not the worst way to die," Hartwig said.

"But there's no worse way to live," said Janusz.

"What do you mean?"

"Living knowing that you'll freeze to death."

They said no more because they had to save their energy. After that, they'd find more carts, more bodies. On two occasions they found entire groups by the roadside who, having stopped to rest, to sleep for just a moment, had formed their own cemetery of ice statues. They also found hanging bodies. The Army didn't hesitate to hunt down and punish soldiers who had deserted their ranks in an attempt to survive the war. Neither of them said anything, but Janusz knew that, like him, Herr Hahlbrock must be wondering whether any of those hanging bodies belonged to the soldiers who'd abandoned them to their fate on the farm.

By the time they found the third macabre tableau, and the twentieth, after they'd lost count, just one of the men would get down, without hope, to move the bodies that blocked their path. Nor did they look at the soldiers who, like dangling lookouts guarding the road, stared at them with dead eyes. Even Kaiser was no longer alarmed or curious.

What kind of war was won by an army that killed its own men and left them hanging as a warning? What kind of treacherous weather was it that had connived with the enemy to bring the advancing Russians' ice?

The unusual winter had become the most lethal army, one that encircled them and killed without spilling blood. Anyone who stopped became a victim. Anyone who kept walking would live while they had the strength and the will. That was why so many bodies of children and grandparents were abandoned: because anyone still standing was listening to their body when it said, keep going; you only have enough strength for yourself; all that matters now is your own life.

"How I wish we could help, but we can't. You understand, right, Janusz?" Hartwig said one day, catching him unawares.

Janusz nodded. He understood. Herr Hahlbrock, he assumed, had reached the same conclusion that he had: each to their own universe. It hurt, he didn't deny it, but like his boss, he'd forced himself to be hard. Everybody fights to preserve what is theirs. That was why they kept going, following other battered survivors; that was why they overtook them when a space opened up, but no longer looked, not wanting to see the misery and the forewarning of death in their eyes.

Perhaps it was what had happened when the Army had so coldly forced everyone off the road. They considered us lost, the living dead, reasoned Janusz. They didn't want to see the misery in our eyes. We're already ghosts. They're rushing to save something, but if it isn't their people, then what is it? What else is there, when everything that's happened is their fault?

After the first encounter with corpses, Janusz overheard a conversation between Herr and Frau Hahlbrock: Never let the children open the curtains. Then he'd told her what they'd witnessed. Our food, our blankets . . . it's all we have in the world. We must take good care of it all. She agreed. Erna took more convincing: That's selfish, she said. It's not Christian. It's our lives, our daughter's life, Franz responded.

War transformed everything: a country into pieces, a village into a nucleus, a nucleus into a family, the family into the entire universe. Their universe couldn't save anyone, Janusz understood. Their universe couldn't offer so much as a crumb of bread, because a crumb given away yesterday would be the one they needed tomorrow. He couldn't afford a single minute of quiet sadness for the misery of others. He kept going to save himself and those he fought for. For that, he needed all his energy and concentration.

They navigated with Hartwig's black-market map, and in this way, each day found a place to rest and plan the next leg. The farmhouses were locked, their owners gone, perhaps safe by now. It seemed they'd done as the Hahlbrocks had: set their animals free at the mercy of cold and hungry humans, but also with a chance to live. So travelers like them found the houses locked but the barns and granaries open.

They were no longer alone in the barns: they shared them with other travelers, almost all of them women traveling with children and elderly relatives. Some were tired like they were but satisfied that they hadn't lost anyone yet. Others, with empty gazes, seemed surprised to find themselves still alive but with empty hands, with no more children or elderly to take care of. All of them were hungry.

Janusz stayed out of the conversations. His German gave him away as a Pole, and the looks he received from some people suggested that they blamed him and his people for their misery. They looked at him with the contempt Radosz had told him about. Once, when a boy asked Ilse why they shared their bread with one of *them*, he had heard her say Janusz isn't an Untermensch. She realized that he'd overheard.

"You're not, Janusz," she repeated.

Not to her, but was that how others saw him? As subhuman?

On the Hahlbrocks' remote farm, he hadn't truly experienced that contempt. The soldiers gave him hard looks, but Janusz put it down to the nature of the relationship between guard and prisoner. Being hated by women, old people, and children was new to him. How sheltered he'd been: it only now occurred to him that the only Germans he'd known were the Hahlbrocks. At first, true, they hadn't let him in the house. But that had changed when he'd rocked Edeline in his arms. And even before that, they'd been wary but never made him feel inferior.

Now all these Germans had to share a roof with an Untermensch. Janusz didn't know whether the other travelers confronted the Hahlbrocks about it when they talked around the fire. They shared information. Going that way's not a good idea, they advised. Or: The safest place is Königsberg. All the ships are coming for the evacuation. And the enemy will never take the city, they won't let them.

The majority soon resumed their journey, but a few decided to stop, give in, return home. It was the same either way, they said: behind them, the Russians; ahead, the Americans and the British. Losing is losing. It doesn't matter against whom.

Janusz had no intention of pointing out their error, and he didn't know whether the Hahlbrocks tried. Frau Hahlbrock would give him a good breakfast and then he'd try to sleep, but it was hard now with the noise from so many people, so many children crying, with the laughter of the few that, like the ones traveling with him, still had the energy to play.

The previous day, they'd found the barn full, so they'd been forced to leave the carts outside in the elements, out of their owners' sight. Wanda had been obliged to give in: Kaiser spent those hours in the back of the cart, under one of the children's quilts. Wouldn't the horse blankets be better? Wanda suggested. The horses are using them, her husband replied. They had no choice. The desperation of the other travelers would tempt them to steal the provisions in the cart, which, under the circumstances, must have seemed like a repository of extraordinary abundance. Kaiser had to do his job as a guard dog, but to do so he had to be well fed. There were no mice to hunt in that barn so crammed with humans. Janusz could make a trap with sticks and cord at the edge of the forest to catch Kaiser something to eat when he woke, but they had to give him something before he slept.

"Ham or sausage: just this once, Wanda," said Hartwig.

Hidden from view, they gave the dog a sausage.

"We're all going to smell of wet dog, tomorrow, Hartwig," said Wanda.

"We already smell of wet dog, Mama," said Ilse, and they all laughed.

The second time they heard the dog bark to deter an intruder, Janusz decided to go out and sleep with him.

"No, Janusz. It's too cold," Frau Hahlbrock said to him.

Janusz smiled at her concern. "Each time he barks, he gets up and uncovers himself. I'll make sure he keeps covered."

He went out with a couple of hot bricks, his sack, and his quilt, after announcing in a loud, sonorous voice: "I'm going to the cart, Herr Hahlbrock."

His boss answered in the same manner: "Take the shotgun, Janusz." Nobody else dared try to break into the space that contained the family's entire life.

Keeping Kaiser had proved wise. The dog had seemed to immediately understand his role. With the drivers, he formed a pocket of warmth. He stayed alert. He woke them with a soft whimper if they drifted off while the cart was in motion. We were right to stop the cart, eh, Janusz, Hahlbrock said every night. You can't come with us, Kaiser, Hartwig had told the beast that day in the granary. Jadwiga will untie you in a little while. He'd done it through tears, just as, through tears, he'd stroked his motorcycle almost as much as the dog, just as he'd set all the other animals free. Look, Janusz: everything that I've been . . . it's going with them, he told him. By then, Janusz knew that he *would* go with the family: he'd accepted right away when his boss told him, it's not an obligation, Janusz, I want you to know that; it'll be a very hard journey. I need your help, but only if you're willing.

He hadn't lied: it was a very hard journey. Even harder than anticipated. But Janusz didn't regret it: the other option would've been to wait for the Russians. Where would he be if he'd done that? Alive? Dead? A wolf? He'd taken this step westward with the family, and he'd stay with them until the end. And then? Then he or the destination would decide. But he'd be alive to see it.

It wasn't bad sleeping huddled up with Kaiser under several quilts. For those few hours, he slept deeply, in relative silence. He woke in the afternoon hungry. Kaiser was the same. So Janusz headed into the forest to find the trap.

"Look, Kaiser, your breakfast. Or dinner, I don't know anymore. Do you want to chase it?" he said, letting the rabbit go.

Kaiser ran, excited, after his prey.

The family all ate, then climbed into the cart, hopeful that the next morning they might arrive in Thorn, a walled city, declared a fortress city in Hitler's defense plan. That meant that there would be a major military presence. They could rest there. Find a guesthouse where they could eat something hot, wash. The Soviet advance had supposedly stopped to the south of where they were. The Army stopped them, a woman had assured them that morning, confident that it would mark a turnaround in the Vaterland's fortunes. Let's hope so, everyone said without believing it.

"I think we'll see Thorn in the distance when we turn this corner," Hartwig was saying, when all at once, more than a dozen aircraft roared overhead. Kaiser barked at the sky. Looking up, Hartwig and Janusz saw the bellies of the ferocious birds from the east.

Wanda, alarmed, lifted the canvas to peer out.

"What is it?" she asked, trying not to wake the children.

"Soviet planes. They're heading to Thorn."

The forest was so thick and so close to the road that it was impossible to take the cart off to hide under the trees, so they just turned off their lights, threw a canvas over the three horses as camouflage, and urged them on. Franz did the same. Sure enough, as they turned the bend, the entire city came into view, just as the Soviet planes unloaded their bombs on it.

A little farther ahead, they found a clearing and stopped the cart near the trees. Helmut whined in his sleep.

"Keep him quiet, Wanda."

She closed the curtain to go comfort her baby before he woke his siblings. It was too late: Janusz and Hartwig heard the children's voices and whimpers, but they never took their eyes off the planes in the distance. First, they saw lights, and then the sound of the explosions reached them. In the air, it was all a big party. The aircraft came and went in a leisurely way; they performed a pirouette and pretended to fly away, but before they reached the city's outskirts, they doubled back for more. They made a show of their supremacy as they rained punishment on the earth. And under them, the city shook; it collapsed. Fire. Death. Many stories ending.

Janusz wanted to run into the forest; he wanted to run to his youth, when the worst thing he'd known was loneliness. Now he knew something worse. How many hearts were stopping each second, how many for every one of his own heartbeats? How many deaths all at once? Was this what it had been like for Irmgard and Ilse in Schneidemühl? How long had that bombardment lasted? How long would this one?

After a length of time no one was able to measure, the warplanes stopped their aerial games and left, empty, satisfied. The fires didn't go out with their departure. The damage would continue when the executioners were long gone, even when they were welcomed as heroes back at their base. In Thorn, the deaths would continue.

"They're still dying," Janusz said, unable to contain himself.

"Those poor people."

Janusz saw his own horror reflected in Herr Hahlbrock's eyes.

"What're we going to do?"

"We have to keep going; find out whether the bridge is still there. But not yet. Let's wait for sunrise."

But the cold was more bearable when they were moving. Janusz imagined footsteps in the forest all around. He could feel wolf eyes on them, from the sky now, too. Even the dog's hairs were standing on end.

He guessed Herr Hahlbrock was feeling the same when he said: "Maybe we'd better go; who knows whether that was the prelude to a land invasion?"

Janusz said nothing, just nodded.

They were nearing Thorn when they saw them: thousands of people standing outside a prison camp, by the roadside. Even the horses slowed their pace: perhaps, like them, overwhelmed by the smell of rot.

Women, men, children. Shivering. All emaciated, their heads shaved. They all wore gray rags and were coatless. Some wore a yellow star on their chests. Others an inverted triangle with a letter *P*. They scarcely blinked. None spoke, even in whispers; none looked around with curiosity. There was no surprise at finding themselves there, near a city in flames. Nor did they startle when Kaiser began to bark. Curiosity and misery belonged to living beings. They seemed to have dismissed themselves as dead.

The only voices that could be heard were German ones: *Vorwärts! Schnell!* Get moving!

Hartwig gripped the canvas hard to stop his wife from opening it, her voice asking what was happening, the children whining, all of them sick from the smell.

"Quiet back there!" he ordered. "Let's go, Janusz!"

Janusz hadn't realized the horses had come to a complete halt. They set off before the mass of living dead could surround them.

"Who are they?"

"Jews. All the Jews in the world."

Was Herr Hahlbrock crying? He sounded on the verge of it. Janusz didn't look.

"And the ones with the *P*?"

"Janusz, I'm so sorry . . ."

"Who?"

He wanted to hear it from Herr Hahlbrock's mouth.

"Poles."

*"Untermensch."*

Janusz squeezed the reins hard. Despite feeling Herr Hahlbrock's intense gaze on what could be seen of his oiled face, he didn't jump down to the snowy ground with his feet well protected by the good boots his boss had provided. He didn't raise his body covered in several layers of wool in protest or rebellion. He didn't stop the cart to declare himself a Pole at the top of his voice in a show of solidarity. All he did was keep going, because living was more important. The people behind them were already dead.

Nor was he capable of looking at Herr Hahlbrock, though he knew the man's eyes were begging him to do so.

"Janusz. I didn't know . . . I never imagined . . ."

"You must've known something," said Janusz through gritted teeth.

And he, too, must have known something.

He'd been a child.

But now he knew something worse than loneliness.

# 41. The invasion of the ice army

## The Schippers

***January 14 to February 25, 1945***

Arno had been keeping count with charcoal marks on the wall, which, he presumed, had once been white. That day's mark indicated that they'd been there for three weeks.

He missed the farm, the open spaces. He missed sleeping without being afraid. But that had ended months ago, when the sound of far-off explosions began, and when the squatters, as his mother called them, started to pass through the farm. There were more and more people traveling from far away in search of refuge behind Königsberg's walls. They were freezing and hungry. Some knocked on the door like beggars. Before long, his mother had told him not to open to anyone.

"Why not?"

"I already give everything we have to the government. Let them feed the people."

Government collectors had visited recently. They'd left them with very little: a few hens, the rabbits hidden in their burrows, the ram—but only because he hadn't allowed himself to be caught, and the horse—because Ethel stood in front of it and hadn't allowed herself to be intimidated.

"*Nein.* I need it to plow. If you take it, you take the summer's harvest before it's even been planted."

"Very well. Not the horse, then. How old are your sons?"

With that, the soldiers provoked Ethel's fury.

"You've already taken my husband twice. We don't even know if he's alive. My daughter's youth group dragged her off to Königsberg, where bombs are raining down. Now you want to take my sons? They're not sixteen. Do you want this one, too? He's very tall, though he's not even ten yet."

She took Arno by his coat collar and presented him like an offering, like a ragdoll, because the shock even seemed to make Arno's bones flop: he didn't want to be a soldier. He didn't want to be separated from her. Why would she offer him like this? What if they accepted him? He felt tears about to crash over him like waves.

"Will he do for a soldier, or will you roast him like you did all my sheep?"

His parents had taught him to be quiet during a conversation between adults, but Arno was ready to disobey.

"No, no. We only need men from age sixteen," said the soldiers, much to his relief.

"Then go look somewhere else."

They didn't go, because they hadn't finished with the Schippers yet. Followed by his mother, they went to search for more provisions in the house. Arno stayed outside, clinging to the horse. The animal's warmth comforted him; the tears didn't come. The animal seemed unaware of how close it had come to a new life. Or to losing its life: they'd all heard stories about the soldiers' horse stews. Arno pulled himself together: he mustn't leave his mother alone with these men.

The soldiers left the house with their arms full. They took his father's old coat and shoes, the ones his mother was keeping for his older brothers. They were about to take the quilts from the beds, but a look from his mother deterred them. Finally, they'd gone down to the cellar and taken preserves, sausages, and hams. They'd left only the preserves labeled prunes, the keg of sauerkraut, a sack of potatoes, and one of onions.

"What're we going to do, Mutter?" Arno asked, dismayed. "I don't like prunes."

"I know, no one does. That's why I labeled all the cans of meat as prunes and hid them among the real ones," his mother replied with satisfaction as she stroked his hair. "We'll be all right."

But the day's events and emotions had taken their toll. Now it was she who suddenly lost all her strength. She locked and bolted the front door—the first time Arno had seen her do so—and asked him to help her to her bedroom, where she lay down and didn't get up for two days.

Arno got a message to Helga via her friend Adelbert, but she wasn't allowed to leave her "voluntary" role in the laundry of a Königsberg hospital. His brothers still lived in the house, but the Jungvolk kept them busy all day. So many tasks, and such heavy work, that they no longer boasted about it as they had done before. They were no longer able to perform their duties on the farm. They only came home to wash, eat dinner, and sleep. They were worried about their mother but could do nothing for her: failing to show up for work was tantamount to desertion.

So Arno took care of Ethel by himself. He fed the animals, and he carried the firewood his brothers chopped before leaving in the morning. He remained alert, forever looking out the window, wondering at events beyond the confines of the farm, but with his ears fixed on his mother's bedroom. When he heard her wake, he dropped everything to be by her side.

"I would never have let them take you, Arno. You know that, right? I'd have killed them first," she said each time Arno arrived with her food. "Don't open the door to anyone and don't tell anyone about the preserves. Not anyone," she said before falling asleep again.

On the third day, she got up, thinner, but strong. Ready to deal with everything, like always.

"What's going on over there?" she asked Arno, pointing at the road in front of the farm.

"It's the squatters, Mutter. There's more and more of them."

They walked out together. Arno noted the snow-covered mounds on both sides of the road, an ice cemetery for people, horses, and treasured belongings. Up close, the procession of living people with dead faces, and of dead people on the backs of the living, seemed endless. Most were women pulling or pushing small carts full of baggage, ornaments, children, and grandparents, some alive. This army of exiles, exhausted, hungry, freezing, was part of the invasion of Königsberg, where they couldn't be refused entry: they were all Germans. Prussians.

"Don't they know that Königsberg's in ruins?" his mother said in a low voice.

*"Bitte,"* a girl with disheveled braids said, holding out a rag-covered hand. In the other arm, she cradled a doll.

Arno understood her suffering and her need.

"Shall we give her something, Mutter?"

"No. Let's go, Arno, we have a lot to do."

"But—"

"But nothing. I already told you: we can't. If I give to one, how can I say no to the next? I'm not here to feed all of Germany. My responsibility is to my children. Let's go."

Arno was disappointed in his mother. She'd always taught them to be charitable as the church demanded. But once they were in the house, seeing the confusion and disappointment on his face, his mother said, "You'll understand one day, Arno." Would that also be on the day of his first communion, he wondered? It would be a long time before he comprehended that what his mother had seen in that endless human column headed to the walled city was the beginning of the end.

"We're just getting to know the war now, Arno. What we saw outside is a woman's war. Forget the Vaterland. Women go to war for their children. I'll fight for my children, for you, but I need your help."

That afternoon, he and his mother moved aside all the furniture and the rug in the little living room to make space for the horse, the chickens, and the rabbits, because if we leave them in the barn, Arno, it won't just be the Wehrmacht that tries to take them. The ram remained as the sole guardian of the barn.

"We can't have him in the house. He knows how to defend himself, son."

It was true.

"We can't live with the animals inside the house for long," he said, fretting.

"It won't be for long," Ethel told him.

Her words made Arno wonder what the near future held in store.

After settling the animals in, they went out to his father's carpentry workshop. Arno hadn't been back there since Vater's departure. In the freezing air, he was sad not to make out the smell of abandoned wood.

"Arno. Come on. *Schnell.*"

His orders were simple: to make sure no one steals the cart, hide the runners and the warm-weather wheels under the snow behind the shed. He carefully positioned bricks under the vehicle and removed the runners, the first time he had done this alone. It worked. Meanwhile, his mother took all the tools she could find into the house. When Arno had finished, he saw the miniature horses that his father had carved and the full sacks leaning against the wall, exactly where he'd left them. Before leaving, he'd told Arno he was keeping the family's future in there: Look, Arno, beautiful carvings in Gabonese ebony. When I get back, we'll copy them to make beautiful furniture. We'll be Schipper and Sons, Cabinetmakers.

They hadn't received any letters from his father. His mother believed him dead. Sometimes, Arno did, too. All Arno had left of him was these horses and this wood. He put the horses in a sack and lifted the sacks onto the cart. He covered it all with canvas.

With the animals now inside with the humans, his mother closed the shutters with no intention of opening them again. Then she forbade Johann and Fritz from going to the Jungvolk.

"But, Mutter, we have to dig the trench to the east of the city. It's to protect—"

"Trenches! I told you I'd have to bury you in your own pit one day."

Seeing the mocking expressions on their faces, the look they exchanged that said, look at Mutter blah-blah-blah, she always says the same thing, she gave each boy a cuff on the head.

"What nonsense. I know nothing about battles, but no trench will stop an army of tanks and planes. Your first duty is to protect your family, to help your husbandless mother. You're staying here," she ordered before they could unleash the usual spiel about sacrifice for the Vaterland.

The next day, some other youngsters came for them. They're not going, she said. They have a fever. Goodbye. The second night, they didn't sleep: they heard noises coming from the barn, the ram bleating, thumping blows, screams of human pain, fleeing footsteps on the snow. Fritz opened a shutter, just a crack.

"Soldiers."

Johann rushed to the door.

"Don't open it! They're not soldiers. They're deserters," his mother said, checking that the solid wooden bar was firmly in place. "Make sure all the shutters are secure."

The previous day, she'd taken dusty locking bars from the cellar. They hadn't been used since the Great War, she told them.

Would the deserters think the house was abandoned, free to be plundered? They could open a shutter and poke their heads out so they'd know it wasn't, thought Arno. They could ask them to go, to let them sleep. But his mother wouldn't do anything but shut the family firmly in. And he soon saw that she was right. The invaders didn't care whether there were people inside, Arno discovered. The smoke coming from the chimney was the first clue that there was life between those walls; the locked door was the second.

Gently at first, then with more force, they tried to open it, without success. They tried to kick it down, but the old oak, well looked after by Arno's father and other generations, resisted. So did the locking bar and hinges. They gave up with the door, but broke a windowpane, and the freezing air seeped in between the shutters' thick boards, which also withstood the blows.

"Go hide in the basement," Arno's mother ordered in a low voice as she picked up the axe.

"Go on, Arno," said Fritz, snatching up a poker.

Johann took him by the hand, led him down there, and locked him in, alone, in the darkness. Arno stayed close to the door. He wished he was older so he could help his family. He was almost as tall as his brothers, but height didn't matter if all he could think to do at the first order was to meekly obey, he guessed. Height didn't matter if all he could do there, alone in the darkness, with danger stalking his family, was to stop himself from breaking down into sobs. And it took all the strength he had. He fell asleep during a lull in the strange noises. Then he woke to the sound of a gunshot, not knowing how much time had passed. And he finally cried, because he didn't know if anyone in the world was still alive.

His mother and his brothers opened the basement door. The gunshot had been outside. The soldiers had gone. They were safe, they assured him. For now. His brothers didn't make fun of his tears. They all slept; Arno, still sobbing uncontrollably, with his mother.

When they stepped from the house late the next morning, the ram was gone. All that was left was some blood on the straw.

That day, they packed. That day, they took refuge behind Königsberg's walls. That day, they became freezing exiles. Squatters. That day was the first time Arno saw his mother cry without hiding her tears.

# *42. Königsberg's walls*

They'd seen the explosions and the fire from the farm, but their imagination had been insufficient for the level of destruction. The walled city's cathedral and library were in ruins, as were many other noble old buildings, the squares and parks populated by refugees from outside and inside, too, with so many citizens left without roofs over their heads. But now, the great city of the Teutonic knights was trying to get to its feet, clearing avenues to restore circulation and repairing the water and power lines.

Down the longest, most tortuous road, they managed to reach the hospital where Helga worked. She smiled in surprise but then looked closer. Their journey had only taken them three hours, but the ordeal of recent days and the pain of saying goodbye were bright in all their eyes.

They'd left behind the walls that had given them safety and warmth from their first days in the world. They'd reinstalled the runners on the cart. They'd tied the warm-weather wheels to the sides along with their father's sacks.

It had surprised Arno when his mother gave him permission to bring the carvings. We can't leave them; they're for Schipper and Sons, Cabinetmakers. She replied with a sparing, if you must, but find a way to hang them from the sides. Inside the cart, they'd packed some sacks of clothes and his father's tools. In cages, cocooned in the family's quilts and warmed with hot bricks, they also had the few hens and rabbits they had kept from the Army, and in a trunk, the provisions their mother had managed to stockpile.

Arno! I almost forgot. The Bible: go fetch it.

The family's Bible was the last thing they loaded onto the cart before leaving. They stopped by the widow Hitzig, whom they hadn't been able to visit for a week. We can't leave without offering to take her with us, said Arno's mother, and he was pleased that her sense of charity hadn't been lost completely.

They found the widow dead. She wasn't the first lifeless person Arno had seen. There were plenty of bodies on the roadside, but those were almost covered in snow, and their features and expressions—their humanity—were hidden. The first dead person he'd really been close to was the widow Hitzig. Nothing hid her features transformed by death, her profound sadness. Her loneliness.

The body in the rocking chair was as devoid of life as the ones outside, but at least they hadn't died alone. Knowing themselves accompanied in their final moment must have brought some comfort. Frau Hitzig hadn't known that the Schippers would have fought for her, Arno thought.

They remained silent, lost in thought, until their mother said, let's go, but check the house: the widow would be glad if her things helped us. They didn't find much: her old coat, the quilt that the widow had wrapped herself in before dying, a few potatoes in the cellar, the firewood that Arno had brought a few days before. They took it all. After stripping her of her quilt, they took the time to say the Lord's Prayer.

She'll never feel the cold again, Ethel said.

The cold was only for the living, and no one could be out in this cold if they wanted to stay living. But the Schippers had no choice. They closed the bare front door of the Hitzig house, the one from which Arno had always cleaned the mud that Fritz and Johann themselves, among others, had thrown. They climbed into the cart in silence. Their mother tucked one of their quilts around his brothers, who sat up front to drive. After putting the widow's coat over her own shoulders, she asked Arno to come closer so that Frau Hitzig's quilt-shroud could cover them both. They barely spoke during the journey that usually took an hour, but that day took three.

Arno's eyes welled up when he saw his mother cry crystal tears as she said the only words of the whole journey: More than three hundred years of family history on that farm . . .

He wondered whether he'd ever see his friend Adolf Müller again. They hadn't passed through Adolf's family's land, but the Färbers' farm seemed uninhabited. Were they on the way to Königsberg, too? Only the dog came out to meet them, to scare them off. Unable to block the horse's path, it had returned to its place, to wait for vulnerable people on foot, perhaps. Arno felt sorry for the animal still protecting the property of owners who'd abandoned it.

He couldn't guess what his brothers were thinking. Perhaps nothing, focused as they were on guiding the horse along the improvised path they were making through the thick snow, since the main road was packed with panzers and other Army vehicles. The highway was for the exclusive use of the Wehrmacht, the soldiers yelled above their engines. It seemed as if an entire division was also trying to reach the city that day. Were they also fleeing? Was the war lost?

*Aus dem Weg!* Out of the way, they screamed at any civilian who blocked their path.

They didn't slow down for anything or anyone. Arno saw with horror that, if refugees took too long to pull to the side, the tanks simply rolled over their carts, leaving women, elderly folk, and children crying as their last possessions were crushed by the Army that was supposed to be fighting for them. Without caring that they ran over animals or dead people—or even living ones if they didn't jump from the cart in time.

Sliding across their own fields and then those of their neighbors, the Schippers carefully dodged carts that had ended up submerged in the snow. Even with their cart converted into a sleigh for the winter, it wasn't easy, and sometimes they had to backtrack in order to get around some obstacle under the snow. But they advanced. We've reached the Färbers' farm, Fritz would say. It'll be the Hohlzahns' next, Johann would reply. In this way, they slowly drew the map of their escape from farm to city, the route that they'd traced and retraced so often in better times. They mapped the route for the whole family, and it had never been so cold, never so long, never so sad, never one-way.

As they'd packed, Arno had been struck by the certainty that his father was alive, that he'd come to the farm and find it empty. Leaving would be like abandoning him, like turning their backs on his memory.

"What about Vater? How will he find us?"

"If he comes back, he'll find us wherever we are, but we'll only survive if we leave, son. We can't stay. We can't defend ourselves. It's over, do you understand?"

In the end, she'd agreed he could leave a note written with a charred stick on the wall to one side of the fireplace: *Königsberg*. Without the others seeing, Arno drew a little horse to one side. Would his father recognize the note as his own and not anyone else's?

In Königsberg, Helga suggested they should register at the *Oberbürgermeister*'s office.

"It's where people ask after family members."

After doing so, they went to look for accommodation.

"We'll go to Fräulein Stieglitz's house," their mother told them.

Johann and Fritz knew the way, but because of the destruction they had to take alternative routes. They'd heard about the old woman from their father, mostly about her marvelous furniture. Fräulein Stieglitz would put them up because she owed their father, Ethel explained. And with their father's tools, the boys would help with the maintenance of the house. They'd share their food. They'd take care of her so that she wouldn't suffer the same fate as Frau Hitzig.

They got lost a couple of times before arriving, the second time only because they didn't recognize the destroyed house. But yes, said Fritz, and yes, confirmed Johann: this was it, this bombed-out corner. The whole front of the grand old house had collapsed.

"What're we going to do?" Johann asked.

Arno saw the same question on his mother's face. The sun would set soon.

"Let's go around the back," she said.

Behind the house they found the large door into the garden and coach house, locked with a chain and padlock. Locked, but standing.

"Arno, pass me the axe."

"No, pass it to me," said Johann.

Johann had to deal the padlock several blows before it gave way. Arno shook, reminded of the deserters who had tried to break into their house.

"Mutter. Are you sure—"

"Fräulein Stieglitz is in debt to your father."

They spent the first night locked away in the old coach house, which they shared with their horse and other animals. On the way, a hen had died, but oh well, she was the oldest, their mother had said. They made a fire on the coach house floor. It's almost as cold inside as it is outside, said their mother. Oh well. We'll clean up tomorrow. They melted snow and made chicken soup with potatoes, which their mother—oh well—shared out prudently. We'll make it stretch for tomorrow, too. She kept the chicken bones to make broth another day. They fed the animals. They covered the cages with the elegant but dusty old horse blankets that they found in a corner. They were not sparing with the horse's rations: he was the one who'd worked hardest that day. They brushed him and covered him with his woolen blanket. They heated some bricks on the fire for the hens and rabbits, and others for themselves. They huddled together inside the Stieglitzes' old enclosed carriage, moth eaten and without wheels.

"Sleep. We'll find something else tomorrow," their mother told them.

They were woken a while later by bombs falling closer than usual.

"Oh well," declared Ethel. "If a bomb falls on us, it'll fall on all of us. Sleep. We have a lot to do tomorrow."

Whether from the cold or a bomb, they'd die together, thought Arno. But it wasn't all of them. Two were missing. His father was missing: Had he died alone? And poor Helga, living alone. The girls she shared lodgings with didn't count: they weren't family. Was she afraid?

"Mutter . . ."

"Sleep, Arno. There's nothing else we can do for now."

They all slept that night. They all woke the next morning.

They went out at first light and found an old pit latrine. Like the coach house and garden, the rear of the large house seemed intact. The service door was in place, solid, closed. Johann and Fritz went to fetch their father's tools, and with patience, they managed to open the lock. Inside, the enormous kitchen was covered in dust, but everything was there: the stove, the icebox, the tableware and cutlery, the pans, the empty larder. There were three doors. One led to a stairway to the floors above, but it was blocked with rubble. The second door was blocked, too. The third opened onto stairs that descended to the servants' quarters and the laundry room. There was no damage there and it was less cold than the coach house.

"Our own bunker. We'll stay here. I knew Fräulein Stieglitz would pay us eventually."

"Mutter, what do you think happened to her? Do you think she was crushed?"

"No. These rich people have family all over the place. I'll bet she went to Berlin. Yes, Berlin. She's probably having freshly baked bread and real coffee for breakfast right now. We'll take care of her house while she's away. But, boys: don't tell anyone where you live, understood? It's a secret."

Their mother feared an invasion of squatters.

"Aren't we squatters?" Arno asked her.

"No, not *us*; we're guests of Fräulein Stieglitz's."

In the laundry room, in addition to the modern coal-fired boiler, which would be impossible to get going, there was an old metal fireplace. They inspected it: the flue was working. There was no electricity, but in the laundry sinks there was running water. After dusting, they carried five old mattresses from the servant bedrooms out to the garden. Arno was given the task of beating them with the butt of the axe to free them of as much dust as possible. Then they laid them all on the laundry's clean floor. They put a bucket in one of the bedrooms to use as a lavatory. It wasn't their farm, but it would do very well.

"Far better than all those poor wretches in the squares. Fritz: go get Helga. She can live with her family again."

They'd been camped out there for three weeks now; Arno was keeping count with charcoal marks on the wall. In another room of the basement, every day, he'd drawn a horse for his father. Any possibility of the family joining the evacuation had quickly been extinguished: Königsberg had closed its gates two weeks after their arrival. The city was under siege from the Russians by land, sea, and air. Only its walls protected it, and walls could not keep planes out. With the constant bombings at night, it wasn't easy to sleep.

And now the family had been reduced to three. Johann and Fritz were gone. Now his mother regretted staying in the city: We should've stopped off for Helga and kept going, she said each night.

"To where?" Arno would ask.

"To Berlin, to eat freshly baked bread with Fräulein Stieglitz."

And he, his mother, and Helga fell asleep—for a while—remembering the feeling of peace that the smell of freshly baked bread brought, hoping and praying that, very soon, Johann and Fritz would be able to enjoy it wherever they were.

But then, without fail, the bombs fell.

# 43. Declared men

One night, Johann and Fritz had arrived wet and mud covered. Frozen. Sobbing. Arno couldn't remember seeing them cry in his life.

The Jungvolk was summoning them to work, Johann and Fritz had told their mother early that morning.

"How did they find you?"

"They saw us yesterday when we were in line for bread."

Their mother told them—blah-blah-blah—what she always did about wasting their time digging trenches. They ignored her as always.

"Don't go."

"Anyone who doesn't show up is declared a deserter. Mutter, they're hanging deserters all over the city."

And they'd gone. That night, they returned—in tears.

They hadn't dug: the ditches were already done. But they weren't just trenches; they were graves. Graves that they had to fill with the executed bodies of women old and young, children and teens their own age, older men. Almost all of them naked, all skeletal.

"A firing squad killed them right in the middle of a square. The soldiers told us they were from the Dessau camp."

They'd all heard rumors about Dessau and about other camps in the vicinity of Königsberg. At school, Herr Baumgartner had told them: Behave or they'll send you to Dessau with the Untermensch.

"There was a girl who was still alive. They told some other boys to throw her in. But she's alive, they said, and then a soldier shot her in the head and said, not anymore."

By now, they were all crying, Arno's elder brothers curled up so small they both fit in their mother's arms. Arno and Helga were left outside the circle. They formed their own.

"Living ones have to walk to Palmnicken. Some boys saw thousands of them. Thousands!" said Fritz.

"There's probably another camp," their mother said, stroking their heads while she made the soothing noises a mother makes to calm her children. To calm herself.

"They said we have to go to Palmnicken, too. They said they'd give us food."

"We'll tell them you're sick—"

"They said we have to register with the Volkssturm by February 3."

"You're under sixteen!"

"That doesn't matter now, Mutter."

No one slept well that night. Tomorrow, they'll go, Ethel said into the darkness. They all heard her. But where would they go and what would they do there? the children all wondered. What none of them wondered was *who* would go.

Fritz and Johann had to run, their mother confirmed in the morning.

"Why only them?" asked Helga.

"Because I only have enough money for two train tickets, if that. We'll follow in the spring."

There were objections: We can't let them go by themselves. How will we find each other again? Arno protested. What will happen to you? his brothers asked. No, Mutter, complained Helga. You said we'd stay together, in case a bomb falls on us, Arno said.

Hush, children. It's decided. If they put you in uniform, you'll die. And I'll have to bury you in one of those holes you dug.

Now, none of them ignored their mother's words.

When the Schippers reached the *Hauptbahnhof*, they learned that the train that had managed to leave that morning had been forced to return: the Russians had blocked the tracks. They went to Königsberg's port, where they found a desperate throng.

"You might be able to find a place. But they don't take men," a woman official told her, gesturing at Fritz and Johann. "And don't expect to leave for three days. Or more. But I wouldn't sit and wait: they're carting twenty frozen bodies out of here every morning. Oh. And don't go to the Pregel harbor: the coal ships there want your weight in gold to take a passenger. They're pirates. Don't waste your time."

Fleeing by sea was impossible.

"Some people are heading down the Frisches Haff on foot or carts," said Helga.

But everybody knew that the narrow strip of land that separated the lagoon from the Baltic was a dangerous trek in winter. Even in daytime, it was difficult to tell whether it was solid ground underfoot or just ice. In darkness it was impossible.

"They can go to Pillau and find a ship."

"Mutter, you heard what the lady said. They're not taking men," said Johann.

"But you're not men!"

Just a few weeks back, Arno's brothers would have been insulted by their mother's declaration; they would have defended the manhood they'd been waiting impatiently for. What they'd wanted more than anything was to become men so they could find glory in the war. Now, with the real war on top of them, so devoid of the glory they'd imagined, so full of the horrors that their father had never wanted to talk about, they lowered their eyes.

"They've already declared us men," said Fritz.

On the way back, outside the Hauptbahnhof, they found a woman and her daughters about to set off in a cart down the frozen strip that bordered the Vistula Lagoon.

"We're trying to reach Danzig to find a ship," she told them, "because they say it will be impossible to find one in Pillau." She agreed to take Arno's brothers with them, but not to share her provisions. "We have space for them, and they seem like able young men. But it's dangerous, what with the cold and the Russians. What about the rest of you? You're not trying to get out of here?"

"We'll wait for the weather to improve. But these two will go with you," their mother announced. She turned to Fritz and Johann. "Run to the house to fetch provisions: take four cans of preserves, two jars of sauerkraut, and four potatoes. That should be enough for the journey. Don't stay in Danzig, boys. What's the point if no ship will take you? Head to Elbing. I'll give you some money. You'll be able to buy something there, I imagine, and then travel overland."

Arno ran after his brothers. At the house, while they rolled up their quilts and a change of clothes, he fetched the provisions from the larder. Before they headed out again, Johann and Fritz gave him some instructions: "Don't go out alone, Arno. And don't let the soldiers see you, you hear? You're nine, but you look twelve because of your height. If they see you, they'll try to take you. Don't let them take you. And take care of Mutter and Helga."

Arno said yes to everything. He didn't know what else to say, and, had he known, the words would have stuck in his throat. He didn't know how to tell them that he'd miss them, that he was afraid: Afraid he wouldn't see them again, afraid he wouldn't be able to evade the Army, afraid he wouldn't be capable of taking care of their mother and sister. Afraid he couldn't keep his promises. With each word, in those final minutes before they said goodbye, his brothers tried to make him a man, just as, unfairly, the Army had tried to do with them. But he was just a tall child. He feared for his brothers but also for himself, for the part of the family that had suddenly become his responsibility. When his father had left, the first and the second time, he'd left Arno's brothers in charge. Now, as they left, it was him. It hadn't occurred to him before that Johann and Fritz hadn't been much older than he was now when they first accepted the heavy responsibility.

But he said yes to everything. He opened a drawer and took out a small butcher's cleaver. He gave it to his brothers.

"We can't take this. It's Fräulein Stieglitz's," Johann told him.

"What does it matter? She's dead, and you're going to need it."

They didn't ask how he knew that the woman was dead.

"But don't tell Mutter."

Then he went over to the sacks of wood carvings. He took out two miniature horses from their father's collection and gave one to each of his brothers.

"When we see each other again, you can give them back to me."

Arno didn't walk them back to the lagoon. He felt himself crumbling piece by piece, brother by brother.

Making the most of his mother's absence, he went instead to do the only thing that gave him joy: exploring the ruins under the snow-covered rubble of the once-great Stieglitz house. Down here, he'd found a piece of furniture made from Gabonese ebony—he was almost certain—whose doors were decorated with carvings of geese, partridges, and foxes. Arno recognized it instantly as one of the pieces that his father had spoken of so often.

When he saw it, Arno stroked the dust-whitened birds and foxes. His father had run his hands over them, too, he knew. It would've been impossible for him to admire such artistry with only his eyes. When it came to carved wood, he had to touch. Arno tried to feel some connection, feel the energy that his father might have deposited in the wood. Where are you, Vater? Do you know where I am? But there was nothing there, no message, no clarity.

He was able to open one of the doors. Inside, he found two old books and many strange figurines, wooden dolls, necklaces, earrings, brooches. Arno had never seen anything like it. He imagined that they were fine things, the kind of things that Fräulein Stieglitz would expect to find on her return from Berlin, after the war.

He closed the door reverently and looked around.

The piece of furniture was so strong that it held up what Arno presumed had been the front door and part of the walls of that section of the house. It was so solid that it had created various crevices around it. Arno set about exploring them, always mindful of the time: he didn't want his mother realizing where he'd gone, because he could guess what she'd say: Arno, if you keep going down those holes, I'll end up having to bury you there. In one crevice he found some slippers. In another, he found Fräulein Stieglitz's frozen corpse.

Just as they'd done for Frau Hitzig, he said the Lord's Prayer. Then he thanked her for the use of her house, but he didn't mention it to his mother: it was better that she imagined their benefactor eating freshly baked bread in Berlin.

Arno knew that what he was doing was dangerous; he remembered what happened to him and his friend Adolf Müller when they'd tried to build tunnels and forts under the accumulated snow: sometimes the structure held, sometimes it didn't. On one occasion, their labyrinth had lasted the entire winter. And there wasn't that much snow over their heads, really. When it collapsed on top of them, all they had to do was stand up, come out into the air, and brush themselves off. And laugh.

Not so in the bombed-out mansion. What made some structures hold and others collapse? That was the question each time. That was what awakened Arno's curiosity and drew him back.

Whenever he had time, he went down into Fräulein Stieglitz's tunnels—as he'd now named them in his mind—and he sat to observe: the passages were formed from broken-up amalgams of bricks, from pieces of timber, from the same materials as areas that were impassable.

He marked what he thought had fallen in such a way as to support the weight of what had come down on top, and admired the power of coincidence: if that piece had fallen at another angle, this tunnel wouldn't exist. Or if the ceiling of the room where Fräulein Stieglitz had died hadn't fallen almost whole but perpendicularly, neither the niche nor the woman's intact legs would have been there.

He couldn't spend long under the rubble because it was very cold; because if he was absent when his mother returned, she would ask him where he'd been; and because when the bombs fell, there was a danger that the angles of the pieces that held everything up could change. But while he was there, the absorption with which he tried to decipher that fragile world helped him forget the even more fragile one in which he lived.

# 44. *More fragments*

Arno's mother wasn't the same. Perhaps because she missed the comforting routine of farmwork. Or because she'd been losing parts of herself—one husband, two sons—and all she had left was a fragment: herself and just two children. Now she ate, took care of the animals, and washed the few things that got dirty, but did little else. At night, she spoke of the springs of her childhood. She always ended her stories by saying, and it's all over now.

His mother was lost in the war, and Arno didn't know what to do for her except keep the fire going. But it was becoming more and more difficult. They'd used up the wood brought from the farm. Then he'd scoured the garden and gathered all the dry branches he could find, but they burned like straw. He'd barely thrown them on the fire when he had to go out for more. It was an endless task. Then he'd had another idea, one combining duty with pleasure. Arno had set about the task of gathering wood in the tunnels, the loose pieces that weren't supporting any part of the structure. The boards from the magnificent stairs that were left exposed, and which he'd torn up with the help of the axe, had kept them warm for the last few days.

Arno knew that, very soon, he'd have to set his sights on the piece with the geese and foxes: he could remove the doors and part of the sides without affecting its structural integrity. But his father's memory stopped him. The other option was the Stieglitz's old cart, but each time Arno dared mention it as a source of firewood, his mother objected vehemently.

On February 20, when Helga brought home news that the siege of Königsberg had been broken, that the German Army had managed to open a narrow corridor along the Sambia Peninsula, she discussed the plan with Arno first. It was time to leave, come what may. In Pillau, they'd try to board a ship.

"A lot of people are getting ready to leave the city. What do you think, Arno? Shall we go?"

Was this what being a grown man meant? Having to make decisions for others? But what choice did they have? He'd seen the destruction in the streets, felt the dejection even among the soldiers, whom he observed without being seen. No one believed that Germany's fortunes would be reversed. They all believed they were only there to die, to buy the Vaterland a little more time.

Arno had heard it straight from the mouth of Herr Färber, whom he'd barely recognized in his Volkssturm uniform, pale when he'd always been pink, and emaciated when he'd always been plump. He found him alone on a bench, so despondent that he didn't mind having what remained of a horse as his only company: the head with its eyes and tongue pecked out by the crows.

"Herr Färber?"

The man looked up. "The Schipper boy . . ."

Where was the booming voice Arno remembered?

"Are you all right, sir?"

The man didn't answer.

"And your family?"

"I tried to save them."

He'd attempted to put them all on the *Wilhelm Gustloff*, but they'd only allowed his wife and youngest children to board. Ludwig was fifteen: a man, now. He could fight proudly shoulder to shoulder with the other men, he was told. The father had begged them to allow Ludwig to go with his mother. The Vaterland needs him here, they said. Relieved at saving the majority of the family, at least, but profoundly sad to see them leave, father and son remained in the port until the great warship weighed anchor.

Arno knew the rest of the story all too well. They all knew it. The *Gustloff* had set sail full beyond its capacity—easy prey for Russian torpedoes. The luckiest died from the explosion; the less fortunate drowned. The four captains who were on board and a thousand or so of the nine thousand passengers were saved, but this was hardly reason to celebrate: they'd have to live with the burden of having left those in their charge to die, with the weight of the baby that slipped from their arms, with the instinctive decision to release the hand of a child, or two, to remain afloat. The sinking of the *Gustloff* was a great loss for almost everyone who remained in the city.

Arno knew he should say something, some words of commiseration, but he didn't know what or how.

"And Ludwig?"

Herr Färber lowered his gaze.

"A sniper killed him on his first day. Just like that: one moment his head was on his body, and the next, nothing. I had to search for the pieces in the earth. I buried him in the ditch that we'd been digging. Now I'm alone, waiting for my own bullet to come. Where will it hit me? That's the only unknown." He looked up to fix his eyes on Arno. "Where will your bullet hit you, Schipper? In the belly? In the head? In—"

Arno ran. He couldn't take any more. He spent much of that afternoon in Fräulein Stieglitz's tunnels, trying to banish from his own head the image of Ludwig's shattered by a bullet. He only came out once he'd composed himself. Why distress his mother with news of their neighbors?

Helga, who'd cradled him in her arms not so long ago, was now asking him to decide with her. He'd seen the weight that a decision had placed on Herr Färber's shoulders. What if the same thing happened to them? What if they left and were blown up by a torpedo? What if he had to see his mother die, see Helga drown while he froze to death in the Baltic? Or worse, survived? What should they do? Stay and die of hunger and cold, or leave and die of war? He remembered what his mother told him that day on the farm: this was the other side of war. Both options were war.

Dying on the high seas would be quicker, he supposed. And if they lived, they'd get away from the bullets. They had to fight for their lives.

"Let's go."

They weren't the first ones in line to leave the city's walls. Ethel, normally so firm, had been paralyzed by indecision.

"We could wait for spring," she told them.

The assertion had the ring of a question, a plea: Please, give us until spring.

"No, Mutter. Right now," Helga said, mustering all the firmness her mother lacked.

"But the cold—"

"The cold isn't going anywhere. And we're running out of food. The horse is thin already. But it can still get us there. Let's go before it gets weaker."

"We had to make his feed last," their mother said defensively. "We'll find more in spring."

"It's getting harder and harder to find firewood," said Arno.

"We've been here almost a month, Mutter."

"How're we going to survive out in the elements?" Ethel asked.

Arno and Helga took that as a yes.

They prepared as well as they could. Helga and Ethel boiled all the eggs they had; they packed their remaining provisions. They got the animals ready for the journey. Arno would take care of the firewood.

"Don't touch the Stieglitzes' cart," his mother said.

Before daring to go out with his axe, Arno peered into the bomb-ravaged street. Once, a woman had attempted to tear the axe from his hands. He'd had to hold on tight and run. He didn't want to think about what would have happened had his assailant been a big man. He would have lost the axe and, with it, any chance of survival.

That day, he didn't see anyone on the streets near the house, but even so, he had to be careful. Exploring, he found locked doors on abandoned houses. They weren't Fräulein Stieglitz's, and nobody cared about them anymore: he chose two and chopped them into firewood.

When they left, they took their belongings and just one thing that wasn't theirs: a thin, rolled-up mattress.

"We need it, Mutter," Helga insisted when her mother protested.

"They'll say we stole it."

"Think about it: we don't know how long it will take us to get there," Helga told her.

At night, the three of them would sleep on it together, they decided. On their mother's insistence, they left the house as they'd found it, because we don't want Fräulein Stieglitz saying we mistreated it.

"Or that we stole from her."

Arno thought of the cleaver he'd given Fritz and Johann. Did it count as stolen? He couldn't regret his decision. God would understand.

By the time they began their escape, the line of people leaving the city was so slow-moving that it was as if it stretched all the way to Pillau. There were more travelers ahead of them than behind them. It was cold. Almost as cold as when they'd left home in January, but this journey wasn't like the one from their farm to Königsberg. Freezing, yes. Full of people, also. But much longer. And now they were also a target for attacks.

The Soviets had lost the narrow corridor to the sea, but they hadn't gone away: from their hills or trenches, from their warplanes, they fired their mortars or bombs as if they were doing target practice. The road was full of bodies, of blood, of human parts mixed with animal parts and bloody tree fragments. Not even the new snow managed to cover the trampled, bloodstained ice.

There was no way to protect themselves, nowhere to run. They heard a far-off explosion and saw how everyone, like them, lowered their heads and made their bodies small. But it was a futile instinct: there was nothing they could do except keep going, deafened, surprised that they remained standing. The best protection they had was to continue advancing until they reached the sea. There . . . there they'd face whatever they had to face. As they traveled along this road of death, they couldn't help but wonder, will the next bomb be ours?

They didn't speak to one another more than was necessary, and none of them spoke to anyone else. On the first day, no sooner had they struck up a certain camaraderie with the group of women and children in front of them than they were erased, completely and instantly, by a bomb. All the three Schippers could do was brush off the bloody snow and calm their horse, whose eyes they'd decided to cover. At least they all went together, Ethel said.

In the day, Helga and Arno took turns driving the cart so that their mother could lie down and doze in the back. The one who wasn't driving would join her to multiply the warmth. At midday, they each ate a hard-boiled egg.

At night, they made a fire to one side of the cart and, defrosting a little sauerkraut and some canned meat, they covered the horse with a double blanket, fed it, and asked its forgiveness for the mistreatment and lack of food. Then they heated the animals' bricks and their own. They had some dinner, more out of common sense than hunger: all they wanted was to sleep, for the Russians to let them sleep without bombs for one night. They positioned a sheet of canvas under the cart and, on top of it, the mattress. Then they covered the cart and its contents with the other canvas, so that it hung down on three sides. This protected them from the wind while enabling them to feel the heat from the fire.

And with their backs to the Soviets, in this way, they hid their fire so it wouldn't give away their position.

After the long day, their den almost felt cozy. They slept under shelter, and, between them, they tripled their warmth until sunrise. Every night, they prayed that Vater, Fritz, and Johann were all right. That the Russians would sleep, rest, and let them rest. But the enemy made no distinction between day and night. The bombs fell.

They ran out of firewood after the third night. Arno reproached himself: he should have made more from abandoned doors. He spent much of the next day trying to gather dry branches, but almost an entire city had gone ahead of them: at the roadside, the forest had no more firewood to give. They decided that going deeper into the trees was a bad idea.

"What're we going to do?" said Arno.

"I don't know," answered Helga.

Sleeping without a fire was a death sentence, as so many had discovered.

"We have your father's wood," their mother said.

Helga and Arno were surprised. They hadn't heard such firmness in her voice in days.

"But that's for Schipper and Sons, Cabinetmakers," Arno said.

"Yes, for the Schipper sons. So that they have a future."

"But we can't burn the horses!" said Arno.

"What horses?"

Arno was surprised that neither his mother nor Helga remembered the miniature horses; when he closed his eyes, he could easily recall his father deep in concentration while his hands carved each detail. That night, they lit their fire with some of the cuts that his father had saved from another fire, looking to the future.

Arno stayed awake for as long as he could. The flames might have been the same as any others, but he thought it was the most beautiful fire he'd ever seen. It came from vines, fruit, and flowers of wood. From his father's hope. And how it hurt to burn it! But their mother was right: the cold hurt more.

The journey to the nearby port took them five frozen days and nights.

When they arrived, they had to wait in line for two more days, but they did so with a feeling of hope. They took turns keeping their place in the line while the other two watched the cart.

While keeping their place, Arno witnessed the guards refusing transportation to men. Women and children, said the guard. Only women and children. One family managed to obtain a pass for their son: after begging, the mother took off her ring. Taking it, the guard seemed suddenly to understand that the boy's adolescence had been an optical illusion. The mother kissed the man on the hand.

Was that how things were obtained? Arno wished he'd brought some of Fräulein Stieglitz's treasures from the tunnels. But that *would* have been stealing. Taking jewels wasn't the same as taking an old mattress. Besides, until now, he hadn't known what use they would've been. He regretted leaving them. Now it was their turn to secure a place on the next ship. Then he regretted it even more.

The soldier looked closely at the three of them.

"You and the girl, yes," he said. "But they don't take men."

Fear seeped into Ethel's voice. "My son's underage."

"He doesn't look underage."

"Check his papers."

She went to show him.

"Lady, if you knew how many people come here with false papers, trying to shirk their duty, you wouldn't dare show me yours."

"He's nine years old," said Helga vehemently.

Arno didn't know what to say.

"Next!" said the soldier.

"No!" his mother shouted. "He was born on March 25, 1935. I'm telling you, my son's just nine years old."

"Move out of the way, lady. The ship's about to leave," he said, signaling to two other soldiers.

The soldiers began to push them, but Ethel gripped the counter.

"Wait! Wait . . . my daughter will go." She ignored Helga's alarm and refusal. "Let her go, at least."

The man didn't care about the argument that broke out between mother and daughter. He didn't care about the yes you will, no I won't, or the what am I going to do by myself, or the what're you two going to do. He just gave them a ticket for one passenger and ordered them out of the area.

Arno had never seen Helga cry so much. Or argue like she did all the way back to the cart, without realizing that they were only going there to collect her belongings, to pack two cans of preserves for her.

"Arno, stay here with the cart. Let's go, Helga."

Arno and Helga squeezed each other hard, wordless, not knowing when they would see each other again. Then Ethel took her by the arm to break the bond and led her in the direction of the wharf. Helga walked forward, but looking back, her eyes on her brother. Then they were lost in the crowd.

The time that his mother took to return, Arno spent lost in the void, in the memory of Helga's moist eyes and in the feeling of his own eyes, in his body torn cruelly and suddenly from a dear embrace, from the most familiar embrace he'd known. He lost himself in lamenting the height that made him seem older, his nine years that hadn't yet taught him how certain things were obtained, and especially the jewels he'd failed to take out of respect for a dead woman he'd never known.

When he saw his mother rushing back, he quickly dried his eyes. He would never cry again, he promised himself. He understood what his mother had sacrificed to stay with him. She'd promised to fight for him in her war, and Arno, while upset that Helga was gone, while worried for her and knowing how much she'd be suffering alone, allowed himself to be overcome with relief. Whatever happened, he wouldn't be alone.

"Where're we going?" Arno asked his mother when she climbed onto the cart with a red face.

"To Fräulein Stieglitz's house. She still owes your father."

Driving away from the port, they remained silent. They each stared ahead, unable to look at each other, for now.

"Where is Helga going?" asked Arno when they'd left the port.

"Anywhere that's not here."

"Where?" he insisted.

He wanted to imagine her alive there, wherever it was.

"Denmark."

Where was that? Would she be safe? And what about *them*?

"What are *we* going to do?"

"Wait for spring. What else?"

They weren't alone on the road back to Königsberg, but they managed to make better time. The Russians were firing less. It only took two days and a night to make it back. Only one hen died.

"The youngest one," his mother said.

While his mother cooked, Arno disappeared into his tunnels. Of all of Fräulein Stieglitz's old jewelry that he'd found in her sideboard, he took only three pieces. Would they be enough? He didn't dare take more. He held the fossilized resin up to the faint light, wondering at its age, from what country's forests it had sprung, what history it contained. He made a small hole in the stitching inside the lapel of his coat. He inserted the amber and put the lapel back. Not even his mother would notice it.

That night, they ate chicken soup. They made it last a week.

# 45. Looks

## The Hahlbrocks

***January 21 to February 21, 1945***

The promise had been that they'd rest in Thorn. Then, that they'd stop for a few days at Grandma's house. None of it had happened.

The journey was no longer exciting, even for Freddy, with his vivid imagination. No one had anticipated that journeys could be endless, boring, sad.

They all wanted to be home. They wished they could sleep in their beds, sit at their table, take baths in their tub, laugh with Jadwiga. They all missed Jadwiga. They were all fed up.

The children were fed up with the dark hours of the evening when they couldn't even amuse themselves by drawing on their blackboards; with sleeping in order to escape, more than out of tiredness; with Helmut's dirty diapers. They'd even tired of the stories that Ilse told, because for a long time now, she'd had to repeat her repertoire. When she asked Janusz for a new one, he didn't have the time or the energy; all he wanted to do after driving all night was sleep, eat, and get everything ready to leave again.

"Another day, Ilse."

Janusz had never said no to her before.

After taking care of the horses and Kaiser, the three men chose a place in a corner of the barn or granary, wrapped themselves in their quilts, and rested without moving until hunger woke them.

Kaiser, on the other hand, often ended up in the cart, curled up but alert. He stayed close for Helmut to nap on top of him, for Edeline to put her flowery hat on him, for Irmgard to stroke his back absentmindedly while she read and, impassive, to return Ilse's look. Her father said he'd taken his role as protector very seriously. Ilse agreed: the dog tolerated a woman approaching to ask something, or unfamiliar children playing nearby, but he never allowed a man to approach, no matter how old.

"Yes, Papa, he's a very good guard dog, but if he sees a mouse, he drops everything. He even lets Helmut roll off him!"

Her father laughed, and Ilse was pleased to see him happy, even if just for a moment. Like Janusz, he saved all his strength for the night drives. Ilse had never imagined that a person had to be strong in order to laugh.

In the day, their mother made them keep quiet so that their father, their uncle, and Janusz could sleep and regain their strength. It didn't matter that there were other people in those barns who didn't lower the volume of their crying, of their groans, of their hunger. They all make more noise than we do, Ilse would tell her mother, but she'd reply, the other travelers don't owe your father or Janusz anything, but we do.

Sometimes they found other children to play with or talk to. Most were hungry and cold. Most cried when their mothers told them it was time to go. Ilse could understand why: back into the ice, on foot, in a wheelbarrow, or on an open cart. She would have cried, too.

The first time Ilse realized how others were traveling, she decided to stop complaining about the cold. It was impossible not to feel it. Impossible to prevent it from creeping down her neck and making her nose constantly red and runny. She hated it when her mother told her, Ilse, you must wash your hankie. Or, seeing as you're going to the toilet, wash and put on some clean underpants. And, seeing as you're putting on clean underpants, wash the dirty ones.

Washing a rag or underwear in freezing water made her hands burn, and no amount of rubbing would make them warm again: the only thing that worked was sitting in front of the fire that her father lit before going to sleep. Just pulling down her two pairs of tights and underpants in some outdoor toilet was bad enough. Did she also have to wet her skin? It was very painful. And don't even think about rubbing your freezing backside covered in tights, a slip, and a dress in public, Ilse! We don't do that!

She didn't like the cold. She didn't like how it seeped into her bones, how it made her younger siblings cry when, by dawn, it had managed to steal almost all the heat from inside their sacks. But they were lucky: they had layers of clothes, thick overcoats, wooly sheepskin sacks with hot bricks. While they traveled, they had space to move around a little, so that Ilse could say, come here, Edeline, or, Freddy, get in my sack with me. Smiling, their mother told them they looked like a strudel, and that was how they felt: squeezed together and hot like the filling in a freshly baked pastry. They were so lucky to have their unorthodox cart to insulate them from the worst of the winter.

At no time during their journey had they seen another cart like their family's: covered and flowery inside, less cold than the open air, albeit almost as smelly now as Helmut's diapers. When they stopped to rest, her mother opened the curtains at each end to air out the interior, keeping a lookout for people approaching while she prepared food or washed diapers with the soap for bodies, seeing as she'd forgotten the one for clothes. Aunt Erna took good care of her cart, too, though hers wasn't as protective or as pretty: it didn't have the flowery woolen rugs on the floor and ceiling. The simple canvas covering allowed more cold in, but the heat from the bricks that they used to defrost the food helped a lot, she said.

People eyed their carts. They watched them eat. Ilse had never felt such intense looks before. Uncomfortable looks.

"How is it you even have food for the Pole?" a woman asked her mother one day.

"We prepared for months."

"You doubted the Führer?" The woman seemed offended.

Her mother's response was sharp and offensive in several ways: "You didn't?"

Her mother was tired, too. Ilse could hear it in her voice and see it in her face. One day, after many on the road, she'd seen her without her overcoat while she washed her armpits under the dress that had once been a good fit. Now it was baggy under the arms, around the waist. Ilse noticed that her face had also lost its roundness and its shine. She began to observe that her mother ate, but every day she set aside some of her portion so that one of her children could have more; one day it was Edeline, the next, Helmut, then Freddy, then Irmgard, then her.

They were all tired of being hungry. They'd begun the journey asking for cookies or bread and butter for their snack, still used to life on the farm. Each time, their mother had to repeat, again and again, it's all gone, all gone, all gone, wait till dinner. The little ones didn't understand. They didn't understand why, when they cried with hunger, their mother hugged them instead of giving them food. And they demanded, and they demanded. But her response was always the same.

Irmgard and Ilse had already spoken without lies, without playfulness, and without softness to Freddy: You're old enough to understand that there's no more food till tomorrow, the milk's for Helmut, stop pestering Mama. And with a look, they reminded him every day: You're a big boy now, don't cry, don't whine, hold on. Just as they held on, though they sometimes felt like crying, too, because they missed having a belly full of stew, broth, cheese, vegetables. Now, they ate their food cold, because the smell that the ham gave off as it browned in the pan elicited eager looks from other families and tears from other children.

"Don't think any of those women would share anything with you if they had it," Wanda told her eldest daughters. "Don't look at me like that. To give them something, I must take it away from my own children. I prepared. Why didn't *their* mothers prepare?"

They ate every day, but the five of them stared at their mother when she served them less each time, when there was no bread, when they finished their portions more and more quickly, when they wanted to ask for more despite knowing that it was all gone, all gone, all gone.

After seeing her so thin, Ilse decided to refuse to eat her mother's extra part when it was her turn to receive it. Sometimes she managed, but sometimes she didn't. Next time, she promised herself. But sometimes she managed and sometimes she didn't: her demanding stomach made her forget her resolve.

Whenever Ilse opened her eyes as they traveled at night, she found her mother awake, dealing with something. She tried to help her as much as she could, but she'd found she could only do it in the day. At night, it was better to stay asleep. Those hours lost at night helped her rest her hunger, her boredom, and her fear—a fear that had gripped her since the night when they'd been woken abruptly by the sound of engines above them and by far-off explosions.

That night, Irmgard had been the one to calm everyone down. She even comforted their mother, who was rocking back and forth with Helmut in her arms, saying stop, stop, stop, because stop, stop, stop was her only protection against something unknown, against her first close encounter with violence. Ilse, hyperventilating, was transported to the suppressed memories of a night, years before, when a siren had woken her.

"That sound's a long way off, don't you think, Ilse?"

Did her sister want an answer?

"Don't you think, Ilse?"

She felt Irmgard's elbow dig into her ribs as another explosion thundered in the distance.

"*Ja.* A very long way."

They were the ones who knew about bombs near and far. They were the experts. But Ilse couldn't make her voice sound calm like Irmgard's, so she let her go on.

"See, it's nothing to worry about. Sound doesn't do any harm. It'll be over in a minute, you'll see. Nothing to worry about, nothing . . ."

Ilse was surprised to find herself being soothed. She clutched her doll, but she allowed Irmgard's voice to guide her, just as her hand had in Schneidemühl, trusting that her sister would take her somewhere safe.

When it was all over, when the bombing stopped and the cart set off again, after saying the Lord's Prayer just as it was taught in church, they'd tried to sleep. But suddenly, a stench assailed them all. The first to vomit had been Irmgard, but her mother had followed. The little ones sobbed and yelled. Their father shouted at them to be quiet, and, stunned by the unusual hardness in his voice, they tried.

"Breathe through your mouths," their mother ordered them.

What had the stink been? Where had it come from? No one would answer them.

And so, that day, they crossed the river without stopping in Thorn, without eating stew, without resting in a bed. Without even stopping at dawn, as they usually did. The children heard what the adults were saying without words. They sensed their relief when they found the bridge intact, and their tension when they realized it was so packed that it would be hours before they could cross to the other side.

When they reached another farm at midday, they were all more tired than usual. Their father and Janusz barely spoke. The children were pale and haggard. We're almost at Oma's farm, their mother told them.

"And when we arrive, we'll make broth and take a bath. We'll wash the quilts and boil all of Helmut's diapers."

"We'll sleep in beds," said Irmgard.

"Will we stay at Oma's house?" asked Ilse.

Their mother didn't respond to the statement or the question.

"Mama!" Irmgard suddenly cried.

"What?"

"It's January 21. It's your birthday!"

"We have to celebrate," said Ilse, angry with herself for forgetting.

When their mother said, "No, it's not necessary," and "What are the other travelers going to think?" their father intervened.

"Wanda, some celebrations can't be missed."

That raised their spirits. Ilse took out the paper crown, the one she'd made for Helmut not long ago, though it seemed like a lifetime. Unfortunately, all the packing and unpacking underpants and tights, and the boredom and the weariness and the cold—especially the cold—had made her forget the delicate crown, which she now found folded up between a dirty pair of underpants (one day she hadn't washed them when her mother told her to) and her Sunday dress. She smoothed it out a little and placed it on her mother's head. It was very small on her, but she tried not to move so that it wouldn't fall. There was no nostalgic mention of cakes or cookies when Irmgard served her mother her full portion of ham, and a piece of cheese with peach jam on top. They all smiled, even their father, who drew strength from it, and Janusz—almost—when he gave their mother his best wishes.

*"Wszystkiego najlepszego,"* he said.

"Janusz!" Ilse said, laughing. "You know nobody understands Polish!"

She didn't understand why Janusz's almost-smile disappeared.

"If you don't mind, I'll go to sleep now. It was a hard night."

"Of course. Go," their father told him, serious.

Janusz's departure marked the end of the party, which had only lasted as long as lunch.

When they set off that night, the children's spirits were renewed. Grandma wasn't expecting them. They'd give her the surprise of her life: her grandchildren visiting for the first time! And they'd rest. And they'd take baths in hot water. And they'd eat a plate of hot food. Whatever it was. And the mothers would wash everything. And the carts would stop stinking. But it wouldn't matter anymore because it would be the end of the journey, at least for a while.

When they arrived the next day, they learned that they'd have to continue almost immediately. Grandma's house was just one point on the route. One farm among many, albeit one where they'd be allowed to stay in the warm house, while other travelers stayed in the barn.

"Why, Papa?" Irmgard asked, on the verge of tears.

"Because we have to go fetch Tante Ida and your cousins."

It hadn't been easy to persuade Grandma to go with them. Her son and daughter said to her: Mama, there's no time, you can't stay. But they got nowhere. It was Ilse's father who finally convinced her: The Russians are too close. Do you want a repeat of Nemmersdorf here? The Russians don't differentiate between young and old . . . While Grandma reluctantly packed, Hartwig, Franz, and Janusz replenished their supplies with the little that was available on Grandma's farm. After leaving a potato broth to simmer, Wanda left the delicious smell of the kitchen behind and went to wash and boil the baby's diapers in the barn. Ilse, Irmgard, and Freddy were given the task of opening the granary where their grandmother kept the henhouse.

Bring the two hens and any eggs you find, she told them.

There were two left that only laid eggs without chicks, as some refugees ate the rooster. In the granary, there were two small mounds of corn.

The Army didn't come take their part last autumn, Grandma explained to the other adults. They're not collecting maize from those of us who have it or delivering it to those with cows. I've bartered a little for butter or milk with neighbors who have dairy cows. Longingly, she added, Oh, to be a cow and not go hungry . . .

They slaughtered the hens for soup. They would take the bones with them: You get another very good broth from them, and then you break them and suck out the marrow, Grandma said.

They'd take the eggs boiled. There weren't many: they'd give them to the babies.

They all ate at the table together, much to the annoyance of their grandmother.

"The dog and the Pole can eat in the barn," she'd declared.

Ilse was proud when her father didn't allow it.

"We all eat together, or nobody eats," he said firmly.

Freddy looked up in alarm. "I wang ooo eek!" he cried, breaking the tension with his desperate articulation of hunger.

They all laughed, except Grandma and Janusz.

While the children played or read upstairs in the care of Irmgard and Ilse, the mothers organized themselves for the journey, and the three men slept by the fire in the living room. They gave the horses time to rest, and, at nightfall, they set off again. To Schneidemühl, now. None of them climbed into the cart with any enthusiasm. None of them expected the journey to end there.

A few days later they left Schneidemühl empty-handed. Ilse overheard Tante Ida from the next room.

"I can't leave," she told Ilse's father. "What if Josef comes back and doesn't find us?"

Ilse thought she'd realized that Josef had died. She guessed that her father was trying to say it, but her aunt wouldn't let him.

"No! He might've been taken prisoner. I have to stay where he can find me. And in any case, I don't have any provisions: we can't be a burden on you. Here in the city I can get some things with my rationing coupons. We'll be all right."

They didn't seem all right. Ilse's cousins had gray skin, they didn't even want to play marbles anymore, and, they told her, the siren went off more and more often.

"Nemmersdorf?" Tante Ida said when Hartwig reminded her of the event. "The Russians wouldn't dare do anything like that in a big town like this. Anyway, they won't get through . . . You heard the news: we broke the siege of Königsberg."

And just like that, the other Hahlbrocks were left behind.

"We tried. We can't force anyone to undertake a journey like ours against their will," Ilse's father told her. "And there isn't time to keep insisting."

They would travel west. Now, they'd try to cross the Oder, put the river's waters between them and the Russians.

"Always west, running from the Apaches like the settlers of the Wild West, Freddy," their father said.

But he could no longer excite his son with the promise of future adventures. By now, Freddy understood that the Apaches in his story were called Russians. And this was no tale of heroic adventure.

"The Oder's very close to Berlin. Surely the Wehrmacht will stop them. They won't let them through, you'll see," Irmgard told Ilse in secret.

Ilse hoped her sister was right. That was where they were heading. Tired, freezing, in a cart that smelled awful again.

The only good thing about the situation—as Ilse reminded her siblings every day—was that their grandmother would always travel in the Bendziuses' cart, because, poor Erna, she has no one to help her, as the old woman never tired of saying.

Poor Crystl, thought Ilse, already having to learn how difficult it was to love Grandma.

# 46. An arrival

Wanda met Hartwig's cousins for the first time that morning in early February.

For years, Hartwig had been exchanging letters with a cousin he hadn't seen since the two were single men. They'd been partners in crime as boys, he told Wanda, and years of separation did nothing to dilute such a friendship. The man would welcome them, Hartwig assured her.

But perhaps he wasn't actually so sure, because he asked the family to wait in the cart until he'd spoken to his cousin. They'd arrived without warning, and on farms west of the Oder, people seemed not to understand the turn the war had taken in the east or the consequences it would have on their lives.

Wanda and Hartwig were now on the other side: they'd had two years of peace during the war and then another three years of relative peace. They had been aware of the food shortages, of course, but deep inside they told themselves, if it doesn't happen here, if we have what we need, everything's fine; if bullets and bombs aren't raining on us, we're all right. Those poor other people, but us, we're all right. Now they found that being on the other side was terrible, that it hurt: How could their German brothers and sisters be so blind to the Prussians' suffering? How was it possible that they didn't understand that the fate of one was the fate of all? But at the same time, they'd escaped. They were lucky still, lucky not to experience firsthand the atrocities of the invading army.

The owners of the farms where they'd tried to find shelter on this side of the Oder didn't look kindly upon the invasion from an army of ragged exiles, birds of ill omen who announced the end of the world: The Russians are coming! Here, their farms were still active, their granaries and barns full of grain and animals: there was no space there for human beings who'd disobeyed the Führer's orders not to cede territory, shrinking from the danger of a few bullets. They were sneeringly called *Piefkes*, mocked for their accents and their penury.

They'd been allowed to buy a little milk and cheese, but not enough to replenish their supplies.

"It doesn't matter," Hartwig told Wanda. "We'll be there soon. We'll stay at Wilhelm's until we decide what to do."

In the meantime, they'd had to spend two days with only the trees' foliage as a roof, because they found no open doors. They reached Wilhelm's farm as tattered, helpless, disillusioned outcasts: the Vaterland wasn't prepared to welcome its Prussian sons and daughters as equals.

Wilhelm's was a farm of modest size, but it was still working normally; everything was being prepared for the spring planting. There were Polish Zivilarbeiter working without military supervision, because how could they run when they were so far from home?

Wilhelm had barely recognized Hartwig. Wanda supposed that it wasn't just the years apart. The month he'd spent exposed to the freezing air, with limited rations, had transformed him: as well as being disheveled, he was very thin, his eyes sunken, his cheekbones pronounced. A month's growth of his beard and hair didn't help, either, and his skin was burned and cracked. But he identified himself, and his cousin, after initial words of suspicion, enveloped him in an embrace.

"Cousin Hartwig! To what do we owe this pleasant surprise?"

Hartwig told him. Then the surprise was not so pleasant anymore. There are a lot of you. It wouldn't be a problem as far as he was concerned, but he had to consult his wife, who was in Berlin that day visiting their sixteen-year-old twins, who were now distinguished members of the Hitlerjugend.

"Please just allow us to come in to get warm. We have our own food . . ."

"Ah. Then come in for a while. But tell the children not to get anything dirty. We don't have children in the house anymore and Grethe's very particular."

"Thank you. I know Wanda will be grateful, too. Can we stable the horses?"

He showed them the barn. Once inside, they all climbed out of the cart. The men dealt with the horses, and the women and children saw to the food. Wanda looked at her offspring with a critical eye. She tried to tidy their hair and clean their faces with a wet handkerchief, but it was an impossible task. She did the same with herself. What kind of impression would they make? They looked like what they were now, she realized: down-and-outs begging for a roof over their heads.

"Children, be polite. Don't forget your *please*s and *thank-you*s. Understood?"

They were the same old lessons, but a month in the cart might have erased them. Why not, if it had already erased their smiles?

"And smile."

Hartwig ordered Kaiser to stay near the cart.

When they knocked on the door to the house, Cousin Wilhelm opened with a smile that disappeared when he saw the large group, the Polish giant, the little boy trying to smile with an incomplete mouth.

Wanda was on the verge of turning around and leaving. How dare he judge them?

"Who's that?" Wilhelm asked, pointing at the young man.

"That's Janusz," replied Ilse brightly.

But Wilhelm wasn't asking her.

"He's our Zivilarbeiter," Hartwig said briskly. "A good lad who—"

"He can't come in."

"But—"

"He can stay in the barn with the horses. And he isn't to speak to my workers. I don't want him giving them ideas."

"Listen here, Wilhelm," Hartwig began.

Janusz interrupted. "It's fine, Herr Hahlbrock. I'll wait there."

But Ilse wasn't having it. "We all eat together or—"

"Ilse! *Sei still!*"

Wanda cut Ilse off before she completed the declaration her father had used with her grandmother. The strategy wouldn't work here.

The smiles had been wiped from all their faces. Hartwig and Wanda exchanged looks. They had no choice. None of them had the strength for so much as another hour of frozen wandering. Janusz went to the barn with his portion of ham and cheese.

They ate. They washed a little. They cleaned the bathroom and kitchen so that they wouldn't leave a single trace that could annoy the woman of the house.

She'd do what she could to persuade Wilhelm's wife to let them stay, thought Wanda. She didn't care about pride anymore, she reflected as she sat there in a soft armchair stroking Edeline's hair while she slept peacefully in her arms. Pride, like a beloved dinner set or inherited mirror, loses its value when you're fighting for your life. Just the thought that the woman might refuse to take them in, that they'd have to return to the cart that very day, made her want to cry.

When Grethe arrived that afternoon, she found her living room taken over by strangers looking only a little cleaner than they had that morning.

*"Was ist los?"* she asked, severe.

They all remained silent, expectant, while Wilhelm explained, It's my dear cousin, they're *Flüchtlinge*. He told her briefly about the month of flight, the hardship, the Russians always close behind.

*"Flüchtlinge . . ."* There was contempt in her voice. "The streets of Berlin have been invaded by refugees. Bums. I don't see any Russians anywhere."

"Grethe . . . they have nowhere to go."

Wanda looked at her husband, who'd thought he *did* have somewhere to take his family: the home of his cousin, who would surely offer them refuge before they continued their journey.

"We can work," Hartwig said.

Was his tone pleading, Wanda wondered? Perhaps Hartwig felt the same: pride neither feeds nor warms.

"No. You can't work here," said the woman.

There was a surprised, dense silence. Hartwig was about to defend his professional abilities when the woman went on.

"Only farmers are to stay on their farms. All other men must report to the Wehrmacht. Like my sons did today."

How many veiled grievances were in that statement? How many accusations? Grethe didn't know what they'd been through, and she didn't care. Wanda tried to make eye contact with Hartwig in order to read a promise in his eyes: Of course I won't report to the Wehrmacht. But he didn't look at her.

The couple left them all there, stunned, while they went to argue somewhere else in the house. The Hahlbrocks could hear raised voices, but they couldn't make out the words. What would win: loyalty to family or loyalty to the Reich?

Wilhelm and Grethe reached a compromise. There was a small hunting cabin in the forest that bordered the farm. It hadn't been used for decades, but they believed that the roof remained intact. The only condition was that by the time officials were due to visit in two weeks, Hartwig and Franz must have reported to the Wehrmacht.

"We don't want them accusing us of assisting deserters."

Deserters? What was the woman talking about?

"Go before it gets dark," she snapped.

As they parted company, Wilhelm offered some hay for their horses. And a look full of apologies.

# 47. Light

The cabin reminded him of his childhood.

Janusz was almost certain that, if he summoned his mother's spirit, she would emerge as white as the snow from the living trees. The forest here was different, and in much the same way, the cabin gave the impression of existing outside time and the reality of the world.

Seeing the hidden cabin, he almost believed, thanks to the last traces of childhood that remained in him, that they could stay there and never be found by the war or by Russians or by Germans. The twilight and the mist shrouding the cabin gave it a certain magical quality. But the feeling only lasted for a moment. If the cabin were magical, it would welcome them with a lit fire. The forest's leaves would never rot at the door. It would flush out the darkness that had accumulated inside during years of neglect.

He was furious, not with the cabin, but with himself. Magic didn't exist, it had never existed, not even when his mother's stories had made him believe so keenly. His mother, who'd become a ghost, abandoned him to his fate. He guessed she'd stopped believing, too. If it wandered at all, his mother's ghost wandered a different forest, one where he had only known loneliness. And the cabin there had just been an ordinary hut, where a boy had been unable to bear his loneliness.

"Janusz? Are you all right?"

He had to get down from the cart, not sit there bewitched and motionless.

"*Ja.* Still half-asleep, I guess."

Janusz banished the idea of magic to the darkness, upset with himself for allowing his childish fantasies to get the best of him again.

They would rest in this cabin, but not by the grace of some special power. It would provide walls; it would give them a roof. That was all. After the month they'd had, they didn't need anything else. But the dark cabin couldn't protect them from what was coming.

Wolves of all species were stalking them, and never, not even for an instant, should he believe that they'd given them the slip, or that there was any magic in the world that could hide them from view. He didn't know when, but they'd have to flee. He hoped his boss knew this, too.

Janusz unloaded the little firewood they had. It would take far more than this to flush out the cold amassed over so many years of neglect.

The first thing they did was to inspect and clean the flue. A bird had long ago decided it would be a good place for its nest, which they now removed, evicting a spider and its prey from it. Next, Janusz went to inspect the structures adjoining the cabin: a pit latrine plagued with insects but solid, and a little stable about to be defeated by age.

"Herr Hahlbrock: the stable's not safe for the horses. Shall I take them to your cousin's barn?"

The man sighed. "No. I'll take them. But this one needs to be ready by tomorrow. The less we rely on my cousin, the better. Come on, Franz," he said to his brother-in-law.

Janusz took the axe into the forest and chopped enough wood for the night. When he went to deposit it in the cabin, Frau Hahlbrock was organizing everything: the women would sleep in the bedroom with the children. The men would sleep in the little living room and kitchen.

Irmgard and Ilse, grateful at the prospect of a bed or even a static floor, entertained the little ones while the mothers did what they could to clear the dust and the rodent droppings. Kaiser followed, sniffing everything, hoping to find a mouse dazed by all the activity. And Helmut, tottering, followed Kaiser. Janusz was surprised. When had the baby learned to walk? Sometimes he fell onto his backside, but there he was, attracted by the tail he wanted to pull. The dog dodged, lashed him with his tail, nudged him with a hip. And the baby fell, laughed, and got up again. The game was clearly familiar to them both, but Janusz, normally asleep in the day, had missed it. It was as if they'd lived in parallel realities. And in his, there hadn't been much laughter.

The next day, he awoke surprised to have slept for twelve hours straight. When he went out, the unfamiliar forest welcomed him as one of its own creatures. The new snow crunched under his feet and glowed with the first rays of sun filtering through the high treetops.

Living in the day wasn't the same as living at night. In the night, it wasn't possible to hear the wind stir the leaves without imagining it was an enemy. Being awake while the rest of the world slept had given him limitless time to stare into the void, without any distraction from the short, formless stretch of white road all night, and each day falling into a sleeping trance where he was besieged by the blank stares of all the Jews in the world and perhaps all the Poles, except one.

Him.

Driving through the night, under the weight of infinite fatigue, he could end up thinking he was the only Pole missing from that mortuary. He imagined his brothers' protests: Pole! Why're you living shoulder to shoulder with Germans? Pole! Why did you never try to escape? To fight? To die with pride instead of living deceived like a child? Why don't you join our number? Why don't you die with us?

That was the question that broke his terrible reverie. He hadn't accepted death as a child in the woods, nor when he ran from the Russian voices that invaded his land, nor when he meekly accepted his status as a forced laborer. Should I want to die with my countrymen? No. He refused to accept it.

Why didn't he go when Radosz and the others went? Why wasn't he hanging dead but proud from a tree like Tadeusz, or punctured by a bullet like Józef? Because he wanted to live. Because he wanted to live despite his mother, despite the Russians, the Germans, the Poles. But to do that, he had to deceive himself a little, fall under a spell of his own making. When he'd lived by day in a remote corner of the world, the charm had been easy. On the road in the desolate hours of the night, the magic dissolved.

In the light of this bright day, Janusz knew that he wasn't the only Pole left in the world: Jadwiga remained, at least, and that comforted him. With the sunlight, he could put aside the hard looks, the contempt, and remember instead that it had often been Herr Hahlbrock's voice—Janusz, pass me the reins so you can rest—that had brought him out of his abyss of fear.

After that horrifying night near the camp outside of Thorn, he'd spent night after night lost in resentment against his boss and everyone like him. But now, in the light, he recognized the horror and contrition in every look his boss had given him since then.

Some time after that encounter, he and Herr Hahlbrock had managed to speak to each other again, albeit only in darkness. They'd both wanted to live, and so they'd cast their spell and hidden away in comfort. Even Janusz, who almost never went to the Polish village because it hurt. Who'd decided to stay when Herr Hahlbrock gave him the option to leave. How easy it was to turn a blind eye, whether to the government's cruelty or the suffering of others.

Inside the cabin, the sounds of morning had started: Helmut and Crystl were crying; the older children were stretching.

"Janusz!" Ilse was calling from the front door. "Jaaaaa! Nuuuuusz!"

It was how she'd always called him. Ever since, with her first cry of his name as a toddler, she had ended his loneliness. Janusz smiled for the first time in a long time.

He turned toward the sound of the beloved voice. Now that the magic spell was broken, there was a lot to face up to: everything was new in a world that neither Herr Hahlbrock nor he recognized. Were there many others like them? Were there people who, like them, had chosen to blind themselves in order to live? He hoped that, soon, they would see clearly, too.

Now that *he* saw clearly, Janusz knew that he'd never be able to forget what the German people had done to his own. But a morning like this, with an innocent girl who'd always loved him, reminded him that, while there was darkness, there were always faint rays of light for those ready to see.

Janusz came out from the shade of the trees. Ilse's face lit up when she saw him.

"My papa told me to help you find firewood."

In spite of everything, he was grateful to the Hahlbrock family. They—Ilse—had helped him forget his loneliness. That, too, he would never forget.

There was enough light in the forest now to search for fallen branches, which in turn would make light and heat in that ordinary cabin that was more hideout than home.

"Are you wrapped up warm?"

# 48. Words that are used

Wanda had used up her whole repertoire of words. All of them. They were of no use.

*Tick-tock, tick-tock . . .* She was running out of time. *Tick-tock, tick-tock . . .* Every seven seconds a German dies in the war. Now it could be her husband, the father of her children.

"Don't go. Don't enlist."

They'd been arguing over it for almost two weeks. Two weeks, packed into a rustic cabin that, after the journey they'd traveled, seemed glorious to all of them. The rest had done them good: Freddy's cold was gone, the color had returned to their cheeks, and Janusz's and Hartwig's cracked skin had almost healed, although a black frostbite mark had set in beside her husband's nose. Wanda told their children: Your father's a hero, and that's the mark to prove it. They all agreed, except Hartwig, for whom, it appeared, being declared a hero by his family wasn't enough. Now he'd taken his summons to heart and had decided he'd fight for his country.

They'd already evaded the government for a month and a half. What would happen if they dodged it for another month or two or three? Or until the war ended? What harm would it do? Would their enemies triumph just because one farmer used his good sense, listened to his wife, and failed to enlist?

In that month and a half, they'd also evaded the news. They'd listened neither to German radio nor the forbidden British station, and the information they heard from Hartwig's cousin seemed to emerge more from fervor than from the truth. All the evidence indicated that the end was near. Wanda didn't know what else had to happen for the Reich to surrender so that no more soldiers, or mothers, or children would have to die.

"What's the point in going now, Hartwig? By the time you get there, they'll be sending you back, Wanda would tell him, hoping that sense would prevail."

"Wanda. I have no choice. Nor does Franz. You heard Grethe. What do you think will happen if the officials find us here?"

"We'll hide. We'll disappear into the forest. We'll travel like gypsies."

"Wanda, they took away all the gypsies. And I'm a man. I can't run from my duty like a coward."

It was something else they'd spoken about: the silent condemnation of the women on the icy road, the gossip in the granaries and barns. What right did that woman—Wanda—have to keep her husband with her? How was it possible that all *their* husbands and brothers were fighting or crippled or dead, but look, there's a young one, whole, healthy? Coward.

That was the crux of it. Wanda had been telling him for years: Hartwig, the reason you're not going to war is because you're needed on the farm.

But his brother Josef and his childhood friends had gone. Nothing was left of his life as a young man among young men. It was just him and Franz. Just them, because all the others had heeded the call years before.

"You could hide in the forest while—"

"And what do you think Grethe will do? Let me spend the winter on her property while her sons—her sixteen-year-old boys!—join the Volkssturm? Or Operation Werewolf, if that woman is to be believed."

Grethe boasted that, thanks to men like her sons, Germany's greatness would survive any adversity, and that such was their bravery that they'd been invited to join a secret branch of the Army. So secret that few knew of its existence.

Wanda and Hartwig had heard all about it on the two occasions when they were invited to the house to drink some bitter ersatz coffee.

But only the two of you, Wilhelm told them both times. Grethe doesn't want children in the house anymore. You can leave your kids with their grandmother, can't you?

Yes, they could. And they could leave them with Franz and Erna, too, since the Bendziuses were also not welcome. It wasn't that Wanda wanted to go to listen to Grethe talk endlessly about her sons, who were about to become wolfmen. She went because she had to, and she'd had to stop herself from saying: If this branch of the Army is so secret, why do you know about it, and why're you telling us?

They had to put up with the spineless cousin and his domineering wife. They had permitted them to stay in relative comfort for two weeks, but time was running out. Wanda imagined Grethe counting the days before they had to leave. Then she would turn from reluctant hostess to enthusiastic denouncer.

The day before, Hartwig had gone to visit Wilhelm uninvited, without informing Wanda.

"I told him that Franz and I would leave for Berlin tomorrow. To go register. I asked him to allow you to stay in the cabin."

Wanda wanted to knock some sense into him, but she resisted. Then, for the umpteenth time, she spoke her most used, most useless words in the face of her husband's stubbornness: Don't go.

"Stay for the children, if you won't stay for me. Three of them wouldn't exist if you'd gone to war at the start. None of them might exist now if you hadn't—"

Hartwig cut her off. "I'm doing it for them and for you. If the Army didn't arrest me on the way here, it was only because of the crowds and because they were too busy to bother, with the Russians at their heels. Now the Russians have halted their advance, it seems. But they're coming, as are the British and Americans on the other front. Berlin is not Königsberg. The Army will muster all its resources there, sparing no effort, unforgiving."

"But your children—"

"The government doesn't care about my children, Wanda. I must go, because if they catch us on the road, they'll pull me down from the cart and hang me from the nearest tree, like all those soldiers we saw. And you and the children will be forced to watch. And then you'll be left without a plan, without anyone to protect you."

"Ah, and if you go, we do have a plan?"

Yes, he insisted. Yes, there was a plan. The cabin was tolerable after they'd cleaned and carried out some repairs, particularly on the outbuildings. They'd stay there with permission from Wilhelm, who wouldn't ask Grethe for hers. He'd just inform her, he resolved. When they left, when the deer returned to the forests after the war, and thanks to the improvements they'd made during their stay, Wilhelm could rent out the cabin to hunters from the city. Grethe wouldn't be able to refuse.

There was nothing left of their original provisions, but they had plenty of rationing coupons and some money: some things could be obtained from the nearby village of Halbe, and others could be bought from Wilhelm. Irmgard, Erna, and Wanda could help on the farm preparing hams or cheeses. They'd be paid a small amount of money or in kind. That would satisfy any objections that Grethe had. Ilse and Grandma would take care of Freddy, Edeline, Helmut, and Crystl. Ilse would help Janusz with the animals and firewood.

Shouldn't Janusz work on the farm? No, never. Wanda understood: it had been made clear from the beginning that the young man would have to stay in the forest. He mustn't be seen by Grethe or any of the other workers.

"And, Wanda, when the soldiers do come, you must make sure they don't find out he's here. They'll take him."

"They can't do that! Janusz has been with us since he was little more than a boy."

"Janusz belongs to the Reich, not to the Hahlbrocks. The day we left the farm, we stole him."

"But he agreed to come," she said weakly.

"He doesn't even belong to himself. Janusz's wishes are important to us, but not to anyone else. You saw Wilhelm's reaction when we arrived," he said, his face betraying his disappointment with his cousin. "Imagine if Grethe knew. The soldiers will take him, maybe even to a camp like the one outside Thorn."

Hartwig had told her of what they'd seen there. Even if we win this war, he'd said, we'll have to pay the debt in hell. That was what Hartwig called the horror he'd witnessed that night: debt. It was an easy word to say, but it did not bode well for the future.

"You saw it clear as day, Wanda; we were farmers, but we became jailors. I allowed it to happen."

He'd allowed it, but so had she. It was true that she'd declared herself against it, but never beyond the confines of their bedroom, for fear of reprisals. She'd kept quiet. They all had. How uncomfortable it had made her at first and then how normal it had become to have Polish workers on the farm and to live under the eye of Army guards. How nice it had been not to go hungry and not to lose her farmer husband to the war. How easy it had been to forget that Jadwiga and Janusz were with the family not as dear friends but as captives.

In the judgment to come, they couldn't claim innocence. How would they pay their debt?

"Don't go, Hartwig, don't—"

"Look, Wanda, like you say, the war's almost over. I don't think it'll even last until summer. I'm sure they'll send me straight back."

Wanda hung her head, defeated by her own words.

"And then I'll come and find you here or in Hanover or wherever you are. I'll be fine. And you will, too. Don't worry."

Don't worry. How many men had said the same thing to their wives before leaving, never to return? How many wives had, like her, said nothing in reply?

Going with him to pack his small bag of clothes, insisting that he should take his feather quilt, and hearing him assure her that they'd give him what he needed, Wanda understood that she was just another link in a continuous chain of women united across time and every language by the same plea.

Don't worry.

# 49. Three days of silence

For three days, Ilse spoke only when necessary. Only when necessary to Janusz, while she helped him with the firewood. Only when necessary to Helmut, Crystl, Edeline, and Freddy, when she gave them orders or held them when they were hungry. Their stomachs always felt hollow, and she didn't have any more food to give them or any more words to comfort them or any games to distract them. The little ones filled the hollow space with their screams and sobbing, and their grandmother filled hers by saying, Ilse, make them be quiet.

In the evening when her mother returned with her aunt and her sister, who worked on the farm with the odious Grethe, Ilse handed over her charges to their mothers, and kept quiet. She drew or wrote on her blackboard. She read the book she'd brought, though by now she knew it by heart.

Ilse's silence weighed more on her than on anyone else. Her silence was her scream. Her silence was her absent father. Her father, who'd told her: Ilse, I have to go, help your mother, help Janusz with the horses and with Kaiser, take care of your brothers and sisters, take good care of yourself, dear girl. Her silence was her sadness.

He hadn't wanted to listen to her.

"Papa, I don't want to help Janusz with the animals. I'm scared of them. You have to stay. I'm scared that you're leaving."

"Ilse, it's an order. Janusz will show you what to do."

"But—"

"But nothing," he said sternly. "And listen to me: you mustn't let fear win. Do you hear me? You're my brave girl. Brave girls win."

"But they're going to kill you like they killed the papas of all the kids at school, like they killed Uncle Josef."

"Of course they're not. Didn't I just tell you that we brave ones win?" he said with a smile that, years later, Ilse would recognize as forced.

Seeing him leave with Uncle Franz was hard. Freddy and Edeline cried, because they understood, and Helmut and Crystl cried in solidarity: they knew that something big was happening. Irmgard hugged her father, but he said some secret words in her ear that infused her with strength. Ilse envied those words; she wanted them for herself. In that moment, she wanted her father all to herself, like when she was a little girl on his motorcycle, when they did the farm's accounts, when they shared private jokes. She wanted those words so that they'd have the same effect on her that she witnessed in Irmgard: back straight, tears gone. She also wanted the smile that he gave Freddy, the tickles he gave Edeline, and the bear hug Helmut received.

Ilse, who wasn't crying, though she didn't understand why not, hugged her father and said to him again: "Don't go, I'm not brave."

"Oh yes you are."

"When will you be back?"

He didn't answer the question.

"Be brave. Take care of everyone. And I'm entrusting Kaiser to you," he said to her secretly. *"Ich liebe dich, Tochter."*

He freed himself from her arms, and she was happy to have her own secret words from her father. But then she saw him say goodbye to Janusz, to her mother. She saw them being left as empty as she was. She saw her father give Kaiser a final stroke on his back, the dog also seeming to understand, whining with distress as he tried to tear himself from Janusz's grip. She saw her father's eyes taking them all in, as if memorizing them; she saw him turn around—without looking back now—to go to war.

Her father's words helped for a moment, but once he was out of sight, the anger returned. She was angry at him, even if she was old enough now to understand it wasn't the fathers who went but the country who took them.

She reserved a compartment of her anger for the Führer, but a bigger one was allocated to her father and her mother: to him for suddenly revealing to her that he was powerless to say no to anyone, and to her mother for letting him go, and for not hugging him at the end as he deserved, for not giving him his secret words at the last opportunity. But the biggest compartment of her fury, and the part that saddened her most, was reserved for her own forgetfulness. As much as she tried, she couldn't remember whether she'd whispered her secret words in her father's ear. Then she admonished herself for not yelling them at her father when he turned away, when he climbed on the cart that would take him to the train to Berlin.

If she'd yelled them—*Ich liebe dich auch, Papa*—perhaps he'd go to war with the certainty that he was loved, too. If she'd yelled them, perhaps he would return sooner. He *would* return, unlike her friends' or her cousins' stupid fathers who'd allowed themselves to be killed or who disappeared. She couldn't remember whether she'd said the words secretly, but what she did know was that she hadn't yelled them when she'd had the chance. She'd kept back the words that, later, in her silence, and later still, when her silence was broken, she would, for years, repeat as prayer: I love you, too, Papa.

She punished herself with silence, but only for three days. The first to grow weary of Ilse's unusual introspection was Kaiser. She would wonder forever whether it had been because, missing her voice, the little ones had cried more and pulled his tail more, or because the dog understood that, in her father's absence, he now belonged to her, or that they belonged to each other. Perhaps those had been the words her father had secretly given *him* before leaving.

On the third day, as she read listlessly, she felt a furry presence beside her. Kaiser was looking at her. Ilse was used to the look. It was the same I-want-to-eat-you look he'd been giving her since she was Helmut's size. You're imagining things, her father always insisted, but for some reason she couldn't recall, Ilse had always sensed that the dog posed a threat.

"Don't eat me, Kaiser."

In response, the dog didn't change the intensity of his gaze, but he opened his mouth and dropped a pine cone, which rolled toward her. Where had he found it? Perhaps in a corner of the little stable where he now slept with Janusz.

"Do you want me to pick it up?"

The dog stared at her, his look unchanged. Expectant. Hungry? Ilse wanted to retreat, ask her mother for help. But her father had asked her to be brave, to take care of everyone. He'd asked *her*.

"I'm going to take it. Look." She moved her hand slowly. "Do. Not. Bite. Me."

He didn't bite when Ilse seized the pine cone, but he continued to stare.

"Now what do you want?"

She knew there were dogs that liked to play fetch. But if she threw the pine cone, it would break apart and make a mess. So she wouldn't throw it. But what else could she do with it? The dog lay down against her to share his warmth. Ilse, surprised, kept the hand holding the pine cone raised. Then her arm tired. Carefully, she let it fall onto the animal's back. He took a deep breath, trembled, and then let out a little huff.

She'd never touched him without shivering, without feeling imminent death upon her. Now she didn't know whether to breathe for fear of setting him off. She was careful with her exhalations and movements, but the dog didn't stir. Then Ilse began to use the cone as a comb, and the dog repositioned himself to give her better access. Each stroke of the pine cone down his back made him tremble, but he nestled closer. Ilse imagined that he was experiencing what she did when Irmgard gave her delicious tickly feelings on her back with her fingertips, so she continued, gently at first, but then harder and more confidently while she brushed dry twigs from his fur.

With her rhythmic movements, with the dog's warmth and weight, Ilse fell asleep. The next day, she woke when Kaiser stretched. Her mother—who else?—had let her sleep right there on the floor, had covered her and Kaiser both in a quilt and even brought her a pillow. Ilse thought she'd never slept so warm.

Kaiser stood and left their shared cocoon. Open the door for me, he told Ilse with his eyes.

"Coming," she said. Before opening the door, she said to him, "Eat well today, Kaiser, so you're not hungry for me, all right?"

The dog went out, and before closing the door, Ilse saw a faint ray of sun reflect off his fur. She returned to her makeshift bed and searched for the pine cone so she could put it somewhere safe. Her father had gone, but she was making her first attempts to obey one of his orders: Take care of Kaiser.

Kaiser had never gone out hunting looking so smart and so handsome, and it was thanks to her not allowing fear to win. She had fought and she had won, and with that certainty in mind, she slept a while longer, reassured.

# 50. Lost stories

"Janusz. I know it's a lot to ask, but please: stay with my family."

He would be their only protection, Herr Hahlbrock told him before leaving, so Janusz must never be seen. If the Army discovered a Zivilarbeiter without a master, they would make him disappear without hesitation.

"You'll stay hidden in the woods. You'll teach Ilse how to take care of the horses and chop wood."

"It's not necessary, I can—"

But it was necessary, Herr Hahlbrock insisted. No one knew what would happen or when. They had to make sure that the family could cope if they were left alone. At that moment, Janusz made his promise: "I'll never leave them alone, Herr Hahlbrock. I'll stay until you return."

Herr Hahlbrock smiled, but Janusz saw the doubt in his eyes. Before leaving, he repeated his plea: "Take care of them, Janusz." Now it was the women who worked and brought home provisions: milk, butter, flour, bones for broth, potatoes, soap. The grandmother boiled the two babies' diapers, and for that she needed large quantities of firewood, which Janusz and Ilse obtained. While they searched, he set traps that often came to nothing. When they did catch something, the dog looked at Janusz expectantly.

"Sorry, Kaiser. This rabbit's for the family. Find another for yourself."

And the dog would shoot off after some airborne trail.

Once, a cat fell into the trap. That day, Crystl was sick, so the grandmother had stopped Ilse from going with him.

Idle girl, she'd snapped. Always running off and leaving me with everything. You're staying.

How grateful he'd been that Ilse didn't see the white cat with its mournful gaze. She would have set it free. Janusz killed and skinned it.

"What's this?" the grandmother asked before immersing the animal in boiling water.

Janusz stared hard so she'd understand: I won't tell you what it is, there are children around.

"It's a rabbit, Frau Bendzius," he said with his most precise pronunciation.

The grandmother clearly preferred a full belly to the naked truth.

"Ah. Looks like an old rabbit. We'll have to boil it longer, so it softens, don't you think?"

That night, there were only expressions of appreciation for the hunter and the cook. No matter what fell into his traps, Janusz decided, he wouldn't hesitate to take it to the table. Meat was meat: the children needed it to fill the bottomless hole of a growing body, and the adults to feed their hope, though he supposed that everyone, like him, remained hungry.

The next day, he and Ilse went in search of firewood. Kaiser scouted up ahead. Ilse seemed exasperated.

"Not even Kaiser pays attention to the stories anymore. I don't tell them like you do, and they're all bored of the same ones. Why won't you tell me more?"

"Because there's a lot to do."

Ilse frowned. "You always say that: because there's too much work or it's too cold, you're too tired, you don't have time. Because you're out of breath walking in the snow. But you're never out of breath, Janusz, I know it. You just don't want to anymore, do you?"

Ilse was right, smart girl. All she needed to add was: Because you're sad and because you don't have any more stories to tell. That was the simple truth.

His mind had once been a repository full of story seeds ready to germinate, but they were gone. What he didn't know was whether he'd gradually lost them on the long journey, or whether they'd abruptly withered on the outskirts of Thorn. Perhaps, distracted by shock and horror, he hadn't noticed the stories, like docile prisoners, obeying the German orders: *Vorwärts! Schnell!* Perhaps they'd all joined that march of death.

Had he been aware of the exact moment of their loss, would he have been able to defend them, to protect them? Would he have had the strength to persuade his stories to stay inside him? Or would he have let them go?

He didn't recognize himself. Without the new, unborn stories, he didn't even want to revisit the old ones. They belonged to another life.

"I'm sorry, Ilse. I've been distracted with everything there is to do. I told your papa I'd take care of you all. Maybe when the war's over, ja?"

She didn't respond. Could she sense his drought, his emptiness? The truth was, Janusz missed his stories, he was sad that he wasn't the person he had been, and he hoped to recover them when calm and sanity were restored to the world.

When the bullets and the looks of contempt stopped, when words like *Untermensch* were removed from the world forever, the stories would return.

# 51. Neighbors

## The Schippers

***February 25 to March 26, 1945***

His mother had always been strict, but never as much as since their return to Königsberg. At first, she'd forbidden Arno from leaving the house because they'll see you, they'll take you, a bomb will drop on you, you'll fall into a ditch, and I'll have to blah-blah-blah.

But it was impossible to abide by such a decree if they were going to survive in the frozen city. And the bombs had stopped, so instead a feeling of relative security fell on the few remaining inhabitants. The Army might know what had happened, but people like them knew nothing. The Russians had given up, perhaps. They hoped.

After the first few days back, in which Arno and his mother felt they'd earned a reprieve, they began to approach the bottom of the keg of sauerkraut and the sack of potatoes. Despite living in Fräulein Stieglitz's kitchen, with the persistent cold the hens weren't laying as many eggs as they ordinarily would, and the rabbits didn't seem to want to mate. It didn't matter how many times Arno's mother told them if they didn't have babies soon she'd turn them into stew; the rabbits paid no mind.

Now that the siege had been broken, the city was receiving supplies again. So his mother had begun to send him out when it grew dark for more firewood, and later, during the daylight hours, for soap, bread, milk, and sausages, but come straight back, Arno. Don't trust anyone. And drop everything if a soldier speaks to you. Run.

Arno always ran back, even if no one spoke to him. He knew that his mother was waiting. That she'd been waiting for him from the moment he left through the garden gate.

Sometimes he returned empty-handed, sometimes with his knapsack swinging with the three hundred grams of bread allotted per coupon, or soap, or some old potatoes. But empty or full, the lines were the lines, and Arno couldn't make them move any faster. The city might have felt empty compared with before, but it was still home to tens of thousands: city dwellers reluctant to leave their homes, refugees like them from the surrounding farms, the old and young who would be its last line of defense. Sometimes, when it was his turn, the bakers (or the butchers or the dairymen) looked at Arno with pity as they hung up their closed signs.

"Sorry, lad. There's not a crumb left."

His mother didn't understand why it took so long, because she refused to leave the house.

"If we both go, Mutter, we could—"

"No. If we leave the house unoccupied, someone will find it," she said. "And they'll break in and steal everything. Or when we get back, we'll find intruders sleeping on our mattresses and our hens boiling in someone else's pot, you'll see."

Arno went out every day for firewood, but he did so with the axe down his pants, to protect it from covetous eyes. He hooked the metal head on his belt so that the long handle hung down the side of his leg.

It wasn't a forest of trees that he searched; it was a plentiful forest of doors and furniture. First, he focused on the bombed-out houses. But it was dangerous to enter the damaged structures, so one morning, he had decided to try one of the most intact, with an eye to saving the few carvings he had left from his father's collection.

Arno felt like a thief. Other than Fräulein Stieglitz's, he'd never entered a house without being invited. With a blow of his axe to the doorknob, he was received by the freezing air and smell of a family that had locked up with faith that they'd return. He was received by luxury like he'd never seen: the walls covered with tapestries, furniture with mirrors and ornaments, and a large spiral staircase.

Before beginning to hack, he explored the whole house. He imagined his own fractured family living between these walls. He would slide down the banister on the big staircase, doing a great leap at the end. His mother, a good seamstress, could take in the fine clothes that the lady of the house had left in the wardrobes. They'd sleep in the room with the big bed that had a canopy and red curtains embroidered with gold thread. They'd light the enormous fireplace and would never be cold.

But then he thought about how much wood they'd need to keep such a fire burning, to keep the enormous, high-ceilinged room warm. So he abandoned the idea and concentrated on his original mission: chopping up the doors.

When he went down with his first load, an elderly woman was standing motionless at the bottom of the stairs. She gave him a severe look, without saying anything. His heart leapt out of his chest. Was she the owner?

Arno halted his descent, but he didn't know what to do. His mother had always told him, if they see you, run. But to run, he'd have to give up the precious wood. If he ran, he'd abandon his axe, which was still upstairs. And he would never do that.

"Are you a thief, child?" the woman asked.

"No."

"This house belongs to the Blomeier family. Are *you* a Blomeier?"

"No."

"Then you're a thief," she said emphatically.

"No! I haven't stolen anything."

"And what is that you have there?"

Arno looked at the firewood he'd gathered into a pillowcase.

"My mother's cold," he said. He wasn't taking the fur coat he'd seen in the wardrobe. He was only taking wood for a fire. He couldn't apologize for that.

"I'm cold, too, but I don't go around stealing pillowcases from other people's houses," said the elderly lady.

Arno blinked in confusion.

"We're cold, and we don't have firewood," she said.

"I can give you some of this."

"No, child. You'll bring us firewood every day. The same amount you take to your mother."

"But—"

"We'll pay you."

At that, Arno smiled. His mother would be happy.

"But put that pillowcase back. You can hack this house to pieces, but never—get this straight, child—never ruin a woman's bed linens."

Arno didn't understand, but he would obey.

"I don't have any way of carrying all the wood."

"Come to my house. I'll lend you the gardener's wheelbarrow."

Frau Beckmann and her invalid husband lived in a mansion two doors down. The woman only went out when necessary: to stand in eternal lines like Arno; to return, like him, with very little. Her husband never went out. He sat at the window, observing everything: the bombs falling, their neighbors fleeing, the more tenacious ones killing their thoroughbred horses for meat, and an unknown boy who, one day, had gone out in search of fallen trees to chop with an axe that he'd defended from a woman who tried to snatch it. The same boy who now returned in search not of trees but of doors.

"We thought about coming to find you, but we saw you leave on the cart. Then a few days later we saw you return without your sister . . ."

"Helga went to Denmark."

"Now it's just your mother and you," said the man. "And your mother never leaves the house."

"She's taking care of it until the lady comes back . . ."

"We all know that Fräulein Stieglitz is never coming back."

It alarmed him that they knew.

"Bitte, don't tell my mother."

"What's your name?"

"Arno."

"Arno, you're a good son."

The Beckmanns had no children now. The sons had perished in the Great War, and their only daughter had died in childbirth. The new war had taken their servants, even their old housekeeper, who'd suffered a direct hit from a bomb when she went to church.

"I told her: Don't go, Brunhilde. The Russians love big buildings. But she brushed it aside. Someone has to keep praying, she said."

Until recently, they'd relied on the few neighbors they had left, but that had ended once and for all on the day they opened the road to Pillau.

"Even in the war, old money's worth more than new money. And in this neighborhood, it was all old money. The ones who decided to leave the city right away were the first to obtain passage. The ones who took longer also obtained passage the moment they expressed a desire—no waiting in line. They've all gone now, or they all died, as you well know."

Now the Beckmanns were alone, like Arno and his mother.

"My poor wife aches all over. The hours she spends waiting in line, in the cold, are going to kill her. Arno, we have plenty of money, but all the money in the world, no matter how old, can't heat a house if there's no firewood. It can't even fill your belly if you don't have the strength to search for food. If we give you money and our coupons, will you bring us whatever you find? Will you make firewood from all those empty monstrosities and bring us some every day?"

That became his routine: cart the day's firewood from one house to another; run around the city dodging soldiers; buy food if he was lucky, bemoan it if he wasn't, but return home to his mother, who always, no matter how long he took, awaited him with anguish in her stern words.

Spring came, and with it Arno's birthday, but though he'd wanted to find a ham hock to surprise everyone with, invite the Beckmanns for dinner, he hadn't even found bread or milk or cheese. It's my birthday, he told the butcher. Lad, the butcher replied, in these times, every day we live is our birthday. Hock . . . pfft! You weren't even in time for the bones today.

Arno sat in a half-ruined square to lament the hole in his belly, made bigger by the crazy idea of ham hock swimming in his mother's plum sauce. How long had it been since he'd seen a plum? How long had it been since he'd smelled meat in the oven, a sauce thickening on the stove, some freshly baked cookies? Not since his previous life, since a good Christmas, since a time when he hadn't known what hunger was.

He was about to head home when a group of boys stopped near him. It was a rare encounter. There weren't many children in the city. He knew that they were a little older than him even if they weren't as tall as he was. He smiled.

United by circumstance, surprised to find a new boy, they became instant friends. They'd decided they would try to get into the movie theater. To forget how hungry we are, they told him.

One of them, who'd grown up in Königsberg, had been a regular at the picture palace before it closed. Now that the Russians had lost interest in the city, it was open again. Do you want to come? Arno admitted that he didn't have any money to pay for it.

"No one's got money. I know how to get in through the back."

They didn't know which movie would be shown that day, but it didn't matter: they were all exciting, they told him. Arno believed them. If it was true that movies made you forget your hunger, then they must be very exciting. He knew it was time to get back to his mother, but he'd never been to the movie theater and it was his tenth birthday that day. He knew he'd pay the price for it later, but he decided he'd go for a while. Just a few minutes, then he'd leave the screening before his mother missed him too much. Yes. That's what he'd do.

They snuck in without any problem and occupied almost the entire front row.

This is the best row, the boys told him.

First, they played the newsreel. The initial impact was huge. The enormous figures, so real and natural; talking photographs. Adolf Hitler appeared old, spent. His left hand was trembling, though he tried to hide it behind his back. From the voice he'd heard on occasion on the radio, Arno had believed the man was a giant, but he was no taller than the children he was greeting in the footage. None of the soldiers were older than his brothers, but one spoke with a voice as high pitched as Arno's, as childlike. It was a boy who'd been made into a grown-up and seemed happy to be one. A child they'd persuaded to become a soldier.

Arno wanted to go home. The newsreel made him remember his absent brothers and the reason for their absence. His own predicament. He was about to excuse himself when the main feature's credits began rolling, the music, the movement. He allowed himself to be seduced by the huge screen, the dim light, the tale of Kolberg: the giant people, the old war that was nothing like the present one, the cavalry, the military bugle, the romance, the hero—oh, if he could be that hero!—who declared: There is no love more sacred than the love for one's country, no joy sweeter than that of freedom. You know our fate if we do not win this battle!

The whole audience applauded the rousing words. Arno did, too, but shortly after, he slumped to the floor, nauseated, vomiting the void in his stomach. The other children laughed. The adults scolded them. One of his new friends helped him out.

"The front row's the best, but also the worst. It happened to all of us the first time. We still get dizzy, but we know how to hold on until the end now. Rub some snow on your face and in your mouth. *Auf Wiedersehen!*"

Arno did as the boy suggested, but when he turned to thank him, he realized that he was alone in the darkness.

Time had never passed as quickly as in that movie theater. The motion picture had made him forget his hunger, but once the cinematic spell had broken, he realized that he'd begun to feel unwell from the moment the first horse had galloped toward him on the screen.

What seemed like a blink had been at least two hours, he calculated. Arno remembered his mother. He closed his eyes and sighed. Then, pushing past the nausea, he ran.

When he arrived, his mother was sitting on her mattress in the dark. She hadn't even tried to keep the fire burning. She didn't yell, she didn't even say her blah-blah-blah. She looked away, and all she said was go to sleep.

When he went to the Beckmanns' the next morning to deliver their firewood, he learned that, the day before, his mother had left the house at nightfall to demand that they return her son to her. They'd assured her they hadn't seen him since that morning.

"You scared us all," Frau Beckmann said.

Now he owed an apology to the elderly couple, too.

"I'm sorry, Herr and Frau Beckmann."

"You can't do that to your mother, Arno," she said. "Besides, what were you thinking of, going to the theater! Russian bombs like big buildings."

"I didn't think. I just wanted to have fun, see my first movie."

"To forget the war for a while," said the man.

Arno nodded.

"I understand, child. There's nothing wrong with taking a break from—"

"There's a lot wrong with not telling your mother," Frau Beckmann said sternly, reprimanding them both.

"Well, that's true," said the old man. "You must tell her. There's nothing wrong with wanting to take a break from the war, Arno. But you mustn't get lost. It's always better to stay close to home or where you're able to run. There'll be time for movies later on."

Arno furrowed his brow. The Russians were gone. When would things get better?

"Remember this: wars are lost or won, but they never disappear. In the meantime, if you need a break, I can lend you a book."

Herr Beckmann lent him two: *The Three Musketeers* and *Twenty Thousand Leagues under the Sea*.

"Big adventures written by Frenchmen, Arno. They're very old copies. They were mine and then my children's. Don't let anyone see them. We don't want government idiots thinking that D'Artagnan, Athos, Porthos, Aramis, and Nemo are Allied spies plotting to attack the Reich."

Arno didn't understand. He'd never read anything that wasn't about Germany or its wars.

"It's a joke, child. They're books from another time. They won't do any harm. On the contrary: if more Germans read them, more Germans would enjoy themselves, and there'd be less war, I'd say. But the lunatic Hitler wanted his war—"

"Kurt . . . ," his wife reprimanded him again.

"Yes. Another joke," he conceded, clearing his throat. "Take them, Arno. Enjoy them and rest. But don't think it gets you out of bringing firewood and bread, eh?"

That day, he was lucky. He bought bread, sausages, and potatoes, which he added to the weight of the two books in his cloth knapsack. Then he found a little hay for the skinny horse and seeds for the hens.

That day, everyone would eat well. Once again it seemed like the war was fading away, but he kept in mind Herr Beckmann's words: Wars never disappear. He understood more clearly when he encountered the boys from the day before, the ones from the movie theater, who, seeing the weight of his knapsack, turned their greeting into pursuit. Hunger was stronger than any friendship. Arno ran, and, because he had already planned his escape route through Königsberg's maze of destruction, they never caught him.

He deposited the shopping in front of his mother as an offering.

"I'm sorry, Mutter. For yesterday. There were some boys, they invited me to the movie theater and—"

Then she looked at him. Furious.

"Oh! You went to the movies . . . And where did you get the money for that?"

"I didn't pay."

How clever he'd thought he was. His mother's face said the opposite was true.

"How many Commandments did you break yesterday? Did you remember God? Did you respect your mother? You stole, that's what you did. You stole from the theater people. Was it fun? What else have you stolen?"

Arno thought of Fräulein Stieglitz's cleaver and the small treasure he kept in his coat's lapel. He decided to break another of the Commandments. He lied.

"Nothing. Never."

"I thought the Army had taken you," she said, her voice breaking.

"I'm sorry, Mutter."

Finally, she seemed to listen to his words. She sighed.

"Wash. We're going to have a good dinner tonight," she said, still serious, as she set to work.

Arno smiled. That was how his mother forgave. That night, he started reading *The Three Musketeers* to her out loud. Herr Beckmann had been right: a German who reads is happy and forgets war. He rests.

That night, they slept in peace. That night, forgiven, warm, and with a full belly, Arno believed what he hadn't for a long time: that one day, they'd be reunited with Johann, Fritz, and Helga. And perhaps also with his father.

# 52. *Sunday*

***March 27 to April 8, 1945***

At dawn, the bombardment of Königsberg resumed, albeit intermittently. Herr Beckmann told Arno that the bad weather was on the city's side. The rain and low mist impeded aerial bombing, but Arno, take care of yourself when the sun comes out.

Arno had spent all winter longing to feel the sun's warmth on his face. He'd longed for the colors to return. Now he hoped the low, gray clouds would stay forever, even if his daily search for firewood became endless, the snow turned to stone, and the hardship became permanent. He was used to living like this now. He remembered the past, when there had been no fear, like something from a dream, anchored to the smells of a kitchen, to the memory of his father and his siblings, all of them sitting together at the table. And he, the youngest, the most protected.

Now, that life was over, and everyone was gone. Now, his only protections were the gray clouds, a city's rubble, his mother, Herr Beckmann's advice, and the old clothes Frau Beckmann had given him for his birthday.

"Oh, Arno! They're a little big on you, but you look like an elegant schoolboy now."

Arno didn't know whether his mother would let him keep the gift, he told Frau Beckmann.

"Of course she will. She'll be delighted to see how well Johannes's clothes fit you. May he rest in peace."

The Beckmanns' youngest child was still in high school when the Great War started, and two years later, he'd been accepted at the University of Berlin. But instead, he joined the Army.

"My poor boy would be an engineer now, but he wanted to follow in the footsteps of his dead brothers, may *they* rest in peace. Don't go, we told him, but sons that age don't pay any attention to their parents. He died like all my boys, on his first day in the trenches in 1916. A waste. Don't tell Herr Beckmann I told you. He doesn't like to talk about it."

Arno folded up his tattered old clothes.

"Why're you folding them? We'll throw them in the fire!"

He didn't care. His mother had already given up trying to mend all the holes. He put down the bundle and put on his frayed coat.

"Leave the coat and boots, too."

"No. Not the coat."

"But you have a new one here. Well, not new, but we kept the moths away. Don't you like it? It smells of camphor but—"

"I do like it. I'll put it on top of mine."

"But yours smells awful, Arno."

Arno knew. He couldn't ignore the warm aroma that emanated from his body and the wool of his thirdhand overcoat, invading his nose with each swing of the axe. But no matter how much the lady insisted, Arno wouldn't budge. He was grateful for the fine underwear, the two pairs of socks, the pants, the shirts, the thick sweater, the mountaineering boots. But he left the house with his old—but treasure-filled—coat under the new one.

Another day, Herr Beckmann called to him from his window. It was very early.

"I haven't chopped the wood yet."

"Doesn't matter. Arno, did you hear the bombs?"

No one could have missed the explosions creeping closer. Last night, it had been his mother who'd urged him to keep reading, for two reasons: to find out how the duel between D'Artagnan and the three musketeers would unfold, and to distract from the bombs.

"It won't be long before the Russians arrive. What're you going to do, child?"

Arno didn't have an answer. "What should I do?"

"I'll watch everything from here. You pack provisions and come for Frau Beckmann before leaving, if that's possible."

"What about you?"

"Arno. My father died in the Franco-Prussian War; my sons, in the Great War. I didn't have a war in my youth in which to die, so this one'll have to do. No, no," he said before Arno could interrupt. "It's not that I want it. It's just that I know it. To survive, one must move. I can't move, but my wife can. She was never a grandmother. Take her so she can be yours."

Arno had never had a grandmother. Of course he would accept Frau Beckmann.

"She already has everything packed," Herr Beckmann said with relief when Arno agreed. "She thinks she's packing for me, too, child. Don't tell her it's not so."

After that warning, Arno and his mother kept all the most important items close at hand, ready to load onto the cart. The horse, frail despite the efforts they made to obtain food for it, still seemed capable of pulling. Arno's mother walked it a little around the garden and spoke to it, as she did with all the animals in her care. So I don't go crazy and so they don't, she admitted to Arno one day. When spring really arrived and the horse could graze, it would regain its strength. It just had to stay alive until the day when green sprouted from the ground.

Despite the bombings, Arno still went out for firewood and food each day. Herr Beckmann gave him more money: Get as much as you can, he said. Hoard food but spend all the money. Don't save, don't be frugal. The Russians won't give you a crumb, and our money will be useless.

Every day, before going out to do his chores, Arno put on his old coat under his new one, folded up his quilt, hid his books between the folds, and headed to the coach house. He packed everything in the cart, from which he took out the axe. Every day, when he returned, he put the axe back in its place in the cart and took out his quilt and books. His mother did the same.

That day, the city center was impassable, even for a boy with agile feet. Arno stopped to watch cautiously from a corner. What remained of the Army had retreated here.

"Keep back," said one of the movie theater boys, instantly a friend once more. "I was the only one who managed to get away. They took all the others."

There was no point explaining that he was only ten years old.

"Go to your mother," Arno told him.

"What mother? Mine left months ago with my younger brothers and sisters."

Arno turned away, grateful to still have his. He had to get back. That morning, like every morning, she'd told him if he had any doubt, if there was any danger, he must run straight home.

For a few days now, the tension had been palpable: the explosions were moving closer, and the soldiers had taken to hunting deserters who'd changed their uniforms for civilian clothing. Arno tried not to look at the crows feasting on the bodies that swung in the wind. The loss of any pretense told him the end was imminent.

He took the shortest route home, but that meant he had to cross the park where Johann and Fritz had seen a soldier give a young girl the coup de grâce before throwing her into a pit of executed prisoners.

Treading on its surface, Arno thought, was like desecrating a grave. The snow hid everything. There was no sign of marks from pickaxes and spades, no evidence of the recently covered pits, or even of bomb craters. But that day, there was something in the air, something that made him hurry, cut straight through, forget his respect and fear, decide that he'd ask for forgiveness, but that he had to pass through.

It hurt him to tread there, and with each step he said, sorry, girl, sorry, girl, and he tried to make himself as light as the crows hopping across the snow without leaving prints, but his new boots left a record for the dead of his slow and clumsy passage.

Then the whole flock of crows took flight, and he wished he could fly with them, make himself small, not be the only dark mark in the center of that tragic place covered in immaculate white. He tried to quickly dig a tunnel like the ones he'd dug with Adolf Müller when he was little, but he wasn't a field mouse or a rabbit, and the aircraft was coming straight for him.

Arno gave up trying to hide. He threw himself facedown on the snow, but then rolled onto his back to look up at the sky. He stared without blinking, without daring to breathe, straight at the airplane that, flying low, was hunting him. He admired it: its propellers, the sound of its two engines, its underbelly, its retracted wheels, its colors, its illegible Russian lettering, the wings that lifted it like a bird. A talking bird, Arno was surprised to discover, because instead of dropping bombs or showering him with bullets, it mocked him.

"Volkssturm boy! Go home to your mother! *Deutschland ist kaputt!* Don't fight, and you'll live to be as old as your Vaterland!"

Then the plane rose higher and left him there. Arno breathed, sunk into the snow, and still without blinking, followed its flight. He hadn't seen bombs under its wings; its only weapon seemed to be its megaphone. It wasn't a warplane; it was a mocking plane. That was all it had wanted to do: make a solitary child want to hide in a tunnel.

Furious but still filled with terror, he kept his eyes on it. When he understood that the aircraft was turning around with the intention of finding him again, Arno ran, without apologizing to the dead now. He ran to hide in the ruins of two houses, crouching motionless at the edge of the park. He didn't want to hear that metallic voice speaking to him in heavily accented German. He didn't want to give the plane—its pilot—another opportunity to make him cry.

Holding his sweetheart's hand one night as they watched fireworks fill the hot summer sky of a very different country, Arno would be struck by his own recklessness of that day. And then the astonishment and the questions would come. Why did a boy roll over to look at the airplane he believed would kill him? Why did he want to see it drop its bomb? Why, for a moment, would he have preferred to be bombed than mocked? Because he'd never seen an airplane so close, because his curiosity and awe were stronger than his fear. Because he still hadn't gotten to pore over books of gears and cogs, machines great and small. And because the bomb would only have hurt once, but the mockery would hurt for the rest of his life.

He didn't tell his mother what had happened. He did tell Herr Beckmann.

"They know there's no resistance now. Do you have everything ready?"

That night, his mother insisted on reading the Bible, but then she said: We'll have some of those musketeers afterward, don't you think?

The first spring sun came out that Saturday, and the Russian planes arrived to celebrate it. Arno and his mother didn't go out for firewood or even the latrine.

That Sunday, the Schippers, huddled together in the bunker that before it became their home had once been the servants' area of an elegant house, couldn't distinguish one bomb from another, one tremor from the next. His mother prayed; Arno listened. His mother said, we're together, mein *Kind*, mein Arno. And while he listened, he recalled the words of the movie hero: You know our fate if we do not win this battle! Fräulein Stieglitz's tunnels . . . You . . . Will there be anything left of them tomorrow? . . . know . . . What would Herr Beckmann say? . . . our fate . . . What would D'Artagnan do? . . . if we do not win . . . What could Arno do? . . . this battle! . . . Nothing.

That night, there was neither the Bible nor any musketeers to distract them.

The next morning, with the first break in the bombing, and against his mother's wishes, Arno went out. Fräulein Stieglitz's garden was intact, though the snow was gray from the dust. The horse had kicked the walls of the coach house, but when Arno offered it some hay, it was content enough and ate. Arno took his axe and went out onto what remained of the street with more caution than usual. He had to ask Herr Beckmann what to do. Was it time to leave? If he found anything made from wood on the way, he'd take them some, he decided. But he had to hurry. He could hear the machine guns of a pitched battle to the south. He guessed it was the Russians trying to invade the city.

As Arno turned the corner, he already had his hand half-raised to wave to Herr Beckmann at his window. But his hand dropped, and the air rushed out of him. There was no window. There wasn't even a house.

He ran home, collapsing at the door. His mother was out with the horse, and he was glad. He didn't want to see her, didn't want to be seen. He couldn't breathe, couldn't think. His body was splitting in two. Then he peered into Fräulein Stieglitz's tunnels. Still there. He crawled in. He breathed in dust, but there among the admired geometry that formed well-traveled paths, he was able to think again and recognize the pressure in his body for what it was: pent-up tears. He didn't want to let them out inside his labyrinth; they would be so fierce, he thought, they'd shake the foundationless structure and bring it down.

He wondered whether tunnels had been left under the Beckmann house. He wondered whether, if he explored there, he would find the two of them as he'd found Fräulein Stieglitz.

It was his first experience of people dear to him dying violently because of the war. He understood that many died every day, but he didn't know them. The Hitzig widow's death didn't count anymore: it had happened in another life, when his original family was still his world. With the Beckmanns, out of the rubble, he'd created a new family.

How long had that family lasted? He didn't know, exactly. Arno still marked his days on the underground wall in Fräulein Stieglitz's house, but he'd stopped counting them, stopped grouping them. Now he measured time in finds, in chases, in losses. One day, he'd gone out for firewood, and he'd returned with grandparents. That had been the biggest of all his finds: a family that lasted from the day it was found until the bomb. A lifetime.

Until he saw the beautiful house turned into a pile of bricks, he didn't know what it felt like to lose everything. He'd lost his old life, too, but gradually. With one heartbreak, and then another, and another, it had faded away. He missed his father, brothers, and sister every day. But perhaps they had only been scattered; perhaps they still lived. Perhaps.

In his new life, he'd lost everything all at once with the remote and anonymous press of a button while he wasn't looking, while his mother held him, while he was thinking about . . . what? D'Artagnan's heroism? *He* would've gone to rescue his grandmother at the sound of the first plane. He would've plunged into the rubble and found her as soon as the bombing stopped.

Perhaps any brave man would've run to rescue Frau Beckmann. Perhaps Arno, had he been older, would have arrived in time, dodged bombs and flying rubble, and deposited her in one piece in his mother's arms. But Arno hadn't known how to leave his mother's arms; he hadn't known how to open his eyes when the explosions had pummeled his ears. He was still a ten-year-old boy, afraid, not a hero.

On one occasion, he'd asked Herr Beckmann if he wasn't afraid of being killed by a bomb. Because, no matter how much his mother told him, if we die, we'll die together, Arno *was* afraid.

Son, bombs are like lightning; they never strike the same place twice.

Arno was reassured. It meant that no more bombs would fall on him and his mother because they lived in a bombed-out house. But he'd forgotten the Beckmanns.

Anyway, if they fall, Herr Beckmann had continued, don't you think it could be because you've been chosen to leave this life and go to the next? I'm not afraid of being killed by a bomb. What frightens me is living and knowing that I've lost everything. All I have left is my wife and you, Arno. Don't forget that.

Arno didn't know how to respond to those last words. I should go, my mother's calling, he'd said, stammering. Days later, he was still unsure how to reply, so he'd put the words away. For later. Now it was too late.

Hidden in the tunnels, which were well lit for the first time by the bright spring sun filtering through the gaps, with his heart as broken as all the houses, Arno hoped that the old man was right and that he'd been chosen to leave this life to go to the next, accompanied by his wife. Later, he'd say the Lord's Prayer for them, but he didn't yet have the strength to bring together those words as dispersed as the dust. Why did words fail him when they mattered most? Why hadn't he told Herr Beckmann everything he felt? He rued his silence. Herr Beckmann had given him advice and a grandmother, and now it was too late to tell him: Let's go together.

That day, the old man had declared his affection for him, but a few days before, he'd also given their closeness an expiry date that would depend on the Russians. Arno hadn't been ready to fully comprehend Herr Beckmann's explanation: I can't move, but you can; I don't have a future, but you do. With those half-understood words, he'd given him a vision of the future that Arno had lost, though he didn't know when or where. When did he stop believing that his father would return? When he saw the look of despair as he left? On the way to Königsberg? And when did he stop believing he'd be reunited with his brothers? From the moment they said goodbye?

In Königsberg, Arno had learned to live day to day, to say: Today I found firewood, I tracked down food, I'm not so hungry, today was a good day. He'd stopped thinking, when I grow up, when I have my first communion, I'll understand everything, just like Helga promised. Herr Beckmann had managed to make the child dream again, to plan and make vows such as, when I grow up, I'll never be hungry or cold. All other vows depended on that first being fulfilled. But the second was: When I grow up, I'll find my family.

But the future wasn't what Herr Beckmann had promised. And bombs weren't like lightning: the neighborhood was proof of that. And he'd miscalculated. They hadn't had time to flee as the old man had planned: watching through his window while a new family of three—a grandmother, a daughter, and a grandson—went off to start a new life.

For the first time, Arno understood that no one knew everything. Not Helga, who'd had her first communion, not his mother, not even Herr Beckmann. He would mourn that day's loss forever, but if there was one thing he learned from the experience, it was that war was like that: it bombards, but whoever emerges from the ruins better get up and carry on living. He had a future; Herr Beckmann had been right about that. He wasn't going to give it up again for anyone or anything.

He couldn't do it alone, but he wasn't alone. They were a decimated family—a boy and a mother with a faulty heart—but the war hadn't killed them. Not yet. They were obliged to make a future even if it was just for two. He'd speak to his mother; he'd tell her about the Beckmanns' advice and warmth. About their death. About Fräulein Stieglitz's tomb, the piece of furniture with the foxes, partridges, and geese, what it still contained and what he'd taken. He would confess he'd carried a small treasure of amber in the lapel of his coat ever since their return from the port. He hoped she'd understand; he hoped she'd let him keep it. It could mean the difference between life and death, he would make her see. Together, they'd make a plan.

He crawled out of the tunnel and went out into the garden. Above him there was only the sun's rays in the freezing air, and all around, the strange smell of a destroyed city. In the distance, he could hear artillery. The battle wasn't moving closer yet. It wouldn't be long before it did. *Deutschland ist kaputt,* the pilot had said, mockingly perhaps, but truthfully. The battle for the Vaterland was lost. No words from any hero of the big screen could change their fate; no words from any hero were as valid as those his mother had said in that other life: What we saw outside is a woman's war. Forget the Vaterland. Women go to war for their children. I'll fight for my children, for you, but I need your help.

Together, they'd fight.

How natural it would've been for the Arno of before to yell Mutter! And how natural her reply would have been, also at the top of her voice: *Was ist los?* But that before was gone. The now demanded low voices, discretion, stealth. At all times.

He went to the stable where his mother, on her knees, was trying to gather up the hay stalks that had escaped the horse's mouth to give it perhaps another mouthful.

*"Mutter, komm,"* Arno whispered to her.

Alarmed, she whispered back.

*"Was ist los?"*

# 53. The collapse of the walls

***April 9, 1945***

The next day, the German commanders surrendered to the Soviets. The great walled city, referred to by the Führer as an "invincible bastion of the German spirit," had fallen, marking the official defeat of East Prussia.

The world would learn about the event from the Russian press. In Germany, they would try to silence or minimize the news. Let it not be said at home that Adolf Hitler had lost not only the German offensive but now even the defense of the Vaterland itself.

It would take much longer for the world to admit and bemoan what happened next, what happened inside the walls of the former fortress of the Teutonic knights and throughout the region once called Prussia, after its surrender to an army hungry for revenge.

# 54. False promises
## The Hahlbrocks

***April 1945***

Wanda opened her eyes. It was half past five in the morning. Time to get up.

Every day now, she and the other women milked the cows, fed them, and cleaned the barn because, without warning, the Army had taken away all the Polish Zivilarbeiter.

What do they need them for, Grethe had wondered.

They didn't need them, but with the Russians so close, they feared that they'd escape and join the battle against their masters. The Army had gathered them to make them disappear. All except Janusz. He was safe.

It doesn't matter, said Grethe. The spring is late, so there isn't so much work yet. I suppose they'll send us some new ones for sowing time . . .

But even in a winter that refuses to go away, there's a lot to do on a farm. Wanda was used to hard work but of another kind, inside the house. Farmwork exhausted her, wrecked her hands. Irmgard, still just fourteen, woke up whimpering every day: her entire body hurt. Erna was the same, but the worst was that the strenuous labor had stopped her milk. Crystl cried and Erna cried: she'd taken it for granted that, so long as she had milk to give her daughter, the baby wouldn't die of hunger. "Now what am I going to do?" she asked Wanda.

"Stop crying, for starters," she replied. "And the same to you, Irmgard. We're going to work; we're going to save. The war can't last much longer."

"And then Papa will come back . . ."

Wanda smiled, but she didn't respond. She wouldn't make unfounded promises. Hartwig returning was her deepest wish, not a certainty, just as the Führer's promises that they'd win the war had been only that: a wish.

What's going through the Führer's mind now that he's surrounded by Russians, Britons, and Americans, she wondered. Would he one day ask forgiveness for lying to them all in his efforts to deceive himself? On the farm, Wanda turned on the radio at every opportunity, less to hear the news—much of which she didn't believe—than to hear an improbable apology.

But so far, nothing. So far, the radio had all been music, encouragement, pleas for solidarity in the final war effort, and tales of hardship everywhere. More and more hardship. The war consumed everything. Even the youth of her eldest daughter, whom she no longer wanted to deceive.

Enough! she told herself that Sunday before dawn. No more complaints, Wanda.

Wanda took a deep breath and threw off the warm quilt in a single movement. She got up. She splashed freezing water on her face and quickly brushed her teeth. While she dressed, she heard noises in the kitchen.

Curious, she went out. Irmgard and Ilse were still asleep in the living room. Kaiser was following Janusz as he paced anxiously in the kitchen.

The young man looked at her.

*"Was ist los?"* Wanda whispered, surprised to see him in the house so early.

"Frau Hahlbrock. We need to get out of here. Let's go, now."

Hartwig had told her to listen to Janusz.

"Why?"

"I went out walking and reached the defense line."

"Again? Janusz, you know how danger—"

"The Army's expecting something, Frau Hahlbrock," he insisted. "They're reinforcing with a lot more troops and tanks. The Russians are coming."

"And if we wait . . ."

"We risk getting caught up in the battle here. Have you heard anything on the radio?"

She shook her head. They hadn't said anything. But they wouldn't.

"All right," Wanda said, exasperated with herself for trying to put off the inevitable. "Let's go."

Her family, like Berlin, like the Führer, was surrounded by enemies. Which should they choose? Were some enemies better than others?

Wanda put a hand on the young man's arm. "Thank you, Janusz. But don't say anything to the children or my mother. I'll tell them."

Wanda woke Irmgard and Erna. She broke the news quietly as they walked to the barn: the cows couldn't wait. The women returned with a wheelbarrow of hay for the horses, potatoes, eggs, milk, and cheese, which Wanda added to what they'd saved up.

Next, they said goodbye. Wilhelm told them he wouldn't leave his farm. If he did, he'd have to report to the Wehrmacht. And Grethe wouldn't leave him.

"Besides, Wanda, you're overreacting."

They spent the afternoon packing and cleaning, while Ilse kept the little ones distracted. Then, with Hartwig's map, they made a plan.

"I have a brother," Wanda's mother said.

Wanda had been Freddy's age the last time she saw Uncle Albert. She barely remembered him.

"He has a farm in the north. Near Schleswig."

They studied the map. It would take a long time to travel nearly to the Danish border, and that was without counting the detour they'd have to take to avoid the siege of Berlin. But heading northwest would get them away from the Russians without bringing them closer to the territory that the British and Americans now occupied to the west.

"Do you think he'll take us in?"

"That apostate was never a very good brother, but what choice do we have?"

What choice did they have? None. Janusz was the one most relieved by the quick decision.

"Let's go, then," he said. "Now."

"How will Erna and I cope alone? Who will help us drive the cart?" her mother said.

"You won't be alone, Mother," said Wanda. "We'll all help each other. Janusz will help all of us. We'll travel in short stretches."

"Irmgard can travel in our cart. She can help with Crystl."

"No. My children stay with me."

Grandma Hannah fixed her eyes on Wanda's, but Wanda returned the look, unyielding. It was Erna who broke the tense silence.

"It's OK, Frau Bendzius, you and I will keep each other company."

They marked that night's leg of the journey on the map. Due to the spring daylight, each stretch of nighttime travel would have to be much shorter than the previous winter.

Leaving the cabin, closing the door, was very painful. They'd rested there and regained some strength and some provisions. It was almost as difficult as the day they'd left their own farm. Why? Everything and everyone was on the carts, ready to leave. Everything was clean. Grethe couldn't complain about the guests she hadn't invited.

Wanda sat in the empty space beside Janusz on the driver's bench. The place she would occupy on the journey was the one that had belonged to Hartwig. The void she felt suddenly made sense.

It was Hartwig; it was the part of him she'd kept alive even when she was alone in the cabin they'd shared for two short weeks.

When the cabin's door closed, that chapter closed. The war had forced them to break their promises, to allow themselves to be separated. Not knowing where he was, fleeing the refuge where he'd left them, Wanda felt as if she were abandoning her husband. How would they find each other again?

"Are you all right?" the young man asked her.

Once again, reluctant to promise or lie, Wanda chose not to answer.

"Let's go, Janusz," she said firmly.

They all spent the first few minutes in silence. Even the babies seemed infected by the adults' feeling: the desperation of not knowing what the future held for them.

# 55. Eve's curse

Ilse was surprised when they stopped to rest at an empty granary. Where were all the travelers they'd seen before they reached Cousin Wilhelm's farm? It felt strange, lonely. And it was cold, because lighting a fire inside a granary was too dangerous. Being inside a granary was only a little better than being outside.

That day, when they'd finally settled the little ones, Irmgard woke up, pale, her stomach hurting. Ilse went with her to the outdoor toilet. From outside, she heard Irmgard start crying.

"Ilse, fetch Mama."

"But she's asleep . . ."

*"Ilse, schnell!"*

Alarmed, Ilse ran with Kaiser at her heels. She took over with Helmut, who'd just woken up, while their mother rushed off. Before long, the two of them returned from the toilet with serious expressions, their arms interlocked. Irmgard, tearful, lay down again.

"Mama says we won't travel tonight."

"Do you feel very sick?"

*"Ja."*

"What is it?"

"Nothing."

"With that face, it can't be nothing."

"Ilse, you're too young to understand."

But it had to be serious, because their mother gave Irmgard all the Christmas napkins and even Grandma approached to stroke her hair almost gently. Ilse heard her grandmother say something about enduring the pain of Eve's curse. What was that?

Something bad, judging by Irmgard's face. Ilse couldn't see her own, but the state of her mother's and Irmgard's worried her. Now that they helped Janusz drive the cart at night, their skin was frostbitten: they no longer had the luxury of cod liver oil with zinc because the little bit left was needed for Helmut.

"Anyway," her mother joked, "who wants to go through life smelling like diapers?"

That night, instead of driving the cart, Janusz went out with Kaiser. To set traps, he said. Perhaps they'd catch a rabbit. Ilse fell asleep with that promise in mind. She hadn't tasted meat for a long time.

The next morning, they were sitting on the ground, inside their sacks, sleepy but anxious. Waiting in the cold. Janusz had arrived early with bad news: no rabbits. Helmut and Edeline had runny noses and Ilse was in charge of wiping them, since her mother and Aunt Erna had gone to the farmhouse to ask if they could use a stove to heat bricks, boil diapers, defrost milk, and cook potatoes. They were all hungry. Irmgard didn't speak, but she looked better. Janusz was inspecting the cart. The only one missing was Kaiser.

"Janusz, have you seen Kaiser?"

"A little while ago, around that corner."

Ilse found him eating corn.

"No, Kaiser! *Böser Hund!*"

But Kaiser didn't even look up. Being a bad dog didn't seem to matter if it meant filling his belly.

"You're a dog, not a cow. You'll get a bellyache like Irmgard."

Janusz approached, curious.

"He's hungry," he said to Ilse. "Yesterday, he took them by surprise, but the mice won't come back out until the dog's gone."

"But he can't eat cow food," said Ilse.

"It's not the best thing, but I don't think it'll harm him. Still, I'll take him hunting again. Who knows, we might come back with rabbits for everyone. *Kaiser: komm!*"

# 56. Kaiser and the wolves

Janusz went out with Kaiser that morning to hunt but got sidetracked helping the women with a heavy load they were carrying. Afterward, he looked around: the dog was gone.

Kaiser never gets lost, he told himself. Nevertheless, he went after him. He'd take the opportunity to set more traps. With luck, they'd have rabbit or squirrel for dinner that night before setting off.

He was able to make out some paw prints in the snow, but they disappeared. Kaiser would come find him, he thought. He laid his traps. There was complete silence in the forest.

Suddenly, in the distance, Janusz heard barking; he ran toward the sound. As he got closer, men's voices emerged, excited shouts.

He approached the small clearing with caution. There, five ragged soldiers armed with knives encircled the bleeding dog that they'd tied to a tree by his neck. As much as Kaiser fought to free himself, the rope wouldn't give, and his wild barking was now turning into squeals. A daring soldier managed to drive his knife into the dog's leg, and Kaiser let out a squeal of pain before collapsing, alive but defeated. The pack closed in.

Janusz closed his eyes; he didn't want to see any more. He turned and ran without caring how much noise he made. But even with his back turned, his ears worked and so did his imagination. He'd arrived too late. And what else could he have done, armed only with the cord for his traps? All he could do was run. Raise the alarm.

He called to her from a distance.

"Frau Hahlbrock."

He was out of breath from the run, the cold starting to freeze his sweat-soaked hair. She approached.

*"Ja?"*

"Kaiser went hunting without me. But I found him."

And he told Frau Hahlbrock how. She turned pale and bent over a little, as if punched in the stomach. That was how he felt, too: as if he'd taken a blow whose effect wouldn't subside. Janusz thought he should help her sit, offer her water, but she recovered in an instant.

"Janusz, fetch the gun."

"Frau Hahlbrock, what're you—"

"Bring it loaded. *Schnell!*"

Janusz led her to the clearing in the forest. Frau Hahlbrock didn't stop cautiously at the periphery: she strode into the clearing as if it belonged to her, like a forest goddess, armed with her fury and a double-barreled shotgun.

"Halt!"

The men stopped immediately, accustomed as soldiers are to fear and obeying strong voices.

"That dog is mine."

They'd interrupted the soldiers while they butchered the animal. Kaiser's head was set to one side, and his skin had almost been separated from his body.

"It was a wild dog."

"Liars, as well as murderers? My dog had a collar. That red one there."

"You don't know what it's like to be hungry," one sniffed.

"We're Prussians. Do you think we came this far without hunger?"

"Not enough, or the dog wouldn't have made it here alive," another sneered.

Wanda stood firm. Inspired, Janusz tried to do the same.

"That dog is mine."

"What difference does it make now?"

"You're going to give it to me."

They laughed.

"To give it a Christian burial?"

"To eat, seeing as you've done us the favor."

Their laughter stopped. Janusz stared at her, almost as red faced as the men.

"And if we don't?"

"If you don't, my son will run to alert the battalion we saw a short distance away," she said, gesturing at Janusz with her eyes. He nodded. "They'll find you, and when they do, I can assure you, you won't be hungry for much longer."

The men exchanged looks.

"We could share."

"Yes. We could. You'll give us the hind legs. We'll leave you the rest."

Before the men could protest, Wanda aimed the shotgun.

*"Schnell!"*

She and Janusz walked away, fast, without speaking. He followed her with a skinned leg in each hand, making sure the blood didn't drip on his pants. They felt unspeakably heavy. Frau Hahlbrock carried the shotgun, but she seemed to struggle with its weight, too, her breathing loud and then labored. Was she crying? Janusz wasn't sure. *He* wasn't crying, yet.

"Don't take those into the granary," she said breathlessly. "Gather branches, make a small fire near the edge of the woods. I'll tell Erna to bring the pot and a knife to cut the meat from the little *deer* you caught. Understood?" She waited for Janusz to agree. "I'll send you some potatoes and an onion. I'm sorry to ask you to do this, Janusz, but you're going to have to cook the stew. I don't feel well. I'm going to lie down for a while."

Janusz nodded, unable to find his voice.

"Janusz? Those men—" She paused. "I've never been so scared in my life."

Janusz looked at her with admiration.

"They weren't men, Frau Hahlbrock. They were wolves."

# 57. With empty hands

If she closed her eyes, she could still see Kaiser's. Dead, looking at her. And that was why Wanda scarcely slept anymore. She was glad: it meant she drove, and Janusz and Irmgard could rest.

What would she say to Hartwig? The same thing she'd said to the family, to Ilse? That it was time to go and the dog hadn't come back. That they'd heard at the farm the Soviets were close. That they'd already lost a day there—because your little girl became a woman—and they couldn't waste another minute.

Would he cry as Ilse had for hours? It was better than admitting they'd made the most of his meat. Better than telling him that, when they all congratulated the great hunter and cook, Janusz said nothing, just lowered his gaze; that, smiling and grateful, they all devoured their meager portions; that Ilse said, Kaiser will love the bones, and Janusz choked on his mouthful; that no one realized he was missing until the end, until they climbed on the cart and Ilse asked, where's Kaiser?

How could Wanda admit to Hartwig that, though she'd refused the stew Janusz prepared that night—Grandma Hannah eyeing her and the dish knowingly—on the second day, hunger won out, and she ate gratefully?

The stew lasted them seven days. Now, another week later, they all ate their boiled potatoes with nostalgia for Janusz's venison. The children would ask, when will you trap us another one? They're not easy to find because of the war, he'd reply.

He was asleep on the bench beside her, exhausted. Erna's cart had gotten stuck in a muddy, half-frozen rut made, Janusz thought, by military trucks. Pulling it out had been difficult, despite the horses' strength. Now Wanda was holding the reins, and she knew that she was heading in the right direction, but she didn't think they'd reach shelter before daybreak. Tomorrow would be May 1, and the closer they got to summer, the earlier dawn came. That lost hour had cost them. It was a dangerous mistake. They'd spend the day in the forest, she decided.

She looked up at the sky. Nothing. Perhaps around the next bend they'd find a safe place to stop, she thought. The forest made way for the road, but nothing else.

"Janusz."

She was sorry to wake him.

*"Ja?"*

Wanda almost laughed at the young man's efforts to pretend he wasn't sleeping.

"It's all forest here. I don't think we'll find anywhere to pull off."

She could see the dawn now.

"What shall we do?"

"Stop."

"Yes, but where? Help me find somewhere."

When they turned the next bend, the forest's shadows vanished. Ahead, they saw military vehicles abandoned on the roadside. But Wanda was confused. If they were abandoned, why did she hear the sound of engines?

Just as someone called to them from inside the forest, Janusz leapt up.

"We need to get off the cart. Now!" he said, pointing at the sun.

Wanda pulled back the canvas while Janusz jumped down to grab the horses.

"Children! Wake up! There are planes coming. Get out, quickly! Irmgard, get Edeline. Come on, Freddy. Ilse! Ilse! Pick up Helmut."

The sound was growing louder. Wanda climbed down from the cart. Irmgard got out with Edeline. A soldier gestured at the two girls to take shelter in the forest, and they ran toward him. Ilse, awake now, clambered into the front with Helmut in her arms. Freddy followed. Wanda held up her hands to receive her children.

"Freddy. Come on. Quick! Ilse, pass me Helmut."

The first bomb fell: a nearby truck exploded. The horses ripped their reins from Janusz's hands and bolted, taking the cart and half the family toward aircraft that were coming for more.

Wanda was left in the middle of the road with empty hands held high, and all she could think to do was yell: "Don't let go of Helmut, Ilse! Don't let go!" Her throat tore, but she didn't feel it. The terrified horses were dragging the cart at full speed, bumping along the battered road. "Don't let go of him!" She wanted to run after them, but Janusz stopped her.

The engines droned. For a moment, the cart seemed to float, then crashed back to the ground. Earth and metal flew in all directions. And there Wanda stood, in the middle of the road, with her hands empty.

"My children!"

Janusz pulled her away.

"Don't let go of him!" He led her into the shadows of the trees. "Don't let go!" He laid her on her front on the forest floor. But she never took her eyes off the road, never even blinked, until earth rained on her, until she was covered in pine needles. With her eyes closed, she finally forgot Kaiser's dead eyes, that vision displaced by the terror on Ilse's face in that final moment they'd had to look at each other. That, and her own empty hands, broke Wanda's heart.

# 58. The geese

The world exploded. Her mother was there and then not there. But as she disappeared, she yelled, don't let go of him, and that cry rang in Ilse's ears louder than the horses' screams. Louder than hooves and wheels slamming against the hard earth. Louder than the engines overhead, than the thundering explosions, than the fires that banished the iciness from the air, than her brothers' sobs.

Don't let go of him, Ilse! She wanted to shout, I won't let go, with the same force she used to grip Helmut, but forming words would have weakened the conviction in her arms. And the cart was intent on tearing her brother from her, on throwing them into the air, but she fought with everything she had in that blurred, frozen, burning world that suddenly enveloped them.

The horses' initial jolt had made her fall back on the bench that was still warm from her mother and Janusz. With her arms full, she could only use her shoeless feet to try to gain a foothold on the smooth floor.

And Helmut cried in her arms like he'd never cried before, and Freddy cried behind her, and the flock of furious geese approached in unison, pouring their rage and their hot, thick, pink-lake urine down on them, showering everything, and her arms were useless for protecting the baby from the viscous liquid.

The cart tossed relentlessly. The horses galloped and shrieked. But now Helmut had stopped, Ilse realized, relieved. Hush now, she thought. Hush now. She nestled him into her shoulder a little more snugly. She was running out of strength in her arms, they were cramping, but don't let go of him, Ilse, don't let go of him, don't let go. She crossed them tighter over her brother's little body. Her ears hurt from Freddy's continued screams and from the explosions. Hush now, Freddy, like when he was a baby, but Freddy didn't hear her. And the geese kept coming, and the horses kept running, and she couldn't say to them, hush now, horses, you can stop now, let me down, let me rest.

One of the horses tripped and the cart jumped, throwing Ilse onto the wooden floor. But she didn't drop Helmut, who, lying against her shoulder, remained asleep. The world lost its blurry quality, it came back into focus, it stopped amid fire and ice. The sky was clear of geese. Ilse leaned back against the bench, relieved: it was over. It seemed.

But the horses kept shrieking. Ilse was still skittish with the large animals. She barely dared brush them. How did Janusz console them when they screeched like this? What did he say? But she couldn't remember their docile horses making such sounds before, horrible sounds that seemed to be subsiding now, thanks to a soft voice speaking to them.

Janusz?

Ilse got to her feet using only the power in her legs. Hush now. She wouldn't let go of Helmut for anything, not even to get up. She wouldn't wake him.

The gentle voice didn't belong to Janusz. It was a stranger, a soldier. When he saw her, he seemed surprised.

"*Kind!* Are you all right?"

Ilse wanted to tell him to lower his voice, that he'd wake her little brother and make Freddy cry. But she couldn't. And Freddy was already crying. She just nodded.

"Do you want to pass me the baby?"

*Don't let go of him, Ilse!* Her mother's words still rang in her half-deaf ears. The man had a kind face, but even so, Ilse shook her head.

"I'll lift you down. Is that your brother crying in the back?" he asked as he carefully deposited her on the grass. "What's his name?"

She wanted to tell him. But she couldn't. If she tried, she'd drop Helmut. She looked at the forest. She was tired. She'd like to rest against a tree, but the man went away, and she didn't move from where he'd left her. Then he returned, Freddy howling in his arms. He was bleeding. Poor Freddy.

"Can you walk, princess? We must hide in the trees, quickly. Fihn!" he called to another soldier. "Get this cart off the road."

*"Jawohl, Kapitän!"*

The horses didn't want to move. Ilse knew it just from their cries. She was supposed to be taking care of them. She'd do it once she was able to lay Helmut down.

"Quickly, princess!"

Her arms ached, her legs shook, but she obeyed.

# 59. They always pass twice

When the airplanes passed, Wanda wanted to get up right away. Janusz held her.

*"Nein,"* said another man taking shelter under the trees. "These British always come back."

And he was right: the engines faded, then they returned with the same fury. The second time, Wanda pressed her face against the earth.

She didn't try to get up this time. She'd fought and she'd lost everything.

"That's it. They're gone," someone said.

And then voices could be heard everywhere in the forest. They rose from the earth, like hers. Wanda heard some crying that belonged to her. Edeline. Edeline and Irmgard! They *did* make it down; she'd seen them. She'd forgotten.

"Irmgard!" She looked at Janusz. "Find them!"

He charged off, returning quickly with both girls. Edeline threw herself on her mother. Irmgard looked around for her siblings and then looked at Wanda with the unanswerable question. Her eyes filled with tears.

"We don't cry, Irmgard. Look at me," Wanda insisted, though her voice trembled. "We don't cry."

She freed herself from Edeline's arms and got up. Edeline wanted to be carried, but Wanda had to save her strength.

"There'll be more explosions. Some of the trucks carried munitions," one of the soldiers told Janusz, who nodded without saying a word and revealing his accent.

If it were just her, Wanda would run. If it were just her, a bullet could hit her, for all she cared. But it wasn't just her, and she had more children to find. Or pieces of children? No. She couldn't think about that. She had to save her strength.

Janusz followed, carrying Edeline, without looking at Wanda. She didn't look at him, either. She fixed her eyes on the road that her children had disappeared down. With each step they took through the thick curtain of smoke, of burned forest and hot metal, Wanda was afraid of what she'd find.

Irmgard reached for her hand, but Wanda couldn't bear contact with anything, with anyone. The smoke filled every part of her, made her eyes water; those tears weren't hers, no: they were from the smoke.

But then Irmgard said, "Look, Mama," and she gestured at the frozen earth, sprayed everywhere with blood. Blood had pooled in the hoofprints of three runaway horses. Her horses. Her children.

Farther ahead, they found Ilse's doll sprawled in the middle of the road. Irmgard picked it up. Then Irmgard's blackboard, Ilse's shoe, Helmut's sack, mud covered.

Irmgard gathered it up. But all Wanda was searching for was bodies. Helmut's. Ilse's. Freddy's. *Meine Kinder,* she wanted to scream so that her children knew that their mother was searching for them, so that the world knew that a woman had lost her children, but she remained silent.

They'd traveled hundreds of kilometers, but the one they traveled that day, on foot, was the longest. Edeline clung to Janusz's neck, as if afraid he'd drop her, leave her. Irmgard hopped over the puddles of blood. Little by little, out from the trees, out from the smoke, came soldiers who'd managed to escape their vehicles, dazed, surprised to be alive. Some helped the wounded; others dragged the dead. Wanda silently followed the trail of blood, pushing past each curtain of smoke.

Up ahead, they heard a gunshot, a great weight falling, a horse's frightened whinny. Wanda looked at Janusz, who picked up his pace. She did, too. Then they saw the cart, still a hundred paces away. Wanda stopped dead: the canvas cover was riddled with bullet holes.

Wanda ran. She left everyone behind.

*"Meine Kinder!"*

Breathless, in a blink, she was there. She opened the rear curtain and climbed in. Splintered wood, ripped carpet, spilled blood. The sunlight entering through the thousand perforations. But no bodies. She felt hope rise alongside the despair.

She went out to the front and found a terrible scene. Before her, broken horses. Behind, on the canvas, the contents of their bodies spattered by the bullets from the sky. How could her children have survived if these enormous animals were in pieces; if the left one was lying still; if the middle one, wild, was soaked in blood; if the right one's innards were on the ground?

She slumped onto the bench, her eyes darting frantically. They searched among the men emerging from the forest, who looked with pity and then away. The soldier holding her horses' reins was speaking to her, but she didn't hear, she didn't understand.

"Ilse! Freddy!"

The soldier climbed onto the cart.

"I told you. Your children are over there."

*"Meine Kinder?"*

"*Ja.* Come. I'll help you down," he said and took Wanda's shaking hands. "Careful now. One more rung. Schulz!" he called. "Take this lady to her children. Give her your arm so she doesn't trip."

"Mama?"

Janusz and the girls had caught up.

"Come, children. Let's go find the others."

*"Nein!"* said the soldier. "The young man can go with you. Leave the girls here. We'll take care of them."

Wanda saw that the man couldn't look her in the eye. What was waiting in that forest? She took a deep breath and detached herself from Schulz's arm. She straightened.

"Irmgard, stay with Edeline," she whispered.

"But, Mama—"

"But nothing. Sit by the cart. Perhaps a good soldier could do us the favor of fetching a quilt?"

They had to pry Edeline off of Janusz. As they followed Schulz, the little girl's pleas rent the air: "Don't go, Mama! Janusz, stay with me!"

Before entering the forest, Wanda took Janusz's trembling hand and squeezed it; he squeezed back.

Just a short ways into the dim woods, her Freddy's choked pleas rose up even louder than Edeline's.

"Ngo! Eck go! Ngo! Ilhe! Huher! Huher!"

What were they doing to him? Wanda released Janusz's hand. She left Edeline's screams behind and ran toward Freddy's.

The first thing she saw was Ilse with blood-soaked hair, wrapped in an enormous military overcoat. She was on Freddy's back, pinning him down, stroking his bloody hair, saying, "Don't cry, Freddy, don't cry." But he was crying. Screaming. Behind them, a coatless soldier had pulled Freddy's pants and underpants down to the ankles that two other soldiers were holding. Pincers in hand, he was picking at Freddy's backside.

"Freddy!"

Freddy, in his panic, didn't hear Wanda's hoarse voice, but Ilse did, almost getting up to run over.

"No, princess," said the soldier. "Don't move. Thank goodness your mother's arrived! We need her help, don't we?"

She approached and knelt beside her children. She stroked Ilse's cheek, and then rested her own cheek against Freddy's.

"I'm here, Freddy. Everything's going to be fine."

"Huher! Ick hurkh!"

"I know, I know it hurts, but it'll be better soon, you'll see. There, there. I'm right here, but I'm going to help the doctor. No, no, I'm not going anywhere, I'm right here with you."

Wanda looked to the soldier standing over her child.

"How bad is it?"

"He's a very lucky boy. There are several wounds, but none very deep. They'll need stitches, though. A trunk had landed on top of him. I've already pulled out some shards of wood. He also took a blow to the head that will need attention."

"Ilse?"

"Your daughter's unhurt. I checked when I took off her coat."

"Mama?" said Ilse in a small, unrecognizable voice. "I didn't let go of him."

For a moment, Wanda didn't know what she was talking about. Then she did. The soldier quickly looked away, returning to his work.

"Where's Helmut?" she asked in her broken voice.

She looked around frantically.

"I didn't let go of him. He fell asleep, Mama."

"Helmut!"

"I'm sorry," the soldier said, directing his gaze to the base of a tree behind him, out of the children's sight.

She'd forgotten that Janusz was with her. He was sitting there to one side of the tree, hugging his legs. Lying beside him, Wanda saw, was Ilse's brown coat. It covered what they'd laid directly on the ground.

"My son!" The fraying thread of her voice finally broke.

Would her body break in the same way? The pain suggested it would. Wanda held herself around her ribs to keep herself in one piece.

She walked slowly toward the coat, fearing what she'd find under it. Knowing what she'd find under it.

"I didn't let go of him, Mama." Ilse's voice sounded more tired each time she said it.

Wanda stopped. Ilse was her child, too. The one who hadn't let go of her brother. She needed to be comforted.

"I know," Wanda rasped without turning. "You didn't let go of him, my girl."

The boy that was crying, injured, needed her, too. The girls sitting at the edge of the forest. They were all waiting for her. And the baby that slept under his sister's coat was also waiting for her, but with no urgency now.

She approached. Ilse's coat collar had a furrow burned into it where the bullet had skimmed past. Another hair's breadth and Wanda would have lost Ilse, too, with the same projectile. She knew at that moment that, one day, she'd find the strength to be grateful that she'd only lost one of her children. But not today.

Wanda knelt. She uncovered Helmut. Janusz looked away and groaned, almost a protest, but she had to see her son, touch him. Just then she remembered she hadn't changed his diaper before the attack, that she hadn't defrosted milk to give him when he woke. She'd find the forgiveness she needed another day, too. Right now, she'd be angry with herself for letting her baby sleep in a wet diaper. Angry that she hadn't changed it for him one more time. Just one more time.

She forced herself to look at the baby that would never wake up. The bullet that had skimmed Ilse's coat had hit him in the head. She remembered the carnage splashed on the cart's front curtain. Life of her life, flesh of her flesh. What harm had Helmut done for the world to condemn him to die? What had his parents done? Live. That was all. For living where and how they had lived, now they had to pay their debt. She hoped that the world considered it settled.

The baby lying there didn't look like the one who had smiled at her as she'd laid him down to sleep in the cart. He even smelled different. But this was his hand, his ear. He was hers. And he was waiting. But she had other children. She refused to pay her debt with another. She covered her Helmut. She wrapped her arms around the parts of her body that were trying to scatter and got up. With her mutilated voice, she said what had to be said.

"Janusz. Go to the cart and see how the girls are. Then bring me Helmut's bag and the medicine box. And bring the Christmas tablecloth, too. It's in the sack on—I don't know where anymore."

Janusz furrowed his brow. "What for, Frau Hahlbrock?"

"To give him a Christian burial."

Janusz turned and left.

Wanda went to hug Ilse. To take care of Freddy.

# 60. Dying in winter

Winter is not a good time to die. The pickaxe with which the young man tried to dig the grave wouldn't penetrate the frozen earth; its impact echoed in the silent forest.

They had to break up the ground, go deep. The body was waiting; the flesh ice was waiting. Leave me here, it said to the woman who'd been its mother with each whistle of the improvised shroud in the freezing wind. She heard, understood, consented, but she refused to crumble: there were still living bodies to watch over and others, also living, moving ever closer by land and air, who wouldn't hesitate to kill the rest. They had to flee.

"Quickly."

The ground gave way at last to the pickaxe; it gave way to the young man's strength and the mother's will. They dug deep to bury the body well. There was no time, but they were leaving a child she'd fought to protect all his life. She would make sure he was well protected here, too.

She laid him in the bottom herself. Together, the young man and the mother covered him well with the dark earth ice. They consigned him forever to the soil that had witnessed his death.

Then they left without looking back. Without saying a prayer. Without even a few loving words. Without leaving a marker to indicate the place where a beloved life had ended.

They had no time. They had to put one foot in front of the other. They had to make the cart wheels turn again. There were other lives to protect.

Winter is not a good time to die, but in that winter that was so dark, so long that it clawed back any promise of spring, nor was it a good time to live.

# 61. The last Germans

## The Schippers

***May 1, 1945***

The destroyed house hadn't caught the Soviets' attention. It was just one among the many they'd destroyed from afar. In the madness of the conquest, the invasion, the pillage, nobody kept an inventory of destruction, which was why the house had become invisible.

It was better for the victors to explore the structures stubborn enough to remain standing; it was better for them to encircle the surrendering Army, better that the German soldiers began their long march to the gulag as prisoners of war. Better also to find the Prussians hiding in basements, schools, and hospitals; to kill some, rape many, strip all of their shoes and watches. Better, once the initial violent urge had been satisfied, once the officers had brought some order, to set fire to everything.

Ethel and Arno Schipper waited. They knew they'd be found one day. What they didn't know was how to survive when they were. They hid in Fräulein Stieglitz's tunnels when they heard jackboots near, but they couldn't spend all day or night there, so they crept in and out like the rats that had begun emerging at the onset of spring.

Their life consisted of a before and an after. Before and after the Russians came. Before, it had been difficult, uncertain, but the air they breathed belonged to them. After the Russians came, they woke up each morning surprised to see another day. One day, then another day, then another, until the day they were found.

Königsberg's last day.

If the Russians discovered them, they'd kill them, but the cold would, too, if they did nothing to drive it away. After several days shivering, eating what little they had frozen, they decided that a small amount of smoke among all the pyres wouldn't give them away. But they needed firewood.

They started with what they still had close by. When there were no unfamiliar sounds on the street, Arno went out to the coach house to break up the Stieglitzes' old carriage. What does it matter now? his mother said. The woodworm that had been attacking it for years helped. With a single blow he broke the door, which shattered into splinters. But blow by blow, day by day, soon all that was left of the carriage was its space in the coach house and their memory of the first night they'd spent in Königsberg.

So he had to go out for more. Take the risk.

Arno went out feeling like one of the rats he'd observed inside the tunnels, determined not to be detected. Outside, there were no tunnels, but there were labyrinths of rubble, and he knew them better than anyone. He didn't take the wheelbarrow: they'd sacrificed that to the fire, too.

He'd return to the Blomeiers' house for the pillowcase that Frau Beckmann had stopped him from taking. It was past the time for worrying about such things, his mother said. They were living in a bubble of time, an in-between when insignificant things like sins couldn't stand in the way of survival. Goodness was for before, and it would be for afterward, too. They still took out the Bible each night and read. But as for the Commandments, Arno, for the time being, you'll love God and honor your mother, but that's it.

"So take the pillowcase and only carry what you can run back with."

And that was what he did, but each time, he had to go a little farther away. And the days passed, one by one, but they passed. And in that bubble of time his mother said they lived in, hunger didn't show them the same mercy that the Commandments did; it didn't make an exception just because the enemy was prowling outside.

The eggs had run out and the hens had stopped laying. So they ate one, rationing it. Then they boiled the bones twice more and cooked the last potato in the feeble, tasteless broth. Fruit preserves were now just a memory from better days. They scraped the bottom of the sauerkraut keg with their fingernails and peeled off the scraps of dry cabbage that had stuck to the sides. Then they broke the keg into small pieces and, before throwing them on the fire, sucked them until they tasted of nothing except old wood.

They had one hen left, but Ethel didn't want to kill it. She'll lay more eggs, she said hopefully, but the hen wouldn't lay. The rabbit was finally pregnant, so its buck was superfluous, and they ate it. They boiled its bones twice, too, but now they had nothing to add to the broth. That day, after the last boil, his mother broke open the bones and said, Arno, suck out the marrow.

The same day, Königsberg's last, as he darted among collapsed walls, Arno was struck by a smell that promised to fill the hole in his stomach. The Russians only caught him because the aroma reeled him in like a fish on a hook.

Arno had watched them from afar, hidden, he believed. There were three men, but he didn't see the smiles or notice how relaxed they were. He only saw the pieces of fried ham they passed around. His mouth watered and his stomach groaned, but he couldn't take his eyes off it.

Suddenly, he felt a hand seize him by the coat collar.

“Что ты здесь делаешь, мальчик?” said the man with a cavernous voice and the appearance of a bear.

Arno dropped the firewood. The hole he felt now wasn’t from hunger; it was much bigger than that. It made him shake from head to foot.

“Ответь мне, мальчик!”

He didn’t understand what the bear was saying to him.

“What’ve you got there, Little Sasha?” asked another man in a friendly tone and excellent German, putting down his ham and approaching.

*“Ein Spion, Kapitän.”* The bear’s accented German was harsh.

“Are you a spy like Little Sasha says, boy?”

Arno shook his head, but the bear shook him some more.

“Отвечай!”

“Yes. Answer me, boy. Were you spying on us?” His tone didn’t change.

*“Nein! Ich bin kein Spion!”*

“If you’re not a spy, then what’re you doing here?”

“Отвечай!” the bear commanded again.

“I was just gathering firewood, and I smelled your food and—”

“No, *Junge*, what’re you doing in Königsberg? All the Germans left yesterday.”

Arno almost forgot his fear. *“Was?”*

“We went up and down the streets announcing it. Where were you that you didn’t hear?”

“At home.”

“And who do you have at home with you?”

If he didn’t respond, would they expel him from the city alone? If he gave away his mother, would they hurt her?

The bear shook him again.

“My mother’s very sick!” Arno wailed. “It’s her heart. She doesn’t leave the house, and I take care of her. We didn’t know we had to leave.”

He was supposed to take care of her, but he’d informed on her.

"You're the last German in Königsberg, Junge. You and your mother, unless we find more strays," he said, looking at his men, disappointed at their inefficiency.

"We'll leave!"

"We'll escort you home."

"Kapitän, please don't hurt my mother!"

"We Soviets are gentlemen, Junge. Didn't you know that? Walk."

With no alternative, Arno led them to Fräulein Stieglitz's house. If they killed them, they'd die together, he thought. On the way, he tried to hide his limp: he didn't know how they'd react if they discovered the axe he still kept concealed inside his pants. Before going in through the gate, the captain asked whether it had always been his home. Maybe he could see the grandeur and wealth of days gone by, Arno thought.

"No. My father worked for Fräulein Stieglitz. Kapitän?"

"Yes?"

"Please let me go in by myself, so my mother doesn't get frightened."

"I'll go in with you, but we'll leave Little Sasha and the others outside, yes? I'll be a gentleman."

"Do you promise?"

"Word of honor," said the man, looking him in the eye.

There was something in his gaze that made Arno believe him. The soldiers stayed on the street. Arno and the captain closed the gate behind them and went in through the kitchen door. His mother wasn't there. In the cages, only the hen remained. The rabbit's was empty. Where could she be?

"Did she go out?"

"*Nein.* She never goes out."

Arno opened the door that had once led from the servants' area to the main part of the house, where everything had collapsed. A small opening at floor level led into the tunnel. He crouched down and called, his voice trembling.

"Mutter? *Komm, bitte.* There's a captain here who wants to talk to us."

"Coming," they heard from the depths of the tunnel.

"What's in there?"

"Fräulein Stieglitz's tomb," said Arno.

His mother came out with a knife in her hand, but she was shaking so much that Arno snatched it from her easily.

"*Nein, Mutter.* It's nothing to worry about."

"No, nothing to worry about, Frau . . . ?"

"Schipper," she said, trying to firm up her voice.

"Frau Schipper. I'm Captain Aleksandr Solzhenitsyn," he said with a formal bow. "It's an honor." Then he looked at Arno. "We found your son . . . What's your name, Junge?" he asked, smiling.

"Arno."

"Arno was lost, so we brought him home."

"I wasn't lost!" Arno objected.

"A little lost, seeing as all your people have left the city." He ruffled Arno's hair as he said it.

"All our—?" His mother ran out of either words or air, Arno wasn't sure.

"You need to leave the city today," the captain said seriously. "We'll escort you to make sure you get out safely."

"Where will we go?" his mother said, fearful.

"Out in the open air, to wander like all the others. The Soviet Union doesn't care as long as you're not in the city and it doesn't have to feed you."

He observed while they packed the hen's cage and the empty one.

"Is that everything?" he said, surprised.

"We have a cart in the coach house."

The cart was ready to leave, as always. It was the horse they were worried about. They'd already discussed the possibility that it wouldn't be able to pull them, but that day, Arno's mother whispered in the animal's ear while she fitted the harness to its debilitated body, and it pulled the cart when she asked it to. She was the only one who rode. Arno walked shoulder to shoulder with the captain to the city's nearest exit. In his company, they had no trouble. With the open road ahead of them, his mother told Arno to climb on.

"Kapitän, thank you."

"Don't thank me, Frau Schipper. I wish you luck and hope that the war ends for you soon."

"That the war ends. For everyone," she said.

The last Prussians in Königsberg turned away from the man and the city.

"Mutter? What're we going to do?"

"Let's go home. If it's still there."

# 62. History
## The Hahlbrocks

***May 7, 1945***

The world would mark April 30, 1945, in its history books, but not because of an aerial attack on a country road, or because of the end of a life that had barely begun.

The history books record that day as the suicide of the German chancellor Adolf Hitler, along with his wife, Eva. In Berlin, the conversation centered on his will and testament: Who had been left with what? Some didn't want their assignments, and took their own lives, too. Some handed Berlin over to the Soviet Army on May 2, and others did the same with the rest of Germany on May 7.

In no history book is it written that it was on that day, May 7, that Wanda's injured child was able to take his first steps, or that her traumatized girl was able to uncross her arms a little and move without so much pain. That it was on that day that their mother, knowing the immediate danger had passed, would wake up in a borrowed bed and cover herself head to foot to try to create a cocoon of oblivion, but fail, because two questions played and replayed in her mind.

Where's Helmut?

Abandoned in the forest in an unmarked grave.

She'd answered the first question for her daughter: You never let go of him, but he died; he's with God now; it wasn't your fault; you must understand that, Ilse. They weren't geese; they were warplanes. You must understand that.

And Hartwig? Where is Hartwig? Somewhere where he already knows everything, perhaps. Where he knows that his son died, where he knows what is to come, the full debt his family will have to pay. Sometimes, a terrible hope passed through Wanda's mind: Yes, perhaps he has died, too, so he already knows, and I don't have to tell him.

Moments like that one are never recorded in history books. Or in family histories. That recurring moment, full of sorrows and regrets, full of phantom feelings in her hands, which will attack her with identical force every morning for the rest of her life, was one that this mother with the weight of the world on her would keep silent forever. She would never tell anyone how, with those blood-covered hands, she'd wrapped her baby in the Christmas tablecloth, and the blood soaked into the linen and painted new red flowers on the tablecloth already stained with plum jam, Helmut's favorite, because in all the time since they'd last used it, since that breakfast celebration—*eins, eins, eins*—those hands hadn't taken the time to wash it. They'd thought they'd have time later, those hands.

You mustn't leave anything for later, Wanda berated them every day after that day, digging her fingernails into her palms in punishment.

She kept it all to herself; she kept the tears—all of them—to herself, because she had to protect everyone: she was the mother with the weight of the world on her shoulders.

You mustn't leave anything for later, she told herself on May 7, as she'd tell herself every daybreak. And she came out from her cocoon as she'd do every morning of the rest of her life. Despite the cold. Despite the pain.

# 63. Goodbye

## Janusz

***April 30 to May 10, 1945***

When Janusz reached the cart to collect the things Frau Hahlbrock had asked for, the second horse lay dead. With a brief look, he thanked the soldier who'd put the creature out of its misery. With another, he saw that the girls were all right. Edeline was asleep in her sister's arms. Janusz tried to smile at Irmgard.

They only had one horse left. Though it was soaked in blood, he could tell it was uninjured. He found everything Frau Hahlbrock wanted. Before returning to the forest, he spoke to Irmgard.

"Fräulein Irmgard, your mother asked me to tell the soldier that the horses are her property."

She hadn't said anything about it, but Janusz knew her. She wouldn't allow anything to be wasted under any circumstances.

"That she wants to take the legs, at least two. She said they should wrap them in the blankets. And if you can, straighten up the inside of the cart."

"And my brothers and sister?" she asked.

But Janusz had already turned away. He pretended he hadn't heard.

He didn't know which steps were harder: the ones he'd taken without knowing what lay ahead or the ones he took now, aware of what awaited beyond the trees. The first time, walking with Frau Hahlbrock, his heart had halted. It started again when he saw Ilse, blood soaked, but appearing unhurt. He wanted to run to her and lift her into the air, take her somewhere safe, but Freddy was under her, injured. Anyway, it wasn't for him to react in such a way; that was for the mother.

But then he'd spotted Ilse's coat spread on the ground, and once again his heart stopped. It broke for the dead baby, so cheerful and active the day before. It broke more when he saw the comprehension in the eyes of his mother, who after touching Helmut's body had to return to Freddy, who was calling for her.

But Ilse.

Ilse was alone in the confusion. That was her bloodless, invisible wound. I didn't let go of him, she said, but each time she said it, the statement sounded more like a question. She was the same when he returned from the cart, staring into the tree-filled void.

When they'd finished stitching Freddy's legs and hip, they told her to get up. But she couldn't, however much she wanted to. Then Janusz went to her. He lifted her in his arms, and she held him while he rocked her with each step to carry her away from Freddy's persistent crying, to return to Helmut's side. He couldn't leave him alone. He thought he could feel a sob emerging, but when he looked, Ilse's eyes were closed but dry. Good. Better that she didn't see Helmut.

"Are you all right?"

"I didn't let go of him, Janusz," she intoned. And then, "I'm so tired . . ."

Janusz took the huge overcoat off her, then removed his own and laid her on it, wrapping her up in a ball.

"It's all right, Ilse. Rest," he said, patting her on the back with the hand that didn't hurt, as he'd seen his own mother do so many times with his sick sister. "Shh, shh, shh. *Odpocznij, kochana dziewczyna.*"

Rest, dear girl. She immediately fell asleep. Janusz sat like a sentinel between her and Helmut. He wanted to remember the lullaby that his mother sang, but too many years had passed, and his hand hurt.

"Shh, shh, shh . . ." He continued his patting.

A few steps away, Freddy was still crying. They'd cleaned the wound on his forehead and were already stitching it. Poor Freddy, Janusz thought, then immediately tensed up when Schulz approached and sat beside him.

"Kapitän Fischer went out to the cart when he heard the horses. Did you know, he competed in cross-country riding at the Berlin Olympics? He hates to see horses suffer. But he found this brave girl there." The young man gestured to Ilse.

"*Ja.*"

"But she wouldn't let go of the baby. Only when Kapitän Fischer said her other brother needed her did she let him take this one," he said, pointing to Helmut's body. "The older boy's going to be fine. The Kapitän isn't a medic—ours was killed a month ago—but he knows all kinds of things."

"Shh, shh, shh . . ."

The friendly thing would be to respond, Janusz supposed, but what could he say that wouldn't betray his accent?

"Where are you all from?" Schulz asked.

Janusz kept his eyes on Ilse. "East Prussia," he said in a low voice, as if trying not to wake the girl.

"So why aren't you in the war?"

There it was. Janusz tried to make eye contact with Wanda, but she was focused on Freddy. Janusz looked Schulz in the eyes and continued to pat Ilse's back.

"I'm a Polish Zivilarbeiter," he confessed. His head swam.

The young soldier's eyes widened and he glanced around to see if anyone had overheard. He looked at Ilse and Janusz's hand on her back.

"I thought you were a deserter. The Kapitän doesn't take kindly to them. But I don't know how he'll react if he finds out you're a . . . Don't tell anyone else. Do you understand? You might be the last Pole in Germany, or this far west, at least. I won't tell anyone, don't worry, but—why're you still here?"

"I promised I'd take care of the family," Janusz said, amazed not to find himself being arrested.

At that moment, Wanda arrived with Freddy in her arms. She sat beside Janusz and laid Freddy beside Ilse. Quiet sobs continued to emerge hoarsely from his chest. Schulz said goodbye: the regiment was preparing to move out.

Once Freddy was asleep, with her eyes on Helmut's body, Wanda asked, "What do we have left, Janusz?"

"We have the children, one horse, and the war behind us."

And ahead of them, but neither of them said it.

"I don't know whether my mother's still alive. Or Erna and Crystl. I only remembered them when we were pulling splinters out of Freddy," she said with the withered voice her screams had left her with.

He'd forgotten, too. "Do you want me to go search for them?"

She took a deep breath. "No. The most important thing now is to fetch a spade. And a pickaxe. We must bury him before it gets dark."

"I'm sorry, Frau Hahlbrock."

"Don't say it, Janusz."

And she stood up.

"I have to change his diaper."

"Frau—"

"Please fetch the spade. Take Ilse and then come back for Freddy."

Ilse didn't wake when he laid her down in the cart. He assured Irmgard she was all right, just in shock. The soldiers had already taken their part of the horsemeat. The two legs that Irmgard had requested were wrapped in a blanket. Janusz tied them to one side of the cart. With the other blanket, he covered the blood-soaked driver's seat as well as he could. He partially untied the spattered canvas and folded it back over itself on top of the cart. It was both all and the least he could do.

When he returned for Freddy, Frau Hahlbrock, an expert in such maneuvers after being on the freezing road for so long, was changing her baby's diaper while protecting his body from the cold.

Janusz carried Freddy to the cart, then checked the horses' reins and adjusted them for a single animal. When he returned to the woods, Frau Hahlbrock had her little son's body on her lap, wrapped in the Christmas tablecloth. Her gaze was absent. Janusz could see that she was rocking him. Or herself. He approached.

"Shall I help you . . . ?"

"Don't touch him!"

Janusz took a step back. "No. Of course. Where do you want it?"

She chose the tree she thought was the most beautiful.

"No more bombs will fall here," she said softly.

He hoped it would be so, and dug without respite between the enormous roots, though he could already see, as well as feel, that the fingers on his right hand were broken, swollen, out of place. It had happened when he tried to cling to the reins when the horses bolted. Each blow on the icy ground was slow torture. She took turns swinging the pickaxe. In silence.

Persuading the owner of the next farm to open his door to them wasn't easy. The children were asleep in the cart, Frau Hahlbrock with them. Janusz knocked on the door before dawn. The old man who opened it pointed a shotgun at the giant with a foreign accent. Not even the offer of horsemeat persuaded him to listen. Frau Hahlbrock had to go and plead their case. Then, the man and his wife invited them into the house. There were beds for everyone.

"Except the Pole. He can't come in."

After putting Freddy and Ilse to bed, Janusz headed to the barn, as usual. He didn't sleep. He heated water to wash the horse covered in its companions' dried blood. He went out to fetch snow and covered his aching hand in it for a while. But the state of the cart prevented him from sleeping. It bore witness to death. He dismantled it. He'd have to wash it all, especially the canvas, which he boiled with soap in a large earthenware pot.

At noon, Freddy's and Ilse's intermittent crying reached him. What was wrong with Ilse? The old man had left the house, but he hadn't answered Janusz's questions. He'd just taken the frozen horse legs when they were offered to him and walked away. Later, without so much as glancing at him, he'd left to fetch a doctor.

When Irmgard eventually came out, Janusz approached. She was crying.

"Fräulein Irmgard—"

"Janusz." She seemed startled, as if caught doing something wrong. "I had to get out. My mother says we don't cry, but we're all crying, except her."

"How's Freddy?"

"In a lot of pain. My mother says the sulfa powder will stop any infection; the doctor says he'll be all right."

"Ilse?"

"No one understands what's wrong with her. She can't uncross her arms. She can't walk. She won't open her hands. She cries whenever someone tries to help."

"Can I see her?"

"I'm sorry, Janusz. The Kochs won't allow Untermensch in their house." She said it frankly, but with sadness.

"Don't leave her alone, Fräulein. Don't try to uncross her arms. Rub them like we do with horses. Put her in a hot bath and rub her all over."

Irmgard went back into the house, but Janusz stayed close. When Wanda walked the doctor out, Janusz heard him say that Ilse would need massages and hot compresses.

"What did the child do? What did she carry?" the old doctor asked.

The weight of the world, thought Janusz.

Her mother didn't answer.

"Frau Hahlbrock?"

"Yes, Janusz?" Wanda's voice hadn't improved; it sounded like a stranger's.

"Could you ask Herr Doktor to examine my hand?" he asked, holding it out.

Both Frau Hahlbrock and the doctor looked at his hand with astonishment. His ring finger and little finger had a grotesque, twisted appearance, and his entire hand was inflamed.

"Janusz! How did that happen?"

"The horses. I didn't want to let go of the reins."

She looked at him with understanding and sympathy.

"Can you help him, Doctor?"

"I'm Polish," Janusz told him as a warning, as a plea.

The doctor looked at him and took a moment to answer.

"The human hand has twenty-seven bones, and I know them all. And it has been a long time since I've seen a case as interesting as yours, young man. Come." He gestured toward the house.

"Would it be better in the barn, Herr Doktor? The stove's lit; it's not too cold . . ."

He understood.

"I'll follow you."

The doctor had done a very good job. It had hurt when he'd realigned the fingers and metacarpals, but he distracted Janusz by teaching him the names of each broken part. He'd told him to keep the splint on for three weeks, at least.

"It's nothing that rest won't fix. And you, Frau Hahlbrock: rest, and gargle with salt water."

Because of the children, they had no choice but to do as the doctor said, staying on the farm to recover. Within days, Janusz's hand had improved notably. Time and rest helped Freddy and Ilse, too. Both were walking now, and with Irmgard's massages, Ilse could almost fully stretch out her arms and open her hands.

She kept him company while he scrubbed the cart's blood-soaked, hole-riddled canvas and rug for the third time. Janusz hadn't wanted her to see it, but he soon saw that Ilse was protecting herself: she spoke about everything except that day and looked everywhere except at the scars the bullets had left. Nor did she ask him to tell her stories or to tell her where he thought Kaiser was, as she usually did.

The next day, Frau Hahlbrock asked him to take her to the nearby town.

"The doctor thinks he's found my mother."

They went in the uncovered cart. They both missed its old solidity, the weight behind them, the flowers inside. It felt strange to travel so light. When they reached the doctor's office, they found Grandma Hannah with Crystl in her arms. The old woman cried with relief when she saw her daughter, and with pain when she learned about little Helmut.

"Oh, my girl, Erna's in a very bad way," she said through her tears.

Erna Bendzius had bullets in both legs, she told them. They'd amputated them, but she'd already developed septicemia. The doctor had put out an emergency call, trying to find penicillin, but he warned the family it was probably too late.

Grandma stayed with her daughter-in-law. Crystl traveled back to the farm with Wanda and Janusz, sleeping in her aunt's arms. That night, they learned that the war had ended. There were no celebrations. They spent the next two days going to and from town to visit Erna.

On the second day after peace was declared, Franz Bendzius met them at the hospital. He'd arrived too late: his wife had died.

"He deserted," Wanda told Janusz on the way back to the Kochs' farm. "He's been searching for us for weeks. He found Erna through the hospital registry."

"And Herr Hahlbrock?" Janusz asked hopefully.

Wanda shook her head. "Franz said that, when they enlisted, Hartwig declared himself an expert motorcyclist, and they sent him to the eastern front, as a lookout. Do you think he deserted, too?"

Janusz shook his head: Hartwig Hahlbrock wasn't the type to desert anyone or anything.

"He deserted us—like all men who go to war." Into these words, Wanda injected all her bitterness. She didn't let Janusz object.

"I told him: You're a farmer. But he wanted to be more than a farmer. Remember when Ilse was little, when she said that her friends' fathers were fools for going to war? Well, it's true: war is for idiots. Gullible idiots dying for honor. And then, what's left? Women without husbands, orphaned children. A country in ruins. A debt to pay."

What debt? What was she talking about?

"Janusz, you must go."

He felt the words like a blow.

"I—"

"I know you feel obligated. But you're free now. The war's over. You won."

He'd won?

"I didn't win anything."

"Maybe not; I'm sorry. Maybe nobody won. And we brought you a long way. Forgive us. Now you'll have to go all the way back."

"No, Frau Hahlbrock. I can't go. I promised Herr—"

"That promise means nothing if he's not here to see it kept. He's not here anymore, Janusz."

How could she be so cold, say it flatly in her rasping voice, not even looking at him?

"All the more reason I should stay until you reach wherever you want to go."

"The Kochs want us to stay here. We'd work. They'd leave us the farm, they say. They don't have anyone. Their only condition—"

"*Nein, Frau Hahlbrock!* Don't stay here. The Russians are still coming."

"—their only condition is that you leave." She paused, let her words sink in. "Don't worry. We won't actually stay much longer. But, Janusz, remember Wilhelm and Grethe? Look at the Kochs. People will tolerate your presence even less now that they've lost." She paused again, and Janusz didn't know what to say. "Believe me, when the Kochs made the offer, I was tempted: my own home again, my own land again. It would almost be a miracle."

Wanda's ruined voice grew thick, but she caught herself before the tears could rise.

"Janusz, I am profoundly grateful for what you've done for us, but my children come before you, before me, before my husband—alive or dead. My children are everything. We won't stay here, but only because you're right about the Russians. I still have to take my children somewhere safe."

She wasn't looking at him. She wasn't even blinking. Her voice was losing strength; Janusz had never heard her talk so much.

"Wherever we go, we'll depend on people's goodwill, and there isn't much of that left. We're landless Germans, Janusz. We're refugees in our own country. Nothing will be easy; nobody will want to share anything with us. Well. Only the Kochs, because they have no one and they live far away from everything." She almost smiled. "I'm sorry, Janusz. But you have to go."

"But—"

"Go. Tomorrow."

The force of those words plunged them into silence for the rest of the journey.

"Can I say goodbye to Ilse?" he said when they reached the farmhouse.

"What did you give that girl? Ever since she met you, it's been Janusz this, Janusz that. What did you give her?"

"I gave her my stories, Frau Hahlbrock."

She nodded. "Ilse and her stories . . ."

There was another silence.

"May I say goodbye?"

"No. She's already suffered too much. I'll explain that you had to leave urgently."

The next day, Wanda came out before dawn to see him off. In addition to his quilt and sheepskin sack, she gave him their cords for traps, a spoon, a cup, a knife, and a small axe. She gave him a ham she'd taken without asking from the farm, and two boiled eggs. She also gave him a sack to put it all in.

"If you go home, give my best wishes to Jadwiga."

He nodded. The silence that followed was clumsy, dense. She broke it.

"It was a terrible winter, wasn't it? But the sun is out now, Janusz. Remember us with affection. That's how we'll remember you. I hope you have a good life. Goodbye."

# 64. From Königsberg to Kaliningrad

## Arno

***May to July 1945***

They crossed their own fields, still partially snow-covered in the shadow of the wooded perimeter, trampled, and flattened by Russian feet and machinery. Nobody had bothered to remove the decaying bodies.

"Cover your nose and mouth, Arno."

Arno obeyed in a vain effort to keep out the stench and the flies. Finally, they arrived. They were home. To their surprise, they found the house almost intact. Arno's mother took the key from her overcoat, where she'd kept it since she locked the door the day they left.

Arno watched as she inserted it, turned the knob, and pushed open the door. He'd never felt such joy. At that moment, he really believed that the war had ended, and with the war, the cold and the hunger. He believed that, like any day when he returned from school or chasing the ram, he'd walk in and be able to take off both coats, his boots. That his father would be waiting with the fire lit, soup on the stove, a loaf of bread in the oven.

But they were met with darkness, emptiness, and more than ever, the terrible and inescapable absences.

His mother examined everything, surprised that not a single Russian bullet had touched the house, that no soldier had made it his own. She checked: there was water in the tap, but no power. It doesn't matter, thought Arno. We have plenty of oil lamps in the basement. His bed was as he'd left it; the armchairs in the living room were still against the wall. The message he'd left for his father remained. It wouldn't take long to make themselves comfortable.

"We can't stay here," his mother said.

"Why not?" Arno asked, alarmed—angry, almost.

"Because they'll see us and take it away."

"But it's ours!"

"Arno, I'm yours and you're mine. But that's all. Our war will continue even when theirs has ended. We've already said goodbye to this house. We aren't coming back. We'll stay in the barn or the workshop. But we'll take some things that might be useful. Here."

She pulled the rabbit from inside her blouse. She noticed Arno's surprise.

"Well, what did you expect? I wasn't about to leave her to a Russian stew, especially when she's finally pregnant."

They set up camp in the workshop: his mother thought they'd attract too much attention in the barn, which was visible from the road. They took some oil lamps from the basement. In one corner, they found two cans of preserves they'd missed when they left in a hurry. They really were prunes and not meat, but if Arno hadn't liked the fruit before, now it seemed delicious. They took towels and two mattresses. They brought the horse, the hen, and the rabbit in there, too.

They'd live like they had in Königsberg: his mother would stay inside, and Arno would make his rounds for firewood. The snow would disappear soon.

"In the meantime, I know where those lazy brothers of yours left potatoes and onions unharvested, like they do every year. They'll be old and frozen, but they'll do. Go find them tomorrow when there's no one around."

"What about the bodies?"

"Leave them be."

The forgotten crops were exactly where his mother had told him they'd be. Arno scoured every corner of their fields, dodging bodies and saying furtive prayers. Then he ventured onto other farmers' abandoned land, taking care not to be seen, even if there was nobody left to care. He found just enough to sustain his mother and him. A few days after their return, the rabbit gave birth to twelve young.

"We'll live," his mother told him, smiling.

In the early summer, after the snow had finally disappeared, Arno found the strawberries where his mother told him they'd be. He went to check every day, willing them to ripen. The wait seemed endless, but his wish finally came true.

His mother gave him a few each day, but the rest she made into preserves. It was difficult to do without sugar, but she managed. By the time the fields were green, the horse had lost the desire to graze. Arno cut grass and took it to the animal, but it ate very little.

"He's old. And ill-treated."

Arno felt his mother's sadness.

"Arno, go to the house and fetch the box of sausage-making things. Make sure nobody sees you."

He went and returned with care, since more and more people were passing by the farm. What did his mother need a meat grinder and pigs' intestines for? When he returned, he understood. She'd sent him so he wouldn't see, wouldn't intervene. She'd cut their beloved horse's throat, though not without first positioning a metal bucket to collect the blood. The horse was looking at her in silence as its life drained from its body.

"Mutter!"

She didn't turn around. She only had eyes and words for the dear animal that had pulled them back and forth so many times.

"I'm sorry," she said as she stroked it, looking into its eyes. "I'm sorry. The worst part's over, handsome boy. There, there . . ."

Arno didn't know who she was saying it for, him or the horse or herself. All of them, maybe. Before the horse fell, she fastened its hind legs to the pulley chains.

"I don't know whether we'll be able to lift him, just the two of us," he said.

"I don't know, either. But we'll try."

The pulley was for loading heavy things onto the cart. It would hold the horse's weight, but only because the animal had left half its body mass in Königsberg. Arno was surprised by his own strength. Before, he would have called one of his brothers. Before, he would have let his mother do half the work. His mother never stopped talking to the horse. If the effort had been too great, she wouldn't have had the air to speak.

By the time they'd managed to pull it to an almost-vertical position, the horse had given everything its heart could pump: two buckets of blood. It died with a great final snort.

"We'll make *Blutwurst*."

They only had onion and the coarse deicing salt his father kept in the workshop. No pepper, no cloves or ginger. Horse instead of pig.

"It doesn't matter," said his mother, seizing the saw. "The important thing's the blood and meat. Arno, go to the forest and see if you can find any old chestnuts or walnuts from last year."

He only found a few, but his mother used even the ones that had been nibbled.

"Chopped up inside the sausage, no one will notice. Would you notice, Arno?"

"No, Mutter," said Arno, surprised by her newfound energy. "Why're you so happy?"

"I still want to live. And today I'll eat, and I'll live. And so will my son."

When it stopped wanting to eat, the horse had told them this was as far as it would go.

"We had to help him die, Arno. And he'd be happy to keep helping us, son, I promise you."

They managed to fill all the pigs' intestines for sausages. There was even some left over to make potted meat that Ethel marked as prunes.

That night, they ate, grateful. Then they took the musketeers out once more.

In preparation for hot days, his mother asked Arno to go to the house for her two summer dresses and more underwear. He tried on clothes from his brothers' trunk, but the pants were too short. Was he that tall already? He took one pair and two shirts, but put on the clothes Frau Beckmann had given him. He left his coats, his brothers' clothes, and his winter clothes in a corner of the workshop.

"Why're you leaving things like that, child?"

"They're folded neatly."

"I told you, they'll come and drag us out of here one day. Keep everything important in your sack at all times and keep the axe where you always keep it. Just like in Königsberg. Nothing's changed."

That was what he did. It wasn't much, but they were important things: the books Herr Beckmann had given him, their Bible, his clothes. Wrapped in his new overcoat was Fräulein Stieglitz's kitchen knife that he'd taken from his mother when she came out of the tunnel, a few remaining scraps of his father's Gabonese wood, and the miniature horses. He laid the Beckmann boy's coat underneath everything, but on top, he put his old one: the most important one. He sandwiched some provisions in between. His mother kept her belongings and provisions hidden between quilts in two more sacks. And how right she had been, thought Arno on the day they came for them.

The previous day, he'd been searching for more strawberries at the edge of their fields when a slight woman strode up to him, furious.

"What're you doing here?"

"I live here," he replied, not knowing what else to say.

"I know who you are, Schipper. Do you think I don't recognize you?"

How did she know him?

"Take me to your parents."

"Only my mother's here."

That seemed to please her.

The two women recognized each other.

"It's Frau Filipek, Arno."

Frau Filipek? He remembered her plump and jovial.

"You played with her sons."

"And where are they, Frau Schipper? I only have the girl and the little one now."

"We searched for you . . ."

"Oh yes? For how long?"

His mother said nothing.

"I only came back to see if any of my sons were here. They released me when the war ended."

"The war's over?"

"For me it is, since May 7. But for you it's barely started," she said with evident pleasure. "You lost. Your people are being taken away in freight trains like livestock. Like you did to us Poles and the Jews. Let's see how you like spending twenty-four hours without being able to sit, soaked to your shoes in piss."

"Frau Filipek, I can assure you that we never wished you any harm—"

"I didn't wish you any, either, but that was six years, one husband, and six children ago."

And with that, she left.

"Arno," his mother told him, breathless, "make sure everything's packed. It won't be long now. We won't eat tomorrow, I'm sure, so tonight we'll have a good dinner."

She kept two rabbits: a female and a male. She set the rest free. That night, they killed and cooked and ate their one remaining hen. Arno struggled to obey his mother when she told him to leave nothing on his plate. It had been a long time since he'd seen it so full. They poured the stock into a bottle. They filled another with water.

As his mother had predicted, they came for them before noon the next day. They were permitted to take only what they could carry. They picked up the three sacks stuffed full. Arno's heart ached at leaving his father's tools. The soldiers ordered them onto a truck. The journey felt long, suffocating, but the hardest thing was not knowing what awaited them at the end.

"We're in Königsberg," another passenger said when the heavy canvas opened momentarily.

"Königsberg?" their guard said with a sneer. "Königsberg doesn't exist anymore. You're in Kaliningrad."

It all happened just as Frau Filipek had described. They were taken to the Hauptbahnhof and herded into a freight car. When it was full, the doors were closed, but the train didn't leave until two hours later.

Before getting on, their sacks were inspected, but they'd packed dingy underwear, quilts, and coats on top. Arno flinched when they moved his overcoat, when they touched one of his father's ebony cuttings, but they found nothing objectionable or desirable, like the valuables they found in other people's luggage. The guards did not object to the two rabbits that peered out at them when they opened his mother's sack. No one thought to search his body and he was so accustomed to carrying the axe down one leg that he didn't even think of it until an hour into the journey.

"Mutter, I need to pee."

"Hold it a little longer."

"I can't."

"Undo your pants, I'll cover you."

As he did so, Arno felt the axe and had an idea: he took it out and made a hole in the thick timber boards of the train's floor. Then he knelt and, protected by his mother and his sacks, was able to relieve himself quite tidily and modestly. Others wanted to use the makeshift bathroom. If they took turns and moved carefully, nobody would have to wet themselves.

"Break the door open," an old man said when he saw the axe.

But Ethel refused.

"Who's going to jump out of the train? You? And where are you going to run if you survive the fall?"

But before long, his mother told him: "Break a board, son, just a little. Make us a window so we can breathe." He did it, and they all felt better for a while. They spoke. Where are you from, where did they find you, how many children do you have, move over so I can use the hole, how many of your sons died in the war? They all had the worst story, or all knew the worst. Then they fell silent. Some cried, some collapsed. Meanwhile, the heat from their bodies triggered a reaction: the dormant fleas—hidden in the wood of that German train that had transported so many people to concentration camps—woke up.

# 65. A separating door

***July to August 1945***

They were heading west, they determined by peering through the improvised window. We're going to Germany! Where else? the passengers said.

Arno and his mother had positioned their sacks vertically at their feet and managed to sit on them without taking up extra space. They took turns dozing while the other kept an eye on their possessions, but only until the fleabites became impossible to ignore. They took care of the hidden rabbits as best they could, gave them water, and then drank water and chicken stock in little sips themselves, careful not to be seen.

"We'll ration it, Arno, and we can't give anyone any," his mother explained in a low voice. "We don't know how long this journey will take."

They had their axe. They had their quilts, the rabbits, the sausages and canned meat. And he had his coat in his sack. With all that, they'd be all right afterward, his mother whispered. For the time being, water and stock—nothing else. Arno felt sorry for the people who had nothing, not even water. Several died on the way, including the old man who'd wanted to escape.

When the train slowed as it entered a village, his mother put the piece of wood from the wall back in place so the Russians wouldn't notice the damage. Then they stopped, and soldiers made them all get off.

"Where are we?" Arno asked.

Up ahead, someone saw the station signpost.

"We're in Görries. Germany!"

*"Meine Damen und Herren,"* a Russian said in German with a harsh accent. "*Willkommen!* You have arrived in the new Soviet zone."

They didn't know what that meant, but by that afternoon they would discover that the Allies had already divvied up the whole country. It wasn't just Prussia that no longer existed: all Germany had crumbled.

They were all taken to the village square, where they were inspected individually and as families.

"Name and age?"

"Arno Schipper," he told the official. "Ten."

"You're very tall," he replied, squinting at him and then at his papers.

"That's how he's been for ten years, and no longer," said his mother.

She said it in a relaxed manner, but Arno could hear the tension in her voice. Would it be a repeat of the scene at the port?

"But not as tall as the boys of the Soviet Union," said the man.

He gave them a piece of paper in Russian that they showed to another official.

"That way," he said, indicating a corner of the grassy square where some other small groups were already standing.

The war hadn't touched the village. Everything was intact, the square's trees thick with leaves. It was like a world he'd once dreamed about, Arno thought. They sat in the shade of a tree. Away from the others, his mother took out the rabbits so they could stretch their legs a little and nibble the plants. When night fell, they took out their coats and quilts, but not the sausages.

"I'm hungry, Mutter."

"I know. Have some stock."

They waited there for two days, not knowing why. They saw trucks arrive and take groups away but didn't know where they went. They spent the time plucking fleas from each other one by one.

At last, they were taken to a three-story house.

There, a stern woman told them to follow her to the top floor. His mother carried the lightest of the three sacks. Arno took one up and then returned for the other. Ethel was still out of breath when he climbed the stairs for the second time. In the room the woman had assigned them, there was a single bed, a small window, a desk, a chair, a small wood burner, and nothing else.

"I'm Frau Hammerschmidt."

"I'm—"

The woman didn't let her finish.

"This was my son's room. In winter, you'll find your own wood for the burner."

"I'm sure we'll be gone before winter," his mother was quick to say.

The woman scoffed and went on. "You don't have a bathroom. Under the bed, you'll find a bucket. Throw your business in the pit every day, do you hear? I don't want filth in my house."

"We're not dirty people."

"You smell like a latrine."

"And so would you if you hadn't had water to wash with for more than three days," his mother said, indignant.

Arno remained silent, shocked by his mother's aggression. Afraid the woman would throw them out.

"There's water from the well downstairs, too," Frau Hammerschmidt went on. "I'm opening my house to you because our new masters ordered it. Nothing better go missing."

"Where can we cook, take baths?"

"There's an empty coach house you'll share with the family that now occupies my second floor. You may cook there, if you can find firewood and food."

She closed the door hard behind her.

"Keep away from that woman, Arno."

"How long will we be here, Mutter?"

"I don't know. Not long, I hope. The governments must be trying to swap prisoners."

"I hope it won't be long, too. And yes, keep away from me, child," called Frau Hammerschmidt through the thin walls.

They'd always talk in whispers, they agreed. Arno went down for water and to throw out the contents of the bucket that was now their lavatory. He found another bucket that he washed and filled from the well before carrying both upstairs. They both washed. How nice the water felt on his face.

Then they ate.

"This sausage is delicious," said Arno.

"Arno!" his mother hissed. "Don't even mention that word. Or the woman will make us pay rent with—our things."

They organized themselves. They opened the little window to let in the warm summer air. Arno went up and down every day with empty buckets, full buckets. Frau Hammerschmidt yelled from wherever she was: I'd better not find your filth splashed all over the place, child. Arno only said guten Morgen to Frau Kleber and her daughters on the second floor. They responded without fail but always sounded sad.

His mother slept in the bed, he on the quilts after reading three pages of the musketeers: Just a bit at a time, his mother said, almost as anxious for more as he was. Every day, they packed as if it were their last. They kept their provisions under a floorboard.

Arno went up and down and out to explore the village. He never took longer than promised, but every day, his mother was waiting with stern words. He told her about everything he'd seen: it was summer, and the sun was warming the earth like he'd believed would never happen again. It was a nice village, with more and more Russians arriving, and not just soldiers, now. Families arrived and chose the apartment and the business that they wanted. The Russians had a butcher shop, but only they could buy meat, because German money not fit to wipe backside anymore, he heard the butcher say in stilted German. The Russians also had flour for bread, and the bakery smelled of Arno's childhood, so he always hung around there, though the baker chased him away. And Arno went up and down, and his mother waited for him.

Arno went up and down, and one day, he reached the lake. He bathed and washed his clothes in the freezing water, albeit without soap. On the way back, a soldier gave him a piece of chocolate and he was tempted to eat it right then, but he didn't tell his mother that when they shared it that evening.

One day, fifteen days after their train journey, Arno said nothing on his way down, not even good morning to the Klebers. He dumped his bucket into the pit and then went to the well. He looked down to the bottom, then turned around, sat, leaned back, and closed his eyes.

His mother was waiting for him with breakfast, his mother was waiting for him afraid, his mother went down to look for him, his mother found him where he sat. His mother was about to scold him, but she saw the marks on his face, on his torso. Her son was burning up.

His mother tried to get him inside.

"What's the matter with the boy?" the landlady shouted.

"He has a bit of a fever, that's all."

But the woman saw the marks.

"That's typhus. Nobody comes in here with typhus!"

"It must be chicken pox," his mother said, though she knew it wasn't.

"It's the Jewish plague. You flea-ridden exiles brought it here. You're not coming inside; this house is clean," Frau Hammerschmidt said, walking backward to get away from them.

"Let us in or I'll go tell the authorities you threw us out."

"You can't let the boy die like that," Frau Kleber said indignantly from the second floor.

Frau Hammerschmidt, equally indignant, reconsidered.

"Very well, let nobody say I threw a child out to die like a flea-ridden dog on the street. But he's not my responsibility, and I don't want the infection going up and down my house!" She focused on Ethel. "The boy can stay, but only if you keep him in the storeroom. Strict quarantine. Do you understand? Do you *all* understand?" she called up to the second floor. "If he lives, he lives. If he dies, he dies. It's that or the street. And if you want, shut yourself away with him, but if you do, don't come back out, even for water."

His mother didn't argue. She dragged her son upstairs to the second door on the third floor. She opened it and led him in. There was space in the storeroom for her son. She sat him down. There was a little window; he wouldn't be completely in the dark. She went to fetch a bucket, a bottle of water, and his quilt. She made a bed for him near the door that would separate them. She laid him down. She held a cool compress to his forehead. Then she went out to wash her hands, change her clothes, and ask herself over and over, why him and not me? But first, she closed the door. Then, she made herself a bed outside, because she wanted to be close, to hear each breath, each groan, each whimper, answer each time he said Mutter and each time he said, *Hier bin ich, Vater.* I'm here, Father.

The first night, nobody slept in that house of thin walls.

In moments of consciousness, the boy realized he was somewhere strange, and he called for his mother, crying, afraid. He banged and he kicked, but nothing happened, nothing moved, he could never get out. In that place, it was always night, he was always lost, and he ran and he searched, and he ran and he choked. In that place, he was lost, but so was his father, so was his sister, so were his brothers. And they all yelled for him. They were all searching for him, but in that place, no one heard him; there, everything hurt, everything burned, everything froze, everything broke. And his mother wouldn't stop. She wouldn't stop with her orders: Drink, drink, drink. *Nein, Mutter: ich bin so müde.* I'm so tired, let me sleep. *Nein, nein.* But she never took no for an answer, and the boy cried.

⚘

What he didn't know was that his mother cried with him. He would later learn that she used those moments to tell him, in the strongest voice she could muster: Sohn, drink water, drink water. Water, water. That she passed a bottle through the door that she immediately closed, because the landlady was listening. That she knew when he obeyed and when he didn't. When the fever overcame him.

On the second day, the mother went to see the landlady.

"Do you know where I can find medicine?"

She laughed.

"Medicine, from the Russians? If you'd gotten the Americans a few weeks ago, maybe. All these people do with sick people is quarantine them in a warehouse outside the village."

So she went back to her son. The second-floor neighbors, moved by their plight, shook off their sadness to take water up for them both, so that the mother didn't have to go up and down, so that she didn't have to leave him. And sometimes, peaceful, free for a moment from the fever's delirium, he asked for his mother, and she said, I'm here, Sohn. Drink water, drink.

Sometimes he obeyed, but sometimes he didn't, and then she came out with her commanding voice. And sometimes he obeyed, but sometimes he didn't.

And the days passed, and sometimes no sounds came from inside, and then his mother pressed her ear against the door and managed to hear a sigh, and breathed again. And from outside, she told him the stories of his childhood. And sometimes she pressed her forehead against the door and cursed herself for not going in. But if she fell sick, who would take care of him? If she died, who would mark her son's grave?

The days passed, and the peaceful stretches were longer, and then when she stuck her hand in to take out the water bottle, she also set down a little plate with a spoonful of fruit preserves on it. And she'd say, drink water, eat fruit, drink water eat fruit.

Why're you wasting food on a dying boy, the landlady complained from downstairs, but the mother closed her ears.

Sometimes, the neighbor from the second floor kept the mother company. She told her that her eldest was pregnant, but only Hilde, thank God. "My younger daughter isn't, nor am I. There were twenty of them. Russians. Three days in that basement. They took turns, came back. They tore my youngest. The fevers come and go. How did you save yourself?"

"My boy saved me."

"Mutter? Are you there?"

"Ja, Sohn, I'm here! And you're getting better, do you hear me? I can hear it in your voice. Drink water and you'll get better. And eat your fruit."

The second week, they came for her. If she wanted a home and bread, she had to work, the Soviet official said. What work could she do?

"I can cook."

"Everyone can cook."

"I can bake bread. I can cut and grind meat. I can slaughter animals."

They assigned her to the butcher, effective immediately.

"My son's in quarantine . . ."

"But you're not. You will work."

In the mornings, she filled his water before she went out.

"I have to work, son. I'll be home soon."

At night she returned exhausted, but with a piece of bread for each of them. Three hundred grams, to be as precise as the butcher was when he paid her. She gave it to him with the butter she'd gotten from the landlady in exchange for preserves. She broke it into small pieces. And miraculously, her son bit, chewed, and swallowed. He began to ask her to let him out, and to speak in full sentences.

"We lost Vater in the war."

"Yes. We lost him, son."

"But he's not dead. We have to find him."

"We'll find him when you get better."

Or:

"Let me out, Mutter, Vater's talking to me."

"What's he saying?"

"That he wants to see me."

Before going to work, his mother locked the door. And she said: You must stay in there until you're better, son, and I must go to work. And every day, she asked, why him and not me, God?

One day, her son sat up. He knew where he was; he knew he was sick. He was hot. There was light. Was it early or was it late? He tried the door, but it was locked.

"Mutter?"

He shook the door.

"Mutter? Open the door!"

From outside, he heard a woman's voice. It's your neighbor from the second floor, it said, and for a moment he struggled to remember. His mother was working, his mother would be back. He had to be confined because of the infection. Drink water, child. Eat your bread. And he ate all the bread and got up, slowly. He opened the window to let in air and to get rid of the smell.

I'm bored, it stinks in here, I stink, he told his mother that night, and he didn't know that, outside, his mother smiled.

# 66. The lost doll

## Ilse

***October 1945***

"We're leaving today," Ilse told Freddy.

He didn't believe her because she'd said it every Sunday for five months now. She told him because their mother, in turn, told her: Maybe next Sunday, Ilse. She clung to those words.

It was June by the time they'd reached Uncle Albert's farm. The war was over, but nobody was celebrating. After finishing a lunch of cabbage broth, the children were told to go out and play, a message Ilse understood: the adults need to talk. Uncle Albert and Aunt Olga, Grandma, their mother, and Uncle Franz stayed inside.

Ilse followed Edeline and Freddy out. Irmgard carried Crystl, who was crying. Mama, she yelled to Wanda, but Edeline, almost four now, said yet again, she's not your *Mutti*, she's mine. There was no happiness inside or out. Nor were there games: they all felt the absence of Helmut. And Aunt Erna. And Kaiser. And Janusz. And Papa.

Five months later, Ilse still fantasized that Kaiser, lost, had found the family's trail and would follow them with his nose wherever they went. But they'd been here so long, and Kaiser hadn't shown up. She always looked up when she heard a dog barking, but the bark was never his.

She also fantasized that her father was returning on a new motorbike the Wehrmacht had given him. Back home, the sound of a motorcycle had always meant her father's return. Now, British and American motorcycles were everywhere, but it was a long time before Ilse's heart stopped accelerating, before her mouth stopped yelling, then saying, then sighing *Papa* each time the familiar sound reached her ears.

Sometimes she imagined Janusz watching over them from a distance. But her mother insisted, Ilse, Kaiser found a new home; when your father arrives, it won't be by motorcycle; Janusz was needed in his country, he wanted to see Jadwiga, he said he'd write one day. I know, Ilse, I know, but he had to go.

In the daylight hours, Ilse still imagined Helmut learning new words. Maybe Aunt Erna had become his mother, like her mother with Crystl, and he'd be happy, as always. But at night, she dreamed of him still in her arms, and she heard herself saying, I won't let you go, I won't let you go. She woke with her arms crossed over her chest, tight and painful. And empty.

One night before they reached Uncle Albert's, her mother had had to stop the cart because she was groaning in her sleep.

"Ilse, wake up. Ilse! Shh, shh. It's over now, Ilse. Shh."

"Where's Helmut?"

"He's not here, Ilse. Remember?"

"Did I let go?"

Her mother said, "I already told you: you didn't, and it's not your fault, you must understand that, Ilse. Enough, now. He's gone. He's with your grandparents and aunts and uncles, and we're here and we must carry on. Do you hear?"

Yes, she heard, and she listened. But she woke up every day with her arms crossed, tight, painful. Empty. Years later, when Ilse held her own child, the memory of that old pain would come rushing back. Her sweetheart, the only person in the world who knew, who understood, would wrap his arms around her from behind, easing the weight and her tears.

That first day, the adults had decided: Uncle Albert couldn't afford to keep them all on the farm. They'd go to the nearby village to find accommodation and work: since the Zivilarbeiter had left, everyone needed laborers. But Albert and Olga would help: they'd keep Ilse and Freddy.

"No, Mama! Don't leave us," said Ilse, fighting back tears.

"I have to, Ilse. You'll take care of your brother. And you'll mind your manners."

Then she turned to Freddy, who was crying.

"You must listen to your big sister. And stop crying. We don't cry, Freddy."

"I hoo cry, Huher."

"Then Ilse will teach you not to, won't you, Ilse?"

From then on, every night before they slept, she told him not to cry, to keep it all in.

"Aer?"

"I don't know where, Freddy. Inside your body there's a place where you keep everything. Sometimes I think it's in my belly, sometimes in my heart, sometimes in my head. I don't know."

And since then, once a week, on Sunday, they saw their mother, whose sun-toasted face was painted with a big smile, and no one told her that Freddy hadn't learned not to cry yet, or that Ilse was exhausted after walking behind Uncle Albert's tractor all week, barefoot so she wouldn't ruin her shoes, collecting the potatoes that escaped the machine, because in this house anyone who wants to eat has to work, child.

"Except Freddy, because he's only five and he's injured," she said each time, to remind Albert of his agreement with Wanda.

"Well, that's what you get for abandoning your land: you end up as down-and-outs."

Ilse never told her mother how afraid she was of the guards and dogs that made sure nobody stole so much as a single onion from the fields. Or how she always tried to leave one or two under a tree for the children that peered out from the forest with hunger in their eyes.

Nor did she tell Wanda that Uncle Albert constantly insulted the family's choices. Or that he made them say the strange prayers of what he called the true church: the Seventh-day Adventist Church. That their uncle was regularly offered silver, jewelry, fine rugs, and even cut-glass chandeliers, and gave desperate people just a small bucket of potatoes in return. That a woman who handed over her wedding ring wept as she took it off. They never asked: Mama, what does "he who has potatoes is king" mean? Uncle Albert said it each time he made an exchange. Before long, they understood.

Each night after dinner, they went to their bedroom. They drew, read, and wrote, without making noise, on Ilse's blackboard. Freddy often cried himself to sleep.

"Ooh you hink Huher eh uh gecause ee cry he os?"

No. Ilse didn't think their mother had left them because they cried the most. To comfort him, she repeated the explanation their mother had given: they had to stay because she didn't have enough space or food for everyone. This way, she'd know that two of her children would eat. Irmgard was working, too, and Edeline and Crystl were too young to be left, so it had to be Ilse and Freddy.

On Sundays, when their mother visited, Ilse understood. By Monday, she didn't, though she pretended she did. She forced herself to tell Freddy: This is our way of helping Mama. But she went to sleep wondering if maybe Mama had left them because seeing them made her sad; if seeing them made her think about what happened to Helmut.

When Freddy was asleep, Ilse did her own writing for a while before she got into bed. Her old doll on the side table was the only witness to the letters that always began: *Liebe Mama.* By dawn, Ilse had always made the words disappear, because they were hers and nobody else's. She carried them away as chalk dust on her hand, and they disappeared into the earth behind the tractor. Ilse planted her words and harvested new ones for the night. With each step through the black mud fertilized with chalk, she organized the inventory of everything she'd lost: war, Jadwiga, house, Papa, Aunt Erna, Helmut, Janusz, Mama, doll.

Irmgard had picked up Ilse's doll from that road on that day. The first day Wanda left them to work, she'd cleaned it a little and decorated the table with it, to keep the children company.

Ilse hadn't touched it. Or looked at it. It had fallen on the road that day when she lost her brother. No one should have picked it up.

Jadwiga, house, Papa, Aunt Erna, Helmut, Janusz, Mama, doll, *that* Ilse.

War.

# 67. The burden

## Janusz

***May 1945 to March 1946***

He went into the forest.

He went because he said he'd go. He said he'd go because he felt rage boil in his stomach. She'd called him her son to the men who killed the dog, yet now she cast him out? After coming so far? And without even letting him say goodbye? It was leave or explode, yell, climb the cart and claim his place on it. It was go or be a burden.

He went, but only a short distance at first, separated from them by an invisible wall. Wanda Hahlbrock's words pursued him. He'd won, she said, but Janusz knew he'd lost everything.

He'd just stay to see them leave, he told himself. Despite what she'd said, he still felt the promise he'd made Herr Hahlbrock, the bond implicit in it: You belong, you're needed.

They left in the day, because the protection of the night was no longer needed, and then he also began his journey. But in the shadows, through the trees. His direction was determined by the cart in which he'd lived for the last six months and the family that he'd made his own.

Where was he going to go, alone? He, whose only direction in life had been given to him by this family?

He was no longer the boy who'd come out of the Białowieża Forest, but the old loneliness was back, imposed. And he didn't feel strong enough to bear its return. Now, though Janusz stayed among the trees, he couldn't take his eyes off the road, compelled to follow. He remained bound to the cart that had become his entire universe, just as he'd been bound to his mother's forest, waiting for her return or her ghost. But she'd never arrived. And now the cart was leaving.

It carried a universe that didn't include him.

If he looked the other way, into the depths of the forest, he'd lose it. Everything was in that direction: a new Poland, his old language, his forest. But loneliness was there, too; the memories of lost childhood. Choosing that direction would weaken the only tie that sustained him, that bound him.

He feared, too, that the old forest would shun him, that his mother's ghost would appear and chastise him: What have you done with the boy I left? What have you done with the stories I entrusted to you?

"I lost them, Mother; I left them scattered on the road. Life trampled them."

Where had his cultivated innocence, his imagined belonging, his chosen universe disappeared to? Where, after seeing that *P* on the chests of those condemned to death and feeling it sewn onto his own skin with each show of contempt? Where had they gone after he witnessed the horror of bombardment, after the beloved dog's death had been imprinted on his mind and his tongue, after seeing Ilse and the children disappear, after throwing himself on Frau Hahlbrock to protect her, after hearing the horses that he'd taken care of for so long scream, after sitting beside the dead body of a cherished baby, after carrying Ilse and believing that life would go on this way and one day being informed that no, *he* was the burden?

Scattered on the road with his stories.

All he had, he'd thought, was the family. He felt their losses as his own, and when Frau Wanda had referred to him as her son, the knot had only tightened more.

But go, because you'll be a burden. He didn't want to be one.

I'll go, he said, and he made her believe it. But it wasn't so easy.

He followed them north until they reached the farm that must have belonged to the grandmother's brother. He saw the door opened to them; he noticed the old man's reluctance to let them in. He saw Ilse greet her great-uncle without smiling. He saw her turn around and look to the forest before going in. He saw the door close behind her.

He treasured that final glance, but the closed door was his signal. They had come this far together; the girl was safe. Then, Janusz turned around and faced the depths of the forest; he would walk in *his* direction, in the direction of loneliness.

He would detach himself from everything. He would be a wolf now.

Sometimes he walked, sometimes he rested. But he always went east, and never on roads or into villages. And the farther east he went, the more Russian voices he heard. Stay away from the Russians, Janusz: that hadn't changed.

He slept under the trees; he set traps. Now that the war was over, life was returning to the forest, so he was never very hungry. In summer he'd found fruit, in fall some walnuts, and he was glad he didn't have to share with anyone. The months passed.

One freezing night, a pack of wolf children came out from between two trees. Their feral eyes seemed to gleam through the mist, and he thought they'd attack him like those other wolves had attacked Kaiser, but then he realized they were looking at his squirrel.

"Want some?"

Wary, they ventured out. There were nine of them. Some had coats. Others wore German helmets too big for them. None, not even the youngest, showed any trace of the softness of childhood. The only light in their eyes was the reflected fire over which the squirrel was now turning brown.

He gave it all to them. He also gave them the rabbit meat that he had left over from the previous day. It wasn't much for so many, but no one complained. After eating, they all lay down to sleep. Only the eldest, who looked twelve or thirteen, sat down by the fire.

"Who are you?" Janusz asked in German.

"My mother was killed by Russians and I was left alone," said the child. "The same thing happened to the others, or they were abandoned, or they got lost in an attack. Some of them don't remember where they're from."

"And you?"

"I remember," the boy said.

But he didn't tell him. Instead, he said he'd gathered them all together during the last snow. But the group kept changing; even the day before, they'd been ten: a girl had fallen into a river's freezing current. They hadn't tried to find her.

"And where do you get clothes, coats, blankets?"

"From dead people and their suitcases. When the snow melted, the fields were full of them."

Then they slept, too. Janusz thought the pack would go on their way the next morning, but no: they looked at him with the same vacant expression as the day before. He set several traps and caught two rabbits that he skinned with his knife. The youngest ones accepted their ration only from their leader's hands. And Janusz saw that there was light in their eyes when they looked at him.

They walked slowly west. The older children sometimes carried the younger ones when they got tired or the mud became too heavy for them. They didn't accept Janusz's offer to carry them, and he didn't mind the slow pace: he was in no hurry to arrive anywhere, and he'd rather retrace his steps than leave them near the Russians. At the first settlement they reached, he'd hand them over to the *Bürgermeister*.

These children might not ever find their families, but they could return to their own people. What would have become of him had he, at twelve, found someone who took pity on a wandering boy? But no one did. Perhaps, by the time he reached the farm, it was too late for him. When the Germans caught him, had his eyes been absent? Had they been as empty as these children's?

They stayed with him for ten days, and he almost got used to their company and their silence. He taught them to make traps and fire. One day, he tried to tell a story, but he didn't know whether it was because he'd forgotten the right words or because the children didn't know how to pay attention: none of them sat still for more than ten words. He didn't try again, because words mustn't be wasted, or they escape and die. Maybe the little ones understood that, too, because they never said a word to him or even to one another. The ones that could speak, like the nameless leader, told him that the forest was full of children like them, children of the war.

"Wolf children," Janusz told them.

They seemed to like the name.

The next morning, they were gone. The wolf children had taken his knife and one of his cords. Something else died inside him. A wolf I am not, he told himself. He hadn't been one even when his mother went away forever, like the mothers of those children had. He'd immediately started searching for company. And he would never have run away. With someone else's knife and cord.

He turned around again and walked east. He wouldn't stop again. His destination was in the east, in the silence of the trees. And so, step by step, autumn ended and a harsher winter than the previous one arrived.

He found a ruined shack near a lake. He'd have to hole up there or he'd lose his remaining toes. He fixed the hut's roof with pine branches, filled the gaps between the wooden boards with mud. Inside, there was an old stove. He patched up the flue with the same mud, and tested it: good enough to warm his nights without suffocating him. He took stones from the lake to heat on the stove. They wouldn't last for as long as bricks, but they'd help. He wouldn't freeze to death.

When spring came, Janusz knew only because of the forest's signs. In his time there, he hadn't uttered a word in his mother tongue or any other. He hadn't sung. He'd counted only his toes—eight, still—and his years. He was twenty-two, he calculated. And he was an old man. Where had his youth gone?

It had turned to dust, like everything else.

# 68. The forest giant

## Arno

***March 25, 1946***

That day, Hilde Kleber's baby died. Fate, the cold, malnutrition, sadness; they all had an opinion on the causes of death. His mother had died in childbirth, but he'd tried to live, and his grandmother had done everything she could to help him. They'd called him Helmut, a good German name, so that when he grew up, Frau Kleber said, he'd never suspect his Russian blood.

Helmut had clung to life in order to cry and to squander what little life his young grandmother had left. That was what Frau Hammerschmidt said. If she had any compassion, she'd help him die. And let us sleep!

The baby's grandmother had eagerly awaited the arrival of March. She was certain: if Helmut could just have one sunny day, he'd survive. But no sun came, and the baby's time ran out. All because of the Russians, said the grandmother through her tears, who'd planted children in German bellies but provided neither warmth nor food.

She refused to bury him in the village grave for that winter's many dead. She'd suffered enough having to bury her daughter in the one for those who'd died of typhus. And Frau Hammerschmidt refused to allow the baby's spirit to haunt her, so she hadn't permitted his burial in the yard.

They prayed; they performed funeral rites. They wrapped the body in the light blanket that had been his only possession in life. Then they put him in a sack, and with a final blessing from the grandmother, Arno went out, leaving his mother and the Klebers behind.

As always, he carried his axe. It would have to do.

"Choose a beautiful place, child," Frau Kleber said to him.

Arno hadn't been to the lake since the previous summer. In those two weeks of fever and imprisonment, he'd grown weak, lost too much weight.

"But I think it all went to your bones, son: look how much you've grown!"

It was true. Arno had struggled to adjust, still making calculations based on his old height, so that he stumbled everywhere and hit his head against the sloping ceiling of his room and the stairs.

Having regained his strength over the past months, if not his weight, and acknowledging his new size, he'd been forced to go out to look for work with his boots cut open to make space for his growing feet.

"We'll try to get another pair."

The first thing Arno saw that day was the sign for Herman Götz, *Schuster*. The cobbler told him he didn't need an assistant, despite the mound of shoes on his table waiting to be fixed.

"Almost all of them belong to Russians. *They* pay. Not much, but . . ."

"I could bring you firewood."

"Where from, if no one has any? No. Off with you, now. I have a lot of work to do."

Arno left. He walked around the village cutting plants that he thought the rabbits would like to eat, stuffing them into his knapsack. Then he sat in the square to observe.

The Germans wandered aimlessly, their pace dictated by hunger. They peered through store windows that the locals perhaps remembered full and accessible. Now there was nothing for them there. Only Russians went into the one coffee house that remained open, all of them with a cigarette between their fingers, some holding hands with German women who wore makeup and painted-on smiles. Arno thought of Helga, in Denmark, pretty, hungry. That was if her ship had ever arrived, if she had lived.

He had to find a way to help his mother, who, every day, arrived home weak with her apron soaked in blood from the butcher's, and very occasionally, with a scrap of fat or a stolen bone with a little meat stuck to it.

"Remember what I told you about the Commandments, Arno?" Ethel said as she sat down to eat, exhausted. "Remember that every day."

He went back to the cobbler the next day and the next. The answer was always the same. He shook his head while trying to light the last of his cigarette butt.

"You like to smoke?"

The man gave him a sarcastic look.

"What do you think?"

"Do you want me to get cigarettes for you?"

"Where from, if no one has any?"

"The Russians do."

That made the man's face light up.

"I'll give you fifty grams of bread for each one you bring me."

"Does it matter if they're half-smoked?"

"Pfft! You see me dying and you think I care about a little Russian spittle?"

From that day on, Arno devoted himself to trailing Russian smokers: eventually, they'd throw away the butt, and he'd collect it from where it fell. Then it occurred to him that he could clean the tables at the coffee house for free. The owner, a Russian, accepted happily.

Almost nobody left anything on their plate, but when something was left, even a crumb, Arno ate it. If there was coffee in a cup, he drank it. With one hand, he swept the grains of sugar sprinkled across the tables into the other hand. He savored every grain. But first, he raided the ashtrays.

Soon, the cobbler was no longer his only customer. Many greeted him with a broad smile. They knew what Arno did to get the butts and, though it seemed simple, they never dared adopt his methods; a child following Soviet soldiers wasn't a threat, but a grown man doing it would be guaranteed a bullet between the eyes. They were happy to trade with Arno so that they could smoke without risking their necks.

In this way, Arno obtained firewood when it was impossible to find his own. He bartered for a potato here, an onion there. He managed to surprise his mother with a birthday gift of ten misshapen, sprouting potatoes.

When she saw them, his farmer mother smiled like she hadn't for a long time. The potatoes made her forget to say what she always said before going to sleep: Maybe they'll let us leave tomorrow. Amen.

"How lucky we are to be farmers in a village full of city people who don't know gold when they see it," she told him after allowing herself to be hugged.

And so he procured some more, and more onions, too. They planned to celebrate Arno's March birthday by planting. In fifteen weeks, with the help of the sun, they'd dig them from the earth, multiplied. Arno had already built the rabbits a wooden cage. With better weather, they might soon be able to take them out to the coach house: the doe was already expecting her first litter.

And with the prospect of enjoying this rare bounty, Frau Hammerschmidt had allowed them to use her backyard, coach house, and, once a week, the kitchen.

"To use it every day, you'd have to bring me a beer, child."

After that, he always tried to find one, but nobody traded those for cigarette butts.

But then little Helmut had died on Arno's birthday, and so, that March 25, instead of planting onions and potatoes, he would plant the baby far away from everything so that he'd only hear his mother's and God's voices for the rest of eternity.

"Why aren't the Klebers coming?" he'd asked his mother before going out.

"They're very weak and don't have warm clothes, Arno. They wouldn't survive going there and back."

And that was why he was assigned the task, because while his old coat was now short on him, the one from Frau Beckmann covered his arms and reached down below his knees. For three cigarette butts and his old boots, the cobbler had given him a bigger pair that had belonged to an old villager felled by typhus.

Arno found the spot he remembered from his visit the previous summer: among the trees, with a view of the lake. Here, there would always be clean air and fresh soil, and the rainwater would never stagnate. In addition to the voices of the child's mother and God, there would always be birdsong and squirrel chatter. Soft words, songs, and laughter. It was a good place.

He took out his axe and drove it again and again into the still-frozen earth. Sweating, he took off his big overcoat and then the old one. At last he reached the depth his mother had recommended. All the words had been said, but after laying the little body in its grave, Arno added a Lord's Prayer.

"You would've liked this world without war," he said when he finished covering the baby.

He said it with confidence, though in reality, he didn't remember such a world.

He sat there for a while, allowing the air to dry his sweat before he put his coats back on. Then he saw it: a cunning arrangement of sticks.

A trap. The engineering was simple but brilliant. He forgot about putting his coats on. He approached to examine it. He was about to move the trigger stick to observe the trap in action when he heard a gruff voice.

"Don't do that, please."

Arno spun around. A bearded giant came out from behind some bushes. His blue eyes contrasted with his long, tangled black hair.

"It took me some time to build it."

Arno found his voice.

"I'm sorry."

"Are you a wolf child?"

"A what?"

"A wolf child."

"No. I'm just a boy. Are you a giant?"

He smiled.

"Some say so. You're very tall, too."

"But not as tall as Russian boys. A guard told me." Then Arno stopped. "You're not Russian, are you?"

The giant didn't seem to like the question.

"I'm Polish. Are you sure you're not a wolf? You're alone, in the forest. Burying someone. Your brother?"

"No. A baby that was born sick in the house where I live."

"And its mother?"

"She died. What are wolf children?"

The giant told him a story about wolf children who roam the forests and bewitch unsuspecting travelers, and who might disarm traps that aren't theirs.

"I didn't do it, you saw. But I'd like to learn to make traps like this."

The giant didn't respond.

"Will you teach me? Then I'll never go hungry again."

After a moment, the giant nodded.

"But if you steal my cord, I'll come after you wherever you go."

Arno swore he'd never stolen anything in his life. He hoped the lie didn't show in his face.

The giant showed him various types of traps. Arno practiced until he was sure that he'd mastered at least three of them. Grateful for this new skill, Arno went to his old coat and, from the opening that he'd made in the lapel one day in Fräulein Stieglitz's tunnels, he took out an amber teardrop. He knew the Fräulein would approve of the use he was making of it. But he also knew what his mother would think if she knew: Each of those jewels could mean our freedom; don't waste them. He'd never given any away, but the giant's lesson was invaluable: it meant they could eat. It meant survival. That was well worth an amber drop.

"Thank you for the story and the lesson."

The giant grimaced.

"It wasn't a story."

But Arno pressed on. He'd never given anyone except his mother a gift. What were the right words to use?

"On behalf of my mother and me," he said as formally as he could, "I'd like to give you this; it belonged to a very dear woman."

"It's not necessary. I don't want paym—"

"It's not payment, it's a gift."

The giant looked like he was about to turn down whatever it was, until he saw it.

"It's amber," he said.

He took the gemstone and admired it; he stroked it.

"My mother says it's amber from the Baltic."

"*Ja.* It's a tear. One of Queen Jurata's."

Arno didn't understand.

"Do you like it?"

"I do. A lot. Thanks."

He kept stroking the drop of tree resin while Arno, now shivering, put on his coats and gathered his things to go. His mother was surely waiting with stern words.

"Boy: What's the baby's name?"

"Helmut."

The giant gasped, then sank to his knees and broke down in tears. Arno had never seen anyone cry that way, so openly, so profoundly it would touch even the birds. He never wanted to cry like that.

He fled. When he arrived at the house, his mother wasn't stern; she welcomed him with a smile.

"I was about to come find you. The Red Cross brought a letter: Johann and Fritz are alive!"

In celebration, they ate the last of their potted meat.

"Now that we've found our family, maybe they'll let us leave."

That night, they didn't read *Twenty Thousand Leagues under the Sea*, the other gift from Herr Beckmann. They read the letter again and again. There were only a few words and they never changed, but they savored each one. *Liebe Mutter,* they began. His brothers were well and working on a farm near Hamburg, not so far away. They were alive.

Suddenly, there was a future. In the months they'd been living there, Arno and his mother had heard they'd be allowed to leave soon. But they didn't know how long *soon* was anymore. Perhaps the concept was different in Russian. Would the Russians really allow them to go? His mother would ask tomorrow.

As he went to sleep, Arno thought that he'd never known such joy. Then he remembered the bottomless sorrow he'd witnessed that day. He should never have left the giant like that.

The next day he went back, but the giant was gone: he only found an empty shack and, over the baby's grave, a name on a cross: **Helmut**.

# 69. Honor thy mother

***December 24, 1946***

Arno arrived later and later now. Each time, he heard in his head his mother's stern blah-blah-blah: One day, I'll have to come find you and they'll tell me, oh, yes . . . the tall boy? We saw the Russians put him on a train to Siberia!

She needn't have worried so much: everyone in the village knew him now, even the Russian officials. They never mentioned Siberia: they only said that one day he'd be reunited with his family. Like his mother, he didn't believe that anymore: months before, when the officials had knocked on the door to say that all children under the age of twelve had to report to school the next day, they'd lost all hope.

His mother had insisted that he mustn't spend too much time away from the house or that woman will dig up all the potatoes and eat them before they're ready, you just watch. Going to school meant leaving his post, but the order also came with an incentive: they'd give him three hundred grams of bread there.

And, Arno, you're still very thin, his mother had said.

Frau Kleber, who never went out because she was taking care of her daughter, said she'd make sure the landlady didn't go near the potatoes. They trusted her. Still, that night, Arno couldn't sleep. Nor could his mother.

"What's on your mind, son?"

"It's been a long time since I went to school. What if I don't remember the lessons?"

"You're going to show those Russians what a German boy is capable of, do you hear? You'll go, and who knows? You might get a teacher who can finally answer your questions." She paused. "I'm more worried about something else."

"What?"

"Educating a child costs money. Why would they do it if they were going to let you leave?"

Sometime in the night, they fell asleep, but with a new knot in their stomachs. The paper of his brothers' letter was already as soft as fine fabric from all the unfolding, reading, and refolding. Softened, too, by the tears that ran down Ethel's face when she read it alone.

They had written a reply, but the Russians decided everything: the paper to write on, the pen, the absence of an envelope. The Russians would put it in an envelope later and pass it on to the Red Cross, the officials told them. But the only honorable Russian had been that captain in Königsberg, Ethel said. Her letter was short and discreet, because they'll read it, no question. They were well, she wrote, and anxious for the day when they'd be reunited. She signed it *Mama.*

None of my children call me Mama. So they'll recognize the sign.

What sign? Arno never understood. A sign that she loved them without having to say it in front of the Russians?

At school, instead of teaching them about Adolf Hitler, they talked about Josef Stalin, and punished any child who, stuck in the lessons of the past, declared that the Führer was better.

He committed suicide so that he wouldn't have to admit his faults, the teacher told them, and so that the world couldn't punish him for washing his country's children—you—with soap made from human bones. Jews' bones, to be precise.

Arno went home that day in shock. When his mother arrived from work, he told her about the soap.

Tall tales. How could soap be made from people?

Instead of German grammar, they started teaching them Russian. Instead of telling them to recite "The Badonviller-Marsch," they made them memorize the socialist anthem, "The Internationale."

The teacher took every opportunity to thrash anyone who insulted the Soviet Union, didn't pay attention, or failed to learn the lessons. And so he beat them often, because the children paid more attention to their bellies than to Stalin. The teacher gave them bread, but Arno had learned to calculate accurately by sight and with his stomach: of the promised three hundred grams, he only gave them a hundred and fifty. Many of the children stopped going. His mother told him that under no circumstances would she let him play truant.

"Why not, Mutter?"

"Because if we must stay here, you must earn the Russians' trust. And if they send us back to our Germany, you'd better not arrive ignorant. So study."

He spent the mornings at school. In the afternoons, he resumed his cigarette rounds. The cobbler was always his best customer, because as Herr Götz himself said: A cobbler has customers all year round, dear Arno. Learn a trade, lad.

"My papa wanted me to be a carpenter, but in the war—"

"Yes, well. Who needs furniture in a war? Whereas, war or peace, no one goes without shoes. Do you want to be a cobbler? I do need an apprentice."

"No, Herr Götz, I'm sorry. My mother doesn't want me spending even more time out of the house."

"And how is she? I haven't seen her for a long time."

Arno had traded cigarette butts to get his mother new boots, and she'd had to be measured. She didn't care if they belonged to a dead woman, she told Götz. As long as they didn't go with her to the grave.

That made Herr Götz laugh, and since then, he'd always asked after Ethel, such a fine woman, such a good sense of humor. Tell her to come whenever she wants, he said. She never returned.

"What for? I'm a married woman."

Arno had seized on that: Did it mean she believed his father still lived?

"No, son, it means I have no idea. And, for as long as that is so, I'm a married woman."

Lately, Arno hadn't varied his routine except for one thing: he didn't return at his mother's appointed time, not even on Christmas Eve. He went to school and paid attention, just as she'd ordered. Then the cigarettes, the visits to customers, sometimes trapping small game like the giant had taught him, and then . . . then he lost track of time. He went to the square where they'd waited after their arrival. He looked west: sixty kilometers separated him from his brothers. He could have walked it if the Soviets and the arrival of another winter hadn't stood in his way. His teacher had taught them to make a compass with a leaf, a needle, and water, but he'd still freeze to death. Besides, he had to stay where he was so that his brothers knew where to find him.

He lost track of time on purpose because there was no one at home now to remind him that the Russians send unaccompanied children to Siberia. There was nobody waiting for him and, just by her presence, telling him every day: You're not alone; you and I are in this war together; I'll fight for you.

That last night, they'd gone to sleep hungry but happy: the next day, they were going to harvest the crop and slaughter the first of their seven rabbits. It wasn't big, but bolstered with some potatoes, they would have enough for a good dinner and even some to give to the Klebers.

Arno promised he'd find some butter to complete the banquet.

"Good night, Mutter."

"See you tomorrow, Arno."

The next morning, he was surprised to be the first to wake. And his mother hadn't gotten up in the night to add wood to the little burner, he noticed. Arno tried not to make any noise while he washed in the cold, dark room. That day, he had a Russian exam, so he reviewed vocabulary in his head while he combed his hair and dressed. When he'd finished, he said, "Mutter?" She didn't respond. He squinted in the half-light; he spoke again, he approached, he touched her. She was freezing. He sat beside her; he pulled up the covers.

"Mutter?"

He could turn on the oil lamp, but what for? He knew what he'd see. On the day of little Helmut Kleber's death, his mother had told him: There's no life without death. He'd understood, but the dead had always been at a distance. First away from Prussia, then from the confines of the farm, away from their basement, even when thousands of bombs fell, they fell on the Beckmanns. Away from the protective circle his mother created each time she said: If we die, we'll die together. And those bombs had stopped falling, they'd endured that terrible train journey, the typhus was gone, they'd overcome his mother's flu last winter, and they'd survived, despite everything. Then they'd received proof of life from his brothers, and Arno had felt that it was just a matter of time: their war was won. They'd fought, and they'd come out on the side of the living.

But the war's dangers and his mother's feats of endurance had made him forget that she'd been fighting another war since before he was born. Now, in the night, the bomb she had always feared, her bomb, had fallen. It didn't take him, despite her promises. They hadn't died together. And they hadn't gone home together.

Arno saved his tears for later. Honor thy mother: What would she want? For him to live. To eat breakfast. To harvest the potatoes, first and foremost.

He stood, added wood to the burner, and went to school, not because of the exam, but for the piece of bread, his breakfast. Then he went home and dug up the potatoes. His mother would be happy: there were eighty, not very big, but potatoes nonetheless. He put them all in a wooden crate he'd made for the purpose and hid it from Frau Hammerschmidt. Then he went to visit the cobbler.

"Arno, my friend! What brings you here so early? Have you collected my cigarettes already?"

Arno looked at him without answering.

"What is it?"

Like Frau Kleber, Arno didn't want to bury his mother in that winter's mass grave. He knew the place she'd like. Herr Götz helped him arrange everything. They'd need the milkman's cart and three other men to move the body and then dig.

"They'll want paying."

"I'll pay them."

The men wanted a week's worth of cigarettes. He would deliver, Arno assured them.

While the men prepared, Arno went home to get his mother ready. Honor thy mother: she wouldn't want strange men to see her like this. He shifted her onto her back, combed her hair, kissed her, and then, after placing the old copy of *The Three Musketeers* in her crossed arms, he wrapped her from head to foot in the widow Hitzig's old quilt.

Then he went to see Frau Kleber and gave her the news. He didn't accept her hugs, but he did accept her words of admiration.

"She was the bravest woman I've ever known."

Hearing this, Arno felt a lump in his throat that wouldn't leave him for a long time. It prevented him from saying: Yes, his mother was the bravest person he'd known, too. Honor thy mother, the painful lump reminded him, moving down into his chest in an attempt to break his ribs.

"Will you say a few words for my mother, Frau Kleber? She would like that."

"At the cemetery?"

"Here, like with Helmut."

She went to fetch the priest who'd arrived in the last month from Tilsit.

After a simple ceremony with the women of the house and Herr Götz, the priest told Arno that his mother must be given a Christian burial on consecrated land, in the cemetery.

"The place we're taking her is a cemetery, too," he said. He remembered the giant's tears. "And it's consecrated."

Once his mother was in the ground beside little Helmut, Arno asked the men to leave him alone.

"All right, kid, but don't be long: it'll be dark soon."

While he covered her with the consecrated soil, he spoke to her. He made her promises and poured out all the words that the living never say because they think they'll live forever and because it hurts to look at each other when they say them. He said them crying like the giant. And he said them angry like an abandoned child. The winter birds were infected with his sorrow and joined in, and Arno was pleased, trusting that their echo would reach the place to which his mother now flew.

"You'll like this place, Mutter," he said when he felt calmer. "Nothing will ever block the view of the lake from here. In summer, the sun will come through the branches, and the rain will run over you but never stagnate."

Honor thy mother.

"I'll go, Mutter. I'll go as soon as I can, and I'll find my brothers. I promise."

When he got home, he ate a piece of bread his mother had saved. There was a knock on the door. After some more words of sympathy, Frau Kleber said: "Arno. Frau Hammerschmidt said that she was going to tell the authorities that she had an unaccompanied child in the house."

At Arno's look of alarm, she went on: "Don't worry. I told her you're not alone. That we're your family. And I told her what your mother would've said: If she dares, she won't be getting her weekly potato or the rabbit bones you would've given her. That last bit was my idea. But it convinced her. At least, I think it did."

He went back to his mother early the next day with a cross marked with deep lines, so that her name would never be erased from the earth: **ETHEL SCHIPPER.**

The Soviets didn't come for him that day, or the next, or any other.

And now it was Christmas. Another one. And there he still was: they neither took him away nor sent him to be with his brothers. And he arrived home later and later. He tried to provoke stern words from his mother, but there was only silence. He was greeted by an empty bedroom, a potato that Frau Kleber had boiled, his copy of *Twenty Thousand Leagues under the Sea*, his mother's Bible, his father's horses, and a letter written on gossamer-thin paper, marked with the tears he never saw his mother spill.

Honor thy mother.

# 70. Christmas

## Wanda

***December 25, 1946***

Looking into the new mirror—a shard she'd found outside a bombed house—Wanda didn't recognize herself: Almost two years of farmwork in relentless summer sun and dry winter air had weathered her wan skin. Her chestnut hair had gone almost entirely gray. Her body had lost its soft curves. Knowing it was due to hardship, not age, didn't help one bit.

Nor did her sorrow. Sorrow was what had drained her vitality more than anything. Some heartbreak installs itself in the body to feed on the soul: it was sucking her dry from the inside like the vampire in *Nosferatu*, a film that had terrified her as a young woman.

Nobody would believe that just three years ago she'd sustained life in her belly. She wouldn't believe it herself if she hadn't brought that life into the world, held it in her arms, nursed it, and buried it; if her child's laughter wasn't still ringing in her ears, if she wasn't woken at night by his voice, his *"eins, eins, eins,"* his *"ich, ich, ich."* His toothless "Mama."

All the sleepless nights were consuming her, too.

With her physical changes and mutilated voice, Hartwig wouldn't recognize her when—if—he returned. More than a year had passed now since the end of the war, and still no news. The Red Cross knew nothing, and Hartwig's name never appeared on their list as either deceased or prisoner.

"Is he on the list of soldiers?"

Yes, they told her at the offices of what remained of the Wehrmacht, he was.

This was important, because rumor had it that, once on its feet, the new German government would pay pensions. Her pension as a war widow—or Hartwig's as a veteran—would depend on his name appearing on that list.

You must understand, the lack of information is due to the confusion and ferocity of the last days of the war, the military officials told Wanda.

And if he had in fact been sent to the eastern front just before the advance on Berlin, the chances of finding him, alive or dead, diminished. The Soviets were the least cooperative of the Allies, they told her. And thanks to the docility she'd learned during the Nazi years, Wanda didn't dare reply, if you already knew it was the last days, why did you take him? What purpose did it serve? Why did another family need to lose a father?

On good days, it seemed as if half of Germany's men remained prisoners. On bad days, like today, she knew that the whole world, her world, was a prisoner.

Where could he be?

Every day, they learned of soldiers returning after completing their sentences abroad. And that meant the family served a life sentence of hope. Because just as someone began to give up, reconcile themselves, news would come: lots of prisoners returning from France or Denmark today. The worst thing was when he wasn't among the groups that arrived from the Soviet Union, many of them presumed dead but returning alive. They returned with information that there were hundreds of thousands of Germans still there. Subjected to forced labor, mistreated, infected with typhus and dysentery, on the verge of death. One of those could be theirs.

He was paying their debt. They were all paying it. Ilse and Freddy's six months of separation were over, but they didn't believe her when she told them everything would be fine. She could see it in their eyes. Neither her sacrifice nor the time had restored them, helped them regain their joy. They hadn't understood that, in leaving them at Albert's, she'd sought to protect them from real hardship.

At first, the work on the farm outside Hohenlockstedt had earned Franz, Irmgard, and Wanda each enough food to sustain one person, not a family. What was scarcely enough for three they stretched to six.

As part of their pay, they could stay in the barn. The war was over, but for them, it was as if they were still on the road, in permanent flight, in permanent hunger and cold. The locals didn't look kindly on outsiders with strange accents, even if they spoke German. They were trespassers in their own country.

Prussia and its people had been so distant for so long that, here, no one regretted their loss, no one missed them. They were too busy surviving the hunger and the cold or burying the dead, who continued to fall. The war was still claiming victims, even without a single weapon being fired. And every day, more German refugees arrived, uneasy invaders. Exiled pilgrims in search of a country, unwelcome.

It was difficult to live in the wagons and not feel as if they could have to leave at any moment. Franz, Irmgard, and Wanda studied the map every night. They asked the paper covered in lines, borders, and cardinal points: Is there a better place for us? No answer came.

In any case, they'd been lucky to find work: the farms had lost their Zivilarbeiter, but even so, there were fewer jobs than there were unemployed people. But soon, Franz had found work at the local blacksmith's, and the Bürgermeister had assigned them a home: the small second floor of the forge adjoining the house of the blacksmith and his family. It wasn't much better than the barn, but it was theirs for as long as the Bürgermeister said it was, no matter how much the blacksmith's wife objected.

"Dear lady, we can't have Germans living like gypsies. Until we can think of another solution, we must all make sacrifices," he told her emphatically.

And so, they traveled in the carts for the last time. They unpacked them and settled in. After dismantling their covers, Franz returned the wagons to the farm. The rugs, though perforated, would help to improve the appearance of their new home, to warm the atmosphere. The farmer would pay for the carts and horses little by little with flour and eggs. Wanda could continue to say hello every day to the brave but now nervous horse that had borne them to safety.

Weeks had passed before they were sent the military bunk beds promised by the Bürgermeister's office. When they arrived, Wanda decided that it was time to go fetch her missing children. And then, there they all were: four in one bedroom and four in the kitchen of a house that didn't belong to them. They had to use the outdoor lavatory, but their landlady kept it locked.

Take pride, Wanda heard her father's voice say. You're Prussian like Queen Wanda. You have the heart of a warrior who defends her land. But her fight was not for that disputed land but for her family. That's enough, Wanda told herself. We're together. No one's about to starve or freeze to death. Those of us who are here are well. That's all that matters.

She put away her sorrow for a moment. She ran her hands over her silvery braids. She closed her eyes. She painted a smile across her face and turned around.

Their Christmas feast was in front of her. The children were sitting at the little table made from irregular planks of wood, drawing on their blackboards. She remembered packing the fine tablecloth so she could surprise them all on their first Christmas. Wanda shook her head. Had she thought a banquet would be waiting for them at the end of the journey? If she'd ever imagined that tablecloth's true fate . . .

The smile disappeared. It was their second Christmas without Helmut, Hartwig, and Erna. There would be no gifts and, for dinner, only potatoes and cabbage. It's enough, Wanda, it's more than we had last year. Now there was butter, she reminded herself, and bread and salt, which they hadn't had even the day before. Those who were there were together, even if thc table was too small to gather around at the same time. A reason to celebrate. She put the smile back on.

"Who wants to sing 'O Tannenbaum'?"

Irmgard smiled, playing along. She'd been exposed to as much sun as her mother, but her freckled skin still knew how to recover. Wanda hoped that time would erase her daughter's memories of working bent over to sow the fields. This new life had already erased Edeline's and Crystl's memories of their old one. They'd stopped asking for Helmut. They'd sing even if they didn't know the words. Freddy looked at her, serious, but ready to follow her lead even in song. Ilse didn't look up from her blackboard. The amount of time that girl spent writing!

"Ilse." The girl didn't stop. "Ilse!"

Ilse looked up with her new gaze. Profound. Sad. Always sad. Wanda could hardly believe that she was the same girl who, two years ago, had organized the Christmas carols and, a little later, an improvised birthday party. The most beautiful party; the last one of that life.

It was time to begin their new life.

"Ilse, shall we sing?" Wanda said with a real smile.

Her daughter shrugged.

"Come on. Some celebrations can't be missed, and some songs can't wait for another day, especially at Christmas."

Ilse smiled.

# 71. Stories

## Ilse

***December 25, 1946***

Ilse was angry. Sometimes, the sad anger simmered under her skin; sometimes, in her chest. It had started the day their mother came for them at Uncle Albert's farm, but she didn't understand why, since that was what she'd wanted more than anything: for her mother to come and say, it's time to go. Perhaps she'd kept the anger inside for so long that it had filled her body and now it overflowed.

Sometimes, it was less painful to remember her father, Helmut, and Janusz than to listen to her mother's unrecognizable voice, to look her in the eye. Sometimes, her mother seemed more lost than they were, because Ilse's memories gave them life, but reality had robbed her mother of hers. The woman who Wanda was now blotted out Ilse's memories of the strong, happy woman she'd once been.

The woman who made her angry pretended. She spoke to them all—even Grandma—softly, with simple words, and with half-truths, as if they were stupid. She smiled in the same way. Her smile was always a lie.

And she'd stopped fighting. She allowed herself to be cowed, especially by Grandma Hannah. Grandma had stolen from Ilse, and her mother had allowed it.

At the beginning of December, Ilse had received a birthday gift from her father's elder brother, who, according to Grandma, was rich because there wasn't a single butcher in Germany those days who wasn't. The card said: *For our dear niece Ilse, from Gunter Hahlbrock and family.* So it was she who opened the package that arrived from Hanover for her eleventh birthday: an enormous salami that left everyone speechless. But it was her grandmother who took out a knife and sliced a small piece for each of them. She put the rest away.

"I'll keep it," Ilse said. "It's mine, Oma."

"Selfish child. I'm keeping the rest for your uncle Franz; he works hard and needs to eat."

Ilse looked at Uncle Franz, who said nothing because Grandma's decree suited him. Then she looked at her mother, who didn't say anything, either.

Ilse wanted to say, Mama and Irmgard work hard, too; it's my gift, and I want to share with everyone. She put her anger away with her tears.

Since then, she hadn't seen a single piece of her birthday salami, hadn't even seen Franz eat any. He must have hidden to do it. Grandma hadn't even brought it out to share on Christmas Day.

Her mother was looking in the mirror with a desolate expression and Ilse watched as she decided to bring out her false smile.

"Who wants to sing 'O Tannenbaum'?"

Softly, lying, as if speaking to idiots. No. She wouldn't even look at her.

But then her mother said what she said and smiled for real, and Ilse's anger dissolved; it stopped simmering. She put her resentment away again. For another day.

She sang, she ate cabbage and potatoes, and then she offered to tell one of Janusz's stories for the little ones. Her mother's honest smile gave her the courage, even though it hurt, because Janusz's absence would always hurt. Where was he? Why had he left without saying goodbye? But she would be brave, like her mother with her real smile was.

"Which do you want? The one about the fox or the one about Queen Jurata, queen of the Baltic, who cries even now, buried under her castle of amber?"

Put like that, everyone, even the adults, wanted to hear the tale of Jurata. That night, they dreamed of Prussia, but all the stories and dreams in the world couldn't make it real again.

# 72. The amber teardrop

## Janusz

***December 25, 1946***

Walking with the wolf children had taught him he was no wolf. Talking to the boy in the forest had taught him that, while solitude had been imposed again, he didn't want to be alone. The amber teardrop had shown him a part of his past that he wanted to recover. The tears he'd shed for another Helmut had moved him to search for a salve for all the wounds he'd kept hidden since leaving the security and delusion of the farm. He had started out crying for Helmut but continued for Herr Hahlbrock and his family. For Ilse. For himself.

And so he wandered for months. He traveled south on a freight train. He found other young men there, lured by the changes that were taking place. A whole region that had once been German was now given to Poland as compensation for the eastern territory the Russians didn't want to return. The biggest loser was Germany, but closely followed by Poland, which the Russians prevented from regaining its original shape after years of persecution. Many Poles were sent to Breslau and told it was their new home. Perhaps it could be a new home for Janusz, too.

But he'd never been in a city: it seemed enormous, and it was in ruins. He belonged to the forests. But he spent a few days with his new traveling companions. He acted as interpreter, since everything was written in German.

The night they went to the massacre in the square was his last in Breslau. The moment Janusz saw Radosz on the stage, drunk, a knot of repugnance formed in his throat. Radosz, among the Poles being honored for their service as partisans. What was a wolf doing in the city? And with ten Germans kneeling at his feet, adjudged to be guilty, though Janusz didn't know of what. Of being in what was now named Wrocław instead of Breslau? Of having survived the war?

The crowd stifled him with its warmth. He'd never seen so many people in his life, never been so crammed in. Owing to his height, nothing impeded his view of the stage, the knives they took out, the axe in Radosz's hands, the severed head in Radosz's hands, the pleasure on the face of Radosz, the city wolf.

And if there was a spasm in the cheers around him, they immediately returned. Louder. It suffocated Janusz, who ran without caring whether he trod on toes, elbowed chests. He ran and kept running until he reached the city's outskirts, where he vomited.

Thereafter, Radosz invaded his dreams, turning them into nightmares. The only thing that calmed him was holding the smooth tear of Jurata he'd gotten from the German boy and stroking it. He must return to the forests, he decided. Perhaps, in them, he'd escape his nightmares.

That fall, he crossed the Oder and then the Vistula. He followed the compass in his feet, all the way to the Hahlbrocks' farm. He thought he'd find it taken over by another family, but no. It was deserted, though not intact: vandals had torn out its windows and doors and left its empty interior at the mercy of the elements.

He went inside his old hut. It didn't smell of him anymore, or of Kaiser. It smelled of stale urine, of wounded animals. Vegetation was growing inside, reclaiming territory lost in the ancient war against humans. He didn't enter the house. It was better to preserve the memory of their last breakfast, the whole family together, the smiles and the laughter that crackled despite the war outside.

Jadwiga was still here, he remembered. She'd also shared that day with them. He'd look for her.

The village seemed devoid of life. Everything was closed. Her family's house looked deserted. He knocked anyway. To his surprise, Jadwiga's mother opened, looking much older than before.

"Pani Nowak, do you remember me?"

"No."

"I'm Janusz. Jadwiga's friend? You invited me to spend Christmas with you one time . . ."

"Of course! But no one's going to recognize you with that beard, lad."

Janusz laughed. A little.

"I was looking for Jadwiga. The last time I saw her—"

"Oh! My Jadwiga, my poor girl . . ."

Pani Nowak burst into tears. Jadwiga had never made it home. They found her the day after the family left, sprawled in a ditch by the side of the road, surrounded by broken dishes, with the glass from a golden mirror piercing her throat. Raped by several men. One of them, shocked and dismayed, since they'd agreed to attack only Germans, like in Nemmersdorf, had later confessed. It was a group led by the Hahlbrocks' old Zivilarbeiter. Neither Jadwiga's pleas nor the fact that she was a Pole had stopped him.

"Radosz," said Janusz in the thin voice the heart allows when it shatters like a mirror.

"That's the one."

He felt in his pocket for Jurata's tear, clung to its smoothness. Had he known it in Breslau, he would have climbed on the stage, snatched the axe, and driven it into his head, though not without first giving Radosz the opportunity to recognize him: the boy, the głupi, the one who doesn't understand anything. Now he understood too much.

He'd go back. He'd go back and kill him, Janusz promised himself.

Jadwiga's mother told him that everyone had left.

"The Russians don't want us here. They cleared us from our own land. But I couldn't leave Jadwiga alone. Who would take her flowers? The Russians know that, at my age, I'm not going to fill the place with kids. They'll let me die here. That's all I ask."

Janusz stayed with her for a while longer, debating whether to tell her that the Hahlbrocks had loved her daughter and left her a buried treasure. Tell her where it was. But in the end, he decided not to: What for? Pani Nowak lived waiting to die; she seemed resigned to it. She didn't want another person's treasure or need the problems that it would bring if she were discovered with it. Best to leave it underground, in the dark.

Then he left. He went deep into the forest, then slumped to the ground. He couldn't take another step, couldn't bear to shed another tear, so he clung to the amber teardrop. He had thought he'd lost everything on the journey west, but now he realized that there had still been more to lose. Run from the Russians, his mother had said, and he'd fallen into German hands. Now he was returning to live among Poles. Russians, Poles, Germans, British: they all had blood on their hands; they had all become wolves.

I'll go back, he promised himself. I'll kill him. And he imagined a scene worthy of his country's tales: a giant with a wolf's eyes came out from the trees and, with a swing of his axe, killed a national hero.

He wouldn't do it. He wasn't a wolf. He'd let them keep their hero and let the hero keep his memories, which would follow him to hell. If he did that to Jadwiga, who was of his people and whom he'd known for years, what had he done to all the unknown women—all the Germans—he must have found? What would he have done to Frau Hahlbrock and Irmgard had they not left when they did? To Ilse?

And the image of Ilse, dead at the hands of Poles, plagued his mind. She was safe, he thought, but if they'd left an hour later . . . But no.

Something had warned them to go earlier than planned that day, and Ilse lived, though he'd never see her again. Ilse, his adopted sister; Ilse, to whom he'd given his stories. Then he understood that, maybe, though he'd lost his stories, they hadn't been left scattered on the road. Maybe he'd just entrusted them all to a girl with chestnut braids, who wouldn't let them die. Just as his mother had done with him.

Janusz fell asleep with Jurata's tear clenched in his fist. Later, the song of the wind whistling through the trees woke him. The breeze carried a familiar scent. It spoke and Janusz understood. With a smile, he got up and followed it. The moon lit the way.

It was another long journey. The longest of all. At last, he arrived. He could hear Christmas carols being sung in nearby Palmnicken, but they weren't for him. His was the music that came from the sea, the siren's voice, the voice of the amber queen. Jurata. Jurata, who sent out her song of tears with each piece of amber from her castle under the sea. She had sent a tear that had reached him inland, in life. He, believing he'd lost his stories, had taken a long time to understand.

To live, he had to die. His mother had said it before leaving, but he'd thought she was only referring to frostbitten toes. But now, Jurata was calling him. Now he understood. The same thing must have happened to his mother, who only stayed as long as necessary. Only until her daughter died. Only until she lost all hope. His mother's ghost never roamed the forests; it became a wave in the eternal ocean.

To complete his task, to deliver to safety the little sister that life had given him, Janusz had taken a little longer to reach this shore. His destination.

On this journey, he would only take the teardrop, take it back to its owner.

He undressed. As the breeze had promised, he didn't feel the cold in the air. Or when the water reached his knees, or when he introduced his whole body into the gray sea.

Jurata's song was in his ears. To hear more clearly, he stopped kicking. Stopped swimming. Breathing.

He'd never known such peace. He wouldn't feel the cold anymore; he wouldn't feel the loneliness.

He opened his hand and let the teardrop fall.

And he followed.

# 73. A stranger

## Arno

***June 1947***

He wasn't on the first convoy, but he'd be on the second. Arno didn't want to spend another day in that place.

"Why go?" said the Russian official with a smirk. "Not happy in your Germany? Russians here, English there. What is difference?"

"My family's there."

"Family here also. It says you travel with mother?"

"My mother died in October."

"No record here," the man said, irritated.

"We reported it. It must be written somewhere else."

The man rustled the pages, scowling.

"Please put my name down for the next truck to Hamburg. And put Frau Greta Kleber and Fräulein Irma Kleber, too."

"No truck to Hamburg. And no space for so much lady."

"Please. Any truck to the British zone border will do."

The man huffed with indifference.

"I can pay . . ."

The man's eyes flickered. "What you have for me?"

"When you put me on the truck, I'll give you a gold-edged amber medallion."

"Rich boy? What else you give me?"

"That's all I have. But I need to be with my family."

"All right. In square at eleven. Is one hour. You be on time?"

He ran home.

"Frau Kleber! It's time to go!"

Frau Kleber came out.

"What did you say, Arno?"

"They've started taking people to the British zone. I got spots for us on the next truck."

"We can't, Arno, Irma's fever won't go down."

The fever that had come and gone since twenty Russians attacked her.

"But she'll get better there. There'll be medicine, for sure."

"She can't stand up." Frau Kleber couldn't hide her sadness: for her dying daughter, for the missed opportunity. "Arno, we're not coming. Will you be all right?"

"*Ja.* I'll take two rabbits and a few potatoes. I'll leave you the rest."

Frau Kleber, once a fine lady of Königsberg, was now a good farmer. They wouldn't go hungry, and, if things continued, soon she'd be able to sell some at the market.

Arno, faithful to his mother's instructions, kept his sack packed every day. He only had to add his quilt, and he'd be ready to leave. How right she had been: there was never time to pack.

With the sack over his shoulder filled with everything he owned—the Bible, his and his mother's papers, potatoes, and two rabbits in a wooden box—he said goodbye to the Klebers. He was glad he didn't have to do the same with the landlady, who was out.

We'll see each other soon, they said.

"Thank you for everything. Say thank you to Frau Hammerschmidt. When you come, find me."

"We will."

There was no time for more. He had to stop by the cobbler's.

"Herr Götz! I'm leaving."

"You did it, then? Very good, Arno."

"Why don't you come with me?"

"To do what? I was born here. And I'll die here. Besides, who else will take care of your mother's grave?"

Arno thanked him. The cobbler didn't let him go without new shoes.

"Well, they're not new. They belonged to a young man who went off to war without paying."

They both laughed and then Arno set off at a run. He arrived in time. Just. The official was anxiously scanning the supplicants who didn't have a seat. The remaining three spots on the truck wouldn't go to anyone until the boy with the fortune arrived.

"Boy! You almost late. Ladies?"

"They're not coming."

"No discount. Same price one or three."

Arno invited two women to join him.

"Same price one or three," he said before the man could object.

Once on board, Arno gave him what he'd promised. The official held the medallion up to the sunlight.

"Mosquito!" he said, grinning at the insect trapped forever in the amber.

"Two mosquitoes," said Arno.

He left him searching for the second tiny insect. Arno took his seat in the truck and they set off. The journey seemed endless. His brothers' letter, which he carried in his shirt pocket, was over a year old. What if they weren't on the farm near Hamburg anymore? What if they'd given him up for dead?

Once he was on the other side of the new border, he'd figure out what to do. He was afraid, but he'd been more afraid every day since his mother went away.

At the edge of the British zone, they were handed over to the German authorities. Arno produced his papers, and they registered him. The women had somewhere to go, so they thanked him again and said goodbye. He was taken to a refugee camp.

Two weeks passed without news. Questions occupied Arno's mind and his time. What if the officials didn't find his brothers? What if his brothers didn't recognize him? Or he didn't recognize them? Sometimes, he could feel them near his memories, but their faces slipped stubbornly away.

What would he say when they asked about their mother? What if they were angry at him for not taking proper care of her?

"Schipper! Arno Schipper, age twelve!"

"That's me!" He jumped up from his cot.

"Bring your things. They've come for you."

From a distance, he recognized Fritz first. The moment he saw him, all the dislodged memories snapped into place.

"Arno!"

His brothers ran to meet him. They hugged him, overcome with emotion. He pressed himself against them, his eyes closed to hold in the tears.

"Look at you! So tall!"

"You're taller than us now!"

Then a voice outside their circle made Arno's body quiver.

"Hello, Arno."

The man was looking at him pleadingly. He had certain familiar, beloved features. But his nose protruded too much; his eyes were like an owl's. Even his size was different. Diminished.

Arno separated himself from his brothers and ran into his father's arms.

"Vater? We thought you were dead!"

*"Mein Sohn! Mein kleiner Helfer!"*

The hug was different, too: their torsos, almost the same height now, fitted together in a new way. But the voice was his father's. And the words from childhood: My little helper . . . Arno began to cry, unwilling to hold it back any longer.

"Vater? I lost Mutter in the war."

# 74. Texas bound

## Karl

***May 1, 1945***

It was time to sleep. The night's reading was finished.

They closed the book, but comments continued in the dark. It's always sunny there, some said. It's never cold. They might meet Winnetou, many of them dreamed that night, and they'd be as daring and as heroic as Old Shatterhand, protagonist of the novels that the Führer had sent his officers before the Americans came down on them. To infuse them with courage and ferocity.

Those books were among the little they had, aside from the rags their uniforms had become. That spring, their jackets sometimes doubled as pillows. But the prisoners treasured the novels. They took turns reading out loud. Under the spell of Karl May's words, they were transported from the cold mud of their prison in northern France to the dust of the Mescalero Apache lands.

In that place of adventures, they won every battle, their feet were never infected, they were never hungry. They escaped from the reality in which they lived behind barbed wire, in which they'd lost, and someone else had the weapons, and they were aimed at them.

Karl let himself be transported, too; why not? May's stories were exciting. He dreamed of riding bareback, of galloping free across the endless prairies. But sometimes he could transport himself without the help of any novel. He went home and hugged his children; he sat by the fire; put on new socks his daughter had made; cooked a full, thick broth and served it hot. No one makes it like you do, Vater, everyone would say, and he'd go to sleep warm and full, looking forward to waking at dawn.

But soon, the guards said, they'd be transported to a place called Texas. They'd cross the ocean and become cowboys, the German prisoners joked. But Karl didn't want to go there even for grand adventures. He didn't want to be farther from his country, though he knew it was lost. Though he knew he was lost.

On the first day of his return to war, Karl had been afraid they'd send him back to the eastern front, but he was posted as a cook with a panzer division patrolling between Belgium and the Netherlands. He was the newest member of the division and quickly grew weary of being an object of curiosity. They say you have a bullet inside you, Schipper, is it true? They say your wife had you doing the cooking, Schipper, is it true? They say you go to sleep crying, hugging woolen socks, Schipper, is it true? Karl Schipper endured the questions and countered with his own: They say you should always be nice to the person who makes your food, soldier, is that true? That made them laugh, and it shut them up.

After almost a year, during the harshest winter ever known, they were sent to the Ardennes Forest.

The battle had begun in December, when the German Army had taken the Allies by surprise. We'll win this one for sure, said the soldiers Karl cooked for. He said nothing. It was what they'd said in 1941, before they'd lost it all in the ice. So much so that they had to drag ruined veterans like him back to war.

But in the new year, the questions turned serious: They say that you haven't received any provisions for two weeks, Schipper, is it true?

"Look at the broth, soldier," he replied.

It hadn't been two weeks without provisions, it had been three. The broth was little more than hot water.

They were hungry and cold. He was, too, but not as much as the others. He peeled potatoes, carrots, and onions, and ate the skins. He boiled bones for broth and sucked them afterward. For as long as the bread lasted, he divided it and took only his ration, but he ate the crumbs that each slice left on his board. He went to sleep cold but warmer than the others near his cook's fire, ready to heat water for the officers' tea; he had the socks Helga had given him again before leaving. So yes: he slept hugging spare socks; he slept with warm feet and his face covered to protect his eyes, which sometimes watered.

He didn't live in the path of bullets, but he knew a bomb could fall any day. He wasn't on the battlefield, but he understood: if there were no provisions to fill bellies, nor would there be bullets for rifles or gasoline for tanks. Once again, he had to witness soldiers celebrating when a horse died.

"Look at the size of the leg we brought you, Schipper! You can make one of your famous stews."

Yes, his horse stew was famous, and he celebrated, too, because hunger was an immediate problem to which the body demanded a solution. But he also understood that an army that depends on horses and is forced to eat them is not on course for victory. And he knew that the enemy's horses weren't dying—they only had motorized vehicles.

And he listened: the officers gathered in his kitchen because it was the only place to escape the cold. On January 13, he learned of the Soviets' savage advance in East Prussia, and in the nights that followed, he lay awake in terror. What was left of his country? What was left of his family?

The decision to withdraw from the Ardennes was made on the night of the twenty-fourth. His unit was captured as it fled.

Under the Geneva Convention, they can't hold us here for more than a few months after the end of the war. But if they send us to Texas, we'll disappear forever to roast in the sun. Just you wait, Schipper: we'll turn as black as those guards, Marius Dold said to him every night.

His new friend was young. Almost as young as his sons, in fact. He'd been a soldier for less than a year. Marius told Karl he was meant to run his family's pharmaceutical company. To soldiers suffering from trench foot, he'd say: Such-and-such would cure that. And to those who had previously kept the hunger, cold, and fear at bay by means of the magic pill, he said: Ah well, you'll just have to put up with the withdrawal symptoms, my friend.

No one listened to Marius. What use was it hearing about remedies for their ailments if they couldn't get any?

The ones in withdrawal were the ones Karl felt most sorry for. They trembled, and not just from the cold. Some were delirious. But hunger was a distant memory: their bodies were being consumed. They only wanted the drug.

They're handing them out in the medical tent, Schipper, an officer had told him one day, back before their capture. You'll feel reborn.

Karl's slumbering addiction had stirred, but he resisted it. He wouldn't succumb: hunger and cold could kill him whether he felt them or not. And if they didn't, a second round of withdrawal would.

"You never took those, did you, Schipper?"

"No."

"Good for you. They're a total lie," Marius declared.

Karl did listen to him. The young man knew a lot of things that Karl had no idea about, like the Geneva Convention, for example. He also knew English but made sure the guards didn't find out, so they'd continue speaking openly in front of them. That was how they knew the Americans wanted to send them to Texas to turn them into cowboys. It was how they knew that East Prussia had surrendered and that it wouldn't be long before Berlin fell. And it was how they knew, that day in May, that Germany's days were numbered, and, therefore, they would only be prisoners a few more months. What would they return to? Karl was determined to scour every corner of the country for his family; if they were dead, he'd search for them in the ashes. He'd find them. He'd bury them together. He'd mourn them, and then perhaps he would be consumed by the magic pill until he was dead, too.

Like Marius, he wouldn't let them send him to Texas. Very soon, when he was freed, he'd walk east, walk every kilometer that separated him from his family, but he could only do that if he survived his imprisonment. So he had to survive.

Ethel. Helga. Johann. Fritz. Arno. Arno. Arno. With their names on his tongue, their voices in his ears, and their faces behind his eyelids covered in socks, he managed to sleep.

# 75. France

***May to June 1947***

Karl survived another two years of forced labor and mistreatment. Marius didn't. He'd died in April, a day before they were informed that they'd finally be freed.

Their plan had worked. Karl found some herbs that, taken as tea, had given them stomach cramps and diarrhea. The effect of the herbs soon passed, but not before the Americans had taken them off the cowboy list. They didn't want to export diseases to Texas.

"Wait and see, Schipper: in a few months, we'll be dining on a Frankfurter *Rindswurst* with sauerkraut, washed down with *Schwarzbier*."

That was his dream. Karl's dream was eating his wife's Blutwurst again. His own blood sausage was better, but he wanted to sit at the table and for dishes piled high with food that someone else had prepared to appear in front of him.

Two years later, he still clung to that dream; it was what had given him hope and the strength to endure the prison camp and then the life that followed, when he was handed over to a French farmer eager to take full advantage of his forced servitude. Karl remembered hearing about the Polish prisoners who'd been forced to work on German farms. Had they been treated humanely? Karl hoped so.

Their other option was clearing mines. They'd go home sooner, and their rations would be better, the Americans promised.

"No way," Marius told him. "Clearing mines will get us out of here sooner, but in little pieces."

And so the Americans loaned them to the French, who took them to the farm.

"It'll be fine," Karl told Marius. "I'll teach you."

The farmer, the new owner of their time and their bodies, didn't care what such-and-such a convention had to say about prisoners of war. Months passed, and no one showed any intention of letting them leave. For Karl, working on his wife's small farm had been easy. But now, it was impossible to sow seeds with such a weak body and such nagging hunger that a man was forced to eat some of the seeds seasoned with a little soil; to find nests of earthworms and salivate in anticipation; to steal scraps meant for the pigs—in particular, the potato peels, which he would boil with wild herbs and place for himself and his friend between their meager bread rations, so that they could pretend they were eating a sandwich, which they washed down with the starchy potato-skin broth.

Schipper, Marius told him, how lucky I am to have you. I know all about pharmaceuticals, I speak several languages, but I'd have starved alone.

But starvation isn't the only thing that can kill a man: so can a devastating condition that begins with stabbing pains in the abdomen. It's like I'm being knifed, Schipper, Marius said. A condition that continues with medical assistance begged for but never provided, in violation of the Geneva Convention. After that, more forced labor. Followed by a burst appendix. By peritonitis. By agony.

It would've been better to die from a bullet, said Marius. Or from the cold, thought Karl.

Just can't take any more pig food, Schipper, Marius said with what remained of his strength and his sense of humor.

Karl had carried him to the mass grave for German prisoners. Marius's body looked the healthiest of anyone lying there, Karl thought before turning away. All that effort to survive, for nothing.

Another emaciated prisoner was brought to replace Marius, but the next day, the soldiers told Karl that he was leaving. He didn't make friends with the man, but he passed on his survival secrets.

The transport took him to the German border, where he was registered. They would look for his family. He accepted the offer to stay in a refugee camp. He'd eat, he'd build up his strength. If his family wasn't found in the next month, then he'd set off to search for them himself.

One day, he was told he had visitors.

Fritz and Johann. They all cried, especially him. With joy. With sadness. They told each other their stories. The boys took Karl back to the farm where they lived and worked.

A month later, they received news. Arno had been found, the letter said.

"And your mother? And do they mention Helga?"

"They don't say anything else," Johann told him.

"It must be a mistake. Mutter would never leave Helga and Arno by themselves."

"Yes. It must be a mistake."

And they went to find them, but only Arno was there.

And they told each other their stories. And they cried.

# 76. Two paths cross

## Ilse and Arno

***September 1948***

She felt sick. It was the first day of school, but she hadn't been in class for almost six years.

"Ilse! Time to go!" Wanda called from outside.

Freddy was excited for his first-ever day of school; he'd spoken of nothing else for days. But Ilse lingered at the kitchen table in the new clothes Uncle Gunter had sent from Hanover. Ready, but reluctant to move. She would have to, because their mother wanted to walk them at least part of the way and they had to leave now or she'd be late for her job at the cardboard factory.

The new government, her mother said, had a special plan for children who'd missed a lot of schooling. A lot of the kids will be just like you, you'll see. Besides, you read and write every day. And you taught Freddy. If you can read, you can do anything, my girl.

She'd take her old blackboard and a pencil that her mother had bought her. We'll see what else they ask for, and we'll buy it. Ilse saw how she struggled to say those words. Buying was like a foreign concept.

After people spent many years bartering and scrounging to feed everyone, that summer, the government had given each citizen sixty Deutsche Marks: the new money, as Grandma called it.

They'd celebrated as if they were rich: they'd gone to buy ice cream and some secondhand shoes for Edeline. But their mother had saved the rest so that she could get them all the things they needed for school. Hence the new pencil. Take good care of it, Ilse!

After so much deprivation, everything happened so quickly that it made their heads spin. The day they had ice cream, Ilse had overheard her mother say that sweets weren't for poor people, and that she couldn't risk spending a single mark more.

In a conversation not meant for Ilse's ears (she wasn't trying to spy, but in that little apartment above the blacksmith's, you couldn't sigh without everybody knowing), her mother told Grandma that she'd gotten used to a life of going without. She was accustomed to having just enough to sustain their bodies. To living between those dark walls, those inadequate windows. To sleeping beneath two children in the metal bunk bed. She was accustomed to always fearing the worst. The Soviets were refusing to reach an agreement with the other occupying governments. What if they fought over Germany? What if war started up again? Ilse's stomach had tightened when she heard that.

Finally, her mother had been able to leave her job on the farm for one in a factory that would pay her with money. Very soon, she told them, she'd be able to exchange the savings she had in the bank in old money for new. It wasn't much, but they'd be all right. Perhaps their father's military pension would arrive soon, too, and perhaps they'd be given a subsidized house. They were on the list.

The war had ended, but there was news on the radio that worried her mother and Uncle Franz. Ilse, as always, listened. If the war restarted, would they have to run again? Would she have to stop going to school? She was afraid of going back, of how hard it'd be to lose it again.

From outside came the most common sound on the streets: a motorcycle. She didn't look for Papa anymore when she heard it. But that morning, she heard a message in the engine's purr: Get up, Ilse, work hard, be brave, take care of your family. Everyone heard the motorcycle, but her father's words were hers alone.

She got up from the table and went out. Wanda said goodbye when they reached the street that led to the factory. Ilse walked the rest of the way with Freddy. She hid her fear, walking with a firm step.

She'd been afraid many times, but she'd survived the war, two bombings, more than six months wandering, a life without a father, without the brother torn from her arms. *Liebe Mama:* if her mother read the letters Ilse wrote and erased every day, she'd cry. They'd cry together, perhaps. But we don't cry, Ilse. No, Mama. We don't cry. That was why she wrote, so that I don't cry. And so her letters were never really for her mother. They were for no one, they were for vanishing into the air, so that the tears dried before they formed. She'd written and erased the lists of questions and fears on her blackboard each night. Her newest and most immediate one was school.

But when she was afraid, Ilse had her father's words and Janusz's stories to protect her. Like that day, as she went into the school. They all looked at her. They stopped talking, then whispered to one another. They pointed at them. They pointed at Freddy. Ilse felt her anger come out from where she kept it.

She hid her fear, squeezed her brother's hand, and walked in with a firm step.

---

He made his bed and put his nightclothes in a trunk underneath. He was very tidy—that hadn't changed—but he no longer kept everything in his sack, ready to run. It hadn't been easy to break the habit his mother had instilled. Where are you going to go? his father had asked him. If we needed to escape, I'd tell you. Don't worry, son.

And so Arno endeavored not to pack every day, but he still woke in the middle of the night with his heart racing, listening for bombs and his mother's breathing. It wasn't easy to get back to sleep each time he woke and rediscovered the void she'd left. Not at all easy to be forever awaiting her now-beloved blah-blah-blah.

He still felt her presence all the time. He still remembered her two Commandments: Love God and honor your mother. Now all ten had been restored. He was living in the after, though she wasn't there to remind him of them.

His bedroom was so small that as he rushed to get ready—his father was waiting with breakfast—Arno knocked the copy of *Twenty Thousand Leagues under the Sea* and his miniature horses off the little shelf. The two he'd given Johann and Fritz when they left would be missing from his collection forever. They'd burned them the first night they spent alone, after the cart on which they were traveling, along with the women and horses, sank in the Vistula Lagoon. The boys had been walking in front to make sure that the ice was solid when the Russian aerial attack began, and it was only because they were a pace ahead that they were saved. The story had taken them days to tell. Arno watched how, when one started to speak, sometimes the other told him with his eyes to be quiet.

His brothers had already told their father the part of Arno's story that they knew. Arno gave his account, but he didn't tell them about the Beckmanns adopting him as a grandchild, his heartbreak at their deaths. He told them about his typhus, but not his delirium or imprisonment. He told only his father about Fräulein Stieglitz's tunnels, about the sideboard with the foxes and geese on it, about the treasure he'd found inside, and what he'd used it for. From inside the lapel of his overcoat, he took out the last piece he had left: one more amber drop. It reminded him of the kind giant. He was glad to have this one thing for himself, but he showed it to his father, who told him the story of his last visit to the old woman's house, though he broke down in tears before finishing. It's nothing, he insisted. I'm just overwhelmed by everything I have to be grateful for. Arno didn't tell anyone about how certain they'd been that his father and then his brothers had died, about how, with that certainty, they'd built a life for two. He would never tell his father about the end that his horse met: the pulley, the blood. He only said that the brave animal held on until it had gotten them back to the farm. He let his father guess the rest.

He told his brothers about receiving their letter and their mother's immense joy at knowing they were alive. He gave them the soft paper with the ink that had run from their mother's tears. They kept it between the pages of the family Bible. He didn't tell his father about that bubble of time when only two Commandments mattered: one to love God and one to honor only his mother. Best just to tell him how, so long as Karl's fate was unknown, she'd consider herself a married woman. That detail was the one his father asked him to repeat again and again.

All his father shared was that he'd been a prisoner of war in France, but sometimes Arno caught him with his gaze absent, fixed on the past. Arno knew that his kind and cheerful father was lost, made old, unable to reunite with the man he'd been before the war. Honor your father: Arno didn't ask questions, didn't insist.

Helga also kept nearly all of her story to herself. When they found her at last, she was haggard, emaciated, but happy to see them and happy with her new life: she'd fallen in love with a German shortly before the American invasion of Denmark. They'd worked together on a farm there for almost two years. Once freed, they'd decided to marry and return to Germany. They didn't live in the same town, but the family saw them from time to time. Arno and Helga always embraced for a long time, remembering the hug they'd thought would be their last. Like everyone, Helga was recovering, but did not forget.

Nobody would forget. And nothing was the same.

Arno sat down to eat breakfast.

"Your brothers already left," his father told him.

Fritz and Johann worked as policemen in Hohenlockstedt. Farmwork had only been a means of survival, they said. This was a career.

His father had decided that he and Arno would breed the two rabbits descended from the ones his mother had transported and protected. They're Prussian rabbits, he'd say proudly. How they'd survived the odyssey of the war to send two descendants such a distance with Arno years later was a mystery that would fascinate his father forever. The rabbits would multiply, and they'd use them to barter for flour, potatoes, and other essentials. He aspired to nothing else.

Arno observed with sadness how his father limited his life to taking care of him and the rabbits, reading the newspaper, listening to the radio, and waiting for his pension. Wherever he looked or listened, he saw and heard the war. There's no more war, his brothers would insist. Did you forget that we lost? That it's over? Arno didn't like the veiled mockery behind those questions. Some things never changed, like his brothers' lack of respect for their father. Only Arno listened when Karl responded: They say it's over, but wars never die. Look at what's happening between the supposed Allies: they're going to war, and I don't know when, but they'll take us with them! Arno listened; Herr Beckmann had said similar words, and, besides, it was true: the news on the radio and in the papers was alarming.

"Do you have everything?"

His father was more nervous than he was about his return to school.

On his arrival, Arno had handed over the pieces of Gabonese ebony his father had rescued from Fräulein Stieglitz's house. He thought they'd inspire dreams for the future again, but he was wrong. The cuttings were from a life that no longer existed.

"I'm sorry: they're the only ones I was able to save, Vater," he'd told him, dismayed by his father's confusion. "We had to use the rest for firewood. They're for Schipper and Sons, Cabinetmakers, remember?"

The memory lit up his father's face.

"Oh, Arno. Schipper and Sons will always exist, but we won't be cabinetmakers. Not even Schipper has the desire or strength for it now," he said, his eternal carpenter's hands stroking the carvings that he would keep forever after in his bedroom.

Arno had given up insisting that they could trade some rabbits for new carpenter's tools, since he'd had to leave his father's behind when the Russians came to put them on a train in Kaliningrad. When Arno apologized, Karl said he didn't miss them anymore.

"Don't worry. They were important when they were important. I stopped thinking about them a long time ago, son." He showed Arno his hands. "Besides, look: I lost all my calluses. It would be very painful to start again."

His father said that he appreciated the beauty of the cuttings, but he appreciated more that they'd helped his family survive the cold on an almost-impossible journey, and that was the reason he kept them. He included Fräulein Stieglitz in his prayers for the rest of his life, thanking her for being his family's host and savior.

"In any case, forget about carpentry. They'll open the schools soon," he went on. "You'll study, and they'll teach you all about the machines you like so much. You'll see."

Arno had liked that idea. He'd go to school. And he had to admit that if his father was nervous, so was he, a little. He'd have to work against the clock to become an engineer before he was old.

Now the day had arrived. They washed the dishes in silence. His father went out onto the street with him, insisting despite Arno's objections on pointing his bicycle in the right direction. Arno didn't need help, but his father seemed to need to give it. He would have accompanied him to the school gate if Arno had allowed it. But he had his limits.

"You'll be fine. Study hard, son!" his father told Arno when he got on and cycled off without looking back.

Karl Schipper watched his beloved Arno until he was out of sight. The boy filled his heart. But seeing him leave emptied it, filled it with anxiety.

He was just going to school. It would only be a few hours of separation. But Karl's head filled with questions as absurd as they were inevitable: Will I see him again? Will I be alive when he returns?

They'd spent all their time together since being reunited. Sometimes they spoke, sometimes they respected each other's silences, but they always kept each other close. Now that time had ended. First it would be because of school, but Karl knew there were a thousand other ways they would be separated. And that none of them had anything to do with the war, just with the natural course of life. His elder sons assured him the war was over, and they looked at him as if he were crazy when he insisted it wasn't. He couldn't explain to them that, when he closed his eyes, when he listened to the radio, when he slept, when he took care of the rabbits, when he wanted to say something to his absent wife, when he put food on the table, he could still hear the current of the river that had dragged them all away like leaves. He couldn't help feeling that the river of war had thrown them onto this bank only to deceive them, so they'd become complacent until the river burst its banks and dragged them in again.

No matter how one pleads for peace, war never dies, Karl thought, certain that he was right.

Wars leave wounds that can be reopened at any moment.

He turned on the radio. He sat in his armchair. He'd stay there until Arno returned.

When Arno walked into the schoolyard, the first thing he saw was an elegant girl with golden-brown braids, surrounded by boys. He saw the moment when she made up her mind and pushed one of them with unexpected strength, knocking him to the ground. Arno approached, marveling.

"And don't you dare call my brother stupid again. He's smarter than all of you put together," she said. She ran her eyes over all of them, finally coming to him.

Arno didn't know what to say. He was ready to defend her brother, to stop anyone who dared push the girl back. But her ferocious look made him sway where he stood, and the amber flash of her eyes broke something wide open.

❦

Ilse didn't look at the boy blonder than the sun whom the teacher told to sit beside her that first day, and she didn't want to answer his question: Where are you from? She was still trying to level out her breathing after the fight on the playground, to contain the tears of rage. She kept repeating to herself: Nobody's going to make fun of Freddy. Ever.

Where am I from? What does that boy care? she thought, offended.

Together they learned that they both had to stand when the teacher, taking attendance, asked all the Flüchtlinge to rise on hearing their names. She grumbled each time, and it amused him each time, but they stood. Until the day came when Ilse said: No more.

"Now everyone who *isn't* a refugee can stand up, Frau Zegelken."

She said it with such force and conviction that the teacher dropped the humiliating request immediately.

The tall, blond boy was very full of himself, she thought at first. And even though he hadn't been among the boys making fun of Freddy's speech, his presence had colored her impression of him, some part of her brain associating him with that moment, as she'd once associated Kaiser with the geese.

"What did you think of me that day?" she would ask years later.

"That you were the bravest and strongest girl I'd ever known."

But he didn't say that to her on that first day, because in addition to brave, after the incident, she'd seemed full of herself, too: she didn't look at him or answer his questions.

So they just looked at each other out of the corners of their eyes, annoyed.

But life would be patient. He was thirteen, she twelve.

And then they were neighbors.

Ilse's family had been on the list of families in need since they arrived in Hohenlockstedt, and at last a subsidized house became available. One more move after a wandering life, their mother promised, and never again. Ilse liked that certainty: never again. The last stop on the journey they'd begun years before.

They said goodbye—without regret—to the blacksmith's wife. They said see you later to Grandma, Crystl, and Uncle Franz—again, without much regret. They'd still see one another every day, but the two families would have their own spaces, now. They were assigned one of four partitions in a converted munitions bunker. They cleaned. They moved in. They didn't have much: just the almost-empty trunks from another life.

Ilse couldn't believe it, but by the evening, she actually missed Grandma. It wouldn't last long, she decided: she still hadn't forgiven her for stealing the birthday salami.

The next day, her mother told her and Irmgard: Girls, the family next door is all men. Don't even look at them, I don't want any more problems. They promised to obey. Ilse didn't know until the next morning that the neighbors were Arno Schipper, his father, and his two older brothers. Ilse saw Arno leave on his bicycle after saying goodbye to his father. Boy, was he fast!

How she wished her own father were there to see her off in the same way.

Arno's father and Ilse's mother had recognized each other's Prussian accents the moment they introduced themselves. They didn't discuss how they'd left home or how much they'd lost: it wasn't polite to pry into another person's suffering. No one was there without having suffered, they knew that.

In time, Arno and Ilse established a routine: leave for school, each on their own; return to do their chores and homework, each on their own. One day, they realized that they slept on either side of the same wall, that the sounds that she heard through the wall were his, and the ones he heard through it were hers (and her noisy siblings'). They learned to distinguish each other's muffled voices. They never spoke of it in the day, didn't say a word to each other even when both were admitted to the school's special accelerated program, but at night, when it was time to sleep, they knew that only a thin wall separated their pillows. They knocked—*tock-tock*—and they forged a code that was theirs alone: Good night, Arno. Good night, Ilse. See you tomorrow.

One day, Arno didn't ride his bicycle to school, or allow his father to see him off. That day, he walked beside Ilse, matching her steps. They only looked at each other out of the corners of their eyes.

"Would you like to come to the park with me for ice cream?"

When Arno finally asked her out, they were no longer schoolmates. He was studying mechanical engineering, and she was pursuing accounting. Then came the town dance. Arno went because he knew Ilse would be there with her friends. He asked her for the first dance. Neither danced with anyone else for the rest of the night.

⚘

Wanda saw them arrive home holding hands. They looked at each other as they walked. So happy. So different: he so tall, so blond; she, with the modern haircut her mother was so against (it won't be long enough for your braids, Ilse!), looking so beautiful, but so small beside him. They didn't seem to notice: their gazes leveled them, and a knot formed in Wanda's throat.

She would've liked her own mother to tell her: That's how you and Hartwig looked at each other. That's how you loved each other until the last day. But even on the very day—after twelve years of waiting—when Wanda received news of Hartwig's fate, Hannah didn't have a single word of compassion or comfort for her: See what happened? I told you. Why didn't he desert like your brother?

He hadn't deserted. That became clear very quickly. The government had given him up for dead years before, when it started paying the widow of Hartwig Hahlbrock—missing in action—her pension. Wanda had been declared a widow long before losing hope that she wasn't one. And she had accepted it for her children.

But today, Wanda knew for certain that Hartwig had been alive on the last day of the war. On August 20, 1945, he'd been registered at the former Syrets concentration camp near Kiev. The distance between the eastern front and Kiev was considerable. He'd survived the journey; he'd survived another year. The date of his death at the camp was marked as May 13, 1946. The cause: dysentery. He lay in one of many mass graves.

The Red Cross considered the case closed, but she didn't. What had happened to him in that year? What had he done in order to survive? What motivation had he found to get up each day? Did he have any hopes? Did he think about her? She was also tormented by other questions: What had she been doing on the day of Hartwig's death? Did she sense something? Did her heart stop for an instant? She didn't think so. At the moment of her husband's last breath, she might have been bent over picking chard or digging potatoes. Too focused on the family's survival for premonitions.

I'm sorry, Hartwig.

The only thing that comforted her was the fact that Helmut hadn't had to wait long to be reunited with his father. But I didn't lose a single one more, Hartwig, Wanda told her dead husband for the tenth time that day. They were all well: Irmgard works at the cardboard factory, too, now; Freddy and Edeline are in school; Ilse is studying accounting, but she says her best teacher was you, on the farm.

Look at her, Hartwig: there she is with Arno, our neighbor. He's a good boy from a good Prussian family. What a journey they had to make to find each other! It's the first time since you left that I've seen that light in our daughter's eyes. Look, Hartwig. It's a miracle that she's alive. Ask Helmut, he knows. Ilse deserves to be happy. I won't tell her about you today. I don't want to wipe away that smile and that light in her eyes when they've only just appeared. Tomorrow. I'll tell her tomorrow. I'll let her dream today.

Wanda turned away. She went to find Irmgard.

"Don't say anything to Ilse. We'll tell her tomorrow."

And the little ones, too. They all deserved to know, so that their old and deep wound could heal, but there were things that could be left for later.

# 77. The children of amber

From that day on, the two pilgrims never stopped gazing at each other. Her place was with him; his place was with her. What happened to you? I don't want to remember. What have you lost? Too much. What did you see? Everything. Where did you go, Arno? Where did you, Ilse? As far as a war, and as near as the wall between them at night. As far and as near as a vanished homeland. As far and as near as fear and hunger. As far as a city's toppled walls, as near as the breeze from a bullet that ends one life and spares another. As far and as near as chance, which, despite sending them in different directions, had led them to each other.

At last, they were there, where they were meant to be.

With their gaze fixed on each other, they demolished the wall that had separated them. They overcame their bitter memories and the losses that held them captive in the past. With each step, they'd overcome bombs, cold, hunger, the world. They'd reached each other after a long pilgrimage in search of life, of peace. They discovered that when they were together life no longer hurt, and together they dared to believe in a future, even if the postwar world was intent on uncertainty, rubbing their noses in it with each newspaper headline.

On their wedding day, Arno gave Ilse the last remaining drop of amber, in memory of their shared land. "A tear!" she exclaimed.

"That's exactly what the forest giant said," he replied, "that it was Queen—"

"Jurata's tear!" she told him. And she thought of her giant, her Janusz. Could it be that all giants liked to tell stories, or was Arno's giant her . . . ? No. It wasn't possible that in such a big world and on such distant paths they also shared the same giant.

The years passed, and together they made a home that was cool in summer but warm in winter. Whereas alone, apart, in that before-you time so full of stories that they told each other only in fragments, they'd lived in tunnels and barns, in workshops and forges. Unwanted, in strangers' houses. Outcasts in the cold. Refugees. And they believed for a long time that their pilgrimage had ended there, within their own solid walls, with three daughters filled with stories of amber, and three baptisms to irrigate the family's new roots in a land they were claiming as their own.

But they were wrong: those years were just a pause in the journey.

The drop, as he called it, or the tear, as she did, would accompany them on their next pilgrimage: a voyage across the ocean to a new, warm land where they'd spend the rest of their lives. Two more children would be born there. And there they'd lay down roots too deep to sever, roots nestled in that soil that gave the world cacao, vanilla, maize. There, their grandchildren—children of amber and children of maize—would keep alive these stories and the memories of that far-off land whose name was erased from the map after a baptism of fire.

# *Author's Note*

***From Königsberg to Monterrey***

*Tears of Amber* is a fictional novel inspired by real events. Not only by official texts, but also by the accounts of two children and their families who had to travel enormous distances to survive one of the biggest and most terrible exoduses in human history, before coming together in exile.

The real version of this story was told to me by Ilse in my hometown, Monterrey, Mexico, where she and Arno lived until death parted them. In the late sixties, they spent several years in Parras de la Fuente, Coahuila, where Casa Madero, the oldest vineyard in the Americas, imported a corking machine from Germany. They invited Arno—the machine's designer—and his family to supervise its installation, as well as to train the operators. The one-year contract was extended to two, and then three. In that time, Arno and Ilse fell in love with the region, with its people, and with the opportunities they found here. They came because of a machine but stayed out of love. When they decided to set up a factory, they were naturally drawn to Monterrey, an industrial city. It also seemed like fate: they'd begun in Königsberg ("king's hill") and come home to Monterrey (also "king's hill"). There, they watched their children—the three born in Germany and two more born in Mexico—grow up, go to college, marry, have children. They instilled all five with a love for their old country, but also for their new one. They all know themselves to be children of amber, but also children of maize.

The decision to write a novel inspired by the pilgrimage of Arno and Ilse was a very easy one to make. I couldn't start right away because I'd barely begun *The Murmur of Bees*. What I sensed from the beginning was that both novels were connected by "obscurity"—that they would lead me to narrate overlooked events or points of view in otherwise well-known stories: the Mexican Revolution and World War II. What's more, in telling stories set in Linares and East Prussia, I would also tell the stories of Monterrey and Mexico.

I've always believed that a student of history should search for connections, and that there should never be an ending. The history of Mexico doesn't end with the Spanish conquest, the War of Independence, or the Revolution. Arno and Ilse, with their past, present, and future, arrived in Mexico, thereby transforming it and transforming themselves. The same thing happens with many citizens—pilgrims—from all over the world, who've arrived in search of life and peace. They're now part of the history of my city and my country.

Rudyard Kipling said that if history were taught in the form of stories, it would never be forgotten. A literary view of the human experience of the past invites readers into a real, living historical moment, so that the experience of lives and moments distant in time and space become their own.

> *Literature transmits an incontrovertible, condensed experience from generation to generation. Thus, literature becomes the living memory of a nation.*
>
> —Aleksandr Solzhenitsyn

I don't pretend to be a historian or biographer. I'm a novelist: inspiration and imagination prompt me to take alternate routes, and I let them. Like in *The Murmur of Bees*, in *Tears of Amber* I confirm that there's no greater freedom than writing fiction, even when it's inspired by historical events, as mine is.

> *Fidelity to historical reality is a secondary matter as regards the value of the novel. The novelist is neither historian nor prophet: he is an explorer of existence.*
>
> —Milan Kundera

My fiction is anchored to reality, so my research for *Tears of Amber* was extensive. That said, the artistic license I grant myself opens up endless possibilities and gives me the prerogative to mold certain events to better develop the novel and its characters. I attach more importance to transmitting the spirit of an era and a people, to shedding light on the experience of those who don't feature in the history books, than I do to numbers, dates, or the names of important figures who changed the lines on maps and the destinies of their people.

In Schneidemühl, for instance, the real-life Ilse survived a bombing, but not on the date when it happens in the novel: it was convenient to move up this event. I freely merged the timelines of Ilse and Arno's return to school with the reawakening of the German postwar economy. In my narrative, historical figures coexist with people I was told about and with characters from my imagination. I took the liberty of inviting in Captain Aleksandr Solzhenitsyn, famously imprisoned by his own Army for criticizing the violence against Prussian civilians and in particular against women. Over the course of my research, we encountered each other several times, and although Solzhenitsyn wasn't present at the capture of Königsberg (he'd been arrested two months earlier), I wanted to pay a small tribute to his courage and sacrifice. In his years in the gulag, he created a poem (he would commit it to paper later, from memory) entitled "Prussian Nights." In 1970, he was awarded the

Nobel Prize in Literature for his body of work. "The battle line between good and evil runs through the heart of every man," Solzhenitsyn went on to say after he was freed. In that battle, he proved to be the winner.

The novel is sprinkled with examples like this, because *Tears of Amber* isn't the story that Ilse told me, but the tale that hers inspired. Seventy-six years have passed since the war ended. Ilse still possesses the indelible childhood memories that she generously and bravely shared with me, but I had to fill in the gaps, visit other points of view. I had to connect the memories to history and offer them not as memories but as life, with flesh and bone, with the five senses, with games, cold, hunger, pain, fear, determination, joy, love. I'm not a child of amber, but I wrote this narrative about that land with its erased name as if it were mine, because I believe that the history of any place belongs to us all, and the lessons inherent in it are for everyone. We must learn the lessons. We mustn't be blind to what has happened or is happening in other places or to other peoples, regardless of the distance in time, geography, or language.

> *Social problems go beyond borders. The sores of the human race, these running sores that cover the globe, don't stop at red or blue lines drawn on the map.*
>
> —Victor Hugo, about *Les Misérables*,
> in a letter to his editor

# Acknowledgments

This novel wouldn't have been possible without the support and faith of various beloved people. I will start by thanking Ilse, who, in the eight years from when we met for the first time to talk about her life until I informed her that the last page had been written, never doubted that *Tears of Amber* would come into the world and never stopped answering my questions with patience and enthusiasm. I hope that, bookworm that she is, when she reads this novel she perceives the admiration I have for her and for Arno: not only did they survive, but they did so whole, with joy and with their sights set on the future. I'd also like to thank Regine Schipper, their daughter and cherished friend, who often acted as intermediary in my little interrogations and advisor on the German language with which I was bold enough to season this story.

An author writes in the most profound solitude, but to publish, she needs company. I'm grateful to Penguin Random House, my publisher in Mexico, and to Elizabeth DeNoma and Gabriella Page-Fort of Amazon Crossing, along with their great team of editors, for making this publication possible.

A great translator manages to make the border between languages vanish, and I feel very lucky that it has been Simon Bruni who has guided these children of amber to their final destination in English, because I don't think there's a better translator of the intentions of words, of their cadence, and of the human experience. I hope many more projects bring us together.

I'm grateful to my family for their patience, love, and support. They've known about this novel since it came to me in 2010. They were with me when I wrote the first lines in 2014, and neither murmurs nor hurricanes made them doubt that I'd finish it. I appreciate the patience they had when, in the second half of 2017, I did almost nothing but research, talk to them about war, and write. Their faith and presence gave me strength of purpose.

I admit that, while researching for *Tears of Amber* and during the creative process, I had to escape from real life several times. I'm grateful to my dear friends Alejandro and Rocío for loaning me a place where all I could hear was nature, a literary retreat that gave me the space I needed to succeed in my task. I believe that there's a creative force in nature that can be harnessed by anyone who wants to listen with their eyes, see with their skin, and feel with their ears. With *The Murmur of Bees*, this force came from the sea; with *Tears of Amber*, it came from the hills of my land. I recommend the experience.

Infinite thanks, dear reader, for accompanying me to the end.

## *About the Author*

*Photo © 2014 Juan Rodrigo Llaguno*

Sofía Segovia was born in Monterrey, Mexico. She studied communications at Universidad de Monterrey, mistakenly thinking that she would be a journalist. But fiction is her first love. A creative writing teacher, she has also been a ghostwriter and communications director for local political campaigns and has written several plays for local theater. The Spanish edition of her bestselling *El murmullo de las abejas* (*The Murmur of Bees*) was an Audie Award winner and named novel of the year by iTunes, and the English translation by Simon Bruni and narrated by Xe Sands and Angelo Di Loreto was one of Audible's Top 10 of 2019 and a Voice Arts Award winner. She is also the author of *Peregrinos* (*Tears of Amber*), *Noche de huracán* (*Night of the Hurricane*), and *Huracán* (*Hurricane*). Sofía likes to travel the world, but she loves coming home to her husband, three children, two dogs, and cat. She writes her best surrounded and inspired by their joyous chaos. For more information visit www.sofiasegovia.com.

## *About the Translator*

*Photo © Colin Crewdson*

Simon Bruni translates literary works from Spanish, a language he acquired through total immersion living in Alicante, Valencia, and Santander. He studied Spanish and linguistics at Queen Mary University of London and literary translation at the University of Exeter. Simon's many published translations include novels, short stories, video games, and nonfiction publications, and he is the winner of three John Dryden translation awards: in 2017 and 2015 for Paul Pen's short stories "Cinnamon" and "The Porcelain Boy" and in 2011 for Francisco Pérez Gandul's novel *Cell 211*. His translations of Paul Pen's *The Light of the Fireflies* and Sofía Segovia's *The Murmur of Bees* have both become international bestsellers. For more information visit www.simonbruni.com.